A Dirge for the Damned

The Kelk Conflict: Escalation

Book 2 of *The Blacksword Regiment*

by

J. L. Doty

TELEMACHUS PRESS

Published by Telemachus Press, LLC
http://www.telemachuspress.com

Visit the author's website:
http://www.jldoty.com

ISBN: 978–1–951744–25–0 (eBook)
ISBN: 978–1–951744–14–4 (paperback)
ISBN: 978–1–953757–20–3 (hardback)

Version 2022.12.04

KEpuz!po!KJNEFTLUPQ:
Formatted using eTools for Writers 3.8.8, Dec 4 2022, 09:54:43
Copyright © 2013-2016 by J. L. Doty

Printed in the United States of America

10 9 8 7 6 5 4 3 2 1

A Dirge for the Damned

The Kelk Conflict: Escalation

Book 2 of *The Blacksword Regiment*

Damned if I die today,
Cursed if I live tomorrow.

1

Blacksword Patches

WHEN MAJOR TEAL handed John the small envelope containing two Blacksword patches, John stood there in Colonel Brightlaw's office for the longest moment saying nothing. He couldn't take his eyes off the small emblems in the envelope. He had long ago given up hope of ever becoming one of the proud, one of the few, and had purposefully put that out of his mind. He hadn't thought about it in a long time. The Blacksword would always be out of reach for the likes of him. The Blacksword Regiment was reserved for people of superior ability like Macus DeLeon, not for simple schmucks like John Mathius. He had accepted the fact that he would always be one of the meek, one of the many.

Sergeant Omuglu cleared her throat, and John realized he had been standing there dumbfounded and mouth open, like some stupid bumpkin. In a moment of abject terror, he glanced down at his tunic to reassure himself that he hadn't drooled on it, or something else equally as embarrassing.

Major Teal gave him a nondescript smile. "Do you accept?"

John tried not to stumble over his words. "Of . . . of course I do . . . sir."

Teal nodded. "There's no *of course* about it, Sergeant Mathius. You'll be held to a higher standard. If you wash out of the Blacksword, you wash out completely. There won't be any going back; you can't simply revert to ComSecCorps."

Colonel Brightlaw stood to one side appearing hopeful, while Sergeant Omuglu waited behind Teal looking on. Omuglu's face held the classic inscrutability of a DI as she said, "Sir, he won't wash out."

John hoped she was right. "I won't wash out, sir."

Teal's smile broadened. "We wouldn't have offered you the Blacksword if we thought you might fail."

Brightlaw slapped John on the back. "Then it's settled. Congratulations, young man." He gripped John's hand and shook it heartily. The colonel's handshake was neither meek nor soft, and John had to squeeze hard in return just to match it. "And don't think for a moment it's a gift or prize. You earned the Blacksword, so wear those patches with pride."

John thought, *One of the proud. One of the few.* He didn't feel terribly proud at the moment, just humble, and . . . curious.

Teal took his turn to shake John's hand, though not as heartily as Brightlaw, and without the crushing force.

Omuglu didn't shake John's hand, but simply stepped forward. "Colonel, Major, with your permission, may I do the honors?"

Brightlaw grinned and stepped aside. "By all means, Master Sergeant."

Appearing quite solemn, Teal also stepped aside. "After all, you're the one who turned this young man into Blacksword material."

Omuglu shrugged. "I think his background and experiences had something to do with that."

Teal nodded slightly, conceding her the point.

Brightlaw said, "But you moved him beyond those experiences and turned him into a soldier. Without your help he might have turned into something completely different."

Omuglu gave a slight shrug of her shoulders, and John didn't need anyone to tell him the meaning behind the colonel's words.

While Brightlaw and Teal looked on, Omuglu stepped forward and gently took the envelope from John. She retrieved one of the patches from it, then stepped to his right side and knelt down beside him. "Hold still, Sergeant, arms pointed straight down."

John tried to become a statue.

Omuglu produced a small measuring tape then peeled off a protective backing from the patch. "Middle of the sleeve," she said, aligning it carefully, "ten centimeters below the elbow."

Carefully locating the proper position on John's sleeve, she pressed the patch in place. It adhered instantly, and John knew without doubt she had positioned it with the kind of microscopic accuracy only a DI could produce.

Omuglu stood, stepped in front of John and looked him in the eyes. "On the right sleeve the blade is pointed down to symbolize the use of force when needed."

She repeated the process on the left side, kneeling down beside him, positioning the patch with the measuring tape, and pressing it into place. She stood and again faced him. "On the left the blade is pointed up to symbolize that many times force is not the solution, something you demonstrated quite nicely on Reisenar."

John didn't know how much they knew about what happened on Reisenar, and recalling Primatov's caution about saying too much, he had made a habit of simply keeping his mouth shut whenever he heard that name.

Omuglu stepped back a pace and looked John over carefully. Then, with Teal and Brightlaw standing on either side of her, the three of them raised their hands in a salute. John returned the salute and tried not to beam with pride, tried not go grin like a fool, but he failed.

Brightlaw slapped him on the back again. "Well done, lad."

They did more hand shaking and voiced more congratulations. For a moment John thought of that young Kelk woman and how she and her strange comrades didn't shake hands. He wondered if he would ever see her again, though he knew he probably wouldn't.

••••

The orders for Nikaela's new assignment were quite vague. They merely stated that she had been assigned to the staff of Brigadier Skalde Kristdokar, and that any details would be communicated by the skalde herself, or by a member of her staff. It took Nikaela several days to wrap up her assignments on Viktorkinde Prime, though it didn't take long to pack up her possessions. Her berth in bachelor officer's quarters was Spartan at best. To her mind, both her quarters and her lover were temporary accommodations, and she didn't keep anything of real value on the big space station, just her uniforms and a few personal items.

As she packed her belongings, she placed a call to her lover. "I've been reassigned to Hyerdride," she told him. "I enjoyed our time together, and I wish you good fortune." That was the truth. She didn't lie by saying she loved him or would miss him.

"We enjoyed each other," he said. "It was a mutually beneficial relationship, and I wish you good fortune in your new assignment."

She was thankful that, like her, he didn't voice a lie of love and longing.

She rode deadhead on a shuttle down to Viktorkinde, and took a high-speed grav train to the city of Hyerdride, which hosted the largest military base on Viktorkinde. A private note from Kristdokar had instructed her to report to an address a few miles from the military base. It also told her to wear civilian clothing, find an apartment near her new office, and warned her she'd be working incognito for the near future.

Most of her time for the past six months had been spent working in uniform, and she had very little civilian clothing. She still had a few days before she needed to report for duty so she took a detour to a retail district in Hyerdride where she found several clothing stores. She purchased a few attractive outfits that were conservative and appropriate for a professional office environment. But on her way back to the street she walked through a department that offered attire more appropriate for evening wear. She had no intention of purchasing anything there, but always felt a pang of jealousy when she saw vids of young civilians wearing such clothing while partying in night clubs. She had some time to kill, so purely out of curiosity she decided to look around.

A bright blue dress made of a slinky material caught her eye. She paused for a moment and touched the fabric. It had a pleasantly soft texture very unlike its appearance. She thought it would feel good against her skin, and the darker blue of the dress would offset the pale blue of her flesh. It was the kind of dress she would have to wear with almost no undergarments. It was the kind of dress she would never have a reason or opportunity to wear.

One of the store's clerks approached her, a pretty young woman exactly like the attractive young people in the vids. "Mistress, would you like to try that on?"

Nikaela couldn't think of a rational reason to ever purchase such an outfit, and she started to say no, but to her own surprise, when she opened her mouth she said, "Yes, why not?"

In the dressing room she removed most of her undergarments, slid the dress over her shoulders, then smoothed the fabric down her belly and along her thighs. It didn't expose a lot of flesh, but it melted against her body like a second skin and didn't leave much to the imagination. When she stepped out of the dressing room and approached the clerk, one of the young woman's eyebrows arched upward, and Nikaela knew such a dress would never be right for her.

Nikaela stopped in front of a three dimensional projection mirror and turned about slowly, which allowed her to see herself from all sides without craning her neck to look over her shoulder. The dress ended just below her knees, and had a low-cut front that exposed a bit of cleavage, with the points of her nipples protruding visibly from beneath the fabric. It wasn't particularly revealing and the material was not tight or confining, but wearing it, she still felt almost naked.

The clerk stepped back and looked her over carefully. "Mistress, you look exquisite in that dress."

Nikaela looked carefully at her image and thought, *Perhaps I do*. Then again, the clerk might simply be trying to make a sale.

"If I may be so bold," the young woman continued, "that dress, on you, will spark the imagination of any healthy young maestra."

Nikaela turned slowly around one more time, and she thought of that young Commonwealth soldier, her breschkada. He might like the way she looked in it.

She started, and hesitated. Now why had she thought of him? She would probably never see him again, so she tried to put him out of her thoughts.

The clerk asked, "Shall I wrap it up for you?"

Nikaela couldn't think of when or where she would ever have an opportunity to wear it. She shook her head, "No. It's an extravagance I don't need, and one I can't afford."

She returned to the dressing room, removed the dress and put on her uniform, though she did so with some regret. Out in the store proper, as she returned the dress to the clerk she considered it one last time, but shook her head and carried her packages out to the street.

She spent a couple of nights in bachelor officer's quarters on the base while she located a small, furnished apartment within walking distance of her new office. The apartment she selected had a small gathering room, bedroom, fresher, and a tiny kitchenette. She didn't cook, and she wasn't planning on doing any serious entertaining there, so it suited her needs nicely.

She moved into the place the day before her orders required her to report for duty. When she climbed into bed that night, she thought briefly of her ex-lover, and it did not surprise her that she felt no loss at his absence. To him, she had been strictly a convenience for pleasure and to alleviate boredom, and he had been the same to her, but now she had a challenging assignment to fill that void.

••••

"Are you absolutely certain of the sequence of events?"

Kristdokar paused before answering Skalde Supreme Dornmier. As the most senior member of the Larscom Executive Council, the old woman's questions were frequently more instructive than inquisitive, and she appeared to be neutral on the matter of Nikaela Vreekande's breschkada status.

"I am," she said. "I questioned Mistress Vreekande thoroughly. I also questioned Senior Command Superior Thordahl, Command Superior Brynjar, and Oberseergent Geltkarl. As I stated in my report, Geltkarl was the senior NCO in charge of Mistress Vreekande's squad, and rescued the young woman on that subway platform shortly after the incident occurred."

It was not the first time Kristdokar had been summoned to the Hyvaldsborg palace in Emkeldstadt. But to stand before the five members of the Executive Council in closed session, with no one else present, was rare indeed. And while all Kelk held each individual council member in high regard, when all five met together in session, esteem for the body as a whole bordered on reverence. It was therefore customary that when addressing the entire council, one must actually *stand* before them, though exceptions were made for those with infirmities that limited their ability to do so.

Skalde of the Supremacy Veskarson, the only man on the Council, leaned forward with an intent look on his face. "I know every one of us has read your report thoroughly, and viewed the recordings of those interrogations, probably several times."

He glanced at the three more junior members of the Council, Vice Skaldes Nygaard, Tiegnordan, and Haugrund. Haugrund still had quite a bit of pepper in her hair, while Tiegnordan and Nygaard both leaned more toward salt, and not a fleck of pepper remained atop Veskarson's or Dornmier's heads.

By custom, the second most senior member of the five councilmembers chaired meetings of the Council. Veskarson continued. "Some have looked to find fault with your findings, and perhaps been somewhat biased in their considerations. That is natural, given the circumstances: breschkada ... with a Blacksword ... and he breschkada-sa."

Haugrund, a notorious hardliner, slashed a hand through the air. "We only have the young woman's word for what happened between her and that ... commonface."

None of the other council members argued with her, and they all looked to Kristdokar for a rebuttal. She spoke carefully. "I know the young woman well and I do trust her. But I knew that would be a concern, so at my request, she volunteered to be interrogated under deep neural probe. The probe results corroborated her statements."

Tiegnordan said, "It's a shame we can't question the young man as well."

Kristdokar didn't want to even consider that. "I could ask . . . but I doubt they'll comply. And on the off chance they did, I'm certain it would have to be in Commonwealth sovereign territory under Blacksword supervision."

Dornmier shook her head. "I don't think that's really necessary. We do like to attribute all sorts of diabolical motives to the Blacksword, but he was not a Blacksword at the time of the incident, and he is quite young. No, his motives were rather clear."

Kristdokar took great care to keep her tone neutral. "I stand by the facts in my report, which detail the actions of Mistress Vreekande and Maestra Mathius quite thoroughly. I am confident we have the truth of the matter. However, if the Council determines those actions do not make them breschkada, then we all must defer to the Council's greater wisdom, and I will do so without reservation."

"He is not Kelk," Haugrund said, "and there can be no breschkada between Kelk and a common-face."

"On the contrary," Tiegnordan said, "not one of the historians we've consulted rule that out, and most believe it makes the bond even stronger."

Haugrund opened her mouth to say something, but before she could, Dornmier cut her off. "And that bond might give us a bridge to end the hostility that has put the Commonwealth and the Supremacy at odds for a century and a half."

Haugrund pursed her lips and kept her silence. The Executive Council had clearly had this discussion before, and quite probably more than once.

If Kristdokar had ever had any reservations about the validity of breschkada status for the two young people, the deep neural probe results had laid any such doubts to rest. "There is one thing of considerable significance not in the report that I should bring to the Council's attention, something I learned from Mistress Vreekande during the deep neural probe interrogation."

Dornmier squinted at her as if her eyesight had failed, or a wave of distrust had swept through her thoughts. "And that is?"

Kristdokar braced herself for their reaction. "The young man in question is a survivor of Novalis III. And Mistress Vreekande—"

Haugrund shot to her feet as they all shouted questions at Kristdokar. Interspersed in the questions were a few epithets as well. Dornmier ended it by barking, "Silence."

The old woman seldom spoke loudly or in anger, but on the rare occasion when she did, everyone listened. Haugrund had a sour look on her face as she sat down under Dornmier's disapproving gaze. "You were not finished speaking, Brigadier. What more did you have to report?"

Kristdokar hoped she still had a career. "As I'm sure you know, Mistress Vreekande was stationed on Novalis III during her training mission. One day while delivering supplies to one of the rebel factions, she actually saw the young man from a distance. He was a young boy forced by the rebels to be one of their soldiers."

The councilmembers responded with absolute silence. After several seconds Veskarson asked, "Is it possible she was mistaken?"

Kristdokar held her hands out in a gesture of supplication. "It was apparently a very vivid memory, which allowed us to reconstruct much of what she saw. I am convinced she is correct. But I've given you copies of the raw probe data so you can decide for yourselves."

Tiegnordan leaned back in her chair and steepled her fingers in front of her. "Amazing! The bond had formed between them even before they met on that subway platform."

They interrogated Kristdokar on that for more than an hour, though many questions resulted in discussion among themselves, and the *discussion* frequently grew quite heated. In the end even Haugrund, though quite unhappy about it, seemed to have accepted the veracity of Nikaela Vreekande's recollections.

When they finished, they dismissed Kristdokar and the Council dispersed. Nygaard approached her outside the council chamber. "Come. Let me buy you a drink."

They retreated to the vice skalde's office, where Nygaard poured them both a healthy shot of a clear liquid known as kirva. She raised her glass in a salute to Kristdokar. "Your timing on the disclosure of their Novalis III connection was brilliant. I'm not a superstitious woman, but even my pulse quickened when you revealed that."

Kristdokar sipped at her kirva, and relished the taste as the fiery liquid burned its way down her throat. "What about Haugrund?"

Nygaard smiled. "She *is* a superstitious woman. Did you notice she was rather reserved after that?"

Kristdokar winced. "I hope I didn't make an enemy."

Nygaard tilted her head to one side in a shrug. "Emotions are running high on this issue, and you handled yourself well in there."

"It was not easy."

Nygaard gave her a pained smile. "No, it wasn't. And it won't get any easier."

2

It's Complicated

MAJOR TEAL AND Sergeant Omuglu accompanied John when he stepped out of Colonel Brightlaw's office. As they walked toward the lift John glanced Teal's way and said, "May I ask a question, sir?"

Teal nodded. "I'd be surprised if you didn't have a question or two. Ask away."

"You said I'd be held to a higher standard. What does that mean?"

They paused at the lift doors on the eighth floor, but no one hit the button to summon it. Teal turned to face John squarely. "The hardest part about the higher standard is that it's a little vague. For example, if you go out with your friends for an evening of fun, and drink too much, no one will hold that against you. But get roaring drunk in a bar and start a fight, while an ordinary ComSec soldier might get a reprimand and a demotion, you'll probably lose those Blacksword patches."

John recalled that Teal had told him if he washed out of the Blacksword, he would be booted completely out of ComSecCorps.

Omuglu said, "John, there's a fair amount of political visibility to the Blacksword. You walk into a room, and people see that you're wearing those patches, they're going to expect more of you, and you have to deliver."

John asked, "What now? Some sort of really intense advanced training?"

Teal smiled and shook his head. "We already know what your capabilities are. If you have to swim a race you'll probably come in fourth or fifth. But if you have to swim for your life, you'll be the last one with your head above water, and no doubt you'll be helping a couple of your comrades stay alive as well. But you weren't offered those patches because of your physical capabilities, though all Blackswords do have to meet certain minimum requirements in that respect. We selected you for the Blacksword because you think clearly and originally, whether under stress or not. On Reisenar you recognized that your objective needed to change, and you changed it."

Omuglu said, "And that was quite a move, John."

John asked, "So what happens next?"

Teal said, "You're going to spend the next tenday in Blacksword orientation, along with a few comrades from your training regiment."

That sparked John's curiosity. "Anyone I know?"

Teal shook his head. "I don't believe so, though we've watched all of you rather closely for the past three years, and we do have our eyes on a few of your platoon mates. They might be offered the Blacksword in the future, but don't say anything about that to them."

John knew better than to ask who, though he dearly wanted to.

Teal continued. "After orientation you're going to spend a year in O-School, then one year as a very junior officer apprenticed to a more senior officer—in your case, another Blacksword."

John tried to hide his disappointment. "More studying?"

Omuglu closed her eyes and shook her head sadly.

Teal simply reached out and hit the call button for the lift.

The lift must not have been in use because the doors immediately whooshed open. They stepped into it, the doors closed, and a fraction of a second later they opened again on the ground floor. John followed Teal and Omuglu out of the administration building, and out in front of it Teal paused on the sidewalk. "Now comes the fun part of your day, John." He hesitated for an instant, then added, "Or maybe it'll be the hard part."

John frowned and Teal continued. "You have to face your platoon mates wearing those patches." He smiled, turned, and walked away.

Omuglu accompanied John most of the way back to the barracks. "You've done well, John. As the colonel said, you earned those patches, so wear them with pride."

Near the barracks she turned and headed toward her own quarters.

John and his platoon mates were still on leave and had no official obligations. That morning, all but John had received their new assignments, then crowded around comp screens to research their new postings and compare notes. That John had not received an assignment along with the rest had been odd. Carla had said something about, ". . . probably just a clerical thing. You should talk to Omuglu."

No one had said anything, but the surreptitious looks they gave him made it clear they had concluded the lack of an assignment was not a good sign. When Omuglu had told him to report to Brightlaw's office, he had marched there wondering if *killing* DeLeon had finally come back to haunt him. And now he had to face his friends wearing Blacksword patches.

DeLeon sat alone on his bunk, his retinue of sycophants no longer paying deference to him. At the far end of the barracks Carla, Roark, Leeze and a few others sat in a group on a couple of bunks. Their voices had the pitch of excitement and anticipation.

When John stepped into the room DeLeon looked his way. As John walked down the aisle between bunks, DeLeon's head turned slowly and tracked him; his eyes hardened and narrowed angrily. Apparently he had spotted the Blacksword patches and didn't like what he saw.

John approached the group with Carla and Roark, and a few of them stepped aside to admit him among them. Seated on a bunk, Carla looked up at him, her eyes filled with excitement. "*Fearless* is a great ship, John. It's a great posting. I couldn't have asked for better."

Roark asked John, "Did you learn what your assignment is?"

John couldn't think of a way to drop the news that he now wore Blacksword patches on his sleeves. "Yah, I'm going to O-School."

Carla stood up and faced him, standing rather close. "Ooh!" She looked at Leeze Caputto, her closest friend. "He's going to outrank me big time. I bet he thinks he's going to give me lots of orders and I'll have to obey them like a little puppy."

Leeze shrugged and gave John a once-over look. "That could be fun. If you're interested, John, I could do the obey thing." She wiggled her chest at him, which wasn't as formidable as Carla's, but enjoyable to look at nevertheless. "Command me, big boy."

Roark abruptly stood up, his eyes locked on the patch on John's right sleeve. "Shit!"

Carla grimaced and looked at him angrily. "What? What's wrong?"

Someone else said, "Holy crap!"

Carla looked carefully at Roark. He still hadn't taken his eyes off the Blacksword patch on John's sleeve, and her head turned as she slowly followed his gaze.

"Oh no!" she said. "That's not funny, John. You're going to get in big trouble wearing those."

Leeze shook her head. "Carla, I don't think John would joke about that. And he doesn't have much of a sense of humor anyway."

John held his hands up as if surrendering to an armed enemy. "That's my assignment. They offered me the Blacksword."

Carla stood statue still for what seemed an eternity, but really lasted only a second or two. Then she jumped forward, almost knocking John off his feet, wrapped her arms around his neck and kissed him, not a passionate kiss, but a loud, congratulatory smack on the lips that all of them heard. She stepped back, threw him a high-five and shouted, "One of the proud, one of the few."

She wrapped her arms around his neck again, and this time the kiss was quite passionate. John's platoon mates cheered and shouted, but over Carla's shoulder he noticed DeLeon sitting silently alone and giving him a hard, hate-filled look.

••••

Standing at the back of the room, Katrine Primatov listened to Fran Thealone testify before an open session of the Senate Armed Services Committee. The whole event was more of an orchestrated show for the news hypes, providing an opportunity for the senators to showcase their latest issues. The men and women of the committee asked carefully structured questions intended to sound biting and insightful, but in fact judiciously skirted any dangerous subjects that might be problematic for any of the committee members. And Colonel Blacksword, in full military regalia, performed her role like an actor on stage, rarely allowing her calm, studied demeanor to be disrupted, but intentionally showing a little passion or ire when her performance called for it.

Interestingly enough, without having done any homework on the matter, Katrine could easily spot those senators who were up for reelection; their inquiries sounded more like long-winded speeches than questions. At one point Jenine Catarvin rambled on for more than five minutes, and finished without asking anything. A short silence ensued that would have become pregnant had not Thealone asked, "Was there a question there, Senator?"

Catarvin's eyes flashed angrily as she said, "Of course there was, Colonel."

Not for the first time, Katrine wondered how Catarvin always managed to gossip her way to reelection. The woman had repeatedly triumphed in her campaigns, and by dint of longevity had garnered considerable seniority, which counted for quite a bit in the senate. Her constituency must see something in the woman that defied any analysis Katrine might apply.

Senator Silas Palmutter, the committee chairman, lifted an eyebrow and rescued the situation by saying, "I believe that Senator Catarvin was inquiring into the budget expenditures for last year's operations in the vicinity of Reisenar."

Seated at a table in front of the committee, Thealone leaned forward. "There were Blacksword personnel present there, but that was not a Blacksword operation."

Palmutter gave her a smarmy smile. "But it turned into a Blacksword operation, did it not, when your people became embroiled in the unrest on Reisenar? And am I correct that it was one of your senior officers who took command of the situation once shots were fired?" His eyes flicked momentarily Katrine's way, though it appeared no one but she noticed the brief glance.

At least the Armed Services Committee members were focused on the budget, and not the real issues of the Reisenar incident. She hoped that would remain the case when they went to closed session.

Katrine had chosen to wear civilian clothing for this meeting, and had taken a seat in the back row of the gallery. The news hypes ran live coverage of Thealone's testimony, and while Katrine's rank and position were not a secret, the Blacksword patches on the uniform of a high-ranking officer were always an invitation to insert her face prominently into the news feeds, something she really didn't need. She remained seated when the open session ended, and didn't move while the hypes and public onlookers filed out of the meeting room, leaving only the committee members, their aides, Thealone, and Katrine.

When the tall double doors to the meeting room thudded shut, Katrine stood. Jenine Catarvin looked up from something on the table in front of her and her eyes met Katrine's, a vacant look of boredom on the plump little woman's face. Palmutter also looked up, but while he definitely looked her way his eyes did not meet hers. As Katrine crossed the room to the table where Thealone sat, she thought Palmutter might be staring at her breasts. When she stopped beside the older woman, Thealone looked up and acknowledged her with a simple nod.

Palmutter was reputed to be a wealthy and influential man, and a hardline, anti-Kelk hawk. In his early sixties, he had clearly made liberal use of gene therapy to keep the wrinkles at bay, and looked more like a youngish fifty. Gene therapy had probably also been responsible for the thick mane of dark, black hair that grew in a luxurious cascade down to his shoulders. Most women would probably find him quite attractive.

Katrine had never before met the man, nor shared words with him, so today would be their first exchange. And the distance between them was too great to be certain where he'd focused his eyes, or what he had chosen to stare at while she crossed the room. Katrine decided to chalk her earlier concerns up to simple paranoia and give him the benefit of the doubt.

As she sat down beside Thealone, Palmutter said, "Lieutenant Colonel Primatov, thank you for joining us."

Katrine forced a pleasant smile to her lips. "I'm happy to be of assistance to the committee in any way possible."

Palmutter flashed a momentary smile that lasted for the briefest of instants, as if he took some added meaning from her words. "We would like to discuss the Novalis III and Reisenar incidents. You were in charge of the forensic investigation on Novalis III, were you not?"

"Yes, I was," Katrine said, nodding, "but only as it related to gathering evidence for the analysis of the origins of the weapons involved. Forensics in the broader sense is beyond my field of expertise. I merely supervised the teams that gathered the evidence we turned over to the scientists in our laboratories."

"She's modest," Jenine Catarvin said. "As well as intelligent . . . and pretty."

A few of the other committee members flinched with embarrassment. Palmutter made no effort to hide his disdain as he quite visibly rolled his eyes. "We would like to hear the details of the results of that investigation."

Katrine tried not to sound defensive. "I can only give you a limited summary since the clearances for much of that information are higher than the clearances of some of the committee members present."

Palmutter leaned forward and his eyes narrowed. "Are you saying you're not willing to provide the information we require."

Jenine Catarvin gave him a dirty look, and Katrine wondered if the woman might pick a cat fight with her committee chairman.

Fran Thealone answered Palmutter's question. "Senator Palmutter, it was not we who specified the clearances for the information in question, nor we who passed judgement on the clearance levels of the members of this committee. If Colonel Primatov or I violate Commonwealth laws regarding the dissemination of classified information, we would be subject to court-martial, dishonorable discharge, and hard prison time. And if you are instructing us to violate those laws, you would be subject to criminal charges as well. Are you asking us to violate Commonwealth law?"

Katrine was extremely thankful for Thealone's presence. She herself didn't have the seniority or rank to stand up so directly to a senator of Palmutter's status and influence. She would have had to dissemble at some length, and perhaps make an enemy of a very powerful man.

Palmutter slashed a hand through the air like a knife. "Of course not. Let me be more specific. Were the Kelk solely responsible for the unconventional weapons that murdered twenty million people on Novalis III?"

Katrine didn't need to look to Thealone for approval to answer that. "No."

Palmutter nodded. "So there were other interests at play?"

"Yes."

"Were there Commonwealth interests involved?"

That was close to hitting the classification wall, but the way he had worded it meant it didn't cross the line. Katrine looked to Thealone for confirmation and the older woman gave her an almost imperceptible nod. Katrine turned back to Palmutter. "Yes, there were."

"Do you know who?"

"No."

Palmutter gave her a look that seemed to imply he didn't believe her. "Were there Commonwealth interests involved in the unrest on Reisenar?"

That information had never been confirmed, so it had not been suppressed. It wasn't classified one way or the other because it didn't really exist.

"We don't know."

"But you suspect, don't you?"

She shrugged. "There were rumors—nothing confirmed, all unsubstantiated. Don't forget there were almost as many factions on Reisenar as on Novalis III, and they were all trying to play us against the Kelk Supremacy."

Palmutter frowned and looked as if he wanted to pick a fight. "How do you know they tried to play you against the Kelk?"

Thealone tried to answer him. "We had—"

Palmutter raised a hand and interrupted her. "Colonel, with all due respect, I'd like to hear from the officer who was actually present at the time."

Thealone gave him an unpleasant smile and nodded.

"We didn't at first," Katrine said. "But once we captured a few mercenaries and questioned them, we learned the truth."

Palmutter persisted. "And how did you learn mercenaries were involved?"

The proper answer to that would involve using Private John Mathius's name. But even if the young man's true role in the incident on Reisenar wasn't buried deeply in classified files, she still didn't want to expose him that way. Palmutter had the necessary clearances, and she assumed he damn well knew the young man's name, and the most salient details of his actions that night. But there was a lot he couldn't get from those files, and she wasn't about to enlighten him.

She tried to keep the look on her face neutral. "It became obvious we were encountering another player on the field, someone other than us, the Kelk, and the Reisenar natives."

For the next hour the committee grilled Thealone and Katrine on the two incidents. Every senator present threw questions at them, but the most probing inquiries came from Palmutter. And he had an odd reaction to most of their answers, as if he sought something other than the rather sparse information they provided.

When the closed session broke up, Katrine and Thealone held back to let the committee members file out before them. While they waited, the older woman leaned close to Katrine and subvocalized through her implants, "He knew the answers to those questions before he asked them. He has sources of his own."

Katrine subvocalized her own thoughts, "Or he was part of the whole thing from the beginning, and was just fishing to see how much we really know."

Thealone gave her a nasty grin. "He may have been deeply involved, or he wasn't and simply has good sources."

Katrine followed her out of the meeting room, and in the hallway they ran into Jenine Catarvin. She leaned close to Katrine and whispered, "He stares at my breasts that way too."

Katrine started and couldn't hide her reaction. The smaller woman usually wore something that exposed a fair amount of skin in the cleavage area, and was pretty enough that Palmutter probably would ogle her.

Catarvin smiled like a school girl who had just been asked on a date by a star athlete. "It's quite flattering, isn't it? He's very handsome, and powerful."

She turned and walked away, leaving Katrine standing there dumbfounded, and with a desire to puke her breakfast up all over the floor.

3

An Old Friend

ON NIKAELA'S FIRST day of her new assignment, she put on a nondescript business suit and walked to the address specified in Kristdokar's note, which turned out to be a large, square, one-story structure Nikaela thought might have been a warehouse. A sign on the front of the building told her she had arrived at the headquarters of Friedrikdahl Import-Export. The sign appeared to have been recently installed.

The main entrance opened directly into a small reception area, with a young man seated behind a counter, and several empty chairs against one wall. A door in the far wall appeared to lead deeper into the building. Next to it stood a private security guard, a holstered sidearm strapped to his hip.

The door next to the guard opened and two men emerged wearing coveralls discolored by smears of paint. They pushed a cart that appeared to contain large containers of paint, and the place smelled of fresh paint. As they guided the cart across the reception area toward the main entrance, Nikaela approached the young man behind the counter. He looked up from a comp screen and smiled pleasantly. "Can I help you?"

Nikaela felt a bit out of her element. "I'm Nikaela Vreekande. I was instructed to report here for . . ."

She had almost said *duty*, but with the construction workers present, and with everyone in civilian clothing, that didn't seem appropriate. She said, ". . . to report for work."

The young man's smile broadened. "Ah, you're our new comptroller. Welcome to Friedrikdahl Import-Export, Mistress Vreekande."

The ordinary civilian clothing the fellow wore seemed out of place, and there was no doubt in her mind he was all military. And something in the private guard's posture belied the appearance of cheap, hired security. Both men reminded Nikaela of the Special Forces personnel crammed into the assault boat the night they evacuated the warehouse on Novalis III.

The receptionist extended his hand, holding out a plast ID card. "You're to wear this at all times when on the premises."

She took the ID card from him and when her fingers touched it a small emblem on it flashed a bright green. It contained a DNA sniffer, and had she not been Nikaela Vreekande it would have flashed red.

"Excellent," he said. He turned to his comp screen and hit a few keys on his keyboard. "I've just logged your implants into our local system, but it won't be fully up and running for another day or two. Mistress Kristdokar instructed me to tell you to stop by her office as soon as you arrived."

He pointed to the door that led deeper into the building. "Through that door and walk straight to the back of the building. Her office is the only one that's complete, and her name is on the door."

Nikaela thanked him and turned toward the door. The guard opened it and held it for her. As she walked through the entry, he said, "Welcome aboard, Mistress Vreekande." Definitely special forces!

Just beyond the door Nikaela stepped into a large, open area that confirmed her suspicions the place had been a warehouse. The ceiling was easily six meters above her head. A dozen workers were busy at various construction tasks and a lot of furniture had been stacked in a corner of the room. It appeared they had constructed enclosed offices at the back of the building, though as yet only one had a door that could be closed. She walked toward it, and as she crossed the room one of the workers fired up some sort of equipment that emitted an ear-splitting shriek.

She knocked on the door, and because of the whine of the equipment she wouldn't have heard Kristdokar had she responded verbally. Instead, the skalde spoke through her implants. "Enter."

Nikaela opened the door. Kristdokar sat behind a desk and grimaced at the construction noise. The older woman waved a hand impatiently. "Please close the door."

Nikaela did so and the noise level dropped considerably.

Kristdokar pointed to a comfortable chair. "Sit down and relax."

As Nikaela sat down, Kristdokar reached into a drawer in her desk and retrieved a wrapped bundle. She dropped it on the desk and it thudded heavily. The skalde unwrapped it to reveal a small pistol in a shoulder holster. Nikaela raised a questioning eyebrow, and the older woman responded with, "The holster is up to you. If it's not your style, or not to your liking, then don't wear it."

Kristdokar pulled the pistol out of the holster, leaned forward and handed it to Nikaela. She examined it carefully, a grav gun small enough to be easily concealed. It could only fire six rounds, but they would have plenty of punch.

Kristdokar said, "If you want another means of concealing it, talk to the receptionist. He can requisition anything you need. But let me emphasize that you must go armed at all times when outside this building."

Nikaela asked, "It's that dangerous, is it?"

Kristdokar shrugged. "I don't know. It could be. There are a lot of people who will oppose what we are trying to do. We're going to be fighting a hundred and fifty years of emotional bias, so I don't want to take any chances. Just make sure you're always prepared to protect yourself."

It occurred to Nikaela she should make a trip back to those clothing stores. She needed to reconsider her selections with an eye to concealing a weapon.

Kristdokar gave Nikaela a special number. "We're running a secure military network overlaid on citynet. Encode that number in your implants, and as long as you're within ten kilometers of this building, even if citynet goes down or someone tries to jam access, you'll get through to us. But don't use that number for anything short of a serious emergency, because it'll automatically trigger a rapid response team."

Nikaela's enthusiasm rose with each new revelation of the dangerous and clandestine nature of her new assignment. She would now be part of an exciting field operation, and was done with books and studying and lessons and exams.

Kristdokar gave her an appraising look, as if she found Nikaela lacking in some way. "The first thing we have to do is get rid of that atrocious accent you exhibit when you speak Commonwealth Lingua, so I've brought in a special tutor for you. I'll be reviewing your test results regularly to see how well you advance, and I expect you to study hard and progress rapidly."

••••

John's tenday of Blacksword orientation proved to be quite enlightening. Each morning he reported to a small classroom where he and sixteen other new Blackswords listened to Teal lecture them on the regiment's history, customs and etiquette. Logistics, engineering, and support were just as critical to a functioning regiment as were combat fire teams, so Blackswords came in all shapes and sizes. One of John's classmates was a fellow with the last name Silkorski stenciled above his pocket. He carried a few extra pounds around his mid-section and like John had probably not finished boot camp at the top of the physical fitness rankings. But he wouldn't be present if he hadn't proven he could fulfill Sergeant Major Prescott's mantra and, ". . . put on plast and do boots-on-the-ground." John learned the regiment did have its Special Forces unit, Zeta Company, and within Zeta the most capable were assigned to Assault Team Null.

Seventeen soldiers out of John's original training regiment had been offered the Blacksword. All had accepted, though Major Teal told them that was not always the case. If that number was anything close to typical, then with four recruit depots distributed among the more than twenty solar systems of the Commonwealth, they recruited less than seventy new Blackswords a year. With various forms of attrition, that just didn't seem to be enough to keep a regiment fully staffed. John asked about that and Teal said, "We don't offer the Blacksword to anyone until they've at least completed command school. That's a fundamental prerequisite, and it gives us almost three years to watch, observe and see how you perform, react and think. But there are other soldiers from your training regiment on whom we are keeping a close eye, and in the next few years we will likely offer some of them the Blacksword."

The first day of class, when they broke for lunch, Teal had sandwiches brought in. Silkorski approached John and stuck out his hand. "I'm Petra."

John shook the offered hand. "I'm John."

"I know," Petra said.

John had never met the fellow before and wasn't sure what that meant. "You know, huh? The last-man-standing thing?"

A young woman joined them. The stencil on her chest read Moskosa. She had dark-brown skin, but had lightened her curly hair to a shade of soft brown and wore it in a tight buzz-cut only about a centimeter long. She seemed familiar, but John couldn't recall if he'd ever run into her before. She stuck out her hand. "That, and I was on Reisenar. I'm Theila. Hey-You was a friend of mine."

Now John recognized her. The day he had tried to learn Hey-You's real name, Theila had been one of the faces in the window of their barracks, one of those who had dubbed him What's-His-Name.

As John shook Theila's hand, Petra said, "Heard you got messed up pretty bad on Reisenar."

"Yah," Theila said. "But word has it he dished out some serious hurt to those Kelk assholes before they killed my friend."

John shook his head. "It wasn't the Kelk killed Hey-You. It was a bunch of mercenaries."

Her eyes hardened. "Is that why you made friends with those Kelk?"

Petra's eyes widened. "Friends? Really? Isn't that like ... treason or something?"

John carefully recalled Colonel Primatov's instructions on what he could and could not reveal about Reisenar: nothing about powerful Kelk and Commonwealth conspirators, and no mention of the breschkada thing. To make sure he didn't accidentally reveal something he shouldn't, he kept it short and sweet, told them how he'd spotted the mercenary observation posts, realized a third party was involved, and to prove it to the Kelk, gave those coordinates to the Vreekande woman on that subway platform.

"Face to face?" Petra asked. "Do they really have blue skin?"

"It's only a little blue," John said, "but very pale."

Theila asked, "And the red eyes with vertically slit pupils?"

"Red, yes," John said. "That part's true. But they don't look demonic, and their pupils are round like ours."

By that time several of the other new Blackswords had gathered around them to listen. One of them said, "Really weird looking, huh?"

"No," John said, "not at all. Yah, they've got red irises, and their skin is really pale with a little bit of blue in it, but they look human." He didn't add that he had found Mistress Vreekande quite pretty, or that he still hadn't confirmed her tongue was not forked. He really didn't need to confirm that because he was certain the forked-tongue thing was just part of the specious exaggerations about Kelk.

Major Teal called them to order. "Back to work, but we'll keep it casual. If you're not done with lunch, you can continue eating, but we've got a lot to cover."

One thing he emphasized that afternoon was that there was no enhanced rank with being a Blacksword. "Some people think that patch allows them more privilege than normal. You will sometimes see that certain Blackswords are afforded a little more respect than their rank might normally garner. But that's because of the individual man or woman, not the patch on their sleeve. And forgetting that is a quick way to wash out of the Blacksword."

••••

"That's enough for today," Nikaela's Lingua tutor growled. Command Hawk Velkerhaut had arrived at the end of a busy day for the first lesson, and the woman kept Nikaela late, like a young school girl performing penance for some infraction.

Seated at the table in a conference room, Nikaela closed her eyes and rubbed her temples. Velkerhaut had been one of Nikaela's instructors at the academy, and a specialist in Commonwealth Lingua. The woman stood taller than most, with an athletic build and a constantly disapproving demeanor. Nikaela thought that during solitary moments she probably stood at a mirror and practiced scowling at herself.

"I don't know why I'm wasting my time with you," Velkerhaut said as she packed her teaching materials into a briefcase. She snapped the briefcase closed, picked it up, then turned and marched out of the room, shaking her head sadly.

Nikaela's first lesson in Commonwealth Lingua had been more of a test than a lesson. Velkerhaut had quizzed her for two hours to gauge her command of the language. The woman hadn't really given Nikaela a chance, firing questions at her in Lingua in rapid succession. Velkerhaut had walked into the room unhappy to start with, and finished by walking out furious. Nikaela thought it completely unfair that the command hawk had arrived expecting her to fail. But then, she thought it unlikely anything could satisfy that woman.

Kristdokar interrupted her thoughts, speaking to her through her implants. "Mistress Vreekande. My office, now."

Nikaela suppressed a sigh. Velkerhaut had probably gone straight to the skalde, and now Nikaela would have to suffer a dressing down.

"I'll be right there," she said, then stood and hurried out of the room.

The door to Kristdokar's office stood open, but when Nikaela walked in, instead of an angry skalde, she found a woman whose eyes sparkled with excitement. The skalde stood and leaned forward, planting her hands flat on her desk. "We have an incredible opportunity, something I'd given up hope of ever achieving. Go home, change into your uniform, and pack a suitcase; uniforms only. Pack whatever you need for a two-day trip. Then meet me back here."

"May I ask where we're going?"

Kristdokar grinned. "Erikdeg."

Nikaela could not hide her surprise. Erikdeg: one of the most remote and secure facilities on the planet, and the base where she had testified at the tribunal of the five conspirators responsible for the tragedy on Novalis III. She thought of poor Anders Eindride, her superior during that failed operation. When she had discovered the illegal weapons packed in crates labeling them as conventional, he had warned her to forget the matter and never admit her discovery. That had probably saved her career, and he had ended up in a military prison somewhere.

"Why are we—"

The skalde interrupted her by shaking her head. "We're not going to discuss anything about this outside the secure perimeter of Erikdeg."

With her curiosity spiked, Nikaela nodded her head slowly. "Yes, mistress."

She rushed home to her apartment, changed into her uniform, packed a bag, then rushed back to Kristdokar's office. The two of them took a hired car to Hyerdride Military Base where they boarded a small transport used only by officers of flag rank.

Almost two years ago, when Nikaela had gone to Erikdeg to testify at the tribunal, she had traveled deadhead on available transport. The remote location of the facility had meant she couldn't get direct passage, but changed transport twice at other military installations. With delays and layovers, the journey had taken more than three days. But now, accompanied by the skalde, they flew direct. The trip took only eight hours and Nikaela managed to grab some sleep on the way.

The pilot of their aircraft began its descent shortly after sunup. On Nikaela's previous trip to Erikdeg, her view had been confined to the interior ribs and struts of a military transport. But now, sitting at a window, as they approached the base, she watched a barren landscape of empty prairie slide past beneath her. In Nikaela's experience, one or more nearby towns or communities supported even the most remote of bases, but not Erikdeg. It stood stark and alone in the middle of a vast plain, surrounded by a plast wall studded with guard towers and automated gun emplacements.

Their transport settled down on the runway at Erikdeg, then taxied slowly across the airfield. Nikaela hoped the skalde would now enlighten her further as to the purpose of their trip, but Kristdokar remained stonily silent. The aircraft came to a stop inside a hangar at the far end of the field, where to one side a black grav car waited for them.

As they stepped off the transport the car's driver emerged from the sedan, stepped around to one of the car's rear doors, opened it, and stood holding it for them. He said nothing as Nikaela and the skalde settled into the rear seat of the sedan. He closed the door, walked around the front of the car, and slipped into the driver's seat. Then he looked over his shoulder at Kristdokar. "Mistress, SecureMax, right?"

Nikaela thought she did a very good job of hiding her reaction.

"Yes," Kristdokar said, "SecureMax."

Like everyone else, Nikaela had heard of SecureMax: the military prison where the Larscom confined only the most treasonous and despised offenders. But like most, Nikaela had always believed such stories were simply legend and myth. And now it appeared she was about to learn the truth of the matter first hand.

The driver guided the sedan out of the hangar, then down a long access road running parallel to the main runway. He seemed to be heading to an end of the field with no structures or facilities, just an unobscured view of prairie in the distance. He drove past the end of the runway, then turned down a single-lane road that snaked toward the horizon. They never passed through a gate to exit the perimeter of the military base, but after twenty minutes of driving, Nikaela could no longer see any sign of it.

A few minutes later a separate facility with a cluster of square, boxy buildings appeared on the horizon. It had its own perimeter of guard stations and automated gun emplacements, but all aimed inward.

The driver stopped the sedan just outside a security gate manned by guards in full combat armor, which was unheard of for a simple gate guard. The driver turned his head about to look over his shoulder. "I'm sorry, mistress, but I can go no further."

He stepped out of the car, opened the rear door and politely assisted Kristdokar and Nikaela out into the morning sunlight. He pointed to a small parking lot. "I'll be waiting over there, mistress. Just let me know when you're ready to leave."

He got back into the car and drove the short distance to the parking lot.

Kristdokar looked at Nikaela with a painful grimace on her face. "We're here to see an old friend of yours."

4

Absolution

"YOU HAVE A visitor, Eindride. Get up."

Anders Eindride blinked groggily and tried to focus. He recognized that voice, one of the cruelest women he'd ever had the displeasure of meeting.

"I said get up."

Another day of mindless, backbreaking work. The judges who had found him guilty of treason to the Supremacy had sentenced him to ten years at hard labor, though with credit for time served, that had been reduced to eight, and he'd be eligible for parole after five. He had come to realize eight years in this prison were, for all intents and purposes, a death sentence. And he doubted that eligibility for parole would translate into actual release and freedom. Some days he thought a low-gravity gallows would have been far kinder than this.

"Don't make me say it a third time."

Anders sat up in what had come to be an almost conditioned response. The first thing he'd learned in prison was that the guards could be quite cruel. The second thing he had learned was to recognize the tone of voice that preceded the brutality. He suspected the guards had intended those two lessons to sink in, because he had also learned that if he responded quickly when he heard that tone, they frequently gave him a pass on the perceived infraction.

He swung his legs off the bunk and stood. One of his cellmates in the bunk overhead groaned and buried his head beneath his blankets. If they weren't making his cellmates stand as well, then for some reason they had come for him early. Only then did the guard's words sink in.

Anders focused on the blank, closed door of his cell as he asked, "Visitor, who?"

A speaker above the door said, "Don't know, don't care. You know the drill."

He thought he knew the drill, but then he had never had a visitor before. They didn't allow visitors in Erikdeg SecureMax, and he wondered who had the pull to warrant an exception to that rule.

He turned away from the cell door, extended his hands behind him, and back-stepped carefully. He knew when they switched on the augmented programming in his implants, because he didn't care. He didn't care that he was a dead man pretending to be alive, didn't care if they beat him into unconsciousness, didn't care about anything. He felt the cold plast of the manacles click into place around his wrists. The protocols in SecureMax were thorough, if nothing else.

"Step away from the door."

He couldn't have disobeyed even had he wanted to. He didn't care if he obeyed that voice or not, but his feet seemed to move of their own volition, and he took one step forward.

Behind him, he heard a mechanical racket as the plast door slide into the wall.

"Turn around and come with us."

He turned around to face two guards standing just inside the cell door, a tall burly fellow, and a woman holding a neural prod in her right hand. She casually slapped the barrel of the prod against the palm of her left hand a few times and smiled. Under different circumstances, he might have considered her attractive. But more than once he had twitched and spasmed under the sting of that prod, and those memories colored everything about the way he looked at her. She and the other guard backed out of the cell. Anders followed, knowing he should be wary of that neural prod, but he didn't care.

Out in the hallway two more guards waited for them. They paused for a moment and he heard the door clatter shut. One of the guards said, "It's secured," then they marched away from his cell, two guards in front of him, two guards behind him. He should wonder where they were taking him, but he didn't care.

They led him to a small interrogation room that contained a single, bare table with two chairs, one on each side of it. They uncuffed his hands and sat him down facing the door. The chair didn't move in the least, probably bolted to the floor. They cuffed his hands to the arms of the chair and his ankles to its legs, then left him sitting there alone. He didn't care.

He lost track of the time, but he didn't care about that either. And then the door to the room opened, and in walked a brigadier skalde who seemed familiar. It only took a second to recall that she had attended the tribunal that had ended his freedom, though she hadn't played an active role in it. He didn't know her name, and didn't really care.

Behind the skalde, Nikaela Vreekande stepped into the room. He had good memories of the young command boss, and tried to be glad she had escaped the ramifications of his crime. She looked at him sadly, but he didn't care about that either.

The skalde placed a briefcase on the table between them and opened it, which hid its contents from his view. She reached into the briefcase with one hand, turned back to Mistress Vreekande and said, "They're not supposed to monitor this room, but if they ignore the rules and try, now they'll get nothing. It never hurts to assume the worst and take precautions."

Mistress Vreekande remained standing while the skalde sat down in the chair facing Anders and gave him an appraising look. "I'm Brigadier Skalde Kristdokar. And of course you know Command Boss Vreekande."

She reached into the briefcase again, did something, and now Anders cared.

••••

When Kristdokar told Nikaela they had traveled to Erikdeg to see the man who had been her immediate superior on Novalis III, she had managed not to gasp, but it had been a close thing. After that, she had stumbled through security at the main gate of SecureMax in a state of shock, all the while wondering what Command Superior Eindride would now be like. She reminded herself he no longer carried any rank within the Supremacy.

Just outside the door to an interrogation room, Kristdokar stopped and said, "Pull yourself together and listen to me. More than a year ago I petitioned the Larscom for permission to speak with him. They didn't even give me an answer, completely ignored me, in fact. And then, without warning, yesterday I got permission. They didn't give me a reason for their earlier silence, or their sudden change of heart, but I think what we've learned so far about Reisenar, and its likely connection with Novalis III, tipped the scales."

Nikaela hadn't been close to Eindride, but she had always felt sorry for him. He had shielded her from the repercussions of Novalis III, and he himself had tried to alert his superiors to the illegal weapons they supplied to the forces there. He had tried to do the right thing.

Kristdokar continued, "When we first see him he'll probably appear quite strange. They modify their implants with subvert-ware so they can control them absolutely."

When they had enhanced her implants to military grade at the academy, regardless of the denials of the faculty, many of the cadets were convinced the Larscom had included some sort of backdoor in the programming. "How do they get past the personal crypto security? The backdoor that doesn't exist?"

Kristdokar shook her head sadly. "Your instructors didn't lie to you. A backdoor might be exploited by an enemy if they learned how to access it. But here they have physical access, so new inmates are given a choice: relinquish ring-zero access, or we'll open up their heads, burn out the old non-volatile core, and replace it with new programming. Most voluntarily give up their keys. For those who don't, it takes quite a while for the new circuits to grow and mature, but they have plenty of time here, and they're never the same again."

The skalde hesitated, then added, "They gave him ten years at hard labor, with credit for time served. That's far better than his comrades got, but this place is not kind to anyone. Prepare yourself, because the man you're going to see in there is a very different man from the one you knew."

Inside the room Anders Eindride sat in a chair on the other side of a small table, a vacant look on his face. He had clearly been restrained in some way, and when they entered he sat staring at the floor for the longest moment. Only after several seconds did he finally look up and take note of them. But his eyes held the emptiness of despair, and when he glanced toward Nikaela he looked through her with a thousand-yard stare. His cheeks appeared gaunt, and the bones of his face showed quite prominently. She recalled he had been rather handsome, and she had briefly considered taking him as a lover. But while his appearance hadn't changed much, his good looks hung on him like a shroud of sorrow and regret.

Kristdokar placed her briefcase on the table in front of Eindride, opened it and did something with its contents. She turned back to Nikaela and said, "They're not supposed to monitor this room, but if they ignore the rules and try, now they'll get nothing. It never hurts to assume the worst and take precautions."

Then she sat down opposite Eindride, reached again into the briefcase, did something, and the vacant look on his face hardened. His eyebrows narrowed and he looked at them now with wary distrust.

Kristdokar introduced herself, acknowledged Nikaela, then said, "Maestra Eindride, we'd like to speak with you."

He stared at Kristdokar for a long moment. His eyes flicked briefly to Nikaela, then back to the skalde. "That's . . . rather obvious. Why?"

Standing behind the older woman, Nikaela couldn't see Kristdokar's face, but she heard her take a deep breath, and saw her lean back in her chair. "We're investigating the incident on Novalis III."

Eindride lowered his chin and raised one eyebrow. "I thought that investigation was complete."

"We thought that as well," Kristdokar said. "But another incident on another planet appears to be connected to that on Novalis III."

His eyes narrowed angrily. "Another mass murder?"

Nikaela was glad to hear him call those deaths murder. Many in the Supremacy would consider any non-Kelk death merely collateral damage, and would not have applied that term.

Kristdokar shook her head. "No, more like an attempt to start interstellar war between the Commonwealth and the Supremacy."

Eindride shook his head. "We would not do well against the Commonwealth's vastly superior numbers."

The skalde asked, "So you don't agree with those who claim any one Kelk is worth two ComSec soldiers."

He shrugged. "What does it matter if they bring ten soldiers for every one of ours?"

Kristdokar nodded. "Exactly. So that begs the question, why would any sane Kelk want to start such a war?"

Eindride's restraints appeared to prevent him from making any motion other than the slightest of movements. "Again, I ask why you are here talking with me."

Kristdokar turned about, looked over her shoulder, and her eyes met Nikaela's. She said, "Can you answer that question, Mistress Vreekande?"

Nikaela started to say, "No, I have no idea why we're here," but then she realized she did know. She looked away from Kristdokar, met Eindride's eyes, and said,

"Because you tried to alert your superiors on Novalis III. Because you just used the word *murder* when speaking of the deaths of common-faces."

Kristdokar said, "Very good, Mistress Vreekande."

She turned back to Eindride. "I don't know what I can do for you, or even if I can do anything for you. But I needed to know who you really are, though I think Mistress Vreekande already knew that."

Eindride maintained eye contact with Nikaela as he asked, "And why would you help me?"

"I can't," Kristdokar said, "unless you can help us."

"Then how might I help you?"

Kristdokar shook her head again. "I don't know. Right now the Larscom Executive Council is on the fence regarding you. But if I can think of a way you can help, they might be quite grateful."

Eindride shook his head and closed his eyes. "I'm not going to rely too much on the gratitude of those old women."

Kristdokar stood. "Theirs may be the only gratitude you can rely on."

She leaned forward and reached for her briefcase, but hesitated. "One more thing, Maestra Eindride."

He opened his eyes and looked at her squarely.

She said, "You would be wise to forget we ever had this conversation."

He frowned. "Is that a threat?"

"No," she said, "a warning. The people we're looking for appear to be very powerful and dangerous. They are certainly quite ruthless, and I wouldn't be surprised if they can reach extremely far, even into this place."

His eyes widened slightly and he nodded. "Thank you for the warning, Brigadier."

She smiled and nodded once. "You're welcome, Maestra Eindride."

She reached forward, did something in her briefcase, and the vacant look returned to his eyes.

••••

After the two women left, Anders sat for a while staring at the wall. The restraints were uncomfortable, but he didn't really care about that.

Eventually, the four guards came for him and escorted him back to his cell. When they shut off the augmented programming in his implants, and he could care again, he had trouble finding anything to care about. He wanted to care about the strange meeting he'd just had with the brigadier and Mistress Vreekande, but he'd learned long ago that allowing hope to seep into his thoughts only set him up for disappointment.

"Eindride."

At the sound of the female guard's voice, Anders realized he'd been standing in the middle of his cell staring at the wall. He turned around to find the woman leaning against the open doorway of his cell, a minor breach of SecureMax protocols. She stood there slapping the neural prod against the palm of her hand. "That old bitch was really pissed off at you."

That guard could strike out with that prod like a viper, and he'd end up on the floor twitching, and shitting and pissing his pants. He spoke carefully. "I didn't mean to do anything wrong."

She grinned at him. "She was spittin' nails, said you refused to cooperate, said you wouldn't answer any of her questions, just sat there stone faced and called her nasty names."

It took Anders a moment to understand what the woman was saying. Kristdokar had done what she could to protect him. He might get the hot end of that neural prod jammed into his groin, but he could survive that. On the other hand, if the brigadier's enemies were as powerful as she feared, and could get to him all the way in here, they'd hear he had refused to cooperate with the skalde, and he might get to stay alive a little longer.

"Sorry," he said cautiously.

The guard shook her head and smiled rather pleasantly. "That's okay, Eindride. I didn't like that bitch anyway."

She back-stepped out of the cell, and the door clanked shut.

5

Strange Allies

"COLONEL," BRIGHTLAW'S IMPLANTS said, "Private DeLeon is here in response to your summons."

Brightlaw leaned back in the chair behind his desk and said, "Send him in."

A few seconds later the door opened and Macus DeLeon stepped forward smartly. He executed a textbook salute and said, "Private Macus DeLeon reporting as ordered, sir."

Brightlaw returned the salute. "At ease, Private."

Again, DeLeon's moves were by-the-book precise as he assumed the proper stance. He had clearly gone to a lot of trouble to perfect the physical appearance of military discipline. If only the young man had put as much effort into understanding what it took to really be a soldier.

Brightlaw said, "I've read your request for early discharge from the Corps. You do realize such a request is rarely granted, and without a compelling reason you'll be required to complete your term of enlistment regardless of your desires."

A month ago, when young Mathius had beaten the crap out of DeLeon and didn't lose a stripe for it, Brightlaw had expected DeLeon to react in some way. And a few days ago when Sergeant Mathius had returned to his barracks wearing Blacksword patches, Brightlaw thought that would really accelerate DeLeon's desire to act. It would have to be something that denied the validity of the Corps, something that allowed DeLeon to justify his own actions, even if all he came up with was some sort of specious rationalization. No, DeLeon's request had not surprised Brightlaw in the least.

DeLeon said, "Yes, sir, I do understand that."

Brightlaw didn't say that he personally felt such a discharge would be the best thing for both the Corps and Mr. DeLeon. Had the training exercise in which DeLeon abandoned his post been a real live-fire operation, he would have faced a court-martial, a dishonorable discharge, and quite possibly time in a military prison. Brightlaw didn't want DeLeon's parents to go through that, and he didn't think the young man had learned anything from the experience. According to Sergeant Omuglu, DeLeon blamed John Mathius for all of his difficulties. If he remained in the Corps he would most likely find another way to get cashiered, and probably blame Mathius for that as well. Brightlaw needed a good reason to approve DeLeon's request.

Brightlaw said, "Then why make such a request if you know it won't be granted?"

DeLeon refused to meet Brightlaw's eyes as he said, "But I'm aware such a request can be granted if there is, as you stated, a compelling reason . . . sir."

Brightlaw sincerely hoped the young man had some sort of card to play. "If there is a compelling reason, then by all means tell me about it."

DeLeon smiled, and Brightlaw wanted to shout at him to, "Wipe that fucking smile off your face, you little shit," but he held his silence.

DeLeon said, "I've been offered an opportunity to serve as an aide to Senator Palmutter."

Senator Silas Palmutter, not merely an influential politician, but a very wealthy man, and a hardline, anti-Kelk hawk. Palmutter wouldn't have simply offered a Com-SecCorps soldier such an opportunity. DeLeon must have approached the senator's staff, and probably played up the influence he had with his parents. It cost Palmutter nothing to make such an offer, and the senator might think the son of two high-ranking Blacksword officers could prove to be of considerable use. But DeLeon couldn't have set up something like that in just a few days, not across the interstellar distance between Miriteen and Trafalgar. The young man must have approached Palmutter's people a month ago when he lost a stripe and Mathius didn't. He had probably held the offer in reserve while he waited to see what happened, and the Blacksword patches on Sergeant Mathius's sleeves made the decision for him.

Brightlaw asked, "Is that a hard offer?"

"It is, sir."

"And do you have it in writing?"

"I do, sir. And it carries the official crypto signature of the senator's office."

"I'll need a copy."

"I'll forward it to you as soon as I return to my barracks, sir."

Brightlaw nodded. Yes, best for all concerned if he facilitated Mr. DeLeon's exit from the Corps. And the young man would probably prosper in politics; after all, he was that kind of person.

Brightlaw said, "As soon as I receive it, I'll approve your request. You're dismissed."

DeLeon saluted, executed a textbook about-face, and left. Stephen Brightlaw had eliminated one problem for the moment, and prayed he hadn't created an even greater problem for the future.

••••

Katrine and Fran Thealone made their way through the Senate Office Building to the office of Senator Manifort Gascoigne. He had sandwiches brought in and they talked over a casual lunch.

Thealone said, "Mani, are you familiar with the testimony we gave at that closed session of the Armed Services Committee two days ago?"

He shrugged. "I've heard the salient details. Why?"

Katrine said, "We both think Palmutter knew the answers to those questions before he asked them."

Gascoigne said, "We all have our sources."

Thealone leaned forward. "Or he could have been involved in Novalis III, or Reisenar, or both."

Gascoigne squinted at her suspiciously. "Can you prove that?"

She shook her head. "No."

He gritted his teeth as he said, "Then don't even hint at such an accusation outside this office."

She frowned at him. "You don't need to tell me that."

"Sorry," Gascoigne said, "but we're playing with fire here. So you think he knows more than he should?"

Katrine said, "Could be. He was certainly fishing, but not in a way like he was trying to learn something. More like he wanted to figure out how much we know, or suspect."

Thealone smiled at Katrine. "And you did a nice job of giving him some non-answers."

Katrine recalled the way Thealone had stood up to Palmutter during the session. "Thanks for shutting him down when he tried to push the classified thing."

Gascoigne brushed some sandwich crumbs off the front of his shirt and said, "So maybe he was somehow involved and knows more than he should because of that, or he just has good sources."

Thealone shook her head. "It bothers me that he was so interested in learning how much we know. That smacks of guilt, or at least concern, as opposed to curiosity or information gathering."

Katrine recalled Jenine Catarvin's comments after the meeting. "We ran into Senator Catarvin in the hallway after the meeting. She said something that makes me think she admires or sympathizes with Palmutter. She's not a hardliner like Palmutter, is she?"

Gascoigne frowned. "She's been neutral on the Kelk issue so far, but if she's fucking him, that could influence her thinking on the matter."

Thealone's brow wrinkled with distaste. "She's never been much of a thinker."

"She's an airhead," Gascoigne said. "It's embarrassing to sit on committee with her. But I wouldn't put it past Palmutter to fuck her just to get her support on the Kelk issue."

Thealone asked Katrine, "Do you think they're lovers?"

"I don't know," Katrine said. "I don't . . . think so, but I can't be sure."

Gascoigne asked, "What about this young soldier who surprised you so on Reisenar—that Mathius fellow?"

Katrine said, "He's now a Blacksword, and he'll be attending O-School so he'll be here on Trafalgar for the next year. I'll make sure you get a chance to meet him. You'll most likely find him rather unassuming, but don't be fooled by that."

When the lunch meeting with Gascoigne broke up, Katrine accompanied Thealone out of the Senate Office Building. They both had offices in the Armed Services Executive Office Building across the street, but Katrine needed to pack, then get a shuttle up to Trafalgar Prime where a fast hunter-killer was docked and waiting for her. They parted company on the sidewalk.

Katrine maintained a small apartment in the city within walking distance of the rotunda. It was tiny and bloody expensive, but the convenience was well worth the cost.

She enjoyed walking out in the open air, especially on a nice day. And that allowed her to avoid the subterranean tunnels connecting the government office buildings, where an aide on some senator's staff might corner her in an effort to fish for information before a senate hearing about which she knew nothing.

She stopped on a busy street corner waiting for a traffic signal to change, and a large black sedan with government plates pulled up in front of her, hovering on its grav fields. Its windows had been tinted black, so she couldn't make out anything in its interior. A rear window dilated, revealing a man about her age seated in the back seat. He had dark hair and a pleasant smile. Katrine thought of the small grav pistol in the holster beneath her armpit hidden by her coat, but didn't reach for it—not yet.

"Colonel Primatov," the man said. "My employer, Mr. Obradour, would like to speak with you privately."

She hesitated and said, "I'm not sure that's wise."

He shrugged. "All such things are relative. Which course of action do you think will be the least wise: to meet with him in private as he wishes, or to refuse to do so?"

He swung the car door open slowly and stepped out, moving carefully as if he understood it would be unwise spook her. As he did so Katrine stepped back, and she thought again of the weapon hidden beneath her coat. He indicated the open door of the sedan and said, "You have nothing to fear. Please join me."

Obradour was much too powerful to refuse, but she wasn't about to get into a black sedan with a stranger. "How do I know you actually work for Mr. Obradour? Since I don't know you, you could claim to represent anyone you choose."

As if in response to her question, her implants chimed with a secure channel from Fran Thealone's office. "Katrine, Fran here. Tarsik Obradour wants to speak to you in private. I tried to fend him off, but he's pulled some very big strings so you'll have to meet with him. He's sending one of his assistants for you in a sedan. The fellow's name is Mallik."

Katrine said, "Thanks, Fran. He's already here."

They ended the call, and Katrine said to the man standing in front of her, "And your name is?"

He nodded politely and said, "The name's Mallik, Colonel." Again, he gestured toward the open door of the sedan. "And if it gives you any comfort, we won't require you to relinquish your weapon."

"Thank you," she said. "This day is full of surprises." She stepped past him, bent, and climbed into the back of the car.

He joined her, closed the door, and the car sped away. He said, "We won't keep you long, and we'll be sure to have you back at your apartment with plenty of time to pack for your trip."

His pleasant and polite demeanor irritated her no end. "Thank you," she said. "You're most considerate."

They rode in silence after that. The sedan didn't go far and ten minutes later pulled into the circular, covered driveway in front of a high-rise apartment building. A security guard waiting at its entrance opened the car door for her. She stepped out of the sedan as Mallik climbed out of it on the other side. Another guard held the large glass door of the building open. Mallik stepped around the rear of the sedan and said, "This way, please."

She followed him into the building. He led her past a bank of elevators to a single lift that stood alone at the far end of the lobby, with another security guard standing beside it. As they approached, the doors of the lift whooshed open without any discernable action on the part of Mallik or the guard. She followed Mallik into the lift, and she noticed it didn't have the usual array of buttons for selecting a floor, nor did Mallik issue a command to tell it their destination floor. Perhaps he had done so through his implants, or perhaps it went only to one floor. The lift doors closed and an instant later reopened on a large entrance foyer bigger than Katrine's entire apartment.

Mallik stepped out into the foyer and Katrine followed. He pointed to an elegant little table with a vase on it that looked like some expensive antique. "You can leave your briefcase here, if you like."

Katrine almost said, *I like not*, but decided sarcasm would only be detrimental under the circumstances. She put the briefcase on the small table.

He pointed to an arched hallway on the far side of the room. "Please go that way. He's waiting for you."

He didn't say it, but she could almost hear the implied, *And you shouldn't keep such an important man waiting.*

She stepped into the hallway, which was only a few paces long and let out into a large open room with tall, transparent plast windows on all sides. Obradour's penthouse must occupy the entire top floor of the building. The view out over the city of Trafalgar extended to the horizon and almost took her breath away.

Obradour stood at one of the windows looking outward, his back to Katrine. From behind she noticed his close-cropped, pale-gray hair had thinned a little in the middle of the top of his head. He certainly could afford the gene therapy to prevent or correct that, but a man like him probably didn't care about such things.

He turned, and his eyes brightened when he saw her. "Colonel Primatov," he said, speaking softly.

He crossed the room toward her, extended his hand, and as she shook it she noticed his grip was gentle, but not weak or flaccid. She towered over him, probably even outweighed him, though she kept herself trim and fit. And yet, this small man commanded her attention.

"Would you like a drink?" he asked.

She didn't want a drink, but this man intimidated her no end, so just to be polite she accepted. "Yes," she said. "That would be nice."

"Whiskey?"

"Yes, thank you."

He pointed to the windows. "Enjoy the view while I pour you a glass."

Obradour turned to a bar and Katrine crossed the room. The windows extended from floor to ceiling, but she didn't pay much attention to the view as her thoughts focused on why this most-powerful of kingmakers wanted to see her. She heard the clink of glasses behind her, then a moment later he joined her at the window, handing her a glass containing a few ounces of amber liquid. She tasted it, and again he had provided her favorite whiskey.

He said, "It's a magnificent city, isn't it?"

"Yes, it is."

"You know," he said. "We are on the same side, you and me."

She turned her head to look his way. "Is that really true?"

He continued to look out over the city as he shrugged. "In more ways than you think. We both want to protect this city, and this planet, and its inhabitants, and the democratic freedoms we've established in the Commonwealth."

A question occurred to her. It would be foolish to challenge him, but she needed to know his answer. "And your power, and influence, and wealth; you want to protect that as well?"

He turned to face her squarely. "Of course! But does that have to be incompatible with our mutual interests? For example, I don't want war with the Kelk. Certainly, war can be profitable, but I don't need the money, and peace can be just as profitable, and certainly more satisfying. That said, please don't misunderstand me; if the Kelk choose war, then we will give them what they want tenfold."

They stood quite close to one another and she didn't want to tower over him, so she turned away from him and took a step toward the center of the room. She turned back to face him.

He smiled as if he understood what she had just done. "I do know about your young man, this John Mathius. I know all of the details not in the official reports, and I'm not angry at what he did on Reisenar. In fact, like you, I would commend him for thinking outside the box and doing the right thing."

She decided to take a chance. "May I be frank with you?"

He tilted his head ever so slightly to one side. "In answer to that I'll say, 'Of course,' but you'll have to decide if I really mean it."

She simply couldn't figure out how to read this man. "I get the impression you're not driven so much by the way the young man thought outside the box, but more by the fact that certain hidden interests in the Commonwealth tried to finesse us into an interstellar war. It irritates you when someone tries to manipulate you instead of approaching you directly."

His eyes widened and his lips curled into a bright smile. "Touché, Colonel. I knew I would like you the moment I met you. Well, in fact, I knew I would like you long before I met you, because I rather knew just about everything there was to know about you long before we met."

His comment didn't surprise her, though the fact that he would reveal that to her made her extremely wary of the man. Either it had been an attempt to intimidate her, or to pull her into his sphere of influence. She tried not to let her irritation show. "I'm told you're rather hawkish on the Kelk issue, but if that's true, you would be the exception regarding young Mr. Mathius, rather than the rule."

He smiled. "You're thinking of Silas Palmutter, aren't you? My people told me that rather dim-witted Catarvin woman seems to admire him, and that she may be shifting her loyalties his way."

Katrine hated the way Obradour knew everything that happened on Trafalgar, even the little things. "She can be rather . . . bothersome."

He shook his head sadly. "I find it amusing she and Palmutter seem to be gravitating to one another. Did he control himself for once and not indulge in his obsession with women's breasts?"

Katrine couldn't hide her surprise. "He stared a bit—only a little inappropriately. I didn't know it was an obsession."

Obradour lifted an eyebrow. "Don't dismiss him because of his foolish indiscretions. He is a very dangerous man. Should he learn the complete truth of what happened on Reisenar, he'll spread the word to people who don't have the best interests of your young Mr. Mathius at heart. And I do want that young man to live, because he's a natural catalyst."

She wondered if he really meant that. "I want him to live as well, but mostly because he's just a plain, nice kid."

Obradour nodded, "Who can be rather ruthless, I hear."

She shrugged, thinking Obradour could outdo her and John on the ruthless scale any day of the month. "But only when the need arises."

"That's an admirable trait," he said. "Let me make you an offer. Do count on me when you need help. I maintain a rather extensive network of assets who provide me with information. That's how I learn all those things that make me so irritatingly informed. I can't simply put those assets at your disposal because most of them would lose their effectiveness if exposed that way. But if you have a serious enough situation, and you need help, please call on me."

She said, "You surprise me."

He nodded. "Of course I do."

6

Trafalgar

IN SPARE MOMENTS during orientation John did what he could to prepare for O-School. He learned Theila would be one of his classmates for the next year, and Petra had applied for O-School, but been turned down. Petra confided to John, "They told me I could apply again in two years. I don't know if I will."

Most of the curriculum for O-School consisted of mandatory classes, enhanced physical training, and field exercises. When John learned he was allowed one elective class, he had to look up the term *elective*. There hadn't been any choices in his Com-SecCorps training so far. He carefully researched the few optional classes they offered, and at best he managed to find only mild interest in one or two. And then it occurred to him that the one thing he really wanted to learn wasn't available.

Near the end of orientation, as the other new Blackswords filed out of the room at the end of the day, he approached Teal and said, "Major, may I ask a question about O-School?"

Teal said, "By all means."

John wasn't sure how to say this. "For my elective class, they don't offer what I was hoping for."

Teal frowned, and with a bit of impatience in his voice, he said, "Well there's not much I can do about that. You'll just have to select from what's available. What were you hoping for?"

As Teal shrugged into an overcoat, John said, "I was hoping to learn a little of the Kelk language. Maybe some of their customs, and . . ."

John let his voice trail off because Teal froze with one arm in the overcoat. He stood statue-still for a few heartbeats, then he blinked, frowned, and said, "I don't know that that can be arranged. Select one of the available offerings and I'll make some inquiries. But don't hold out too much hope."

John and Carla spent one last night together before she shipped out on *Fearless*. Lying beside her in bed before falling asleep, she said, "I won't ask you if you'll miss me."

"But I will," he said.

"Not the way you miss Hey-You."

He'd never considered that, and he realized she was right. "I'll miss you just as much, but not in the same way. More like I miss family."

She grinned, and he knew he'd triggered her off-color sense of humor. "Kind of like brother and sister with incestuous benefits. I'll definitely miss those benefits. If I'd known incest was this much fun, I would have taken it up long ago, except I don't have any brothers or sisters."

"But I will miss you. You and Roark and Leeze were the first real friends I made after I left Novalis III."

She froze, and only then did he realize what he'd just said. He'd never told any of his platoon mates about his origins.

"Novalis III?" she asked.

Inwardly he grimaced and hoped she wouldn't ask a lot of questions. "Yah."

She lay there for a long moment processing that information. "You were there when they killed everyone?"

"Yah."

"You were one of the survivors?"

"Yah."

"Shit!" she said, sitting up, completely oblivious to her naked body with a casualness John had difficulty adopting. "Shit! I always knew there was something."

She leaned close to him, put a hand on the back of his neck and pulled him close; no kiss, just pressing her cheek against his. "Do you want to tell me about it?"

"No," he said. "Not yet. Maybe someday."

"Okay," she said, and kissed his cheek. "And I'll miss you too."

She shipped out the next morning, and two days later John boarded a ComSec destroyer for deadhead passage to Trafalgar, the capital planet of the Commonwealth. He had a lot of time on his hands during the trip, and his disappointment that he would not learn more about the Kelk surfaced in his thoughts repeatedly.

He did a little homework on the matter, and realized how foolish his request had been. Outside of the intelligence community there wasn't much known about the Kelk, and what little John found was heavily colored by salacious descriptions of their demonic appearance, and tales of their legendary atrocities. Stealing and eating children was still a fairly common theme. He even found a supposedly academic discourse on the horrific methods the blue-skinned monsters used to murder the children, with a nice sidebar on the ritualistic recipes employed to prepare them for the table. The authors carefully documented their sources of information, and John noticed that none of it had been based on first-hand interaction with real Kelk, just other authors who made up their own shit. The Kelk were not a popular subject for academic study, and when it came to learning the language, there were only a few obscure professors who spoke it with any real proficiency.

As the destroyer approached the Trafalgar system, John wondered if the stories he had heard of Trafalgar Prime even vaguely represented the truth. "You won't believe your fucking eyes," one of the destroyer's spacers told him. "Bigger than anything you've ever seen, I'll bet."

Novalis III hadn't warranted one of the big stations, nor did the planet to which they evacuated him. His first experience on a Prime station had been when he arrived at Miriteen for recruit training. But they'd hustled him through the station in short order, and at that time he'd still been in an extended state of shock from Novalis III. He hadn't really come out of that until the exhaustion of basic training set in.

His first solid memory of a big station came from when he, Roark, Leeze and Carla had reported for their first year of active duty aboard the destroyer *Defiant*—he missed the three of them and hoped they were okay. The four of them had gone up to Miriteen Prime a few days early, and he recalled strolling down a wide avenue with the three of them at his side. During the following year *Defiant* had docked at a couple of large stations, but none of them came even close to the size of Miriteen Prime. He suspected the stories of Trafalgar Prime were an exaggeration.

Nevertheless, when the destroyer down-transited into the Trafalgar system, he wandered down to the main mess where the crew had an exterior vid channel displayed on a large screen. He grabbed a cup of caff and sat down with a bunch of other deadhead passengers to watch the ship approach the big station.

It first showed on the screen as a pinpoint of light barely distinguishable from the background field of stars. But as they got closer it took on shape, and as he had expected, it appeared to be much like Miriteen Prime, with tiny little ships maneuvering into position at its docks. And then they got a little closer and he recognized the shape of one of those ships: a massive freighter that provided a scale against which he could now comprehend the size of Trafalgar Prime. Someone gasped as they too came to understand the girth of the enormous station. It could have swallowed a dozen Miriteen Primes.

Allship blared, "Disembarkation in one hour."

John returned to the bunk they had assigned him, packed his duffel, then made his way to the aft personnel hatch. Just as he stepped into line there, the ship's hull echoed with the clang of docking booms clamping into place. One of the ship's junior officers checked him off the list, and he stepped out into the station.

From inside, Trafalgar Prime looked like any other big station. John didn't really have time to spare, so he took a shuttle down to the surface, then a high-speed grav train that dropped him off a few blocks from the O-School academy. With his duffel bag tossed over one shoulder, his implants guided him to the main entrance. He reported in at the guard station there, then followed the directions in his implants to the dormitory building where he would spend the next year.

A non-com seated behind a table in the foyer gave him his room number. The fellow said, "You're bunking with Mayella Forester. She checked in about half an hour ago, so she's probably up there now."

John took a lift up to his floor and followed the directions in his implants down a hallway, looking for his own room. Most of the doors in the hallway were open, and in almost every room he spotted one or more cadets. Those who had arrived earlier lounged about, while newcomers like John were busy unpacking their gear.

When he found his room and stepped into it, his new roommate looked up from unpacking her duffel and smiled. She had chin-length, brownish-blond hair, and bright-brown eyes.

"You must be Mayella," he said, sticking out his hand. "I'm John Mathius."

She shook his hand and said, "Call me May. I don't like the long form, so please don't ever call me that."

She took note of the patches on his sleeves and said, "Blacksword, huh? How'd you get that?"

He was glad for her easy attitude, and relieved she didn't hold him in awe, or something. He shrugged and said, "I'm not quite sure. They just offered it to me."

She squinted and looked at him with disbelief. "You must have done something."

"Well, maybe," he said. "At the end of my active duty year there was this incident on a planet called Reisenar."

Her eyes widened. "Reisenar, I heard rumors about that."

"You did?" he asked, wondering if what she and his other classmates had heard bore any resemblance to the truth.

"Yah. Nothing official, but there were some veiled references in the news feeds, and rumors everywhere. Heard it was a real shoot-'em-up. Some guy ended it by collaborating with the Kelk, or something like that. I heard they locked him away in some military prison. Did you know him?"

John grimaced. He took the word *collaborating* to have a decidedly negative connotation. "I think that was me."

"It was you?" she asked. "I would have thought they'd court-martial you for working with the Kelk."

"It was complicated," John said. He repeated his carefully edited version of the events on Reisenar, and really didn't want to go into a lot of detail.

When he finished she didn't say anything for several seconds, then blurted out, "You're right, that was complicated."

He didn't try to hide the strain in his voice as he said, "I really don't think I'm supposed to talk about it too much."

She grinned. "Okay, John Mathius. My lips are sealed. No more questions."

Unlike boot camp the academy did not demand celibacy of its cadets, but intimate relationships between roommates were prohibited. May was attractive enough, but John didn't want a close relationship at that time so he was content with the prohibition.

John had half-finished unpacking his gear when a male cadet leaned in through their doorway and said, "Belay that, people. It's party time. We're headed down to the strip."

The fellow was quite handsome, with dark, brown hair and striking blue eyes. He hesitated and looked at May more carefully, then stepped fully into the room and extended his hand to her. "Nash Wakeland. And you are?"

May introduced herself, then pointed to John and said, "This is my roomie, John Mathius."

Wakeland glanced at John and said, "One of them hotshot Blackswords, huh?" He was obviously more interested in May than John. "You don't have a stick up your ass, or anything, do you?"

May leaned over and looked at John's butt. "I don't see a stick, and I think it would protrude a bit."

Wakeland grinned, turned about and said, "Both of you, follow me, no excuses."

The *strip* turned out to be a broad avenue a few blocks off campus with bars, restaurants and stores that catered to cadets who wanted to shop or let off a little steam. Wakeland proved to be a nice guy with all the outward charm John could never claim. They had a good time and most of them got a little drunk, but only a little.

When they returned to the dormitory John had a message waiting for him. An hour before lunch the next morning he was to report to his advisor, Lieutenant Commander Chillawan, a male Blacksword officer. The other newly-arrived cadets had similar messages waiting for them.

He had had a good time with his new friends on the strip, and John went to bed thinking he might enjoy his year at O-School.

The next day he reported promptly to Chillawan's office, knocked on the door, and his implants replied with, "You may enter, Cadet Mathius."

John knew he should make a good impression, so he carefully followed the traditional formula, snapped to attention two paces in front of Chillawan's desk, and said, "Sergeant Mathius, reporting as ordered, sir."

Chillawan returned his salute crisply. "At ease and relax. And it's no longer Sergeant Mathius. It's now Cadet Mathius. And with all the extra studies you've got, you're going to have a very busy year, young man."

John asked, "Extra studies, sir?"

"Yes," Chillawan said. "They brought in a special tutor: Professor Emmet Dirkson. He's going to teach you Kelk language and culture, though why the hell they're making you suffer through that crap is beyond me. But none of that extra work counts toward the main requirements of the academy, so that'll be extracurricular. Welcome to O-School, Cadet Mathius."

••••

Anders lifted the sledge hammer and brought it down on the rock in front of him. It shattered into three smaller pieces and a bunch of chips. He lifted the sledge again and broke the three smaller pieces into even smaller pieces. Another day at hard labor, breaking up rocks no one cared about. He even suspected they didn't put the crushed rock to any useful purpose. When he and the other convicts crushed enough, they brought in a heavy grav truck, handed them shovels and made them fill the truck's bed with the pulverized rock. They could crush rock far better with inexpensive heavy equipment, but that didn't punish the convicts properly.

The shadow of a guard blocked the sun for a moment.

"Eindride."

He looked up to the lip of the rock pit. A male guard he recognized stood above him with his fists on his hips.

"Doctor wants to see you, Eindride. Something came back in the blood work from your last check up and he wants to look you over. Can't have you dying on us before you crush your share of rock. Hop to it, asshole, double-time."

Anders jogged over to the equipment truck and turned in his sledge hammer. Then he jogged up the ramp out of the pit. He stopped five paces short of the guard and waited, as protocol demanded. And then he stopped caring.

They shoved him into the back of a grav lift, and he lay there as they ferried him back to SecureMax. Something wrong with his blood work! Maybe he would die. He wondered if they did anything to keep convicts alive when they found something wrong with their blood work. They probably found it easier to just let them die off, but he didn't really care about that.

When they arrived back at SecureMax, they ushered him into an examination room where a doctor in surgical scrubs waited for him. The man told him to sit down on an examination table, and of course Anders obeyed because the altered programming in his implants left him no choice. He thought he would have obeyed them anyway, even if the programming hadn't forced him to. He noticed he left a smear of rock dust, dirt and sweat on the table.

The doctor left the room and a woman replaced him, also wearing surgical scrubs. Something in his thoughts told him he should know this woman, but he just didn't care enough to go to the trouble to recall her. And then he did care, and he recognized Brigadier Skalde Kristdokar.

He looked around the room; the two of them were alone.

She said, "You look like hell."

He grimaced at her. "And you look like you don't belong in those scrubs."

"No," she said, "but they'll do nicely for this."

He pushed off the table and stood. She stepped back, staying well out of his reach. He grinned and said, "Pretty serious breach of protocols, turning off the augmented programming without me restrained, or a team of guards present. Aren't you worried I might try something?"

She gave him an unpleasant smile. "If you did, I'd kill you and we wouldn't have much to talk about after that. But I'm confident you won't, because I'm here to make you an offer."

"An offer?" he asked. "What kind of offer?"

"It would involve early parole. You were the only one who made an attempt to alert us to the unconventional weapons. And you've demonstrated good behavior while here, so we could make the story sound good."

He wasn't sure he trusted her, but he'd do anything to get out of that place. "So you figured out some way I can help you?"

She cocked her head to one side and winced. "Maybe."

"Maybe?" he asked.

She took a breath and let out a sigh. "I have to be honest with you. I haven't come up with anything concrete, but if you agree to try, then we'll parole you and throw you out there."

"I'm not eligible for parole for at least two more years."

"That is a problem," she said. "To be honest, I'm not sure if I can overcome that."

Any hope he might have harbored died with those words. "So regardless of all your lofty promises, I'll just have to rot in here."

"Perhaps," she said. "I don't know. I have some support in the Larscom, but I'm not sure how much, and I don't know if it's enough, at least not right now. But if I can make it happen, you'll be the embittered, cashiered ex-command-superior. And maybe someone will try to make contact with you. If they do, then it would be in your best interests to let me know about it."

He wasn't about to admit to her he would jump at anything to get out of that place. "Or maybe they'll just kill me."

She slowly nodded once. "That's a possibility. But if it works, and you do help us, the Larscom will be very grateful."

He wanted to see if she would lie to him. "And what will that gratitude buy me?"

She shrugged. "I don't know, and the Larscom is not going to negotiate on the issue. Say yes and you'll go back to breaking rocks, then, in a few months you'll be paroled, but under cover you'll be working for me. Say no, and you'll just go back to breaking rocks."

She looked at him carefully for a moment, then added, "But you knew all that anyway, didn't you?"

"Yah," he said.

"You just wanted to see if I'd lie to you, didn't you?"

"Yah."

"Well," she asked, "is it yes or no?"

He grinned as he said, "You already know the answer to that, don't you?"

She grinned back at him. "Yes, I do."

7

Old Allies

OUT ON THE street outside the hotel, rain slanted down at a sharp angle, adding to the gloom of a cloud-darkened night, and filling the gutters with a torrent of water. The first time Katrine had come to Norandyne and experienced such a downpour, she had thought the intensity of the rainfall might flood the street. But the planet's inhabitants had long ago learned to properly manage their overabundant water resources, and the storm drains remained clear and unimpeded. The flow did force them to make certain concessions. Tractioned vehicle transport was virtually unheard of on the planet. When it rained, as it did for most of every day, vehicles that needed to actually make contact with the surface of the road would find it difficult to navigate the river-like flows in Norandyne's streets. The locals relied almost exclusively on grav transport that hovered above the torrent.

The planet was a mud ball, and it rained incessantly, though once or twice every tenday the clouds cleared to reveal a brilliant blue sky and verdant, green vegetation. But such brief respites from dismal, gray skies were few and far between, and Katrine couldn't understand how anyone lived in such a miserable place.

A grav car floated up to the pedestrian quay in front of the hotel, the dark shadow of a lone passenger barely visible in the back seat.

"Miss Fallon."

At the sound of the name of her assumed identity, Katrine turned to face the bell captain, a small man with typically dark, Norandynian features. He wore a tailcoat modeled after styles of a far distant past, and a black, broad-brimmed hat, all classic attire for a Norandynian gentleman, though anachronistic by any other standard. As he crossed the hotel lobby, he closed the front of a greatcoat that extended down to his ankles. "May I help you to your car?"

"Thank you," she said. "That's most kind of you." She didn't need his help, but she always tried to adapt to the local customs, and he would be insulted if a guest of the hotel turned down his offer of aid, especially a woman. Norandynian men tended to be exceedingly courteous to women, which she didn't mind.

He gave her a warm smile. "I'm pleased to be of service, madam."

The air above him shimmered with a tightly compressed gravity field generated by equipment built into the fabric of his greatcoat. He held out his arm and she rested the palm of her hand on his forearm, as was customary on Norandyne. She walked with him as he opened the glass doors at the front of the hotel and stepped out into the slanting rain. The gravity field of the greatcoat kept them both quite dry as he opened the rear door of the car and held it for her. She bent down and stepped into it, sitting next to the car's only passenger. The bell captain closed the door and the car sped away from the curb.

The man seated next to her said, "Colonel, it's good to see you again."

She said, "Thank you for joining me, Major. You've been briefed?"

"Only minimally," he said, a slight note of annoyance in his voice.

"And you're armed?"

"Of course, Colonel."

Katrine reached into her raincoat and pulled the heavy grav pistol from the holster beneath her left armpit. She checked its charge and load, then returned it to the holster. There were certain advantages to the never-ending rain. The heavy raincoat allowed her to conceal a very serious weapon, rather than trying to hide something smaller and less powerful. Unfortunately, it also allowed her opponents to conceal similar weapons that might be used against her.

She asked the major, "How much were you told?"

He lifted his eyebrows in an unasked question and said, "Your identity is Miss Madrid Fallon. I was to pick you up at the hotel, accompany you, be prepared for danger, but not expect it. I was also told to arrange for a very discrete meeting place, then send the address to a particular number."

She said, "The identity is new and clean. I may use it again."

As a senior Blacksword officer, and their most senior asset on Norandyne, the minimal briefing the man had been given was almost an insult. That was the unasked question hinted at by the lifted eyebrows, and it was time to enlighten him further with information she hadn't wanted to transmit by courier.

She continued, "One reason you were selected for this is because you have a reasonably balanced view of the Kelk situation, and can be trusted to act accordingly in their presence." She looked his way.

His eyebrows lifted, he grinned and asked, "Meaning I won't start shooting the minute I come face-to-face with one?"

She grinned back at him and said, "Not just one; probably two or three."

"You trust them?"

She dropped the grin. "Those we're about to meet, I do." His grin disappeared as she gave him a brief and highly edited version of the incident on Reisenar. She finished with, "I apologize that you weren't briefed more fully, but it's extremely sensitive, and absolute need-to-know classified."

He nodded and said, "Now I understand. I'm surprised the young man didn't face a court-martial. Alternatively, someone might have taken him out to some remote place and put a bullet in the back of his head."

"They may yet do that," she said, "though actually he's probably safe. Very few are aware of his level of involvement in the situation, and he's quite junior, so no one is looking his way."

While briefing the major, she had taken great care to exclude all names. If he chose to investigate the incident and went to considerable effort, he could probably identify young John Mathius. But he would have to dig quite deep to do so; that would likely alert her to his curiosity, and she would never again trust him. In any case, he was much too smart to be that stupid.

Katrine said, "Is the man who arranged this meeting place aware of my true identity?"

"No," he said, "nor is he aware of mine, but he's not stupid. I'm sure he has guessed I possess a fairly senior rank within one of the Commonwealth military branches. He will assume you possess even greater authority, either military or political."

"How much can you trust him?"

"He believes quite strongly it is in Norandyne's best interests to align with Commonwealth policies, has even expressed the opinion to close friends that the Norandyne star system should seek Commonwealth membership. Thankfully, he's not an outspoken firebrand on that, which might draw unwanted attention to him, and that discretion makes him an even more valuable asset. He's quite well off financially, so he can't be tempted by money, and he doesn't have any unusual proclivities, so he can't be coerced through extortion or intimidation. And I and my people keep a very low profile, so it's unlikely anyone knows he's working with us."

She said, "Sounds like you keep a close eye on him."

He nodded once. "We do."

"Does he know who we're going to meet?"

"No. I asked for a private and secluded place where I could meet with some people with whom I am negotiating. I told him we'd need to keep everything quiet and out of the public eye. Until a few moments ago not even I suspected the nature of our guests, so he's double-blind."

The grav car pulled up to a square, boxy building and stopped on the pedestrian quay in front of it. The place had a large loading dock with slots that could accommodate several heavy grav trucks. Katrine looked at the major.

Looking at the building, he said, "It's an inactive facility in which our host stores surplus and defunct equipment. It doesn't see daily use."

"Ideal," she said.

She popped the lock on the door, activated the umbrella field in her raincoat, and raised its collar to cover her features as much as possible. She pushed the door open and stepped out into the rainy gloom. A nearby street light barely managed to illuminate the sidewalk in front of her. The major stepped around the car and joined her. He led her to the front door of the warehouse, but paused there, leaned close to her and raised his voice to be heard above the spatter of the rainfall. "Wait here while I make sure it's safe."

"No," she said, shouting the same way he had. "Our guests will be jumpy, and they don't know you."

He nodded, opened the door, stepped aside and held it for her. For a moment she considered reaching into her raincoat to rest her hand on the butt of her grav pistol, but thought it better to keep her hands open and visible. She stepped through the door and stopped just within. Rain hammering on the building produced a constant din that made it difficult to hear footsteps or other subtle sounds, so she didn't hear the major step in behind her, but she did hear the clump of the door as he closed it.

She stood at the edge of a large room with a flat concrete floor. On her left a shadowy assortment of heavy equipment had been parked in a haphazard pattern. In front of her and to her right the floor remained clear and empty. About forty feet above her a latticework of steel and plast girders supported the roof. At the far end of the concrete floor, one dim light illuminated a door that probably led to an inner office. A shadowy figure draped in a heavy, hooded raincoat stood beneath the light in front of the door.

The major stepped several paces to one side to avoid making both of them an easy target for a quick burst of fire. He illuminated the floor in front of them with the beam of a flashlight. They didn't have to worry about the light exposing their positions and making them easy targets; without combat armor to mask their IR signatures, they were easy targets regardless.

Katrine extended her hands and held them to either side, palms out. She started forward and the major matched her pace. Nothing happened as she crossed the distance and stopped a few paces from the shadowy figure standing in front of the office door. Katrine stood eye-to-eye with many men, and she had to look up to meet the eyes of the person in front of her, so she guessed she faced a man. The hood of his raincoat completely hid his features in shadow. If a person wanted to move about unrecognized, on Norandyne heavy cloaks and raincoats were the norm, so a certain amount of anonymity was one advantage of the planet's atrocious climate.

Katrine carefully and slowly reached up, lowered the heavy collar of her raincoat and unbuttoned a few buttons to fully expose her face. In response, the man in front of her pulled the hood of his cloak back. He had dark brown skin tone and brown eyes, his face framed by shoulder length salt and pepper gray hair, with more pepper than salt. But regardless of the makeup, contact lenses, and visual distortion field produced by equipment in his raincoat, she recognized him easily.

During the year since they had last met, Katrine had been intensely practicing her Kelk. She spoke it now as she said, "Command Superior Brynjar, thank you for coming all this way."

His eyes widened a little. "You speak Kelk, Colonel Primatov, and with only a bit of accent."

She thought her accent was far worse than he implied and suspected he was being kind. She continued in Kelk, "Hopefully, I'll do better in the future. But right now my vocabulary is somewhat limited. May we continue in Lingua?"

He switched to Lingua and spoke without an accent. "My pleasure, Colonel."

The major approached them. She introduced the two men, giving the major the false name and rank of Captain Smythe. The major knew not to extend his hand for a shake.

Brynjar stepped aside, opened the door to the office and held it for them. When Katrine stepped into the room she found it contained a table and chairs, but none of Brynjar's comrades as she had expected. The office walls did insulate them somewhat from the sound of the rain pounding on the warehouse roof.

The major followed her in, as did Brynjar, who left the door open. A few seconds later Senior Command Superior Thordahl and Oberseergent Geltkarl stepped into the room. They had chosen to be cautious, had not waited in the confined space of the office where they might be cornered if the unexpected happened.

Thordahl stood a little shorter than most men, while Geltkarl stood about average height for a woman, but had broad shoulders, and like many very senior NCOs, a commanding attitude. They both greeted Katrine pleasantly, and she again introduced the major as Captain Smythe.

After they finished with the introductions Brynjar produced a bottle of clear liquid with a label in Kelk script that Katrine couldn't decipher. Geltkarl placed five small shot glasses on the table, and as Brynjar filled them from the bottle he said, "Kirva, a good way to start a mutually beneficial relationship."

Katrine had heard of the fiery alcohol, but never tasted it.

Geltkarl handed them each a full glass. The three Kelk raised theirs in salute, so Katrine and the major did likewise. The Kelk tossed their drinks back in a single gulp. With some trepidation, Katrine did the same, and fought hard to keep from gasping as the kirva burned its way down to her gut.

Following that little ceremony, Brynjar, Thordahl and Katrine gathered around the table, though none of them sat down. The major and Geltkarl remained in the background. Thordahl asked, "Has there been any fallout at your end?"

"No," Katrine said. "We've carefully sanitized records and reports of the incident on Reisenar, and there's no mention anywhere of the breschkada relationship between our two very junior officers."

Thordahl nodded and said, "We've done the same, though several members of the Larscom are aware she is breschkada, so it may not be as much of a secret as we might hope. In any case, if it's widely disseminated, we don't think our young woman will live long."

Katrine said, "And we fear the same danger exists for our young man."

Thordahl shook his head sadly. "Odd how alike we are: so many of my countrymen hate those who don't share their hatreds."

Katrine said, "I have been authorized to give you a certain piece of information regarding the tragedy on Novalis III."

All three Kelk froze, and Katrine realized she had touched a nerve. "We are under the impression you believe you Kelk were wholly responsible for that tragedy. Is that true?"

They stared at her, suspicion and anger clouding their features, and none of them spoke. She continued. "We have certain evidence to indicate some of the bio-agents used were of Commonwealth origin."

The Kelk remained silent and still. Thordahl said, "Who?"

"We don't know," Katrine said. "The trails all ended in the independent systems near Novalis, sometimes with the convenient death of a local agent or two. Just as on Reisenar, hardline Commonwealth haters on your side and Kelk haters on our side joined with corporate interests on both sides who saw the potential for financial gain. We strongly suspect the same groups were responsible for both Reisenar and Novalis III."

Thordahl leaned forward and planted his hands flat on the table. "This will change much of our thinking on both matters. Are you willing to share the data you have?"

Katrine reached into her coat and retrieved a small comp chip. She handed it to Thordahl and told him the encryption key, finishing with, "Three attempts to decode it with the wrong key, and it will self-wipe in a rather dramatic way. It also contains the coordinates of a communications buoy we've set up just outside of Commonwealth sovereign space, and a special encryption key. The buoy is the first in a relay chain that stretches back to Trafalgar. Get a ship within five light-years of that buoy, broadcast a transition signal on that encryption key, and the encrypted message will land on my desk within a day or two."

Thordahl grinned and nodded his head. "We've done something quite similar." Thordahl reached into his coat, retrieved a comp chip like the one she had given him, and handed it to her. "That contains the encryption key and coordinates of ours."

Geltkarl stepped forward and asked Thordahl, "Please I ask question, Command Superior?" She spoke with a bit of an accent.

Thordahl waved a hand at her and smiled kindly. "Of course, Oberseergent."

She looked pointedly at Katrine as she asked, "You said two junior officers. Your young man no more private, no more enlisted?"

Katrine and Fran Thealone had decided to give them that information as well, so she had purposefully dropped that hint. "No, he's not. He was promoted to corporal, then sergeant, and is now attending our officer school. He is also now a Blacksword, and we have high hopes for him."

Thordahl shrugged. "He is breschkada-sa. That means he is smarter than most."

Katrine couldn't help but smile as she thought of the slightly timid young man who had almost killed their young woman. "Yes, he is. And your young woman is also clearly smarter than most."

Thordahl grinned. "Yes, she is. But we don't tell her that. She needs to learn a bit more humility."

Katrine suppressed a slight chuckle. "And I'd like to see our young man learn to be a little more assertive."

Brynjar said, "It occurs to me we should meet like this regularly, perhaps every month."

"An excellent idea," Katrine said, "though I might not always make the trip myself. Captain Smythe can stand in for me." She'd have to more thoroughly brief him on the events on Novalis III and Reisenar.

Thordahl said, "We'll provide you with a list of subordinates you can trust."

Katrine had a thought. "And let's randomly space the meetings. It wouldn't be wise to establish a repetitive pattern."

They agreed on a time and date for the next meeting. But before that meeting broke up, Katrine had one more piece of information she must impart, something quite sobering. "I should tell you the factions responsible for Reisenar and Novalis III were quite ruthless when they cleaned up after themselves in the independent systems. They killed dozens of agents and provocateurs, and sometimes their families as well. The death toll easily surpassed one hundred."

Thordahl's eyebrows shot up. Geltkarl frowned. Brynjar didn't react.

Katrine added, "Of course, that's nothing compared to the lives lost on Novalis III, but these were all targeted assassinations. And I should add most of them were made to look like an accident."

Thordahl sighed and said, "Mutual hatred does make for strange bedfellows."

They parted, and on the way back to the hotel, Katrine thoroughly briefed the major.

8

Parole

AT THE KNOCK on the door, John stood up from the little fold-down desk in his dorm room, crossed to the door and opened it. Nash Wakeland stood in the hallway with a small cadre of cadets loitering behind him. "Come on, Mathius," Wakeland said. "We're going to the strip to party a little. Join us."

John shook his head. "I can't. I gotta hit the books. And I've got a class first thing in the morning."

In many ways Nash Wakeland had turned out to be much like Macus DeLeon, but without the attitude, or the chip on his shoulder. In physical training, sports, and hand-to-hand combat drills, he outclassed the rest of them. And he seemed to excel at the classroom work without the need to sweat over the books all evening the way John did. More than once Wakeland had organized a little foray to the strip in the middle of a tenday, and more than once John had turned down an invitation to join them. But above all, Wakeland was just a plain, nice guy, without the asshole coefficient of a Macus DeLeon. John wished he were a little smarter, like Wakeland, so he didn't have to spend so much time studying.

Wakeland shook his head. "You need to get a life." He turned and marched away, with his cohort following close on his heels. But a short distance down the hall he stopped abruptly, forcing them to bunch up to avoid running into him.

He looked back at John and grinned, "Next ten-end, you don't get to say no."

John nodded. "Next ten-end."

John closed the door and found May Forester standing behind him. She smiled and said, "You did the right thing, John."

"I know," he said, unable to hide the disappointment in his voice.

She shook her head and her nose scrunched up as if she had just swallowed something sour. "I don't like that guy."

"Wakeland?"

"Yes."

"Why not?"

She waved his question off impatiently. "I don't know. Something about him just doesn't ring true."

He asked, "You're going to help me on the sublight navigation homework, right?"

She grinned. "That's why I'm here. Good old May, the sublight navigation genius. I need to get a life too."

••••

Another day in the rock pit. Another day of mindless, back-breaking labor. Some days it might be a different rock pit and different rocks, but every day was another day like all the rest, and they all blended together into mindless drudgery. Anders didn't really care.

As the sun began to set, Anders lined up with all the other inmates at the equipment truck. He'd been a pick-man that day, and when he finally reached the front of the line he surrendered the heavy pickaxe, then climbed into the back of a big grav truck with a couple dozen of his fellow inmates. They rode in silence back to the facility, no chatter or banter, because none of them really cared about anything worth talking about.

The inmates showered in groups of thirty to forty, and during that time the guards turned off the augmented programming in their implants. Otherwise they'd just stand there staring at the wall and not wash away all the rock dust and sweat. The guards left the programming deactivated during dinner for the same reason. It was so easy to forget to eat when one didn't care about anything. After dinner the guards ushered them back to their cells, then activated the sleep programming. SecureMax had always been a quiet and restful place.

The next morning they woke them at precisely the same hour as the day before, and the day before that, and all the days before that. Anders prepared for another day of the same, but as he and his cellmates filed out of their cell, one of the guards lowered his neural prod and blocked Anders's path.

"Not today, Eindride," the fellow said. "They got something else planned for you, so you get the day off."

He sat alone in his cell for several hours, waiting for whatever it was that had broken his daily routine. He almost wished they had left the augmented programming on. The time would have passed much quicker if he didn't care. Caring had become just another form of torture.

At mid-morning four guards came for him, led by the woman with the neural prod. They followed the protocols precisely, and with his hands cuffed in plast manacles behind his back, and his thoughts sedated by the augmented programming, they marched him to the administration block. They ushered him into a blank and featureless room with two tables, a small one in the middle of the room, and a large one against one wall. They sat him down in a chair at the small table, then cuffed his hands to the chair's arms and his ankles to its legs. They left him sitting there alone facing the larger table at the far end of the room. He tried to care, but it had become so difficult to do so.

Several minutes later two military constables stepped into the room, both carrying neural prods. A female major skalde followed close on their heels, along with a male command eagle. The skalde looked familiar, though Anders wasn't sure from where or when, because he didn't really care.

The skalde sat down behind the larger table, and the command eagle sat down beside her. She looked into Anders's eyes for the longest moment, then said, "Begin recording."

The command eagle said, "Yes, mistress."

At that moment Anders cared again, and he now recognized the woman. She had been one of the skaldes who had presided over the tribunal that found him guilty of treason and mass murder.

She said, "This parole hearing is now in order."

During the clandestine meeting with Kristdokar in the infirmary, she had given him hope this mindless ordeal might end. But it had been hard to maintain hope day after day, then tenday after tenday. And in any case, two months ago she hadn't had the support within the Larscom to get his parole eligibility reduced from five years. He had eventually lost track of the time because he just didn't care.

The skalde said, "Please state your name for the record."

He wondered if that was some sort of trick question. "Anders Eindride."

She glanced toward the command eagle seated next to her and said, "For the record, please read the charges of which he was found guilty."

The command eagle read a long statement filled with legalese and words like *high treason* and *murder*. When he finished, the skalde gave Anders a hard look and said, "What do you have to say for yourself?"

She had caught him off guard. "I ... uh ..." He took a deep breath and tried desperately to focus. "I did try to alert my superiors to the existence of the illegal weapons shipments."

"Yes, you did," the skalde said. "You brought it to the attention of your immediate superior, a command hawk as I recall. And how did she respond?"

Anders had answered all these questions a hundred times before, and he would answer them a hundred times again, if it got him out of this mind-numbing straightjacket they called a prison.

"She told me I was mistaken. I insisted I was not mistaken, we argued heatedly, and she ordered me to bury it and never mention it again."

The skalde sat with her eyes boring into Anders's. Her head nodded very slowly down, and then back up, a single motion. "And what did you do then?"

"I waited," he said, "just a few tendays, but long enough to let her cool down. Then I went over her head to her immediate superior, a command eagle."

"And how did the command eagle respond?"

"She was sympathetic and told me she would take care of it. Then a few days later three soldiers beat the crap out of me behind our barracks. They told me if I tried to go over the command eagle, I wouldn't live to testify against her. But you already know all of that, don't you?"

The command eagle seated next to her leaned over and spoke to the skalde in hushed tones. She listened intently, then leaned back in her chair, steepled her fingers in front of her, and regarded Anders for a long moment.

"That's why we're here," she said. "You made the effort, twice. That's why you were only given ten years, with the possibility of parole after three."

It had been five years, but he didn't say that. Apparently they were all going to pretend his original parole eligibility had been three years. Something must have happened to really scare those old women in the Larscom.

She quizzed him, and made him walk her through every intimate detail of his actions on Novalis III. And he answered all her questions with the same answers he'd given before. After an hour and a half of grilling, she said, "We're going to confer in private."

She and the command eagle stood and left the room. Anders desperately feared he had screwed up his one chance at freedom, and he almost wished they had activated the augmented programming so he didn't care. But he did care, and the minutes ticked by slowly.

When the two of them returned, they sat back down behind the table, she looked Anders in the eyes, and said, "Counting the time served prior to your conviction, you are now eligible for parole, and we believe that no further purpose will be served by your continued incarceration. You will be remanded to a rehabilitation facility in Hyerdride. Make the best use of your time there, Maestra Eindride, because if you fail this, you will not be given another chance."

Anders wondered if that was a stock warning for paroled inmates, or a veiled reference to his vague agreement with Kristdokar. It couldn't be a coincidence that this woman had showed up to parole him less than two months after he had agreed to aid the skalde. And pretending his parole eligibility had always been three years seemed to confirm that.

The major skalde and command eagle left the room with the two MCs following close on their heels. Some unknown amount of time passed, but Anders didn't really care about that, or about anything for that matter.

Eventually, the SecureMax guards returned and escorted him back to his cell. His cellmates were still off somewhere crushing stones in a rock pit. He stood in his empty cell while two guards held his arms pinned behind his back and a third removed the manacles. The female guard stood facing him, slapping her neural prod in the palm of her hand. Only when they turned off the augmented programming did Anders understand how badly they were violating SecureMax protocols. He focused on the prod in the woman's hands, and the meaty clap it made every time it hit her palm.

She gave him a big cheesy grin and said, "They tell me you're leaving us, Maestra Eindride."

His gut tightened with dread. The two men holding his arms must have sensed his fear because their grips constricted painfully.

The woman continued. "Paroled, they tell me." She wrinkled her nose. "That's very rare here at SecureMax, but not unheard of. And because it's so rare, we have a special custom for those who are going to leave us."

Her eyes sparkled as she spoke. "We're going to miss you very much. We want you to remember your time here, so we're going to give you one, last, fond memory to take with you."

She held the neural prod out and looked carefully at its base, then touched the small dial there and set it to maximum. She could have simply programmed it through her implants, but that wouldn't have had the same dramatic effect as doing it visibly in front of Anders and her friends. Then, like the viper he remembered, she jammed the business end of it into his groin.

His guts tightened and spasmed, and as the pain shot all the way up into his chest and throat, he screamed. The two men holding him released him and he dropped to the floor, his body curled around the end of the prod and unable to release it.

The woman yanked the prod out of his crotch, and slowly the pain receded as the guards stood over him. When he could breathe again, he opened his eyes.

Looming over him, the female guard smacked the end of the prod into the palm of her hand. She leaned down, and without activating the prod, used its output end to nudge his chin upward so he met her eyes.

"Just something to remember us by, and to remind you what's waiting for you if they ever send you back to us."

••••

Professor Emmet Dirkson stood only chest high to John, had a wiry frame and probably weighed only a little more than a small woman. He vibrated with energy and gestured with short, jerky motions. He reminded John of a small, frightened animal, but when it came to Kelk language and culture, he proved to be fearless in the extreme.

When they first met he confronted John angrily. "Why do you want to learn about the Kelk? No one cares about the Kelk. Why do you?"

John said, "Well, I—"

Dirkson interrupted him. "Are you one of those Kelk fetish people?"

"Fetish people," John said. "I don't—"

"Yes," Dirkson said, frowning with distaste. "They dress up like Kelk, wear makeup or dye their skin blue. They have parties where they commit all sorts of twisted, disgusting acts. And they think that's what Kelk really do."

John had never heard of such a thing. "No," he said, "I'm not—"

Dirkson said, "I wouldn't waste my time with the likes of you if the government wasn't throwing money at me, you and your stupid deviant friends."

John said, "I met some of them."

"Met who? The fetish people?"

"No."

"Then what are you talking about?"

"I met some Kelk."

"Met some Kelk?" Dirkson demanded, and John wondered what had made him so angry. "You mean you tried to kill them and they tried to kill you. Though, since you're here, I guess you did the killing and they did the dying."

"Well, yes," John said. "It started that way, but we became friends . . . sort of. We—"

"Friends?" Dirkson paused, looked at John with his eyes narrow and hard. "What do you mean by friends? No one makes friends with the Kelk."

John had had a lot of practice relating his carefully edited version of the events on Reisenar, and he could now recite the story without the need to think carefully about what he could and could not say. It would have been simple and easy if Dirkson had kept his mouth shut. But half way through every sentence the little man interrupted him. Sometimes he interrupted to ask a question, which frequently veered them off onto a tangent. Sometimes he interrupted to finish the sentence for John, and he always finished it wrong, which meant John had to back up and start again. And that meant Dirkson would interrupt him again to demand that he explain why he had backtracked. It took the better part of an hour to tell a story that should have taken no more than a few minutes.

When he finally finished, Dirkson said, "Friends. Sounds more like allies. Amazing!"

Dirkson took him seriously after that. John learned that the Kelk language had tenses and genders that changed with the time of day, which made it quite difficult, and he often struggled. His biggest disappointment came when he learned he couldn't use direct neural stimulation techniques to speed up the learning process.

With a sour look, Dirkson snarled, "No one's ever bothered to map Kelk language constructs to the vocal centers of the cerebral cortex. Nobody cares. I've made some effort to catalog the syntactical structure, but I can't get a publisher to fund the coding for direct neural learning. No market, they said. You're going to have to learn it the hard way: memorization and repetition, memorization and repetition, and lots of practice."

John worked at his O-School lessons and training during the day, and twice every tenday spent four hours with Dirkson. Sometimes he managed to join Wakeland and his party friends to let off a little steam on the tenday break, but not often.

9

Old Enemies

AFTER HIS DANCE with the business end of the neural prod, Anders could still walk, but it took more than a day to do so without a limp. They didn't make him return to his cell, for which he was thankful; he really didn't want to find out what other surprises the guards might have in store for him. He went straight from the infirmary to a holding cell in the MC brig on Erikdeg Base. He spent his time there with nothing to do but eat his meals, and walk for one hour each day in the exercise yard under the watchful eyes of two MCs. But it was the first time in a long time he didn't have to struggle to put two coherent thoughts together, the first time in a long time he cared.

He thought a great deal about Kristdokar's last words to him. "You'll be the embittered, cashiered ex-command-superior," she had said. When he looked into his own heart he did find some bitterness. He had tried to warn them, had tried to prevent a tragedy, so in many ways the punishment they had given him just wasn't fair. After all, who could have imagined the scope of what might happen? Had he been prescient, had he been able to predict twenty million lives hung in the balance, he might have done more. It wasn't his fault he couldn't predict the future.

After five days in the brig at Erikdeg, a male command hawk came to his cell. The fellow carried a small duffel tucked under one arm, and the stencil above his left breast pocket read BIRNSON. When the man stepped into the cell he tossed the duffel onto Anders's bunk.

Anders's old reflexes kicked in and he snapped to attention. The command hawk appeared to be well past middle age, with more salt in his hair than pepper. He had a paunch, and stood several centimeters shorter than Anders. He frowned, looked at Anders oddly, sneered, and said, "You no longer hold any rank, so there is no military etiquette between you and me. You do not stand at attention, nor do you salute me. And should you attempt to salute, I certainly will not return it."

Anders relaxed, lowered himself to his bunk, and sat down.

The officious little shit didn't ask any questions, and the interview proved to be more of a lecture than an interview. "You are on parole, which means you are not yet granted full freedom. Nor will we erase the augmented programming in your implants. It will not be activated, but it will be there nevertheless should it be needed again. Is that clear?"

Anders nodded, but said nothing.

That seemed to irritate Birnson, though everything seemed to irritate the fat little fellow. "Once remanded to the rehabilitation facility in Hyerdride, you will have full freedom to move about the city. There are certain restricted areas, but should you approach one, your implants will warn you. Any attempt to ignore such warnings, or to leave the city, will result in immediate revocation of your parole, and you'll be returned to SecureMax. Is that clear?"

Again, Anders nodded, but said nothing. And again, that seemed to irritate Birnson. Anders decided he would not go out of his way to avoid irritating the little asshole.

Birnson continued. "The Supremacy will provide you with gainful employment, and you will spend one month at the rehabilitation facility training for your new responsibilities. After that you will be given a small monthly stipend to augment your income, and it will be up to you to arrange for your own housing. The stipend will end after six months and you'll be on your own financially. One year without any infractions, and the augmented programming will be erased. You will then be allowed to reestablish your own personal crypto security keys. The restrictions on your movements will be reduced, but not eliminated entirely, and before leaving the city you must request permission and file an itinerary. After two years, again without any infractions, all such restrictions will be removed, though you will never again be allowed in a secure military facility. Is that clear?"

Anders decided to see how the fellow would react to a grunt, so he grunted, "Yah."

As he had suspected, that irritated Birnson even more. The little shit continued. "Minor infractions will result in an extension of the one-year and two-year parole periods. Major infractions will see you back in SecureMax without delay. You'll be given a list of all prohibited activities. I advise you to read it carefully and commit it to memory, because even an accidental misstep will be treated as an intentional abuse of your new freedom."

The fellow produced some documents for him to sign. He was tempted to make Birnson wait while he took his own sweet time to read through them carefully, but he decided not to push his luck. In any case, he would sign anything that got him out of that place. He provided a DNA signature, and Birnson pointed to the duffel he had tossed on Anders's bunk. "That's for you. Something to help you start your new civilian life."

Birnson turned and left without another word.

The duffel contained three sets of civilian clothing, nothing expensive or fancy, but certainly adequate to function in civilian life. He stripped out of his prison jumpsuit, and learned to his relief that his new civilian attire fit him properly. He tossed the jumpsuit into a corner, but kept the prison boots they had given him.

They were functional, and he suspected he would now be living a rather frugal life, so it would be unwise to waste anything that came his way.

The next morning, an MC released him from his cell, then escorted him out to the airstrip and onto a military transport. He strapped into a seat in the cargo hold, and was thankful to be the only person present. He really didn't feel like engaging anyone in conversation. He changed transport two times, and four days later he arrived at Hyerdride Military Base.

Two MCs escorted him to the front gate, keeping a close eye on him all the way. They gave him a ticket, a transit map, and directions to the nearest transit station.

An hour later he checked into the rehabilitation facility. They gave him a small, sparsely furnished room with a single bed. That night as he lay there trying to find sleep, he thought of Mistresses Kristdokar and Vreekande. And he again recalled the skalde's words about the "embittered, cashiered ex-command-superior." If the mysterious *someone* Kristdokar had alluded to did approach him, he didn't know what he would do. Could he be the skalde's obedient little puppy and report to her everything he learned? Perhaps her enemies might help him disappear and regain the freedom they had taken from him. But then again, those enemies had been responsible for twenty million lives. If and when the time came to make a decision, he didn't know what he would do.

••••

"No, you have the tense all wrong."

Nikaela wanted to smash the teaching translator on the table in front of her. Her first real Lingua lesson that was actually a lesson and not a test had proven grueling in the extreme. She wanted to shout at Command Hawk Velkerhaut, but she clenched her teeth and kept her mouth shut.

Velkerhaut leaned over Nikaela and shook a finger at her. "I don't know how you passed your exams with such poor command of Lingua, but had I known I would have made you take remedial lessons before allowing you to graduate."

Nikaela's command of Lingua was no worse than most graduates one year out of the academy, but she knew better than to say that to this woman. Neither she nor any of her classmates had taken the language lessons seriously, assuming rightfully that any real interactions they might have with the Commonwealth would be at the point of a gun, or better yet, the launch of a large warhead. It had never occurred to her, and she realized now it probably hadn't occurred to her instructors either, that she might actually have to carry on a conversation with one of them and say something more than, "Fuck you," just before she pulled the trigger.

Velkerhaut said, "The phrase in Kelk is, *I saw the way you looked at me.* Now try again."

Nikaela didn't think it was a coincidence Velkerhaut had chosen that phrase. Someone had probably overheard her last interaction with Private Mathius, or perhaps they had recorded from afar all interactions with the Commonwealth soldiers. Nikaela should have anticipated that, and hoped they hadn't heard her little teasing joke about taking the fellow as a lover. They might think she was actually serious about that.

She took a breath and carefully translated the phrase into what she thought was proper Commonwealth Lingua. The teaching translator then translated her words back to her in Kelk, mimicking any errors she had made in Lingua. "I saw look you had on me."

Nikaela cringed.

Velkerhaut said, "Exactly."

She continued to shake her finger at Nikaela, and emphasized her disapproval with more of the scowl. "I'm not stupid; the civilian clothing, the complete lack of military etiquette. I don't know what you're involved in here, but I'm guessing it's highly classified. And I'm also guessing you're getting special tutoring so you can interact directly with Commonwealth personnel, a very rare thing indeed. I therefore conclude you're going to be representing the Supremacy, and I will not allow you to make us look like a bunch of uneducated, illiterate savages."

Nikaela had never considered it that way. She *would* be representing the Supremacy, and she tried to imagine how she must appear to her Commonwealth counterparts as she stumbled over words in a language that had become the de facto standard for interstellar communications. She lowered her eyes and said, "I'll try harder. I promise I will."

Velkerhaut started; she had probably expected defiance, not capitulation. She lowered the finger and spoke in a softer tone. "Good. I'm glad to see you understand the gravity of the situation."

The older woman nodded, straightened, turned and paced back and forth in front of Nikaela, her voice shifting into lecture mode. "Commonwealth Lingua is an artificial language purposefully developed to be free of historically evolved variations. It's a rich and complete language, so much so it is the default language in regular use in many Commonwealth cultures. But its rules of pronunciation are purposefully clear and straightforward, with extremely few exceptions and almost no idiomatic variations. Some have slipped into the language over time, but very few."

She stopped pacing, faced Nikaela squarely and put her fists on her hips. "It was intentionally designed to be easy to learn."

Her words clearly implied *easy to learn* meant Nikaela should be having an easy time of it, and had no excuse for not progressing faster. Nikaela's implants rescued her. *Mistress Vreekande, you are due in Brigadier Skalde Kristdokar's office in five minutes.*

Velkerhaut cocked her head to one side and looked thoughtful for a few seconds. Her implants had probably given her a similar message. She said, "The lesson is done. But I'm afraid I must report to the skalde your progress is far from stellar. I'm going to ask her to increase your lesson time from one to three hours per day."

Nikaela cringed internally and worked very hard not to let her reaction show. She closed down the teaching translator as Velkerhaut gathered up her materials and walked out of the room. Nikaela followed on her heels and reached Kristdokar's office just in time for her appointment. Now that construction had been completed, the skalde kept the door to her office open most of the time. Kristdokar saw her approach, pointed her to a chair and said, "Sit down. How are the Lingua lessons going?"

Nikaela knew she couldn't whitewash the situation, so she spoke candidly. "I'm afraid Command Hawk Velkerhaut is not pleased with my progress."

Kristdokar calmly asked, "Are *you* pleased with your progress?"

Nikaela shook her head, "No."

"That's a good start," Kristdokar said. "Please elaborate."

Nikaela described Velkerhaut's conclusions about the nature of their mission.

Kristdokar smiled and nodded. "She's a very astute woman. She's also not hard-line anti-Commonwealth."

Nikaela added, "She also said I'll be representing the Supremacy to the Commonwealth, and she thought my accent would make us look like a bunch of uneducated, illiterate savages."

Kristdokar sat without moving, staring at Nikaela with a slight smile on her lips.

Nikaela grimaced. "She's right, isn't she?"

Kristdokar leaned forward and looked pointedly at Nikaela. "You too are a very astute woman. That's why you were smart enough to act upon the unusual information your breschkada gave you on Reisenar. And that's why you're on my staff and participating in this mission. But like most youngsters it can take a little extra time for reality to sink in, and I'm glad it has."

The skalde had both complimented and reprimanded Nikaela with almost the same words.

••••

The academy had an abbreviation for every item in its curriculum. The class on Systems of Commonwealth Governance had been dubbed SysComGov in some far distant past, but the cadets referred to it as BoreGov. The instructor, Major Boremeir, thought his name had something to do with that, but as far as the cadets were concerned, it referred more to his exceedingly dry and *boring* delivery. To stay awake, most of them had taken to downing several shots of strong, black caff shortly before each lecture.

Boremeir sometimes arranged for a guest lecturer, almost always someone in a senior government position of some sort. The most interesting often proved to be career government functionaries. They took the invitation seriously, came well prepared, frequently gave some unusual insight into the process of governance, and had a more lively delivery than Boremeir, though that wasn't much of an endorsement.

On the other hand, elected politicians, especially those who were well known, tended to come unprepared, and more often than not, they sounded more like they were running for reelection. That was John's expectation when he took his seat in the lecture hall that morning. Boremeir had scheduled Senator Silas Palmutter to deliver the lecture, and since the senator chaired the Senate Armed Services Committee, failure to attend could seriously affect one's grade.

The lecture hall had a capacity of about two hundred. Tiers of seats ascended upward from a stage that contained a podium and some chairs. John arrived a little early and took a seat about halfway up near the entrance; when the lecture ended he hoped to beat the rush for the door. As other students arrived the lecture hall slowly filled up with the quiet din of two hundred voices speaking softly.

Boremeir and Palmutter arrived together, and as they descended toward the podium the cadets went silent. To John's absolute surprise, Macus DeLeon accompanied Palmutter, along with a beautiful young woman. The young lady and John's old nemesis from basic training both wore nicely tailored, civilian business suits. When they reached the stage DeLeon and the woman sat down, while Palmutter and Boremeir stood near the podium and chatted.

As soon as DeLeon sat down he looked straight at John as if he knew in advance John would be there, and of course he did. Like all the rest of their platoon mates, DeLeon knew John had left for O-School, and it would be just like DeLeon to have some means of accessing John's class schedule. But what was DeLeon doing with Palmutter? He couldn't just resign from ComSecCorps. He would have to fulfill his enlistment term first.

As their eyes met, DeLeon smiled. Anyone else watching him would interpret the look he gave John as nondescript, but John knew his old platoon mate well enough to see the animosity in his eyes.

Palmutter sat down next to DeLeon while Boremeir took the podium. As Boremeir launched into a flattering introduction of the senator, summarizing his years of service to the Commonwealth, DeLeon leaned close to Palmutter. He whispered something to the senator, and at the same time nodded toward John. The senator's eyes scanned the crowd of cadets for a brief moment, then quickly settled on John. With his implants, DeLeon had probably transmitted an overlay of the seated cadets to the senator, and slapped a cursor right on John's face, though DeLeon's choice of a cursor for John would most likely be crosshairs, like those in a rifle scope.

Boremeir finished his introduction with a flourish and Palmutter stood. As the senator walked to the podium and Boremeir walked to the chairs, they met half way between. Palmutter paused and said something to Boremeir, who nodded, and looked up at John. Palmutter continued to the podium, while Boremeir walked to the chairs and sat down.

As the senator began his lecture, which immediately began to sound like a speech at a campaign rally, John's implants chimed with a message from Major Boremeir.

"Cadet Mathius, the senator would like to speak with you after his lecture. If that means you'll be late for your next class, I'll speak with your instructor so there'll be no adverse consequences."

"Yes, sir. I'll stay behind, sir."

"Very good, Cadet."

Palmutter spoke for about an hour, and John didn't hear a word he said. Throughout the entire lecture, DeLeon never took his eyes off John, giving him a smug look of satisfaction. John considered the possibility he was overly paranoid, but anything that involved Macus DeLeon justified a considerable amount of distrust. What was DeLeon up to?

When the lecture ended, most of the other cadets filed out of the hall, though a few stayed behind to ask a question or two of the senator. Palmutter appeared to revel in the attention. Boremeir would expect John to present himself to the senator, so John waited until the crowd had thinned, then walked down to the stage. As Palmutter continued to talk with a few cadets, Boremeir raised a hand and gestured with two fingers, indicating John should join them.

Boremeir shooed the other cadets away, then said, "Senator, this is the young man you asked about, Cadet John Mathius."

Palmutter beamed a toothy, white smile and extended his hand, "Nice to meet you, young man."

As John shook the senator's hand, the young woman took Boremeir by the arm, saying, "Major Boremeir, I'd like to have a word with you."

She and Boremeir walked to the other end of the stage. The whole situation seemed like an orchestrated effort to get John alone with Palmutter and DeLeon, and John thought his paranoia might be getting out of hand.

Palmutter said, "You and Macus were platoon mates in boot camp, I hear."

The man wrapped an arm around John's shoulders, and with DeLeon following, led him farther away from Boremeir and the young woman.

Palmutter stopped and faced John squarely. "I hear you were deeply involved in that mess on Reisenar."

John thought he already knew the answer, but he asked anyway. "Where did you hear that, sir?"

"Why, from Macus," the senator said. "Said you were badly wounded, and came back with an extra stripe on your sleeve."

Whatever DeLeon had in mind, it would not be good for John. He decided he should heavily downplay his role in the events on Reisenar. Only a few of his close friends had ever heard the real story, and that had been the seriously edited version, and none of them would have passed any of that along to DeLeon. John thought it would be wise to keep to the truth, but only a bit of the truth, a very little bit.

"Yes, sir, I was wounded, but I was just a grunt, a private. I didn't know what went on, most of the time, just got caught in a nasty firefight."

Palmutter's eyes hardened with distrust. "There must be more to it than that, young man. You did get a promotion to corporal."

John shook his head. "I think that was just a standard time-in-grade promotion, sir. You know, stay alive long enough and they give you another stripe. Promotions aren't competitive at that level."

"Yes," Palmutter said. "I guess I was aware of that. But you did work with Lieutenant Colonel Primatov, did you not?"

"Well, yes, sir," John said. Palmutter's eyes brightened as if he had scored a debating point. "She was at the top of the chain of command, and I was at the bottom. So I guess I worked with her as much as any grunt works with a high-ranking officer."

"Sir," DeLeon said. "He wasn't really a standout in basic. Barely got by, in fact."

DeLeon's own ego made him say that, and he certainly didn't realize he might be helping John.

Palmutter continued to press John on the matter, but John stuck to his story.

Boremeir finally rescued John. "Sorry, Senator, but the young man has already missed one class. I have to send him on to his next. If you want to speak to him further, I'll send him to your office at your convenience."

"No," Palmutter said. "No, that won't be necessary. I've learned what I needed to learn."

As John left the lecture hall, he glanced back, and DeLeon gave him the hate-filled look John knew so well.

10

New Friends

DURING ANDERS'S MONTH at the rehabilitation facility, he was required to report regularly to an employment guidance counselor. The powers-that-be had decided that since he had qualified in the military as an inter-atmospheric gunboat pilot, he would make a good grav train driver in the city's transit system. He really didn't see what one had to do with the other, but he kept his thoughts to himself.

They told him grav train drivers weren't called *drivers*, they were called engineers, but like anyone who had ever piloted a gunboat in combat, Anders had trouble with lofty titles for simple jobs. He trained daily on a simulator, and reported twice every tenday to the counselor. She told him he made excellent progress in his training as a driver—*engineer*, he reminded himself.

One month after reporting to the rehabilitation facility, he graduated to apprentice transit engineer. He found a small apartment within walking distance of the transit depot where he reported to work every morning. It wasn't much, just a one-room walk-in with a small kitchenette. All the apartments on that floor shared communal showering facilities, which he didn't mind, because the place met his frugal requirements, and anything was better than SecureMax.

As an apprentice, Anders drove the train with a more experienced engineer looking over his shoulder, a woman named Viktra Kirkdehl. She stood shoulder high to him, had an athletic build, and he found her quite good-looking. But he didn't need any entanglements at that time, and she didn't seem interested, so he put such thoughts out of his mind.

The grav trains and tracks in the transit system were heavily automated, with triply redundant safety interlocks and a centralized control and tracking system. He quickly learned transit engineers were almost redundant, that the most difficult part of his job was remaining awake throughout his entire shift so he could occasionally make the decision to manually intervene. That only happened about once or twice a day, and he longed for the mundane, but still more interesting, aspects of his former life.

At the end of their shift one evening, Viktra said, "Come, Anders. I'm going to meet some of the other engineers, have a few drinks and relax a little. Join us."

He liked the idea of meeting some of his peers, so he said, "Sure, why not?"

She led him to a bar a few blocks from the transit depot, and there they met a small crowd of five other engineers. She introduced them. A tall fellow named Thoran sported a neatly-trimmed full beard. He also wore his shoulder length hair in dreadlocks, which wasn't that common among soldiers, but even more unusual among civilians.

Thoran said, "You don't have to remember all our names, at least not the first time around. But we have a custom here; new man has to buy a round."

Anders had been careful with every penny he earned, and it didn't tax his resources to buy one round of kirva, the clear, fiery alcohol they drank in small shot glasses. Anders learned Thoran had transferred in from another transit depot just a tenday ago, and had taken his turn buying drinks.

Thoran asked, "What did you do before joining the transit authority?"

Anders hesitated because he hadn't considered in advance what he would say to such a question. He wasn't about to tell them he'd been convicted of mass murder and high treason, and had recently been released from SecureMax, but he hadn't thought of a good lie.

"What's wrong?" Thoran asked. "You got something to hide?"

Viktra came to his rescue. "If he doesn't want to say, that's his business. Don't be a jerk, Thoran."

Anders settled on a reasonable lie that wasn't too far from the truth. "I tried the military, but I wasn't good at it. I'm kind of embarrassed they wouldn't let me reenlist."

Thoran slapped him on the shoulder and said, "Never tried that myself, but I heard it can be a hard way to make a living. You at least get a pension out of it?"

Viktra said, "If he had a pension, would he be working transit?"

They proved to be a friendly lot, and they all agreed Anders wouldn't be working transit if he had a pension. They had a few more drinks, but they all needed to report to work the next morning, so they ended the evening fairly early.

Anders followed Thoran out of the bar, and something about the way the man carried himself struck a familiar memory. Out on the street they said their good-byes, and as Anders watched Thoran walk away, he realized everything about the tall, bearded fellow said *military*.

"Never tried that myself," Thoran had said earlier.

There were plenty of ex-military in the city. But why lie about it?

••••

"Your old friend is here in the city," Kristdokar said.

Standing in front of the skalde's desk, Nikaela had to think for a moment to decipher the woman's words. "My old friend? Do you mean the one we visited at—"

"Yes," Kristdokar said, interrupting her with a sharply spoken word. "Yes, I do mean that one. He's been released on parole."

Kristdokar gave Nikaela an address and said, "You don't have to see him if you don't want to. But if you do, you have my permission, though be very discreet about it. We're watching every move he makes, and I wouldn't be surprised if they're watching him as well. It wouldn't be out of character for you to want to see him briefly, but don't say anything that might compromise you or him."

Anders Eindride! For the rest of the day, Nikaela had trouble focusing on anything. She had been diligent in her use of neural stimulation while asleep at night, and had made considerable progress in her Lingua lessons. But that afternoon she couldn't put two words together into a proper sentence, and Velkerhaut grew furious with her.

"What is wrong with you?" the older woman demanded.

Nikaela decided to tell her the truth, though it would have to be an edited version. "I'm sorry, Mistress Velkerhaut, but I just learned an old friend, whom I thought dead, is still alive."

The command hawk raised an eyebrow, her face softened, and for the first time she spoke kindly, "You've had a shock, eh?"

"Yes," Nikaela said. "Yes, a shock."

"I understand," Velkerhaut said. "Why don't you take the afternoon off, and we'll continue again when you can think more clearly. You've made commendable progress recently, so I'll let it go,"—the look on her face hardened and her eyes narrowed—"but only this once."

Nikaela thought carefully about how she might contact her former superior; it never occurred to her that she wouldn't contact him, even if only once. He had protected her, had saved her career, perhaps even her life. And after watching him sit stoically through the tribunal at Erikdeg, never looking her way, never uttering a sound, there remained a few unsaid words between them. If Kristdokar was right, and the mysterious *they* watched him closely, she didn't try to fool herself into thinking she could approach him without being observed. Yet she didn't want to simply go to his apartment and knock on the door, so she decided to approach him on the street.

With her clearances she had considerable access to publicly available civilian records. She quickly learned he had taken a job as a transit engineer, and she noted the address of the transit depot where he reported to work each morning. Given the distance between his apartment and the depot, she thought it safe to assume he walked to and from work. She dug a little deeper and retrieved his shift schedule.

••••

John quickly learned that the extracurricular Kelk lessons meant he rarely had any spare time. On top of his normal studies, for every hour he spent with Dirkson, he spent two trying to complete the extra reading the professor assigned him. The little man kept throwing obscure texts and scholarly papers at him, and he learned a bit about the Kelk culture as well as their language. But three months into O-School, he had rarely joined any of his classmates for a night out on the town. A couple of times he had come close to joining Wakeland and his party friends to let off a little steam on the ten-end, but he just couldn't find the time.

Late one afternoon just before the break, he was seated at the small desk in his dorm room, and struggling with an article on Kelk familial structure. May interrupted him, "I'm going out. Put that away and join me. You need to have a little fun, and I'm just the girl to show you a good time."

May had changed into civilian attire, a simple coat, blouse and slacks, all very attractive. She was certainly pretty enough, and under other circumstances he'd jump at the chance to date a girl like her, but he didn't need the entanglements involved in a prohibited relationship.

There must have been something in John's face, because she leaned forward and said, "Don't worry, Mr. Mathius. I prefer other women, so you're safe with me. Now put the books away, change into some civvies, and lighten up."

He thought about it for a moment. The worst that could happen would be that he wasn't fully prepared for his next Kelk lesson with Dirkson. But none of that counted toward his standing in O-School. "Okay," he said. "I'm game."

May led him to a restaurant where they met Karya, a young news hype May had dated since coming to Trafalgar. Customs on Novalis III had been rather parochial about same-sex relationships, but that was not the case here and John saw both women's eyes light up when they looked at each other.

"My roomie here," May said, hooking a thumb toward John, "he works too hard."

Karya said, "Well you also work too hard."

May shook her head. "Not like him. He's doing all this extra study on the Kelk."

"The Kelk?" Karya asked. She looked at John uncertainly and her nose wrinkled with distaste. "You're not a Kelkie, are you?"

"A Kelkie," John said, "what's that?"

The two young women shared a look, and May said, "He's not as slow on the uptake as he seems."

"Kelkies," Karya said. "People who dress up like Kelk and go to parties. Most of them are kind of disgusting."

Dirkson had mentioned the *fetishists*, but John couldn't believe people were actually that foolish. He had dismissed the professor's ravings as wild exaggeration related to him by a man who didn't exhibit much stability himself.

"You're kidding," John said. "They really do that?"

Karya pulled out a small comp, tapped on its screen, then extended it toward John. "Take a look at that."

She had pulled up a picture from an article about Kelkies. A man and woman had posed for a still photograph. They both had very dark blue skin, and their irises glared a bright red in eyes that appeared absolutely demonic, with vertically slit pupils. Karya said with pride, "I wrote that article myself. Some of them even have their tongues surgically altered so it's forked."

John shook his head. "They look nothing like Kelk."

"Really," Karya said. "They claim their appearance is quite authentic. And how would you know what real Kelk look like?"

"I've met a few."

Karya's brow furrowed with interest. "You have? When? Where? How?"

John hesitated. Providing details to a news hype could get him in serious trouble. May must have guessed his thoughts. She reached out and placed a hand gently on Karya's wrist. "Dear, John cannot divulge details of a combat incident to a member of the media. Anything like that would have to come through official channels."

Karya's eyes hardened, she gave May an angry look, and lifted her chin. "I do not betray my friends by publishing details of personal conversations."

John tried to come to May's defense. "Even if you never publish it, if our superiors heard we told you certain things, they would probably be quite upset. Just trust me when I tell you I have seen them, and up close."

May said, "I'm sorry, Karya."

The look on Karya's face softened. She smiled and said, "Apology accepted."

John said, "But no one will be upset if I give you a more accurate description. Just don't quote me." He then described the general appearance of the Kelk he'd met. "Their skin isn't dark blue. It's actually quite pale, with a slight bluish tint to it. And the pupils in their eyes are not vertically slit. And their eyes don't look at all demonic."

May said, "But still red, right?"

John nodded. "Yah."

Karya said, "So no forked tongues?"

John gritted his teeth and said. "I can't swear to that one way or another."

"Why not?"

"I've never seen one of their tongues."

Karya frowned. "But you said you've seen them up close and personal."

"Yah," John said. "And I've been here with you two for the past couple of hours and I haven't seen either of your tongues."

May stuck her tongue out at him. Karya joined her and they both got a good laugh out of it.

"Yah, yah, yah," John said. "But we didn't have a situation where any of them decided to stick their tongue out at me."

"So forked tongues or no forked tongues?" May asked. "Which is it?"

"I don't know one way or another," John said. "Let me put it this way: I couldn't swear either way in a court of law. But I seriously doubt it. If they had forked tongues, I would think they'd sound kind of funny when they talked, and they don't."

The evening ended nicely with no hurt feelings and a few good laughs.

At John's next lesson with Dirkson he asked the professor about Kelkies. The man snarled, "I'm here to teach you about real Kelk, not about weirdos."

After the lesson John did a little research on his own. Some Kelkies dyed their skin dark blue, and had their eyes modified to glare bright red and appear demonic. Some simply used makeup and contact lenses because they had jobs or something that required them to revert to a normal appearance most of the time. They donned wigs or dyed their hair salt and pepper gray, and they all wore it in dreadlocks—John recalled only about one in ten real Kelk styled their hair that way. And those had all been military, so he knew nothing of the styles affected by Kelk civilians.

The fetish people attended parties, all looking like what they thought Kelk looked like, though John knew they missed the mark by a considerable margin. They made liberal use of certain sexual stimulants, and the parties rapidly digressed. They had even invented strange positions for their sexual acts, some of which required an unusual amount of flexibility, and a few which John thought were not actually possible. Thankfully, there weren't very many such people, but somehow they did manage to find each other.

Many in the Commonwealth government were of the opinion they needed to understand Kelk culture and customs, a subject on which the hawks and doves agreed. The Kelk-hating hawks knew they needed that knowledge to defeat the blue-skinned demons, and the doves wanted that information to try to foster peace with them. Hence, the government encouraged Dirkson and a small group of academics with deep-pockets funding. But they had some difficulty finding scholars willing to specialize in Kelk studies, and several positions remained unfilled, the money unspent.

The Kelk were not a popular subject for study, a situation badly aggravated by the tall tales with wildly exaggerated descriptions of Kelk appearance and demeanor. The fetishists, who represented themselves as accurately depicting the depravity of Kelk culture, didn't help any. On the pretense that they studied the Kelk psyche at their orgies, a few of them even attempted to acquire some of that unspent funding. They were not successful; at least someone in the government must have had a rational understanding of the Kelk.

Four months into his year at O-School, John had gained a limited command of the Kelk language. He wondered if he'd ever have a chance to use it.

11

New Allies

BY AND LARGE, the transit engineers all took their work seriously. Anders once made reference to being a transit *driver*, and by the looks he received from several of them, he learned to never use that term again.

He repeatedly noticed little things about Thoran that led him to believe the man had served in the military at one time, and not for just a year or two. The dreadlocks were certainly a hint in that direction, but that alone would have meant nothing. The fellow carried himself too much like someone who had served for so long, the service had been stamped right into his genetic makeup.

Anders did consider the possibility he had imagined shadows where none existed. Or perhaps the fellow had a good reason for lying. He too might have been cashiered out of the military—though probably not for mass murder on an unimaginable scale—and like Anders simply didn't want to reveal an unpleasant past.

At the end of his shift one day, Viktra approached him carrying a small comp screen. They had become friends, of a sort, though she clearly had no desire to let their relationship go any further than the occasional round of drinks with coworkers at the local bar. She paused, looked at the comp screen and said, "Alfhilde is going on vacation tomorrow, and I need to adjust schedules. Can you clock in two hours earlier than normal, and work a full shift plus two?"

Viktra had enough seniority that she occasionally filled in for their shift supervisor. "Sure," Anders said. "Which route am I taking?"

She smiled, and at that moment his implants shifted into secure-link, encryption mode. She subvocalized, "Brigadier Skalde Kristdokar sends her regards. If you need to communicate with her, you can do so through me."

Anders flinched, which bothered him. His time in SecureMax had dulled his reflexes. He nodded once and left it at that.

His implants shifted back to standard mode, and she continued their conversation about scheduling. "You'll be taking the Capital Line for the day."

"Okay," he said.

She smiled, turned, and walked away.

Anders's thoughts roiled as he stepped out of the transit depot for the walk back to his apartment. He should have anticipated that Kristdokar would set up some means of covert communication. But he had never considered that Viktra might be one of the skalde's assets. Again, SecureMax had dulled his reflexes.

Night had settled over the city, though in early evening the streets were still filled with traffic and the sidewalks with pedestrians. Two city blocks from the depot, Anders turned down a residential side street where both foot and street traffic were considerably less. And by the time he turned down his own street, the sounds of the city were a distant din somewhere far behind him.

He needed to get back to his apartment, close the door, and find enough solitude to think the situation through. He didn't really feel indebted to Kristdokar. Yes, she certainly had had something to do with his release from SecureMax, but then she had worked with the tribunal that put him there in the first place. And he had tried to alert his superiors about Novalis III, tried twice, and suffered a brutal beating for his trouble. No, Kristdokar was just another high-ranking woman playing games with the ashes of his life. He thought if her enemies did approach him, he just might listen carefully to what they had to offer. They might remove the augmented programming from his implants much sooner than the Supremacy's time frame. And they might be willing to ease his financial situation, especially if he agreed to work as a double agent.

Only a few dozen paces from his building, someone said, "Maestra Eindride."

He recognized that voice and paused. He glanced up and down the street to see that other than him, it was deserted. And then a young woman stepped out of the darkness in the shadow of a building, though shadows still hid her face.

He recalled the young, naive command boss from Novalis III. "Mistress Vreekande," he said.

"I . . ." she said, and he heard a tremble in her voice. "I'm . . . sorry about what they did to you."

He shrugged. "It wasn't completely . . . undeserved." Saying that surprised him, given the harsh thoughts that had coursed through his head only a few moments ago.

She took a step forward, the light from a street lamp illuminated her face, and he saw the pain in her eyes. "But you tried to warn them."

Just a few seconds earlier he had made that same argument to himself, and he understood now it had been a hollow excuse. "But I didn't try hard enough, not enough to justify twenty million lives."

"But still—"

He shook his head. "There's no *but still* about it, mistress." He left it at that and didn't voice his final thought.

She stared at him for a long moment. "I'm sorry. I truly am."

"So am I," he said. "But I'm all right now."

"I'm sorry," she said again, then turned and walked away.

He watched her walk down the street, stood there without moving until she turned a corner and walked out of sight.

Kristdokar had most likely sent the young woman to see him, though he'd bet money she hadn't given her a direct order. An offhand suggestion had probably been enough. The skalde knew exactly what she was doing. Looking into the young woman's face had forced Anders to admit the truth to himself.

I should have tried harder.

••••

John didn't think of Hey-You too often, but when he did he had a sad moment. He had managed to put her behind him, though he would not forget her. Still, he didn't date much, mostly because his studies occupied so much of his time.

May and Karya were regulars at the restaurant where he'd first met Karya. It served good food, but being heavily dependent on cadets, it maintained prices that fit within the small stipend the academy provided. John sometimes joined them, though usually because May forced him to step away from the books.

One evening, after they had finished dinner and were chatting over drinks, Karya said, "I should interview some Kelkies about the forked tongue thing."

May looked offended. "Why would you do that?"

Karya's eyes brightened as she spoke. "I'll bet they have all sorts of sensational stories to tell, which always makes for good copy. Then I could interview John's Professor Dirkson, and let him set the record straight."

At an unhappy look from May, she added, "Don't worry, I'll keep John's name out of it. No John Mathius. Never heard of him. Got everything from the Kelkies and Dirkson."

John had a thought. "But will anyone read the story if you're debunking the myth."

May nodded. "He's probably right."

Karya wrinkled her nose. "Yah, readers, and editors, do like the sensational stuff." She sighed heavily. "You're taking all the fun out of it. I—"

She abruptly stopped speaking and her eyes focused on something behind John.

"Mr. Mathius," a familiar voice said.

John's seat placed him with his back to the center of the restaurant. Knowing what to expect, he looked over his shoulder and found Macus DeLeon standing behind him, a pretty young woman on his arm. Rather than sit there twisted about, John stood and faced them as if merely being polite, when in fact he just didn't like having DeLeon at his back. After seeing DeLeon with Palmutter in the lecture hall, John had done a little checking and learned he had signed on as an aide to the senator. John didn't know the young lady with him, but had seen her on campus once or twice in uniform, another cadet.

DeLeon looked John up and down with obvious distaste. "Shouldn't you be studying, or something like that?"

"I probably should," John said, wondering why DeLeon would ask that, "but I needed to take a couple hours off."

DeLeon turned his head slowly and addressed the young woman with him. "He had some trouble as a recruit, needed to study a lot harder than the rest of us just to get by." He turned his head to speak to May and Karya. "Probably wouldn't have made it if he hadn't gotten a lot of help from his friends."

May gave DeLeon an unpleasant smile. "I heard he was the last man standing."

DeLeon clearly didn't like the way she had come to John's defense. "Only because he cheated."

Her smile turned into a nasty grin. "I wasn't at Miriteen, but at the end of basic I had to stand until I passed out too, and I've heard they do something similar at every recruit depot."

She turned to Karya, whose eyes had widened considerably at the exchange. "I can tell you from first-hand experience, it's not possible to cheat and get away with it."

DeLeon's brows had furrowed with anger. "He's smart that way."

May grinned unpleasantly. "But a moment ago you implied he isn't smart."

John struggled to think of some way to deescalate the situation before May stood up and clocked DeLeon. The young woman on DeLeon's arm must have been thinking along the same lines, because she pulled on his elbow. "Come on, Macus. Let's go get that drink."

John said, "Yes, I don't want to keep you from having a good time."

May opened her mouth to speak, but Karya did something under the table.

"Ouch," May said. "Why did you do that?"

Between John, Karya and DeLeon's date, they managed to end it, and DeLeon and the young lady walked away.

When John sat down, Karya demanded, "What the hell was that all about?"

John didn't want to go into a long discourse on his relationship with Macus DeLeon. "He didn't like it that I was the last man standing. He thought it should be him."

May shook her head. "From what I just saw, there was a lot more to it than just that."

John grimaced. "Of course there was, but I really don't want to talk about it."

"Okay," Karya said, "we won't talk about that. But you two have to tell me what this last-man-standing thing is about."

Many of the non-Blacksword cadets seemed a little intimidated by the patches on John's sleeves, and breaking through those barriers sometimes took a conscious effort. May helped in that respect, frequently introducing him to other cadets as her ". . . hotshot Blacksword roomie." Her teasing and casual indifference to his Blacksword patches quickly put them at ease.

In most of John's classes, Blackswords were a small minority. But in a select few, Blacksword officers provided exclusive instruction to the twelve Blacksword cadets present that year. That was the only time he saw Theila, Hey-You's friend. John learned from the other Blacksword cadets that none of them shared their dorm room with another Blacksword. He might never have become May's friend had they not been roommates, and he realized then how their simple, easy relationship had helped him integrate with all of the cadets, not just Blackswords.

May took a sisterly interest in John, chided him for working too hard, and repeatedly told him he needed to get out more and have a little fun. She and Karya jokingly told him they would find him a girlfriend, but they never did anything about it beyond a little teasing. John didn't want a girlfriend at that time, and was glad they limited their efforts to playful banter. May did regularly break him away from his studies, and they went out for a little rest and relaxation, occasionally alone, but more often than not in a larger group of cadets. And John found a couple of opportunities to join Wakeland on one of his party forays.

••••

"Hey Eindride."

Anders recognized Thoran's voice, and turned about to find the tall, bearded man approaching him. Their shift had just ended and Anders was looking forward to dinner and a good night's sleep.

"I'm going out for a drink," Thoran said. "Join me so I don't have to drink alone."

Anders had long ago put aside his suspicions regarding Thoran's past. The man might or might not be ex-military, but if so, it really didn't matter if he had something he didn't want his coworkers to know about. After all, Anders had concealed mass murder on an unprecedented scale, and Thoran had proven to be a nice enough fellow.

"Sure," Anders said. "Sounds good."

The two of them walked down the street to the bar where Viktra had introduced them. They sat down at a small table and ordered a couple shots of kirva.

Thoran said, "Don't see much of you other than work. What do you do with yourself in your spare time?"

Anders shrugged. "Changing careers wasn't easy, had to start all over again."

"Got a girl or anything?"

"No," Anders said. "No girl. What about you?"

Thoran rubbed his beard and flicked a dreadlock out of his eyes. "Yah, I met this girl a year ago. Real alpha female, she is. And expensive."

Anders wasn't sure what he had just heard. "You mean she charges you for—that's illegal."

"No," Thoran said. "Nothing like that. She just makes a lot more than me, so I have to take her to nice places, some I can hardly afford."

Anders took a sip of the clear, fiery kirva. It burned its way down his throat. "You must really like her."

Thoran lifted his glass and threw its contents down his throat in one swallow. He let out a whoosh of air, smacked his lips and said, "Not like that. She's just fun, and convenient."

"So you go to expensive places just to make her happy?"

Thoran shook his head and gave him a big grin. "I like going to nice places too." He leaned close to Anders and spoke in hushed tones. "And I do a little moonlighting on the side to augment my transit pay. Don't let on to management about that."

Thoran leaned back in his chair and regarded Anders critically, his brow wrinkling. "You said you had to start all over again. You mean financially?"

"I mean everything, including financially."

Thoran nodded while rubbing his beard in thought. Then he seemed to come to some sort of decision. "Would you be interested in making a little extra?"

"You mean moonlighting?"

"Yah."

"The same stuff you're doing?"

"Yah."

"What's it involve?"

Thoran didn't answer him, but picked up both glasses, walked across the room to the bar and got them refilled. He walked back and put the full glasses on the table, then sat down. "You said you're ex-military, right?"

Anders nodded and said, "Yes."

Thoran spoke slowly and carefully. "The extra work I'm doing, those kinds of skills come in handy. In fact, they're pretty much a prerequisite."

Anders intentionally spoke with a note of distrust in his voice. "That would imply you have such skills, but you gave me the impression you've never been in the military."

Thoran cocked his head to one side and his dreadlocks shifted that way. "Sorry about that."

"Why mislead me?"

Thoran stared at Anders for a long moment, as if considering his answer. "Some things in a man's past are better left in the past. What about you? Why'd you leave the military?"

Anders grinned and said, "Some things in a man's past are better left in the past."

Thoran gave him a white, toothy grin framed by his black beard. "Exactly! The extra work I'm doing is a little on the edge of legal."

Anders considered that carefully. He wasn't yet certain that Thoran represented Kristdokar's mysterious enemies. It could be pure coincidence that the larger man had transferred from another transit depot shortly before Anders had begun work. But still, to find out he took the next step. "Is it risky?"

Still grinning, Thoran considered that for a moment. "A bit."

Anders raised his glass. "Then I would hope the extra pay is commensurate with the extra risk."

Thoran asked, "How much extra risk are you willing to take?"

Anders hesitated, trying to give the impression he considered the matter carefully. "My financial situation is rather tenuous at the moment. So that depends on how much extra risk your employers are willing to pay for."

Thoran's grin broadened.

12

The Blue Dress

AS A JUNIOR officer Nikaela did not rate one of the enclosed offices at the back of the converted warehouse. She had a desk jammed among a cluster of other desks in the large room between the front of the building and the private offices. Little by little they assembled the team, and many of the other desks now had occupants. Most of them had joined recently so Nikaela didn't know them well. She didn't yet understand what Kristdokar intended to do.

Her exciting and dangerous clandestine assignment had turned into a tedious drudge of sifting through data and statistics, interspersed with the Lingua lessons. Kristdokar hoped to identify some of the organizations and individuals responsible for Novalis III and Reisenar. But after several months of paperwork and Lingua studies, Nikaela's enthusiasm for her new assignment had tempered considerably.

The skalde had elevated Nikaela's clearance level, allowing her to review the deep neural probe data taken from the five defendants of the Novalis III tribunal, which had uncovered tantalizing little tidbits, but nothing concrete. The three lower ranking defendants, the command superiors like Anders Eindride, knew almost nothing—she thought briefly of him and hoped he came out of this okay. The implants of the command eagle and command hawk had been altered, which could only have been done with their consent. Upon arrest, modified software went into action and blocked their memories of certain information so thoroughly that, even had they wanted to cooperate, they couldn't have. The Larscom Executive Council had kept them alive long enough to make sure nothing further could be extracted, then executed them in a low-gravity gallows.

Nikaela had enough clearance to pull information not available for public consumption. She found it interesting that even the highly classified details on Novalis III had been sanitized. After all, she had real firsthand knowledge of what had actually happened.

After sweating over the data for days, she had come up with certain tenuous correlations: organizations, individuals and companies who at one time had had interests on both Novalis III and Reisenar. And some of them might benefit from an unpleasant little interstellar war between the Commonwealth and the Supremacy.

The Kelk could not win such a war, not with the overwhelming superiority in numbers of the Commonwealth. It angered her deeply that commercial interests would choose to profit at the expense of millions of Kelk lives. On an intellectual level she understood the way blind hatred led the hawks to dismiss such loss of life, but the cynical quest for commercial gain infuriated her.

She needed to discuss the results with Kristdokar, so that morning she hurried to work anticipating a bit of excitement. But when she arrived she found the door to Kristdokar's office closed. The skalde apparently had visitors of some sort, and had left instructions for Nikaela to compile all available data on the incidents on Reisenar and Novalis III. Nikaela sent the skalde a message with her findings and a request for a few minutes of the older woman's time, then sat down at her desk and buried herself in her work.

An hour later the door to Kristdokar's office opened and she heard the skalde say, "I'll cut orders to have you transferred immediately."

A familiar voice said, "Excellent, mistress. We look forward to working with you on this."

Nikaela stood. She knew that voice, knew it well, and was not surprised when Senior Command Superior Thordahl stepped out of the skalde's office into the larger room. Command Superior Brynjar followed him, with Kristdokar only a step behind the two men. Thordahl and Brynjar were the only people present in uniform, and both men smiled when they saw Nikaela. They had been her immediate superiors on Reisenar, and she had fond memories of working for them.

She couldn't hide the excitement in her voice when she said, "Command Superiors, it's so nice to see you again."

Thordahl said, "And you, Mistress Vreekande. You appear to have recovered nicely from that business on Reisenar."

"Yes, I have."

Kristdokar said, "I've wracked my brains to figure out a way to reestablish contact with our new friends, but it turns out Maestras Thordahl and Brynjar have already solved that problem for me."

Kristdokar seemed almost jubilant. She leaned close to Nikaela and lowered her voice. "They'll also be joining our team, along with other select members of First Liaison Company. We're going to pick and choose from those who can work with our new friends."

When not in a closed and secure space, they had adopted the practice of referring to Primatov, Mathius, and their other Commonwealth contacts as their *new friends*. Nikaela took Kristdokar's words to mean that they didn't want to recruit anyone from First Liaison with a hardline, anti-Commonwealth attitude.

Kristdokar said to Nikaela, "I got your message that you want to speak with me. Please wait in my office while I see Maestras Thordahl and Brynjar out."

Nikaela stepped into Kristdokar's office while the skalde escorted the two men out of the building. A few minutes later Kristdokar joined her, closing the door. "Sit down," she said. "And relax."

Nikaela took a seat, and Kristdokar asked her, "Have you learned anything from digging through the Novalis and Reisenar records."

Recalling that after the Novalis III tragedy, Kristdokar had twice warned her to forget everything she knew about it, Nikaela spoke carefully. "The classified information on both incidents appears to have been . . . somewhat sanitized."

Kristdokar nodded. "Yes, I'm not surprised at that." She held up a small comp chip. "But Maestras Thordahl and Brynjar have just given me new data, provided to them by Lieutenant Colonel Primatov."

Nikaela recalled the Blacksword officer, a tall woman with dark red hair, and quite good-looking, at least by Commonwealth standards.

Still holding the chip in front of her, Kristdokar stared at it and said, "You and I are going to sort through this information in some detail. I wouldn't be surprised if we find a few surprises."

Nikaela said, "I'll be most happy to assist you, mistress."

Kristdokar placed the chip on the desk in front of her. "Now what is it you wanted to see me about? The message you sent me this morning is rather vague."

"It was meant to be, mistress."

Kristdokar nodded, leaned back in her chair and regarded Nikaela carefully. "I read the message. It's a fairly standard request for further information on seventeen individuals, eight corporations, and six political organizations. I know what I read there. Now you tell me what's not in the message."

The skalde had recognized that Nikaela's message had not been completely forthcoming. "At one time or another," she said, "they all have had connections to both Novalis III and Reisenar. Among the corporations and individuals were corporate offices, partnerships, regular interstellar commerce, and/or trade agreements. Regarding the political organizations, they sent representatives to those planets, or received delegates from them here on Viktorkinde, and they received financial donations from some of those corporations. I should add that those donations were carefully laundered through third party accounts. I followed the money."

The skalde frowned and said, "There must be more to it than that."

Nikaela shrugged. "They would all benefit from a war."

Kristdokar shook her head. "That's tenuous, at best."

"I know," Nikaela said. "But it's a start. That's why I kept the request standard and understated, with no official demands."

"Very well," Kristdokar said. "I'll pass the request on."

The skalde leaned forward and picked up the chip again. "Beside this, Thordahl and Brynjar also brought me some information about your breschkada. He is now a Blacksword. He is attending their officer school and will soon carry a rank similar to yours."

Nikaela asked, "Does that help us in some way?"

Kristdokar said, "It may remove certain . . . impediments." As the skalde spoke, she grew visibly uncomfortable. "I'm going to ask something of you, and before I do, I want you to understand you may refuse the request without any repercussions whatsoever. And regardless of your answer, I will never speak of it again, and no one beyond you and me will ever know I asked it of you."

The skalde had Nikaela's curiosity piqued; she said nothing and waited for the older woman to speak.

Kristdokar spoke slowly. "Maestras Thordahl and Brynjar mentioned that on Reisenar you and your breschkada seemed to develop a certain . . . rapport. Would you agree with that conclusion?"

Nikaela couldn't imagine where this conversation was going. "Yes," she said. "I think we both came to trust each other . . . implicitly. After all, we saved each other's lives."

Kristdokar nodded. "I know you might find this distasteful, but the thought has occurred to me, and so I must ask it."

The older woman hesitated before speaking, then blurted out, "Do you think you might seduce the young man?"

Nikaela's heart started pounding. She blinked rapidly and closed her eyes. "Seduce . . . my breschkada?" She recalled the look on John Mathius's face when she had teased him, but wasn't sure if she could turn that look into desire on his part. She didn't know how he thought of her. In his eyes she might be a disgusting and depraved blue-skinned Kelk demon. She opened her eyes.

Kristdokar nodded and spoke rapidly. "I know it's distasteful, perhaps even downright disgusting. He is a common-face after all, and even worse, now a Blacksword. I wouldn't ask if I didn't think it might help."

The skalde completely misunderstood Nikaela's reaction, thinking her hesitation stemmed from an aversion on her part. "I cannot . . . betray . . . my breschkada."

The older woman continued to nod. "I don't ask that you betray him. After all, we are trying to work with them. But you might learn something."

Nikaela closed her eyes again to consider her own feelings in the matter. She felt no aversion to the young man, as Kristdokar feared. Her hesitation had been her own fear that John Mathius would balk and reject her; after all she was one of those blue-skinned Kelk demons. She knew the kind of Kelk myths Commonwealth children grew up with. She would not like to see that kind of distaste on his face, though that would be a fairly normal reaction for a citizen of the Commonwealth. It would hurt to see him look upon her that way.

She opened her eyes again.

The skalde stood and came around the desk. She took one of Nikaela's hands in a very motherly gesture, and spoke calmly without emotion. "I'm sorry. I never should have asked that of you. I withdraw the request."

The woman completely misunderstood. "If you think it might help in some way . . ." Nikaela hesitated. "May I think on it?"

"Take all the time you need. In fact don't even bother to give me an answer. I can see I've upset you. Take the rest of the day off, and completely forget we had this discussion. Just relax, maybe have a stiff drink, or something."

Nikaela didn't want to take the rest of the day off, but Kristdokar insisted. In short order she found herself out in front of the building, walking down the sidewalk toward her apartment, thinking of John Mathius.

A strangely compelling thought struck her and she halted in her tracks. She considered it for a moment, then used her implants to call a cab. She couldn't stand still as she waited for it to arrive, shifting nervously from one foot to the other, worrying she might have missed her opportunity and it was now too late.

When the grav car floated up to the curb, she hurriedly climbed into it and gave its AI the address. If she were a skalde like Kristdokar, she'd have the authority to override its systems and trigger its emergency mode. It would race down the street flashing an emergency beacon and overriding traffic control signals. But then she'd probably be demoted for the improper use of emergency protocols.

After what seemed an eternity the cab pulled up to the curb in front of the address. She climbed out of it and rushed into the clothing store, then to the department that offered evening wear. She breathed a sigh of relief when she found the blue, slinky dress still there. She didn't need to try it on again. She purchased it, even though it cost two months of her salary as a Command Boss Junior Rank.

When she got back to her apartment she unwrapped the dress and held it up to look at it. Purchasing it had been a stupid thing to do. She would never find an opportunity to wear such a thing, so she put it on and wore it for the rest of the day, thinking a lot about John Mathius.

••••

Well past midnight, Nash Wakeland strolled casually through the lobby of the dormitory. He encountered no one as he headed for the exit, which suited his requirements nicely. It wouldn't be much of a problem if someone spotted him going out. He could drop a hint or two that he had arranged an assignation with that pretty female instructor all the young male cadets found so attractive. No one would question the need to keep such an illicit relationship secret, and it would only enhance his reputation as the handsome party guy. But he still preferred that his fellow cadets remain unaware of his nocturnal activities. Little things like that could plant the first seeds of suspicion, so he chose to slip out unobserved. He walked through the front doors of the dormitory and out onto the sidewalk.

One of Trafalgar's two large moons rested on the horizon in three-quarter aspect, casting dim illumination over a still night. The sounds of the city barely impinged on the quiet of the academy campus. Nash resisted the temptation to sneak and lurk about. If campus security saw him acting suspiciously, they'd probably question him, and there would be a record of his nighttime excursion.

He walked at a normal pace past the main library, then turned left toward the engineering complex. But before he got there, he stepped into the shadows of a narrow walkway between two buildings and paused. He looked up and down the street to be certain he hadn't been observed, then leaned against the building to wait. Five minutes later his employer approached, strolling up the walkway toward him. The man stopped about five paces away and didn't say anything.

As always, they did not speak out loud. Nash subvocalized into his implants, "I'm here as you requested."

The man cocked his head to one side, and in the dim moonlight Nash got a partial view of his features, though he had no doubt the fellow had obscured his face and head with a visual overlay field. The man asked, "Have you had any success?"

Nash needed to give the fellow good news. The money was way too good to pass up, and the fellow had enough connections to get Nash admitted to the academy under a fake identity with a phony DNA signature. "It took a while," Nash said, "but he's coming around, and he trusts me. And I finally got him to come out and party a little instead of burying his face in those damn books."

The man cocked his head to the other side. "I suppose that's progress, of a sort."

"We're only four months into the year," Nash said. "I've still got plenty of time to screw him up."

The man nodded slowly, as if considering Nash's words. "You won't have much time if you fail your transition navigation class and wash out."

Nash hadn't put too much effort into the classroom work. This man also had the ability to fix Nash's grades, or to give him advanced copies of exam questions and answers so he excelled without the effort. Nash demanded, "Why can't you fix that one like the rest?"

Nash caught a glint of moonlight from the man's eyes, and the fellow had clearly not liked that request. "There are some limits to what I can do in that regard. I can boost your scores from middling to good, but someone might notice tampering when it's that significant."

"Then why don't you just screw up some of his grades. He only has to fail one or two classes to wash out, then we'll all be done with him."

The man shook his head very slowly from side to side. "Him, we don't go near. From what we've been able to determine, he isn't that important, so we don't want to overplay our hand. If we learn otherwise, or you screw up your end of this, we may choose to deal with him much more directly."

The man had said, "We," so he wasn't operating on his own. Nash had suspected that all along, because the fellow was all military, but clearly not a high-ranking officer. And the kind of person who could pull the kind of strings this man had, would not meet at night in the dark with a disgraced ex-special-forces soldier. No, he worked for someone more powerful just as Nash worked for him.

Nash asked, "You'd deal with him more directly, huh? What does that mean?"

"I'm not here to answer your questions."

The man's last words had implied they might be willing to employ more deadly measures to meet their objectives. Good.

"I'll get my grades up in that one class," Nash said. "You be sure to keep my grades up in everything else. And I'll be sure to deliver your boy for you."

"We need to see more progress," the man said. "Get him into a bar, get him drunk, and then someone is going to pick a fight with him. It won't happen the next time you get him out, because we want him to get comfortable with you. But when it does happen, you make sure he fights back, and it turns into a real brawl. We'll be watching you as closely as you're watching him."

The man didn't wait for an answer, but turned and walked back the way he had come.

It occurred to Nash it wouldn't be in his own best interests to give the man what he wanted, at least not too soon. They'd be watching him so he'd have to cooperate with their little bar-fight scenario. But the longer he drew this out, the longer he could count on gainful employment. And maybe they'd grow impatient enough to try something more deadly. At some point it would be wise to make sure they understood they could count on him to support them in that, because if and when they proposed something more direct, Nash could raise his prices considerably.

13

No Rest

THE FIRST DAY of winter break John slept in and caught up on six months of lost sleep. Dirkson wasn't going to let the ten-day break between semesters get in the way of his Kelk studies, so John couldn't shake free of the rather eccentric professor. The man had recently introduced him to the differences between Commonwealth and Supremacy laws.

He told John, "The strong matriarchal structure influences almost everything. For example, raping a woman is a capital offense. No prison time, just execution by firing squad. They are rather careful to give the accused due process, but good-bye to any man who gets a guilty verdict. On the other hand, if it can be proven beyond a doubt that a woman knowingly falsely accused a man, she gets the axe."

Other than Dirkson's tutoring, John didn't have too many demands on his time for the next several days. He intended to use the freedom to relax and sleep in every morning, maybe do a little studying, but not too much. Maybe even get a date with a nice girl.

The previous evening he'd gone out with Nash and his cadre of party cadets. John had downed a few beers and was content with that, but Nash had teased him for not drinking more. Then Nash had organized a drinking game. One of the female cadets had ended up on her hands and knees at a toilet praying to the gods of too much drink. John helped her back to the dorm where she made a very drunken and sloppy pass at him. But she stank of vomit, and in any case he wasn't interested.

When he finally climbed out of bed and checked his messages, to his surprise he had orders to report the following morning to the office of Lieutenant Colonel Katrine Primatov. The message included an address for the Armed Services Executive Office Building not far from the Capital Rotunda.

He recalled the colonel as a tall, good-looking woman with dark, red hair, and really nice curves, a lot like Carla's. She outranked him by a couple thousand light-years, so he didn't allow any thoughts of sexuality to impinge on his memories of her, but he couldn't deny the obvious. He did wonder why she wanted to see him, and thinking of that completely ruined his day.

The next morning he couldn't sleep and woke early. He showered, shaved, brushed his hair, put on a freshly laundered uniform, then took the capital subway into the heart of the city. He arrived two hours early, so he bought a brochure from a street vendor. It detailed interesting sights that were a must-see when in the capital. He uploaded it into his implants.

He started with the Capital Rotunda which was just across the street. The brochure told him that the eight tiers of steps in front of it were symbolic of the eight star systems that had originally founded the Commonwealth.

He noticed a pretty young woman in the crowd glancing his way. She had brown hair cut chin length, and when she saw him looking her way, she smiled shyly and looked away. She seemed a little familiar, and he thought he might have spotted her on campus a few times. Then, as now, she wore civilian clothing, so he didn't think she was a cadet.

One block away he stopped in front of the entrance to the National Museum. He was happy to learn his cadet status allowed him free entry. Again, he spotted that young woman, and again she abruptly averted her gaze when he looked her way. Seeing her a second time made him a little paranoid, and he wondered if she had followed him. But then he realized all of the street vendors were probably hawking the same sightseeing brochure, and in all likelihood she had simply followed the same directions. He put his paranoia aside and moved on.

Because of his preoccupation with the upcoming meeting, he didn't really enjoy the marvels of the capital, and recalled very little about them. He vowed to return and take in the sights again when not anxious about facing a high-ranking Blacksword officer.

A half hour before his appointment he made his way to the address he'd been given, a square building six stories high that covered an entire city block. It had been constructed of old-fashioned stone—or perhaps pseudo-stone; John couldn't tell the difference—with tall ornate columns framing an arched entrance built in a grand style.

John climbed the steps in front of the building and subconsciously counted them as he did so; thirty-six. He wondered if that number held some sort of symbolic significance, but didn't have time to look it up in the brochure.

The main entrance opened into a massive hallway that ran straight toward the far end of the building. He stopped and gawked for a moment like some bumpkin from a provincial planet. It occurred to him that he was a bumpkin from a provincial planet. The ceiling had to be at least ten meters overhead, and the hallway wide enough for twenty of his cadet comrades to march side-by-side down its length. The walls had been paneled in some sort of rich, dark wood, and the floor appeared to be tiles of polished natural stone.

A security station blocked the middle of the hallway, with open passageways on either side of it that allowed access to the building's interior. At the station a bored guard sat behind a tall reception desk, and a short line of people had queued up in front of him. Four armed military constables stood behind and to either side of the security desk. As each person in the line gave the guard their name, he directed them to pass by his station either on the right or on the left. Those who passed on the right walked past him without hindrance, while those who passed on the left were scanned by a large apparatus, and their belongings carefully checked. John stepped into the back of the line.

The line moved forward quickly, and when he finally stood in front of the guard he said, "Cadet John Mathius. I have an appointment with Lieutenant Colonel Katrine Primatov."

The guard nodded and looked at one of several screens embedded in the desk in front of him. "You're on the list," he said. "Though next time use the staff entrance and you won't have to wait in line."

John's implants got a request for his crypto ID, he authorized transmission of the necessary sequence, and the guard indicated he should pass by on the right. Apparently, his military grade implants cleared him without further delay.

John's implants automatically connected with the building's security net and projected a virtual overlay in his vision with directions to Primatov's office. He followed the path indicated up the main hallway toward the back of the building, then down a flight of stairs, and along a side passageway to a closed office door.

He stopped in front of it, and double checked his uniform to make sure everything was in order. Then he removed his hat, tucked it under his left arm, and subvocalized into his implants. "Colonel Primatov, Cadet Mathius requesting permission to enter."

"Enter," she said, and the door slid into the wall.

••••

Katrine liked her office in the basement of the Armed Services Executive Office Building. It was large enough to suit her, with room for a couple of guests to sit down and talk comfortably and privately. Most importantly, it was not centrally located, and by that it never drew attention to her. And today that was important, because she didn't want any attention drawn to the young man she was about to meet. It wouldn't do to have him report to either Fran Thealone's or Mani Gascoigne's office. Some news hype might notice, and splash the poor kid's face all over the vids.

When the door to Katrine's office opened, John Mathius marched forward, stopped two paces in front of her desk, snapped to rigid attention, and raised his hand in a salute. Behind him the door hissed shut as he spoke softly, but precisely, "Cadet Mathius reporting as ordered, ma'am."

Katrine glanced toward Fran Thealone, who sat in a comfortable chair behind and to one side of him. The older woman regarded the young cadet with obvious interest as her eyes scanned him from head to toe. Holding his salute, young

Mathius's eyes flicked momentarily to one side, but returned immediately to Katrine. He had executed proper military etiquette, marching forward into her office with his eyes locked straight forward. The way the office was situated, he couldn't have seen Thealone. But he was clearly aware he and Katrine were not alone in the office, though he probably couldn't tell her how he knew that. Given his background, his awareness of his surroundings did not surprise her.

She returned the salute and said, "At ease, Cadet Mathius, and relax."

He did as ordered, but clearly did not relax.

Katrine stood and walked around the desk. She extended her hand, and his eyes widened a little as he reached out and shook it. "Good to see you again, John. It's been what, almost a year since Reisenar?"

He shook her hand with a firm grip, not with crushing force the way some men did when shaking a woman's hand, as if they needed to prove their superior strength. Nor did he hold her hand flaccidly, as if afraid to overpower a woman.

"Not quite a year, ma'am," he said. "But close enough."

She released his hand, gripped his shoulder and said, "There's someone here who would like to meet you."

She turned him toward the back of the room as Fran Thealone stood. At the sight of the older woman, his eyes widened considerably. Katrine had expected that. All three of them were in uniform, and one did not need to be a Blacksword to know that only one bird-colonel wore Blacksword patches with the name BLACKSWORD stenciled above her left breast pocket.

He started to raise his hand to salute her, but Thealone smiled and extended her hand. He awkwardly aborted the salute, reached out and gripped her hand. As they shook hands she said, "It's a pleasure to meet you, John."

He stammered, then said, "Uh, it's an honor, ma'am."

She scrunched her nose up as she said, "Not as much as you might think." She released his hand. "And I'm honored to meet you. What you did on Reisenar was exceptional."

His face reddened. "It seemed the obvious thing to do, ma'am."

"Perhaps obvious to you," she said, "but not to most, eh? For the official reports we heavily sanitized what you did on that subway platform, so I'd like to hear firsthand the details of what happened."

The whoosh of the door sliding open interrupted them. Manifort Gascoigne stepped into the room. "Colonel, and Colonel," he said, acknowledging Thealone and Katrine. Two steps into the room he halted and gave Cadet Mathius an appraising look. "And this must be our resourceful young man."

He crossed to young Mathius and shook his hand enthusiastically. "I'm Mani Gascoigne, young fellow." Cadet Mathius's eyes opened even wider. He clearly realized the hand he shook belonged to a very senior senator.

Thealone said, "Cadet Mathius was just about to give us a firsthand account of his experience on Reisenar."

••••

Colonel Primatov slid a comfortable chair around so it faced a couch against one wall of her office. Then she directed John to sit down in the comfortable chair, though nothing about the situation felt comfortable to him. Colonel Blacksword and Senator Gascoigne, the most powerful Blacksword in the regiment, and one of the most powerful senators in the Commonwealth, sat down on the couch facing him, while Primatov remained standing. John sat on the edge of the chair, and tried not to appear stiff and ill at ease, but he did a poor job of that.

He had now had quite a bit of practice at relating the carefully edited version of events on Reisenar, and the story came without any hesitation or forethought. But a short way into it, Primatov interrupted him. "John, the story you're telling seems to be missing quite a few details compared to what you told me in the embassy that night on Reisenar."

"Yes, ma'am," he said, trying to hide his confusion. "You told me there was a lot I couldn't tell anyone."

She smiled, doing a reasonably good job of hiding what he thought looked like frustrated impatience. "That doesn't apply to Colonel Blacksword or Senator Gascoigne. Please tell them everything. Hold nothing back."

"Yes, ma'am," John said. He thought carefully, but the events of that evening were indelibly etched into his memory. "I was in pretty bad shape when I scrambled onto the subway platform, and I—"

"John," Primatov said. "Start at the beginning, and take your time. You were on a drop boat out of *Defiant*, on what was supposed to be a milk run. I don't think even I have heard the entire story, so take it from there."

John told them of the surprise attack on the drop boats, and of his less than stellar drop to the roof of a building using the grav fields generated by his armor. He told them everything, surprised at how easy it came back to him. They asked a few questions, but for the most part they listened raptly. He finished at the point where he and Lieutenant Komisky stepped into the com room on the second floor of the embassy, and he got his first sight of Katrine Primatov. It hadn't taken long, and he felt a little relieved to have related the full story to someone. He thought of Hey-You.

Senator Gascoigne said, "I have one question. You said one of the reasons you didn't kill her was that you were—and I'm quoting you—'done with murder.' What did you mean by that?"

Any relief he had felt in telling the story disappeared in that instant. His fear must have shown on his face, because Primatov stepped in.

"Senator," she said. "I'm fully aware of the details of John's past, and a sequence of extremely unpleasant experiences he suffered on Novalis III where he grew up. Let me reassure you he has done nothing of which you should be concerned. He simply views certain actions of his in a considerably harsher light than we would; actions that were forced upon him, I should add."

"Mani," Thealone said. "I too know the details of his past, and he's done nothing wrong."

Gascoigne nodded and said, "Good enough for me."

He stood, saying, "Sorry, but I have to run."

They stood with him, and Thealone said, "So do I." She turned to John. "Thank you young man. And you really should be a little easier on yourself."

They did more shaking of hands, Gascoigne patted John on the back, and after he and Thealone left, Primatov said, "Let's go get some lunch. The cafeteria food here is not bad, and I'm buying."

In the cafeteria, seated across the table from Primatov with trays of food between them, John found himself relaxing a little in her presence. She asked him about O-School, and when she asked him about his Kelk lessons, he said, "It's really interesting, though sometimes it's a little difficult to follow Professor Dirkson."

She grinned. "He is a bit of a strange bird, isn't he?"

"You know him?" he asked.

She lifted an eyebrow. "I've been taking lessons from him as well, hoping to mitigate my horrible accent."

They compared notes, and both had a little chuckle at Dirkson's expense. But then John spotted Macus DeLeon a few tables over. DeLeon saw him at the same moment and his eyes hardened. Then he grinned unpleasantly and slowly rose up from his seat.

DeLeon wore an expensive looking business suit, and John braced himself as his old nemesis casually crossed the distance between them. Primatov looked up and smiled pleasantly at DeLeon.

"Hello, John," DeLeon said.

He turned to Primatov. "We haven't met, Colonel. I'm Macus DeLeon, an aide to Senator Palmutter."

She shook his hand and smiled pleasantly as she said, "Nice to meet you, Mr. DeLeon."

DeLeon released her hand and turned back to John. He sneered as he said, "Still wasting your time with that ComSecCorps crap." Apparently, ComSecCorps was now something far beneath his own aspirations.

"Yes," John said, taking care to avoid DeLeon's baiting remarks. "Still ComSec-Corps."

DeLeon's chin rose proudly. "As an aide to Senator Palmutter, I'm learning a lot more than I would as some cadet. After a few years I may run for office myself."

John tried to keep it polite. "Well I wish you luck in that."

DeLeon leaned close to him and hissed, "You can't fuck this up for me like you did the Corps."

John wasn't going to get into that argument so he just grimaced and shrugged.

DeLeon said, "Still no guts."

He straightened, turned his back on John, and walked away.

Primatov said, "He's the one you executed in the sims, right?"

John strongly suspected she knew the answer to that, and he feared her relaxed acceptance of him would now turn sour. "It was all virtual, so it didn't matter. That's what Colonel Brightlaw said."

She smiled pleasantly, put her fork down on the food tray in front of her and leaned forward. "John, when considering your performance in command school we discussed that incident in considerable detail. Sergeant Omuglu was absolutely certain you would have killed him even if it had been real."

John's heart climbed up into his throat, and he wondered if this was a prelude to cashiering a cadet unfit for the Blacksword. If she washed him out of the Blacksword, he'd be drummed out of ComSecCorps completely, and he'd have nothing.

He didn't realize he had curled the fingers of both hands into fists until she reached out and gently covered one fist with the palm of her hand. "We all agreed with Sergeant Omuglu. You would have killed him if it had been real. And I don't think you realize that was one of the reasons we offered you the Blacksword."

••••

When John walked down the thirty-six steps of the Armed Services Executive Office Building, his paranoia made him scan the crowds of people nearby—no sign of the pretty young woman he had spotted earlier. He chided himself for worrying someone might be following him for some unknown reason. On the other hand, she had been pretty, and about his age, and he could count the dates he'd had since coming to Trafalgar on the fingers of one hand, without using up all five fingers. She had twice given him a shy smile before looking away. A part of him had hoped she *was* following him, but not for any nefarious reasons.

Winter break ended and John went back to studying, drilling with the other Blacksword cadets, and practicing his Kelk.

14

Teamwork

AS THE SHUTTLE descended into the outer atmosphere of the planet, the view out the window next to Nikaela jerked and shook. The pilots experienced some turbulence, and a little buffeting, but the boat's internal gravity fields compensated nicely and she felt nothing.

Beneath the shuttle she saw only thick cloud cover. Her view extended several hundred kilometers out to the horizon, but try as she might she could find no break in the gray-white blanket of clouds. It hid every square centimeter of the planet's surface. Then the shuttle descended into the mist and she saw nothing but white, wispy haze.

Still, she stared out the window in fascination, watching the graying tufts of cloud slowly turn darker and darker. By the time they dropped into the lower atmosphere, the cloud cover obscured the sun so thoroughly it could have been twilight on any other planet. Drops of water streaked diagonally across the outside of the window.

Seated next to her, Brynjar said, "Dismal place, is it not?"

She turned to him. "Is it as bad as it looks?"

He grimaced. "Worse."

"Doesn't the sun ever shine?"

He looked past her and out the window. "I'm told they get sunshine about ten to fifteen percent of the time, but all I've ever seen is this incessant gloom."

The shuttle leveled off at about a thousand meters, well below the cloud ceiling. As Nikaela's eyes adjusted to the dimness of the countryside around her she corrected her first impression. Enough light from Norandyne's primary did pierce the clouds to illuminate the terrain beneath her. It reminded her of an exceptionally bright night when both of Viktorkinde's two moons shown full overhead.

A bright light streaked past beneath her, then another, and another. She keyed her implants to get a navigation fix, and learned they were approaching Salvasan, Norandyne's largest city. Then a building about five stories high passed beneath her, and in short order the shuttle streaked above a densely populated area of plast, concrete and masonry structures, not unlike those on any inhabited planet.

Nikaela's implants chimed and the shuttle pilot spoke in bored tones, "We're about five minutes out. We're going straight to the warehouse, so there's no need to cover up, not on a day like this."

That was a relief. They wouldn't have to cover their eyes with contacts, and their skin with makeup.

The warehouse had an empty tarmac parking lot next to it, and the pilot set the grav boat down in the middle of it. Nikaela activated the umbrella field in her coat, then she, Brynjar and six of their comrades sprinted across the tarmac to an open door in the warehouse. A common-face man stood holding the door for them as they filed through it, and once they were inside the man closed the door. Nikaela and the other Kelk stomped their feet and shook the rain off their coats, which produced large puddles of water on the floor beneath their feet.

Nikaela glanced around at her surroundings. She stood in a large room with a flat concrete floor. In the distance an assortment of heavy equipment had been parked in a haphazard pattern, and about forty feet above her a latticework of steel and plast girders supported the roof.

"People," Brynjar called out, and they all turned to face him. He indicated the common-face man standing next to him. "This is Captain Smythe. He is our host here. For the next two tendays, trust his word in all matters."

Brynjar then addressed Smythe. "Is your team here?"

Smythe nodded. "Here, ready, willing and able."

It had been Nikaela's idea to put together a mixed team of Kelk and Commonwealth experts to compare notes, trade data, and attempt to make more headway in their investigation together than they might separately. Had she known such a suggestion meant she would have to spend two tendays in such a miserable place, she might not have offered up the idea. But on the way here she had been told the Commonwealth team would be comprised exclusively of Blackswords, and she harbored a small hope John Mathius would be among them. Who knew what might happen during twenty days of forced confinement?

Smythe said, "Let's throw everyone together and make introductions."

Nikaela pulled off her coat, and her heart beat a little rapidly as she followed them across the concrete floor to a small, walled-off, office complex. But her breschkada was not among those present.

••••

Working the afternoon shift, Anders finished his day late in the evening. When he walked out of the transit depot into the night of the city, he ran into Thoran waiting for him on the sidewalk. The tall man hooked a thumb over his shoulder and said, "I need a drink. Join me."

That had become their de facto signal to meet privately and discuss Anders's possible employment in Thoran's moonlighting venture. Beyond that first time in the bar when Thoran had initially broached the subject, they had now met twice more. Thoran had told him that because of the *sensitive* nature of their extracurricular employer's agenda, he needed to be sure about Anders. To help cement his persona, Anders had dropped a few hints, making it clear he had no fondness for his former superiors in the military. He moved cautiously, and took care not to overplay the bitter, cashiered, ex-officer persona. And from a few minor slipups Thoran had made, Anders suspected his new friend knew far more about his real past than the fellow let on.

As they walked down the street side by side, Anders said, "That woman of yours still costing you too much money?" Anders had begun to suspect the girlfriend was as fictitious as everything else about Thoran. The non-existent woman had probably been no more than a ploy during that first meeting, an excuse to broach the subject of the pitiful pay they received as transit engineers.

"Yah," Thoran said. "I should probably find someone else. I really can't afford her, you know."

At the first cross street they came to, instead of turning right toward the bar where they usually shared a few drinks, Thoran paused and waited. A cab pulled up to the curb in front of him and stopped; he must have hailed it through his implants. He leaned forward and opened the back door, holding it for Anders.

Anders said, "I take it we're not going to the bar?"

"No," Thoran said, his face blank and expressionless. "My . . . other employer wants to meet you."

Anders slipped into the back seat of the grav car. Thoran climbed in next to him and gave the car's AI an address. The car pulled away from the curb on its grav fields.

They rode in silence for twenty minutes as the car carried them into a warehouse district near an airport, then down a poorly lit street. It stopped in front of a run-down, two-story office building. Thoran climbed out of the car and Anders followed him, wondering what would come next. The car pulled away.

As Thoran approached the front of the building the door opened before he got there. Thoran stopped, stepped aside, and indicated the open doorway with a wave of his hand. "After you, Maestra Eindride."

Anders walked forward cautiously and stepped through the doorway into a dimly lit room. The only furniture in the place was a small table with two simple chairs facing one another from opposite sides. The setting reminded him of the interrogation room at SecureMax.

An instant after he crossed the threshold, someone pressed the barrel of a weapon against the back of his head. A man and a woman stepped forward and stopped in front of him, both holding heavy grav pistols aimed at his chest. If he had to guess, both were senior non-coms, the woman a little stocky, the man stick-thin with sharply defined cheek bones. Behind him, Thoran said, "We're going to check you for weapons."

Anders raised his arms. It wasn't Thoran who frisked him, but whoever did made quick, professional work of ensuring that Anders remained unarmed. "He's clean," a male voice said.

Thoran said, "Sit down at the table, Eindride."

The man and woman in front of him backed away to the middle of the room, then split to either side, pressing their backs against the walls there. They had carefully positioned themselves so they would not be in each other's line of fire once Anders sat down in the chair, though in that chair, he would be in a nice crossfire between them. Anders walked forward, pulled out the chair and sat down. By his count, besides the man and woman to either side, Thoran and another man stood behind him.

The woman turned and walked to a door at the back of the room. She opened it, stepped into the room beyond, and he heard her say, "He's here, and unarmed."

The woman returned, followed by an older woman, and even had Anders not witnessed the drama of her entry, the posture of Thoran and the other three made it eminently clear who gave the orders.

The younger woman returned to her place with her back against the wall, while the older woman pulled out the chair opposite Anders and sat down. He saw her face clearly, but had no doubt a distortion field presented a false image to his eyes. It was common knowledge a person under interrogation yielded more information when they could see eye movements, expressions, and other visual cues from their interrogator.

Officer, Anders thought. The five of them working together moved like a well-trained military squad.

At that moment Anders's implants dropped out of the grid. The parole bureau's computers would immediately notify the authorities, and they'd start a manhunt.

"Don't worry," the woman seated opposite him said, as if she read his thoughts. "We've fed your parole bureau a false signal for some time now. They think you walked home and went to bed."

That confirmed everything Anders had suspected. These people had capabilities far beyond some petty criminal organization running a scam with street thugs. His one fear was that they could somehow circumvent the hardwired security circuits in his implants, and force him to answer questions under deep neural probe.

One of the men behind him said, "Mistress, we should move forward expeditiously."

The man's voice had a clear sense of urgency. So maybe they couldn't feed a false signal indefinitely to the parole bureau's computers. Anders hoped that was the case, because he wanted there to be some limitations on the reach of their power.

"Anders Eindride," the older woman said. "Guilty of high treason and mass murder on a heretofore unheard-of scale. Sentenced to ten years at hard labor, with the possibility of parole after three."

That confirmed Anders's earlier suspicion that Thoran had known far more about his real past than he let on. And it also told him there were some limits to their power. They didn't know his parole eligibility had originally been set at five years, and that Kristdokar's contacts in the Larscom had modified the official record.

The woman across the table from him eyed him for a long moment, then said, "Why are you here?"

He took a deep breath, and then he told her the truth. "I'm near destitute. I need money, and work, the kind that pays more than the dregs they give me as a transit driver. And Thoran says you pay good."

He heard Thoran chuckle at his failure to say *engineer.*

She shook her head. "If you were in it purely for the money you would never have joined the military in the first place."

He shrugged and made sure she heard the sarcasm in his voice, "I'm no longer in the military, am I? And a few years locked up in the right place changes one's perspective. Money has come to mean a lot more to me than it used to." He leaned forward, but he didn't want to spook the man and woman with their backs to the walls on either side of him, so he kept his hands at his sides. "And a lot of things that used to mean a lot to me, now mean absolutely nothing."

Again, she shook her head. She nodded toward her comrades. "The minute you saw this setup, and me, you knew Thoran wasn't working for some petty scam artist."

He shrugged. "Well if I'm smart enough to figure that out, I'm smart enough to figure out you're either going to hire me, or kill me. No half way to it, is there?"

She stared at him for several seconds without saying anything. "You tried to warn them."

He leaned forward and didn't have to fake his anger. "And got the crap beat out of me for trying." He glanced at the woman standing to one side, the muzzle of her weapon aimed at the floor. He had no doubt that if he lunged across the table at the officer, the younger woman would raise that pistol in an instant and splatter his brains all over the room. "I wouldn't be surprised if one or two of them are in the room with us right now."

The officer seated opposite him shook her head. "No, the Larscom rather thoroughly purged the command eagle's subordinates. But they showed you mercy."

He didn't have to fake the anger as he fired back at her, "Mercy! My reward for trying to alert them was they put me in that hell hole."

She leaned back in her chair and said, "Yes, I'm aware of the conditions in SecureMax. You know, they encourage the guards to make it even worse."

He worked at controlling his breathing to calm down. "I figured that part out on my own."

"No friends from your past?" she asked. "No ties that bind?"

"Oh I had plenty of friends," he said. "They must know I'm out, but do you see me sitting down with them at a bar, reliving good old times, and sharing shots of kirva?"

He shook his head sadly. "No, I suppose I can't blame them. After all is said and done, they have to take care of themselves."

If they had watched him closely enough, they knew Nikaela Vreekande had approached him on the street that one evening. "You know, that Vreekande woman is the only one who came to see me after I got out. She wanted to tell me how sorry she was."

He had grown truly angry. He leaned forward and pounded his fist on the table. The man and woman to either side raised their weapons as he shouted, "She fucking well didn't apologize for testifying against me at the tribunal." Nikaela Vreekande's testimony had been inconsequential and hadn't really contributed to his punishment, but the angry outburst sounded good anyway.

He lowered his head, closed his eyes, and spoke softly. "No. No friends."

He sat there like that for several seconds, and during that time no one spoke, but more importantly, no one shot him.

He opened his eyes, looked at the woman seated across from him and said, "It's like I never had a past, not one that existed before SecureMax."

She sat there for a long moment, looking at him and nodding her head up and down almost imperceptibly. Then she abruptly stood, sliding her chair back with the backs of her legs. The man and woman to either side tensed, their weapons still aimed at him, but the officer held her hand out and said, "Hold."

Anders sat there beneath her gaze for the longest time wondering if he would live or die. He damn well knew a high-ranking officer when he met one. He would guess at least command eagle, maybe even brigadier skalde.

She nodded and looked past him at one of the two men standing behind him. He expected her to say, "Kill him," but instead she said, "Thoran, take Maestra Eindride out and buy him dinner and a drink or two . . . on me."

15

A Red-Hot Redhead

THE WORK LOAD during John's second semester at O-School didn't lighten up in any way, but he slipped into a groove that worked for him, and he felt a little less pressed for time. On the other hand, he still had the extracurricular Kelk lessons with Dirkson, and Primatov frequently required him to report to her on his tenday break. She called him her aide-de-camp, which was a fancy term for glorified gofer. He liked working for her, and she told him if he did well in O-School, she would see to it he apprenticed to her during the year following graduation.

His duties with Primatov meant he frequently accompanied her to the Senate Office Building and spent a fair amount of time there. Little by little he came to recognize many of the senatorial aides, and befriended a few of them. Interestingly enough, he noticed that, before going to the office of any of the really high profile politicians, Primatov always cut him loose and sent him away. He also noticed that if she saw a cluster of news hypes gathered in a hallway, or outside some committee chamber, she turned and the two of them went the other direction. Or if she must go that way herself, she sent him away before doing so.

One day, during a quiet moment in her office, he said, "You don't like news hypes, do you?"

She paused and frowned, as if considering her answer carefully. "They can be . . . exasperating, John. But when the truth coefficient with some of these politicians drops into negative territory, sometimes the press are the only ones who can call them out on it. And I must confess that can be refreshing."

He had stepped into one of those moments when he could be candid with her. "Why do you avoid them?"

She smiled at that. "I find I can be much more effective if my face isn't splashed all over the vids."

"Why do you send me the other direction when you spot a bunch of them?"

Her eyebrows rose at that and she shrugged. "Think back to that communications room in the embassy on Reisenar. Do you recall the reaction of the captain of *Wicked Fury* when he heard what you had done?"

"Yes. He wanted to see how long I could breathe vacuum."

She nodded. "Unfortunately, there are many like him."

He had not considered that she was trying to protect him, not here, not on Trafalgar. "I understand."

Early that afternoon they walked over to the Senate Office Building, and in one if its main hallways they saw Silas Palmutter and Manifort Gascoigne surrounded by news hypes. Primatov turned to John and said, "Why don't you go back to your dorm early today?"

He said, "Thank you, ma'am," then turned and walked the other way.

At the main entrance to the building he ran into Macus DeLeon and a small group of aides, some of which he recognized, though he didn't know any of them well.

"Well," DeLeon said. "If it isn't Cadet Mathius."

DeLeon's friends had gathered behind him. He turned slightly and directed his comments over his shoulder, though his eyes remained focused on John. "Cadet Mathius thinks he'll do well as a Blacksword. But we all know it's not the brainless soldiers who run the government, don't we?"

One of them chuckled. Another covered her mouth to hide a laugh. They reminded John of the circle of sycophants DeLeon had gathered on Miriteen. John knew three of them, and they were all aides to freshman or junior senators. As an aide to one of the most powerful men in the senate, DeLeon had gathered the less powerful around him as a retinue. Primatov had once told John, "Powerful people who are confident in their power, gather other powerful people around them."

John beamed a smile at DeLeon, leaned forward and gripped his elbow as one friend might grip that of another. DeLeon's implants would have been downgraded when he left ComSecCorps, and only if, and not until, he became something a lot more than an aide, would they be upgraded to their previous status. John had the advantage of full military grade implants.

John squeezed DeLeon's elbow with crushing force, and punched a hard link through his implants to DeLeon's. "Remember what I told you I'd do if you ever abandoned your post again."

DeLeon's eyes widened, and his response came out as an audible squeak. "That doesn't count. I'm no longer in the military."

John released his elbow, and like DeLeon he spoke aloud. "I don't care."

The look the young man gave him was filled with both fear and abject hatred.

John stepped around DeLeon and his sycophantic friends, and walked down the steps of the Senate Office Building. He knew he had just done something stupid and egotistical, but he didn't care. The look in DeLeon's eyes had been worth it.

The battle lines had been drawn long ago.

••••

John hurried down a corridor in the Armed Services Office Building. Karya had some sort of business that morning in the building. As a news hype, she frequently sought interviews with people there. And May had never seen the place before, so the three of them decided to meet for lunch in the cafeteria. After lunch John hoped to give May a short tour of the place.

John met the two of them at the entrance to the cafeteria, and as they walked in they ran into Primatov on her way out. She wore a stylish civilian dress, but she'd been out on some sort of business all morning, and John realized it was the first time he'd ever seen her in anything but a uniform. The dress was nothing fancy, but it made it quite clear the military uniforms didn't do her justice.

"John," she said. "I don't believe I've met your friends?"

John introduced the two younger women. Primatov said to May, "You're his roommate, aren't you? John's told me a lot about you. It's nice of you to help him with his studies."

May's eyes grew quite wide as she said, "Someone had to take the poor guy in hand."

"Well thank you for doing so," Primatov said. She turned to Karya. "And you're the journalist, aren't you? It's a pleasure to meet you as well. And I appreciate the way you don't press John to disclose private details about his work."

Primatov's comment had clearly thrown Karya off balance. "He uhhh . . . I try to keep a clear and well defined boundary between my work and my friends."

"That's quite admirable," Primatov said. "But I've got a meeting in a few minutes, so I've got to run. Please forgive me for rushing out on you."

May and Karya made some noises about it being all right, and Primatov left.

May turned to John, leaned close to him and hissed, "That redhead is your Blacksword colonel you've told me about? I was expecting some pickle-faced broad with a stick up her ass and a hardened plast backbone."

Karya shook her hand as if she had just burned her fingertips. "She's quite a looker, isn't she?"

May's voice grew tight. "You're not supposed to notice that, unless you're noticing that about me. John can look at her ass, but she's way off limits to you."

John said, "I don't look at her ass. She's like—a colonel, you know?"

Both young women curled their hands into fists and planted them on their hips. They stood there silently waiting for John to speak.

John said, "Well . . . okay . . . I mean I do recognize she's good looking . . . and she's got a nice . . . and . . ."

He was just digging a deeper hole for himself. "But she's a god-damned Black-sword colonel."

May and Karya teased him incessantly through lunch. They accused him of studying hard just to apprentice to the *red-hot Blacksword redhead*, which is what they had dubbed Primatov. When lunch ended, Karya tugged on John's arm and said, "You think you could arrange for me to interview her?"

He made an explicit point of mouthing the word *No* without making any sound, then turned and walked away.

John had agreed to go out with Nash Wakeland and a few other cadets that evening. He didn't want to be late, so at the end of the day when Primatov let him go he hurried back to the dormitory. But as he rushed across campus he spotted the pretty young woman he'd seen while sightseeing before going to Primatov's office that first time. She stood about a hundred paces off and seemed to be looking his way. But then she abruptly turned and hurried away, as if trying to avoid him.

That seemed odd, though most likely it was probably something simple. Perhaps she just realized she had forgotten some important matter. But then his implants chimed and he forgot about her completely. "Mathius," Wakeland said. "You're late. Where are you? We're all waiting for you."

"On my way," he said.

"Well hurry up. Lot of impatient people here."

John hadn't gone out with Nash and his friends for a couple of months, and with the arrival of ten-end, he was looking forward to blowing off a little steam. He forgot about the pretty girl and rushed back to the dormitory.

When he stepped off the grav lift onto his floor, Wakeland and his party crowd were waiting impatiently for him. "Move it, Mathius," Nash said. "We're waiting."

They followed John down the hall to his room and stood outside the open door while he stripped off his uniform and pulled on civvies. Then he joined the crowd as Nash led them out of the dormitory and off campus to the strip.

They first needed dinner. Wakeland wanted to eat at a fancy place way beyond John's bank account. "I don't have that kind of money."

Wakeland brushed off his objection. "You're just too cheap—famously so, I might add."

One of the other cadets saved John. "I can't afford that kind of place either, Nash. You must have rich parents, or something. The stipend they give us barely covers a snack in there."

Several others agreed so Wakeland reluctantly capitulated. They got dinner at a much cheaper place, though Wakeland complained throughout the entire meal. Then they walked down the strip to a bar that featured live music and dancing. As they split up and sat down at a couple of tables, John spotted May and Karya on the dance floor. They were clearly enjoying themselves, and completely oblivious to the new arrivals.

When they first arrived there were plenty of available tables and seats at the bar, but as the evening progressed the place filled up. The crowd consisted mostly of cadets from the academy, but mixed in were some civilians and regular military.

Wakeland organized a drinking game, but John had reached his limit so he declined to join in. "Come on, Mathius," Wakeland demanded. "Show us a little guts, for once."

Wakeland pushed and cajoled, but John didn't feel like getting hammered. In fact, he felt like he might have already overdone it a bit, so he wandered over to the bar to get a drink of water, hoping that might clear his head a little. He edged his way through a thick crowd with a bunch of *excuse-me's* and *sorry-about-that's*. John moved carefully, but the place was quite crowded, and in any case everyone accepted a little jostling and a bump here and there, at least everyone but a fellow with strikingly pale, wavy blond hair.

As John tried to get the bartender's attention the blond guy snarled, "Watch it, asshole."

John had barely touched the fellow, a level of contact that wouldn't even qualify as a slight bump.

"Sorry," John said. "It's really crowded in here."

The blond guy stood an inch or two taller than John. He leaned close, probably to take advantage of his height. "Not crowded enough for you to be pushy, shit-head."

"Sorry," John said again. "Really, I am sorry."

At the sound of blond-guy's angry voice the noise level of nearby conversations dropped a little, and the man's next words carried further than a moment ago. "You're the sorriest piece of shit I know."

An anonymous woman said, "He didn't do anything, asshole. Let it go."

The fellow looked over his shoulder, trying to identify who had spoken. John took that moment to turn away from him and catch the bartender's attention. "Just a glass of water," he said.

The bartender leaned close and whispered, "That asshole a problem?"

John shook his head. "Nah. And in any case it's over."

The bartender poured John a glass of water and handed it to him. John turned about, and though he hadn't yet started to move, in that moment blond-guy bumped into him hard. The water in John's glass erupted upward, and he and the fellow both ended up with a big wet spot staining the front of their tunics.

The fellow bellowed, "I told you to watch what you're doing, you fucking idi-ot."

"But I wasn't even moving," John said. "And it's only water."

Blond-guy leaned forward and growled, "You're one of those Blacksword ass-holes, aren't you? Think you're better than the rest of us, don't you?"

The crowd about them stepped away from the two of them, clearing a small space. Nash Wakeland stepped up next to John and said, "You don't have to take that shit from him, Johnny-boy."

John gritted his teeth as he said, "I'm not going to get into a bar fight."

Wakeland turned to the tall blond fellow. "Don't fuck with my buddy here."

Blond-guy gave Wakeland an angry look, but probably decided if John had friends to back him up, he'd be smart to just walk away. He started to turn away.

Later, John chided himself for having allowed his Novalis III reactions to lapse. He'd lived for several years now in a civilized environment where the worst one might experience on any given day was an impolite word or two from a panhandler on the street.

It was a sucker punch. As the fellow turned away, John relaxed a little, thinking the incident had sputtered to an anticlimactic end. But in a flash the man spun back and his fist slammed into John's cheek.

John stumbled back and took two or three people down with him as he fell to the floor in a sprawl of arms and legs. He rolled onto his back and reached up to touch the throbbing pain on his face; his fingers came away with blood on them.

Wakeland leaned over him. "Get up. Don't let that asshole get away with that."

It had been a sneaky blow, reminiscent of his old nemesis Cranoch, and in that moment John's old Cranoch reflexes kicked in. In a single movement he got his feet under him and stood, facing blond-guy in a crouch, ready to take on all comers. The fellow grinned, as if glad to see that now he'd get the fight he wanted.

May stepped between them. "No, John. Don't do it."

John lunged forward, but May wrapped her arms around him in a bear hug and pulled him to one side.

"Let go of me," he shouted.

May hugged him even tighter. "You told me yourself if you got in a bar fight you'd get cashiered. Don't do it. That asshole isn't worth it."

One of John's Blacksword classmates wrapped his arms around the two of them, adding his weight to May's. "She's right. You haven't done anything yet. So walk away from it."

"What the hell's going on here?"

At the sound of the authoritative voice the crowd parted, and four Military Constables stepped into the gap. "Fighting," one of them said. "We don't like fighting."

One of the other MCs looked angrily at John. "You're obviously part of this mess. What the hell do you think you're doing?"

May released John from her bear hug and turned to the MC. "He didn't do anything. He hasn't thrown a single punch." She pointed at the blond fellow. "All that's happened so far is that asshole assaulted him."

John's Blacksword classmate said, "She's telling the truth."

Standing beside him, Karya said, "There's a whole room full of witnesses here who'll tell you the same."

The bartender stepped around from behind the bar and joined them. "That's right, Constable." He pointed at John. "This guy hasn't done a thing." He pointed at blond-guy. "But this jerk has been looking for a fight all night long."

The MCs separated them and questioned everyone thoroughly. Quite a number of bystanders confirmed May's version of events. The MCs cuffed blond-guy and led him away. They released John, and one of them told May and Karya, "Get him to the campus infirmary and get that cut on his cheek taken care of. Then escort him to his dorm room. I don't want to see his ugly face on the street again tonight."

As the three of them stepped out onto the street, John wondered where Nash had gone. It occurred to him Wakeland had disappeared at about the same time the MCs had come on the scene. "I wonder where Nash is," he said.

May said, "I'm almost glad he isn't here, because if he was I'd give him a big piece of my mind right about now."

She looked at Karya. "You saw what I saw?"

"Yah," Karya said, the expression on her face turning thoughtful. She said to John, "It was almost as if he *wanted* you to get into a fight."

"No almost about it," May said, her temper clearly rising.

John said, "He was just drunk. Let's go to the infirmary."

The techs at the infirmary patched up John's face. They applied a little speed healing to the cut, and when he awoke the next morning it appeared completely healed, though he had one heck of a bruise and a very obvious black eye.

He reported to Primatov that day, and when he stepped into her office she took one look at him and lifted a single eyebrow in a silent but sharp rebuke.

He grimaced and said, "Got into a fight last night."

"No you didn't," she said, shaking her head sadly. "An asshole clocked you with a sucker punch, and you didn't fight back."

"You know all about it?"

She grinned. "I know everything, John, especially when it comes to you."

"Sorry."

"Don't apologize. You did the right thing, not fighting back. It was a blatant enough assault you might have gotten away with it, though *might have* are the key words there. You should thank May for stopping you."

"I already have."

Her grin turned evil and malicious. "And if that asshole comes at you again, you have my permission to hurt him, but just a little, and only if you do so quietly and without any fuss. And don't kill him. That would get messy."

16

Time Warp

AT THE END of Anders's shift he passed Viktra in the hallway on his way out of the building. "Good night, Anders," she said, headed in the opposite direction.

"Good night, Viktra," he responded.

Had either of them not used the other's name and simply said, "Good night," it would have been a signal that the speaker had important information to relate. They'd find a way to be alone, even if only for a few seconds, then communicate the information rapidly on a secure link between their implants. But nothing had happened and there had been no developments since his meeting with Thoran's extracurricular *employer*, so that day they passed each other in the hallway without incident. He reminded himself repeatedly that patience and perseverance were qualities that would keep him alive.

When he got back to his small apartment, he had a message waiting for him. It instructed him to report to the parole bureau early in the morning three days hence. He should expect to be gone all day, and arrangements had been made with his employer to excuse his absence.

Why would they schedule him three days in advance? And what would require his time for an entire day? All of his interactions with the parole bureau since his release had been handled remotely. He couldn't count the number of forms he had filled out. And his case officer touched base with him once every tenday, but nothing beyond that. If he had done something wrong or violated some rule of his release, a couple of parole officers would grab him without warning whenever and wherever they could get hold of him, cuff him, and chivy him off to SecureMax in short order. He had no doubt the female corrections officer with the neural prod would be waiting for him.

No, it just didn't add up, and he spent the entire evening and the next three days pondering the nature of that message.

On the day in question he rose early. He didn't want to take any chances so he showered, shaved, and paid particular attention to his appearance. His wardrobe consisted mainly of the three sets of civilian clothing they had given him upon his release from SecureMax, plus a few articles he had purchased on his own. His meager income limited him to functional work clothing, and he couldn't afford to discard an item just because it had become a little threadbare, so his appearance no longer came even close to the dashing young military officer of his past. Perhaps that was a good thing.

The distance to the parole bureau was much too far to walk, so that morning he rode the transit system as a passenger, not an engineer. At least his status as a transit employee allowed him free passage.

He walked the short distance from the transit stop, and paused in front of a window at the parole bureau to check his appearance: adequate at best. He could not put aside his trepidation regarding the coming meeting with his case officer. Had he inadvertently committed some infraction that would extend his parole? He tried to put such thoughts out of his mind as he walked through the front doors of the bureau.

In the lobby a uniformed parole officer sat behind a desk. Anders approached the fellow and gave him the name of his case officer, finishing with, "I have an appointment."

The man behind the desk glanced at a screen in front of him for a moment, then said, "He's been transferred. You've been assigned a new case officer. Office 403, fourth floor."

Anders rode the lift to the fourth floor, then walked down a long hallway to office 403. Inside he found a rather severe young woman with premature gray hair seated behind a desk.

"Maestra Eindride," she said as he entered her office. She pointed to a chair in front of her desk. "Please sit down."

He sat down and she continued. "Give me a minute to review your case."

He sat there in silence for ten minutes while she read through his case file. Clearly, she didn't know anything about him and his past, though he thought it safe to assume that what she saw on the screen in front of her was a heavily redacted version of a lie that hid the real story behind his incarceration.

She looked up from her screen and focused on him. "I congratulate you on making it through your first year on parole without any infractions, not even a minor one."

"But wait a minute," he said. "There's been—"

He hesitated. He had almost corrected her, had almost told her it had actually been less than six months. Perhaps he should just keep his mouth shut and see what happened.

She leaned forward, a frown on her face. "You were about to say?"

"Uhhh," he said. "Uhhh . . . it was nothing. Just a thought that I realized is really not applicable."

She smiled and seemed relieved that she could continue with her discourse. "Today we'll remove the augmented programming from your implants and you'll be allowed to reestablish your own personal crypto security keys."

"Thank you," he said, trying to hide his dismay. "Thank you."

She spoke as if lecturing a child. "The restrictions on your movements will be reduced, but not eliminated entirely. And don't forget that before leaving the city you still must request permission and file an itinerary. Furthermore, some of the prohibitions on your activities have been lifted. I'll upload a new list to your implants after we've finished the modifications."

He shook his head side to side, then decided that might be the wrong answer, so he nodded up and down. "Uhhh, thank you. I appreciate that."

She continued. "And one year from now, again if there are no further infractions, all restrictions on your movements will be removed and you'll be a completely free man."

"One more year," he said. "I'll do my best."

"Good," she said. "Excellent. My job is so much easier when I'm working with a model parolee like you, Maestra Eindride."

It turned out erasing the augmented programming proved to be a rather complex operation. At the end of the day, when it was time to establish his personal encryption key, the tech said, "Think of something permanently etched in your memory. It can be a really good or a really bad memory, but something you'll never forget."

He'd been through the same process when the military had first installed his implants years ago. And back then, to come up with a good thought key he had considered the matter for some time. But now, it didn't take even the tiniest fraction of a second to decide on the memory he would choose.

He recalled the way his body had wrapped itself around the output end of that neural prod, and the way he couldn't let go. He recalled the way his muscles had spasmed so hard he had gripped it even tighter. Gripped it with his jaws clenched so tightly his facial muscles were sore for days afterward. Gripped it like a lover he feared he would lose. Gripped it until the female guard shut it down. And he recalled the look on her face.

A month later, when he got home from work, he had another message waiting for him. Again, it instructed him to report to the parole bureau three days hence, though this time he would only be there for an hour. And again, arrangements had been made with his employer to excuse his absence.

The severe young woman with premature gray hair had been transferred sometime during the month since their prior meeting, their only meeting. And again he had been assigned an even newer case officer, who, like her, was badly overworked and not at all familiar with his case.

Miraculously, an entire year had passed during the month between his two visits to the parole bureau, and he had now successfully reached the two-year mark. All restrictions on his movements were now removed, though they warned him he would never again be allowed in a secure military facility.

"You're now a free man," his newest case officer said as they parted. "Completely free."

Out on the street Anders paused to consider his new freedom. Had Kristdokar arranged to have his records juggled so he could be a more effective asset? But then perhaps his new employer, Thoran's moonlighting employer, the woman who was obviously a high-ranking officer—perhaps her colleagues had juggled the records so the parole bureau would no longer monitor Anders's activities. That didn't make him feel at all like a free man.

•••

Shortly after Nikaela and Brynjar returned to Viktorkinde, they joined Kristdokar and Thordahl in the conference room to brief them on what they had learned working with their Blacksword colleagues on Norandyne. When trying to secure a facility against covert surveillance and monitoring, the effort required to successfully do so, and the odds of a hostile breach, both grew exponentially with the volume of the secured space. Kristdokar's security team had gone to some effort to isolate the entire building that housed Friedrikdahl Import-Export, but only to a certain degree, recognizing they would have to go to impossible lengths to make such a large structure truly immune to a targeted effort. They all operated under the premise that the security for the building probably worked well, but everyone should still assume the worst.

On the other hand Kristdokar had equipped her office, and one conference room, with sophisticated anti-surveillance and jamming equipment. The two rooms were shielded for acoustic, electromagnetic, and transition radiation, then scanned and swept at random intervals, and again immediately before any important meeting. Both spaces were free of any connection to external communications equipment, and in them signals from both citynet and their own private secure network were blocked. Simply put, if one wanted to communicate outside of either room, they opened the door and shouted.

As they gathered and sat down around the large table that occupied the majority of space in the room, Kristdokar said, "Before we get to the main order of business, I want to brief all of you on some recent events."

She turned pointedly to Brynjar and Thordahl. "We have an asset in the field named Anders Eindride. He was Mistress Vreekande's immediate superior on Novalis III during the tragedy there."

Brynjar's eyes widened, while Thordahl's brow furrowed. Nikaela knew she failed to hide her own surprise.

Kristdokar then proceeded to give the two command superiors a thorough briefing on the roles Nikaela and Eindride had played in the tragedy of Novalis III. She held nothing back, even told them of the tribunal at Erikdeg, and the sentences meted out to the guilty parties. She finished by saying, "I've told you this because you need to know Maestra Eindride's background. I managed to arrange his parole about six months ago so he could work for us as an undercover asset."

She then described the terms and conditions of his parole, including the one-year and two-year periods that must elapse with good behavior before he would be granted full freedom.

She let them absorb that for a moment, then said, "As we had hoped, he was recently recruited by someone he believes to be a high-ranking military officer, and whom we believe to be one of our targets. And now, according to the parole bureau's records, those two years have been miraculously compressed into just six months."

Nikaela thought she must have looked as confused as Thordahl and Brynjar. Kristdokar went on to explain how someone had juggled the records in the parole bureau to get Eindride his full freedom a year and half early.

"He thought it might be my doing," she said, "but it was not, and I made sure he understood that."

The four of them sat there for a long moment of silence, then Thordahl said, "It appears our opponents have quite a long reach."

"Yes," Kristdokar said. "They do indeed. Let's all keep that in mind going forward."

Following that they spent the rest of the afternoon reviewing Nikaela's research. They all agreed the data provided by Primatov and her allies had proven invaluable. They had exchanged information several times now, and the time spent in a warehouse on Norandyne closeted with a team of Primatov's Blackswords had produced some interesting results. But it was only on the trip back from Norandyne, with considerable time on her hands, that Nikaela had put together some very disparate, and very disturbing, bits of information.

Kristdokar asked, "So you've been able to establish a connection between a Commonwealth heavy equipment manufacturer and a Kelk arms supplier?"

Brynjar said, "We think so." He looked at Nikaela, yielding the floor to her. Thordahl and Kristdokar turned their attention her way.

"We followed the money trail," Nikaela said. "Transmarin Industries supplies a lot of heavy vehicles and equipment to ComSecCorps, and they have a minority ownership in a shipbuilding firm and an armaments outfit. Norddansk Weapons Systems is a subsidiary of Norddansk Interstellar. They've supplied our military for more than a hundred years, and they're one of the few outfits authorized by the Larscom to maintain equipment and technologies for manufacturing unconventional weapons, the kind used on Novalis III. But they are expressly prohibited from making anything of that sort unless specifically authorized to do so by the Larscom Executive Council."

Thordahl leaned forward and asked, "So if they have the equipment and knowhow, what's to stop them from making it without that authorization?"

The trip back from Norandyne had taken twenty-one days. Brynjar and Nikaela had had quite a bit of time to discuss that subject at some length, and they had agreed Brynjar would field any questions of that nature. He grinned unpleasantly and said, "They're honest people. They would never do that."

Thordahl frowned and gave Nikaela a sidelong look.

Brynjar added, "And one of Norddansk Interstellar's directors is Vice Skalde Tiegnordan."

Kristdokar sucked air through her teeth. "Don't tell me we're fighting against the Executive Council itself."

Brynjar shrugged. "I don't know. You tell me. Did you see any opposition on the Executive Council to the formation of this,"—he waved a hand, indicating the building about them and their organization—"this covert operation?"

Kristdokar shook her head with considerable vehemence. "On the contrary, the few times I was allowed to sit in on a session, they were all quite incensed that someone had end-run them, had made them look bad. They feared loss of face and loss of support among the greater Larscom. The whole mess made the Executive Council look sloppy."

Brynjar nodded slowly and took a deep breath. "Then I think we have to assume if Norddansk is guilty of what we suspect, Tiegnordan likely didn't have anything to do with it. Her presence on their board probably gave everyone a false sense of security, which could have contributed to a lapse in oversight, but hopefully nothing more than that."

Kristdokar leaned back in her chair, closed her eyes, rubbed her temples, and said, "The gods help us if that's not the case. What else have you got?"

Nikaela and Brynjar had rehearsed this carefully, and she continued now with her part of the presentation. "As I said, we followed the money trail. We dug deep to find the connections, but both Transmarin and Norddansk have invoice trails that lead to the same subcontractors on Novalis III, Reisenar, and several of the independent systems in that sector. It's also clear both made a concerted effort to obscure that trail. And it should be noted the methods they used were identical."

Kristdokar hadn't moved and still sat rubbing her temples, her eyes closed. "That reeks of collusion. Anything else?"

"Just a lot of details," Nikaela said, "if you care to go through them."

Kristdokar lowered her hands to the table in front of her. She opened her eyes and looked pointedly at Nikaela, then at Brynjar. "If you keep digging, do you think you can find more?"

Brynjar simply nodded.

Nikaela said, "Without doubt, yes."

She focused her attention on Nikaela. "Then keep at it. If you haven't already done so, I want you to dig up everything you can find on Norddansk. If you need help, just ask."

She lowered her eyes and stared at her hands for a long moment of thought. "And I think I'll pass along what we've learned to our new friends, see what they can dig up on Transmarin."

To Thordahl she said, "While I prepare something, you make sure there's a fast hunter-killer standing by. I want you within range of that communications buoy as soon as possible."

Thordahl nodded and said, "As you wish, mistress."

Kristdokar stood and leaned forward with her hands flat on the table. "I want no hard record of these conclusions. Keep all the data, and keep all the pieces, but I don't want a single computer memory node anywhere in the Supremacy that points to the conclusions we've just come to today. If we need to put it all together at a later time, we'll have all the bits and pieces and we can do so."

She paused and took a careful breath. "I know I probably don't need to say this outright, but I'm going to anyway. Not a word to anyone outside this room. And outside this room, we don't even discuss this among ourselves."

17

Investigation

ANDERS AND VIKTRA decided to pretend they were lovers, which allowed them to spend time alone without arousing the suspicion of the other transit workers, especially Thoran. The pretense also provided the added benefit that they didn't have to rush critical communications. To keep up appearances, Anders frequently spent the night in her apartment sleeping on the couch. On such nights they ate dinner together in her small kitchenette and he got to know her a little. And he found himself attracted to her, the more so as he got to know her. So one evening, after cleaning up the dishes, on a whim, he leaned close to her and brushed his lips across hers. He dare not go further than that, and even then he was pushing the bounds of propriety.

She hesitated, but didn't pull away from him. "You're a convicted criminal," she said. "I shouldn't get involved with you."

Then she kissed him, and that night, and all the nights after, he no longer slept on the couch. His relationship with her made life a little better, a little sweeter.

Anders had now worked for Thoran's special employer several times, and he regularly reported on his activities through Viktra to Kristdokar. They dare not assume her place was free of bugs or other surveillance devices. So they developed the ability to carry on two completely disparate conversations at the same time, one verbally, and one through their implants. One night, after making love, they talked verbally about her childhood. But at the same time they spoke on a secure, encrypted link using their implants.

"They don't seem to need funding," he told her.

"How do you mean?"

"They're not running any scams, they're not running drugs or selling contraband arms. They're not doing anything to make money. But when I moonlight for them, they pay quite well."

With her next words, she seemed to change the subject. "Kristdokar wants you to keep an eye out for anything involving Transmarin Industries or Norddansk Weapons Systems."

"I'm familiar with Norddansk," he said, "but not Transmarin."

"They're a Commonwealth outfit that supplies a lot of heavy vehicles and equipment to ComSecCorps. Like Norddansk, a big outfit, and it occurs to me if either or both are involved, they probably have deep pockets. So it's likely your friends might have all the funding they need."

Anders thought a lot about that conversation, and late one evening, while moonlighting with Thoran, he had an opportunity to get a few questions answered—maybe.

"Hey Anders," Thoran called from the other side of the warehouse. "I need some help here."

Seated in the control cage of a heavy lifter, Anders glanced over his shoulder. Thoran stood pointing at the top of a thirty-foot high stack of large shipping crates. From that distance Anders couldn't be sure exactly which crate his finger pointed to.

Anders hollered, "I'll be right there."

Moving slowly, Anders turned the lifter around. The big machine could easily punch its way through the walls of the warehouse, so slow and steady were the prime rules of a qualified operator. That he had a rating as a heavy lift operator—something he'd acquired in the warehouse on Novalis III—proved to be a bonus to his new employers.

It bothered Anders that Thoran and his friends had recruited him, even though he and Kristdokar had hoped for something like that. He would love to believe he was indispensable in some way, but he had no illusions about his value. He wasn't Special Forces, though he did have the full gamut of military training, a somewhat special skillset they apparently needed. And they couldn't recruit just any former military officer. Their activities limited them to hiring those with the added incentive of disaffection with the Supremacy, anger or bitterness at the Larscom, hatred of the Commonwealth, or simply a willingness to commit criminal acts for personal gain.

It occurred to him that in their eyes he qualified in all of those categories, which probably enhanced his credentials to some degree. But still, he thought it quite likely they could find other candidates for whom they didn't have to go to the additional trouble of falsifying parole bureau records. No, he had missed some part of the equation, and that bothered him, because that could get him killed.

Thoran wisely stepped aside as Anders pulled the big machine up to the stack of crates.

"Which one?" Anders asked.

Thoran pointed again. "Those two on top with hazardous materials labels."

Anders carefully applied power to the lifter and it climbed upward on its gravity fields. When he reached eyelevel with the top of the stack, he saw the two crates indicated.

"Where do you want them?" Anders asked.

"Just down on the floor here," Thoran said, pointing to a spot on the warehouse floor next to him.

Anders selected one of the crates, extended the lifter's jaws toward it, clamped them into the lift cleats on the crate's sides, then raised it a few inches off the stack.

The extra weight on the end of the lift's jaw arms caused it to wobble the tiniest bit, which shouldn't have happened if its feedback systems worked properly. He flagged a note in his implants to check if its maintenance schedule was up to date.

He retracted the lifter's jaws, then gingerly reduced the feed to its grav field generators. He let it descend slowly until it hovered only a few inches off the floor. He eased it sideways toward Thoran, then put the crate down next to him. He repeated the process for the second crate, then parked the lifter, climbed out of the control cage, and joined Thoran next to the two crates.

They couldn't remove the hazardous materials labels, but they could scramble their electronic imprints to make them appear to be defunct outdated stickers, then they covered them with new labels. When they finished, no one would know the two crates enclosed something dangerous. Even Anders didn't know exactly what they contained.

They did a lot of that kind of stuff, changing labels, mislabeling shipping containers, and redirecting them. Everything they shipped out went to one of four addresses on Sarkovie. He had already fed that information to Kristdokar.

When he and Thoran finished with the two crates, they broke for dinner. Night had long ago settled over the city. They walked down a dark street to one of the places that served cheap food to workers employed in the many warehouses in the area. They bought a couple beers and sandwiches and took them back to their building, where they sat on some small crates to eat.

On other occasions Anders had worked with the woman and two men who had been present during his initial interrogation by the officer, and their early distrust of him had slowly disappeared. One of the two men, a fellow named Gaertkine, didn't really share the mindset of the rest and was in it purely for the money. Apparently he had run up some sizable debts, and Anders noticed the others didn't seem to trust him as much.

Anders still knew nothing about the high-ranking officer running the show. But Thoran clearly trusted him now, so he thought he could ask a question or two without raising suspicion.

Around a mouth full of food, Anders asked, "Why me?"

Thoran took a pull on his beer. "What do you mean?"

"Why'd you waste your time recruiting me? I'm a washed-up, cashiered, ex-officer. I don't have any wonderful skills you desperately need. So why me?"

Thoran glanced over his shoulder, then leaned close to Anders and spoke softly. "The command eagle that got the death sentence at your tribunal, the one in charge of your operation on that planet—"

None of them ever spoke the name Novalis III, but when they needed to refer to it, they called it *that planet*. Thoran hesitated, waiting for Anders to acknowledge the unspoken reference. Anders raised an eyebrow, and that proved sufficient.

Thoran continued, "The Larscom cleaned house pretty thoroughly in her organization. We lost a lot of people, the kind we really trusted,"—he lowered his voice—"unlike Gaertkine. And we need to replace them with people with the right mindset and skills. That can be hard to do."

Thoran had dropped the hint, so Anders decided to bite. "What's wrong with Gaertkine?"

Thoran grinned. "The money's good, right?"

"Very good," Anders said.

"Just don't flash it around," Thoran said. "Don't draw attention to yourself. My boss, she doesn't like that."

Anders nodded and said, "Thanks for the warning."

"But that's the point," Thoran said. "You didn't really need the warning. Gaertkine does."

Anders took a chance. "I still don't understand why the pay is so good. What you've asked of me so far, you could get from a lot of people, and for a lot less than you're paying me."

Thoran glanced over his shoulder again, then gave Anders a friendly slap on the back. "Don't worry, friend. We'll soon be making use of your . . . other skills, those that we're paying the good money for."

••••

John had spent enough time with Primatov to know how to read her mood, and when he reported to her office that morning he immediately sensed her calm demeanor had been broken by a little excitement.

"I have something special for you to work on," she said.

"Certainly, ma'am," he said, "whatever you need."

Her eyes seemed to sparkle as she spoke. "Last night I received a tantalizing bit of information from a distant friend. For the time being I'd like you to focus all your efforts on digging up whatever you can on Transmarin Industries. For now, just publicly available information: corporate structure, product mix, any subsidiaries they own, key investors, that kind of stuff."

"I'll get right to it," he said, then made his way down to the desk they had given him in a large bullpen of low-level aides and gofers like him. He thought he'd take a few hours to tie up some loose ends on other assignments. But he quickly learned she didn't care about them, which he kind of already knew, since they were just gofer jobs. She wanted him to drop everything right then and there to jump on Transmarin Industries.

He ran a search of the senatorial and ComSecCorps databases, came up with corporate brochures, financial statements, fiscal reports, and investor reports. There didn't seem to be much there beyond dreadfully boring statistics, so he called an investment broker and made up a little white lie that wasn't wholly untrue. A receptionist connected him to a broker, a young woman named Theresa Vasquez who was probably as low on the totem pole as him.

"My name's John Mathius," he said. "I'm about to graduate from ComSecCorps O-School, and I'll have a real income for the first time, and everyone says I should start investing early, and I've heard Transmarin Industries would be a good place to start."

"That would be an excellent start," she said. "But you don't want to put all your money in one company."

She talked to him about diversity in investments. He asked her what she meant by that, and she used a lot of other unfamiliar terms which confused him even more. He repeatedly nudged her back to Transmarin Industries, and eventually it became clear she had concluded he wasn't going to be one of her biggest clients.

"Listen," she said. "Why don't give me your contact profile and I'll register you with Transmarin for investment updates."

He didn't want investment updates, but he had to play out the lie so he gave her the information, and she promised to call him back if she heard anything. He knew he would never hear from her again.

He sat down with Primatov and they carefully sifted through the limited data he had gathered. But when they finished she leaned back, looked thoughtful, and rubbed her chin like a man stroking his beard. He'd seen her do that before.

"There's got to be more," she said.

John said, "I'll keep at it."

"Yes," she said. "Do that, please. But finals are what . . . next tenday? Don't let it get in the way of your studies."

John ran another search on Transmarin Industries in the senatorial database, and he got a rather curious hit. Charlie Maskers, an aide to a freshman senator from an outer system, had served as an intern at Transmarin. John placed a call to Charlie and he answered immediately, but he wanted to speak to him face to face, so he introduced himself and said, "You going to be in your office for the next half hour?"

"Yah," Charlie said.

"I'll come over," John said. "I want to talk to you about Transmarin Industries."

John used the subterranean passageways to walk from the Armed Services Office Building to the Senate Office Building. He found Maskers seated at a desk in a large bullpen very much like the room where John's desk had been placed among so many others.

Charlie had coal black hair and a permanent five-o'clock-shadow that no amount of shaving could mitigate, though if he were inclined, a little gene therapy could easily take care of that.

After John introduced himself, he asked, "You interned at Transmarin Industries, right?"

"Yah," Charlie said. "About five years ago. Why?"

John kept picturing Primatov rubbing her chin, like a man rubbing his beard, and saying, "There's got to be more."

John shrugged. "Just doing a little homework on them, an assignment I got from my boss."

Charlie shook his fingers as if he had just burned them, the same way Karya had. "That hot redhead, huh?"

John didn't try to deny it. "Yah," he said, "the hot redhead."

"What's she like to work for?"

"She's nice, but all business." John needed to keep Charlie focused. "Transmarin. Tell me about Transmarin."

Charlie shrugged. "Not much to tell."

And there wasn't much to tell. At Transmarin Charlie had had even less responsibility than John did as Primatov's gofer, slash, aide de camp. They spoke for half an hour, then agreed to find a chance to have a beer together sometime.

At the end of that day John accompanied Primatov to a joint meeting of the Armed Services and Foreign Relations Committees. Primatov, Fran Thealone, several high-ranking ComSecCorps officers, and the senators from both committees sat around a very large table made of some richly dark wood. As Primatov's aide de camp, John sat behind her, while Macus DeLeon sat behind Palmutter and stared daggers at John. John tried to ignore him, but doing so proved to be exhausting.

Late in the afternoon the senators decided to go to closed session, and all but the most high-ranking aides were dismissed.

Primatov turned around and spoke softly to John. "I know you've got finals coming up. Go home, get a good night's sleep, and focus on your studies. And try to ignore that unpleasant young man sitting behind Palmutter."

The end of John's year at O-School was approaching rapidly, and John wanted to do well in final exams. "Thanks a lot, ma'am," he said.

John filed out of the room with the other aides and assistants, though DeLeon remained seated with a smug look on his face. Apparently Palmutter considered him important enough to keep him around for the closed session. Certainly, DeLeon consider himself important enough.

As John walked to the transit station near the Senate Office Building, he spotted that pretty young woman far down the street walking his way. He really wanted to have a word or two with her, maybe even ask her out on a date, so he stepped into the shadow of a kiosk that dispensed sightseeing brochures. Since she was already headed his way, all he needed to do was wait patiently.

About half a block from him she abruptly stopped and turned toward the entrance of a building. Her lips moved as if speaking to someone hidden from John's view. And then the blond asshole who had sucker-punched John in that bar stepped into view. She and blond-guy had words and she seemed a little angry. But blond-guy grabbed her arm, and they both turned and walked away together.

She was probably dating that asshole.

John kept an eye out as he walked to the transit station, and as he rode the grav train back to campus, and during the walk back to his dormitory. Thankfully, he didn't see any sign of either of them.

18

Strange Bedfellows

THE CAPITAL ROTUNDA always gave Katrine pause. Built in an antique style with old-fashioned carved limestone, the dome a hundred meters overhead was meant to be a testament to the architect's ingenuity and engineering prowess. But Katrine knew that hidden beneath the stone were modern building materials such as hardened plast struts and condensed pseudo-stone supports. Nevertheless, that knowledge did not lessen the grandeur of the structure.

To cross the open rotunda floor Katrine edged her way carefully through crowds of gawking tourists. She had an appointment with Senator Gascoigne for lunch in his office, and to a capital insider it might seem strange she had chosen to take the long way to get there. But Katrine's face had not been regularly splashed across the vids along with noteworthy headlines, so the tourists didn't recognize her, and didn't hinder her. On the other hand, well known politicians avoided the rotunda for that very reason. She had learned long ago if she used the more private, subterranean passages beneath the capital buildings, she frequently encountered those same politicians, and they often hindered her. The rumor mill still overflowed with misinformed guesswork about the Reisenar incident, and they would probe her for details she could not reveal. More often than not, the long way proved to be the short way.

Outside the rotunda she walked down the eight tiers of steps symbolic of the eight star systems that had originally founded the Commonwealth. She crossed a busy street, then climbed the steps to the entrance of one of the Senate Office Buildings. Her military grade implants allowed her to bypass the security station, and once inside, to her chagrin, she ran into Senator Jenine Catarvin.

"Colonel Primatov," the plump little woman said. "What a coincidence. I haven't seen your pretty face since you testified before the Senate Armed Services Committee."

Katrine smiled, nodded and said, "But you and I have crossed paths quite often at meetings of the Intelligence Committee." She always thought it ironic that Catarvin sat on the *Intelligence* Committee.

Catarvin shook her head and waved a hand. "But that doesn't count. We haven't had a chance to chat one-on-one, girl to girl as it were, and I have wanted to bend your ear on a couple of matters. Could you indulge me for a few minutes?"

It occurred to Katrine that maybe it wasn't a coincidence they had just accidentally run into each other. She had no desire to *chat* with the woman about the latest capital gossip. "I'm sorry, but I have an appointment I mustn't be late for."

Catarvin's smile disappeared, she leaned close to Katrine, and her entire demeanor hardened. "Come now, Colonel, I'm really not the plump, little, vacant, airhead everyone believes. Plump and little, yes; vacant and air-head, no."

Katrine leaned back and took another look at the woman. A little overweight, yet still pretty, she looked at Katrine with a hard piercing gaze. The senator tilted her head slightly to one side. "I see I've surprised you. I like to maintain that image. You'd be amazed what you can learn when people dismiss you out of hand." She gave Katrine a smug smile. "A very important person wants to meet with you in private. Tell Mani you'll be a bit late for lunch."

No, there was nothing at all coincidental about their meeting this way. In that moment Katrine revised all her thinking regarding Senator Jenine Catarvin. She nodded and said, "Let me contact Senator Gascoigne's office and warn them I won't be on time."

Catarvin's demeanor shifted back to that of the vacant air-head. She gave Katrine a vacant, air-headish smile and said, "Of course, that's only the polite thing to do."

Katrine keyed her implants, got through to Gascoigne's secretary, and was immediately put into contact with the senator himself. "Something important has come up. I'm going to be a little late for lunch. If you need to cancel, I certainly understand."

"I'll slide lunch out an hour," Gascoigne said. "You'll be my excuse for cancelling a meeting with a bunch of pushy lobbyists."

She broke the connection and turned to Catarvin. "You have my undivided attention, Senator. You said someone important wants to meet with me."

"Yes," Catarvin said, maintaining the air-head smile. "Come with me."

She took Katrine by the arm and led her down the main hallway of the Senate Office Building. Catarvin prattled on and kept up a steady stream of chatter as she turned them down a side hallway. By the time they stopped at an office door, Katrine had learned of a recent scandal involving a ranking member of the Senate Finance Committee. He had apparently been found in bed with three prostitutes of mixed gender, two of whom were reputed to be several years under the age of consent, and the third just barely old enough.

"It's very hush-hush," Catarvin said. "So don't tell a soul you heard it from me."

A brass plaque on the door where they had stopped declared it to be the offices of Senator Silas Palmutter. Katrine and he had never met unofficially. She had testified before him while he sat on the Senate Armed Services Committee, and he had questioned her at length, but they had never spoken privately.

Still flashing that vacant smile, Catarvin said, "Trust me, dear. You're going to find this quite interesting."

She opened the door and stepped through it. Katrine followed her into a reception room that contained four desks. Macus DeLeon sat at one. He looked up, caught her eye, and grinned at her with an unpleasant leer. A young woman seated at another desk smiled and said, "Good morning, Senator Catarvin, Colonel Primatov." She pointed to a door on the opposite side of the room. "Senator Palmutter is expecting you, so please go right in."

When they stepped into the next room Palmutter rose from behind a large, ornate desk. His gene-therapy good looks and shoulder-length black hair did not impress Katrine.

As Palmutter stepped around his desk, his blue eyes focused on Katrine's chest and remained there, even as he and Catarvin traded air kisses. When the length of the Armed Services Committee chamber had separated them, she had been able to convince herself she had been wrong about his fixation. But now, up close, she could not deny that he seemed unable to look anywhere else, and freely exercised what Obradour had referred to as an obsession. It was at moments like that that Katrine wished she were less endowed and not so curvy.

With the air kisses completed, Catarvin pirouetted and aimed Palmutter at Katrine. "Lieutenant Colonel Primatov, I know you and Silas have spoken officially across the breadth of the committee room floor, but we both felt it would be good for you two to meet in a more intimate setting."

Katrine wondered how much intimacy Palmutter hoped for, but she kept that thought to herself.

Palmutter took his eyes off Katrine's chest, stepped forward, took her hand, and for the first time looked her in the face. "A pleasure to meet you, Colonel."

She stood a few centimeters taller than him. He had a deep, resonant voice, and Katrine wondered if gene therapy had been responsible for that as well. He said, "I'm quite glad Jenine arranged this meeting."

He maintained eye contact with her as he spoke, but his eyes kept glancing down to her chest for brief moments, as if her breasts were a temptation he could not resist. Tarsik Obradour had referred to Palmutter's fixation with women's breasts as a foolish indiscretion, but up close Katrine found it obnoxious and exceedingly distasteful. She wanted to reach out, grab him by the balls, and squeeze as hard as she could. It would give her a great deal of pleasure to watch him squirm as his face turned red while she made his cojones turn blue. It took an effort to smile pleasantly and pretend she didn't notice.

"Come," he said, releasing her hand. "Sit down, relax."

He pointed to a couch on one side of the room. Katrine sat down, and Catarvin sat next to her. Palmutter remained standing, and she realized then he had maneuvered them into a position where he stood over them, eliminating her height advantage. She wondered for a moment if he had done his homework on her, learned she stood taller than him, and planned that maneuver in advance.

Standing over them he said, "You must be wondering why I asked Jenine to arrange this meeting."

Katrine shrugged. "The thought has crossed my mind."

He continued as if reciting a prepared speech. "Here you are, a very important Blacksword officer, and I a senator of some small influence, and we've never met except in the presence of a room full of my peers."

Palmutter clearly had something specific in mind, and was working his way slowly toward it. Katrine decided if she didn't help him get there, she'd spend all afternoon sitting there with him sneaking surreptitious glances at her boobs. She just might get fed up enough to do the ball-squeezing thing, which wouldn't be good for her career. "Well, now we have met. Did you have anything specific you wanted to discuss?"

He stopped pacing and faced her squarely. "Straight to the point. I find that very attractive in a woman." For an instant his eyes flicked toward her breasts, but he forced himself to look into her face. She swallowed hard and kept her mouth shut as he continued. "In the last year you've been a key player in two very important Blacksword operations."

Now that she knew where this was going, she decided not to help him further. "And which operations are you referring to, Senator?"

"Novalis III," he said, "and Reisenar."

Katrine had been ready for that, and she gave him the stock answer she and Thealone had agreed upon. "Novalis III was not an operation, but rather a tragedy to which we responded after the fact. And Reisenar was just a nasty incident."

His eyes narrowed, and for the first time since she had entered the room, they didn't flick toward her breasts. He spoke with a hard edge to his voice. "On Novalis III you commanded the military side of the forensic investigation. And on Reisenar you were the ranking officer present during that . . . nasty incident. What really happened there?"

She didn't like the way he loomed over her, and decided to make use of her height advantage and do some looming herself. She stood and approached him to make her superior height even more obvious. "Senator, I haven't checked, but I have no doubt you have the proper clearances, and therefore have access to all the records, reports, and data available on both of those incidents. I don't know that I could add anything further."

His lips curled upward in a faint, unpleasant smile. "I'm not a fool, Colonel. It's clear to anyone with half a brain"—he glanced momentarily toward Jenine Catarvin still seated behind Katrine—"that even the classified stuff on those two incidents has been sanitized. I want to know what's not in those reports."

She recalled the way he had questioned her and Thealone during a closed session of the Armed Services Committee. She and her superior had both come away with the impression he already knew the answer to his questions, and was really more interested in gleaning how much they had figured out. If enough hawks like Palmutter learned the true details of what happened on Reisenar, a certain young ComSecCorps cadet presently attending O-School would probably not live to graduate.

"Senator," she said, choosing her words carefully, "for me to embellish on what is already in those reports would be wholly inappropriate, and probably illegal, especially in this venue." She flicked her eyes up and back. Catarvin had clearly not revealed her true nature to Palmutter, and if he still thought her to be a vapid air-head, Katrine hoped he would not hold it against her when she refused to speak in front of the woman. She felt bad using Catarvin that way, but only a little bit.

He looked at her for a long moment, then his eyes flicked toward her breasts for an instant and his smile softened. Still looking downward he nodded, and seemed to be talking to the bumps on her chest as he said, "Perhaps another time."

"At your convenience," she said. "But please do go through the proper channels if you wish to arrange another such meeting."

"The proper channels," he said. It was not a question.

They stood there for a long moment, no one speaking, him staring at her breasts. Then he broke the silence. "Well I thank you for coming to meet with me. It's been a pleasure. And I'm sure we'll run into one another again."

At the clear dismissal Catarvin stood, and Palmutter escorted them both to the office door. But he paused before opening it and turned to face Katrine. "You know, Fran Thealone has commanded the Blacksword now for more than six years. I would guess that in the next year or two she'll retire, or advance to a higher position, and we'll be looking for her replacement. And while I know you're aware I sit on the Armed Services Committee, did you know I advise the Promotion Board when it comes to key positions? And don't forget that promotion to such a position requires senate confirmation and a vote of the Armed Services Committee." He lowered his eyes to look at her chest and they stayed there as he continued. "I wouldn't be surprised if your name came up."

"I doubt it," she said, pretending to not understand the implied bribe, and struggling mightily to ignore his ogling. She had to get out of there before she turned the ball-squeezing idea into a ball-crushing incident. "There are three other Blacksword officers who carry the rank of full colonel, or its naval equivalent of captain. I think it's safe to assume their names will come before mine."

His eyes finally looked away from her breasts and he smiled. He opened the door and escorted them through the small reception room, then out to the hallway. When he closed the outer door and Katrine and Jenine Catarvin stood alone in the hall, the plump little woman said, "He's a bit of an ass, isn't he?"

Katrine started, and the senator continued, "You know, I told you before the old fart looks at my breasts that way too. I guess he's not that particular because I'm not that much to look at, but a tall beauty like you was a real treat for him. And you do have all the right assets."

She took Katrine by the arm and marched her down the hallway away from Palmutter's office. As they walked Catarvin leaned close to her and spoke conspiratorially. "By the way, I didn't mind that you used my vapid, air-head image as an excuse to deflect his questions. It can be quite effective that way, and we should work together more often. I'll divert their attention with the air-head thing, and you can divert their attention with those gorgeous tits, though that military uniform covers them up far too much. You should wear civilian clothing more often and show some cleavage. With some flesh showing, you wouldn't have needed the help of my little persona to divert Palmutter's questions, though he's probably alone in his office right now jerking off, or maybe humping that pretty aide of his while thinking of you."

Katrine couldn't think of any sort of response to that. Catarvin continued, "Have you considered taking him as a lover? You never know what you'll learn between the sheets, and I'm not talking about the way he pleasures you. Come to think of it, he's probably had gene therapy for that as well, so he might be pretty good in that department, if you can get past his rather irritating personality."

"I . . ." Katrine said. "I think not."

Catarvin's eyes narrowed. "Are you not into men? Well if you're into women, take me as a lover. I'm quite good in bed, you know, with either sex. Just ask my husband, or any of his mistresses for that matter."

Katrine would have sworn that the day could not hold any more surprises. "No, I'm wired . . . for men . . . but . . . not him."

Catarvin stopped and gave her an evil smile. "You're blushing. That's rather cute, you know."

The little woman turned and started to walk away, but hesitated and turned back. Her voice hardened as she said, "Dear, do be careful about outing me. If it became known that I am not what I appear to be, I would be most unhappy. And I'd also be of no use to you. You have my permission to tell Fran Thealone and Mani Gascoigne. But leave it at that, and swear them to secrecy."

She adopted a vacant look, smiled, turned, and walked away, leaving Katrine standing in the middle of the hallway with her mouth open.

When Katrine got to Senator Gascoigne's office, he was waiting for her with sandwiches. "Well," he said. "What was so important?"

She placed her briefcase on a chair, then pulled off her uniform coat and tossed it on top of the briefcase. "You won't believe it when I tell you. I need a stiff drink."

He asked, "Drinking in the middle of the day?"

She nodded. "If my days continue to be anything like this one, I may take up drinking as a full-time activity."

19

Connections

WHEN ANDERS GOT off shift he joined Thoran for another night of what he thought would be more moonlighting. The tall man had thrown a heavy duffel over one shoulder, and instead of taking the transit system to the warehouse district, Thoran said, "I need a drink. Join me." Their special signal!

Anders raised an eyebrow.

In response, Thoran nodded his head to one side and said, "Come with me."

They walked a few blocks from the transit depot, then Thoran hailed a cab. Just like the night the high-ranking officer interrogated Anders, Thoran leaned forward, opened the back door and held it. "After you, friend."

In that moment Anders feared he had slipped up and said or done something to give himself away. If that were the case, Thoran would certainly be armed and ready for anything Anders might try, so he really had no choice but to play along and hope for the best.

Anders climbed into the back seat of the grav car. Thoran climbed in next to him, placed the duffel between them, and gave the car's AI an address. The car pulled away from the curb on its grav fields.

They rode in silence, and twenty minutes later the car pulled up to the same run-down, two-story office building where Anders had first met the officer and Thoran's other special friends. Thoran hefted his duffel and climbed out of the car. Anders followed him, wondering what would come next. The car pulled away.

The last time Anders had come to that address, as Thoran approached the front of the building, the door had opened before he got there. But that didn't happen this time.

Thoran punched a code into a crude cypher lock, the door popped open, and he walked in. Anders followed.

The small table and two chairs were still the only furniture in the room. Thoran tossed the duffel on the table where it landed with a heavy thud. He rifled through its contents, retrieved a heavy grav pistol, and handed it to Anders. Thoran grinned. "I told you you'd soon earn that really good pay."

Anders checked the charge and load on the weapon while Thoran retrieved another from the duffel for himself. A little later the female member of their team arrived, the stocky non-com. His initial guess about her had been right. They didn't talk about their pasts much, but he had learned that Erika Kristensen presently bore the rank of hauptseergent.

Thoran said to Anders, "You've been on the receiving end of it so you know the drill. You and Hauptseergent Kristensen will take the side positions."

Kristensen had brought her own weapon. She slid one of the chairs away from the table and sat down, saying to Anders, "We've got a little waiting to do."

Anders sat in the other chair, while Thoran stood near the door and watched the street through a window. A half hour later Thoran said, "They're here."

Anders and Kristensen returned the chairs to the table. She took a position to one side of the door, and pointed Anders to the other. A few seconds later Thoran opened the front door and held it.

When a man stepped through the doorway, Kristensen stepped forward to stand about three paces in front of him. Anders joined her, stood beside her, and like her, aimed his weapon at the man's chest. Thoran frisked the fellow, then declared, "He's clean."

A fourth member of their team, apparently the man who had recruited the fellow, stood behind him and said, "Sit down at the table."

Kristensen put her back against the far wall of the room, so Anders backed up to the wall opposite her, careful to take a position that didn't put any of his teammates in his line of fire.

In so many ways it was a repeat of the evening in which they interrogated Anders. Kristensen walked to the door at the back of the room, opened it, stepped in, and Anders heard her say, "He's here, and unarmed." The older woman must have entered the building through a different entrance.

She walked in, sat down opposite the fellow, and questioned him at length. The man hated all things Commonwealth, and to sate his hatred had killed a number of civilians as well as ComSecCorps soldiers. The officer finished by telling his recruiter to take him out and, ". . . buy him dinner and a drink or two—on me."

Once they left, Thoran asked the officer, "Any further instructions, Command Eagle?"

"The usual," she said. "Just keep a close eye on him until we know there won't be any surprises."

After she left, Anders offered his weapon back to Thoran, but the tall man said, "No, you keep it."

Thoran retrieved a small valise from the duffel and handed it to Anders. It contained a maintenance kit and tools for the grav gun, and was large enough to hold the heavy pistol as well. "If you need anything more," Thoran said. "Just let me know."

Thoran hired another cab and the two of them rode back to the transit depot, which was within walking distance of Anders's apartment.

"Command Eagle," Thoran had called the officer. Anders decided to spend the night with Viktra.

••••

Katrine's lunch with Gascoigne lasted for more than two hours. Her revelations about Jenine Catarvin's assumed persona surprised him as much as they had her.

He shook his head and said, "I wouldn't have believed it. She plays that airhead role to the hilt. I always wondered how such an idiot managed to get reelected. She has a fair amount of seniority in the senate, you know."

Katrine's thoughts on the woman had oscillated back and forth since the two had parted. "We only had a brief time together without Palmutter present, but I think she's quite intelligent. It must not be easy to maintain that false persona so effectively. I wonder if I should try to develop a closer relationship with her."

His eyes widened, "You mean take her as a lover as she proposed?"

"No," Katrine said, "no. I don't work that way. I think I should get to know her a little better, see if she can be helpful in some way."

Gascoigne grimaced. "That could be problematic. She has historically been uncommitted on the Kelk issue, but has recently made noises that lead many of us to believe she's shifting her sentiments toward the hardline side. And lately she's spent a lot of time in the company of hawks like Palmutter. That didn't surprise me too much because I considered her a vapid idiot. On the other hand she revealed herself to you in a very specific and overt way."

"Exactly," Katrine said. "She could have accomplished her mission to divert me to Palmutter's office without giving herself away. So she had a reason for doing so."

Katrine leaned back in her chair and recalled the effortless way Catarvin had shifted personas. "Do you think it possible her newly acquired hawkish sentiments are a ruse as well?"

Gascoigne nodded. "You and I are thinking alike here. And if that's true, from inside the hawkish ranks she could be a valuable source of information."

As Katrine left Gascoigne's office, the two lobbyists whose appointment he had cancelled hovered over the desk of one of his aides trying to reschedule their meeting.

Out in the hallway she thought of Tarsik Obradour and the meeting in his penthouse overlooking the city. He had referred to Catarvin as dimwitted. Katrine felt some triumph in the thought that the plump little woman had fooled even that man, who in so many ways seemed all-powerful. Yes, she must get to know Jenine Catarvin better.

••••

John received a message telling him that registration for investment updates gave him access to Transmarin's Investor Database systems. The message included a boilerplate welcome with a lot of flattering language implying he was a brilliant investment tycoon, and they were quite grateful that he would consider investing some of his vast wealth in the company. He quickly learned there wasn't any information there he couldn't find in other public databases, but Transmarin had assembled all the facts and figures in one place, with a customized search engine that made it a lot easier to sift through the data.

It didn't take long to assemble all the details Primatov had asked for. She hadn't instructed him to look for connections to the Kelk, but he knew that was at the top of her mind, so he gave that a shot as well. Unfortunately, the closest he came to linking the company to the Supremacy was a press release. One of their senior managers had been disciplined for going overboard at a Kelkie party. He had gotten quite drunk, wouldn't take *No* for an answer from a scantily-clad young woman in a revealing Kelk costume, had come quite close to assaulting her, then been arrested by the police. The release included a statement on the company's policies regarding tolerance of diversity in the pursuit of interpersonal relationships, intolerance of the manager's belligerent and forceful behavior, and a disclaimer of any policy whatsoever when it came to Kelkies and their somewhat questionable activities.

John found some very indirect connections to the Supremacy through Sarkovie, Reisenar and Norandyne, but nothing that stood out as suspicious or untoward. In one of his searches he stumbled across Palmutter's name. A mid-level manager had donated to his campaign fund, though not in any substantial way, and certainly nothing close to the vast wealth Transmarin hoped John would come up with. He focused on that, and found over thirty managers who had made similar contributions to the senator's reelection. The total added up to a substantial sum, and all of them worked in the same division: Transmarin Missile Systems.

With a little more work John learned that Executive Vice President Lawrence Strikland ran that division of Transmarin. John dug deeper, and found nothing suspicious about Strikland in Transmarin's Investor Database. He reverted to the public information systems, and learned that Strikland had personally donated substantial sums to a senatorial advocacy group named: Nonpartisan Group for Unbiased Transparency in Commonwealth Electoral Processes. NGUTCEP's mission statement contained a lot of aspirational rhetoric, but nothing of any substance that might give John an idea of what they stood for. However, without exception, opinion pieces published by its members demonstrated a decidedly anti-Kelk posture. The group had also spent money with various news-feed organizations supporting Palmutter in his last reelection. Mr. Strikland apparently supported a hawkish stance on the Kelk issue, but didn't want to be known publicly for that.

John decided to call it a day. Finals were looming, and he had some cramming to do. He didn't think he'd see Primatov until after he finished his exams, so he'd wait until then to report his findings to her.

••••

"You're doing much better," Command Hawk Velkerhaut said. "Good."

That was probably as close to a compliment as the older woman would ever get. For the past months Nikaela had worked hard on her Lingua, and her accent had steadily improved. But Velkerhaut never let up, and the days spent under her tutelage still proved to be long and arduous. And even after such a minimal acknowledgement of Nikaela's efforts, the woman ended the session that day with, "But just because you've finally begun to show some small improvement, don't you dare think you can relax your vigilance. As we go forward I expect you to work just as hard, or perhaps even harder."

Velkerhaut left shortly before noon. Nikaela stored her Lingua texts and translators in her desk. Then she walked to the secure conference room where she joined Kristdokar, Thordahl, and Brynjar for a scheduled meeting that would include lunch. She was the last to arrive so she closed the door.

The security team had just swept the room. But with the door now closed, the four of them each pulled out instruments of their own. They then quietly swept the room again, each of them covering the entire volume completely so they had four-way redundancy, in addition to the security team's efforts. They paid particular attention to a tray of sandwiches and cold cuts that had been brought in for lunch. Then they scanned themselves and each other. At that point they each put together a small plate of food, then sat down at the table.

"Anything new?" Kristdokar asked, aiming the question at Nikaela.

Since she had been the one to uncover the disparate connection between Transmarin and Norddansk, she had become their de facto expert on sifting through the data.

"Not much," Nikaela said. "I may have another Commonwealth-Supremacy connection, but it's still quite tenuous, so I think it's premature to bring it up at this time. And I've added a few more threads to the connection between Transmarin and Norddansk, but it doesn't change what we already suspect."

"I'll trust your judgement in that," Kristdokar said. "Take your time and make sure you're right." She leaned forward to emphasize a point. "But don't take too much time."

She looked at Thordahl and Brynjar and asked, "Do either of you have anything?"

Brynjar shook his head, and Thordahl said, "Nothing here."

"Okay," Kristdokar said. "With Maestra Thordahl's help I transmitted our suspicions to our new friends and they're looking into Transmarin. Nothing back from them yet. I've also checked up on Vice Skalde Tiegnordan, though I should add I've been very discreet about it."

Thordahl asked, "Anything interesting?"

"Nothing dramatic," Kristdokar said. "Publicly, she's clearly not an anti-Commonwealth hawk, and she's expressed a number of centrist views. So she isn't politically or ideologically motivated, unless her entire public life has been a ruse.

And she's quite wealthy, so there isn't a financial incentive. She's aware of our operation—all of the Executive Council are, by the way—and gets regular reports on our activities, though no one but a very small circle of our new friends, and the four of us in this room, are aware of our recent discoveries and conclusions."

She hesitated for a long moment. "I'm just not sure what to do."

Thordahl asked, "Then why did you bring it up?"

From anyone else, such a question might have been interpreted as insubordinate. But the command superior had a way of helping them see through the chaff when struggling with an issue.

Kristdokar shrugged uncertainly. "I'm wondering if we shouldn't bring her into our confidence."

"No," Brynjar said flatly.

Kristdokar and Thordahl both gave him a sharp look and he softened his tone. "If we're wrong about her, there'd be no going back and it would be suicide. And I don't see that she can really help us at this stage. I see no reason why we shouldn't wait a little longer, and gather more data before taking such an irrevocable step."

Kristdokar closed her eyes and said, "I guess I have to agree with you there."

They discussed the issue from several angles, but always came back to the same conclusion. They would wait, gather more data, and possibly act upon it at a later time.

20

Unknown Enemy

AT THE END of the last of day of finals, John trudged back to the dorm, thinking he might join some of his friends to let off a little steam. But as luck would have it, his implants chimed with a message from Primatov. She wanted him to report to her office first thing in the morning.

Finals had been five straight days of last minute cramming in the evening, followed by grueling exams the next morning. The punishing pace was broken up only by meals, sleep, and a quick shower each morning.

When he got to his dorm room he found May dressed in civvies. "It's over. We're done. We made it."

He couldn't hide a grimace. "If we passed."

She punched him in the shoulder. "Don't be so negative. They long ago weeded out those who weren't going to make it. Come on. Karya's working late tonight. She's going to join me after dinner, but I don't want to eat alone, so let's go catch a bite somewhere."

"I'd better not," he said. "I've got to report to Primatov first thing tomorrow."

She shook her head like a disappointed parent. "Well you've got to eat. At least join us for dinner."

"Okay," he said, holding up his hands as if she had aimed a weapon at him. "I surrender. But just for a couple of hours. I'm bushed, and I need a good night's sleep."

John changed into civilian clothing and they went to a restaurant and bar frequented by a lot of academy cadets. Just inside the door May ran into a friend of hers, a young woman with brunette hair, blue eyes, and a pleasant smile. They paused for a moment to chat briefly.

The place was already crowded, and as May introduced John to her friend, he stepped aside for two men who came through the door behind them. John glanced their way, and his eyes met those of one of the men. The fellow seemed unpleasantly familiar in a way John couldn't place. But when the man realized their eyes had met, he grimaced and abruptly broke eye contact with John.

Now that was odd, John thought. He recalled the man's face for a moment, and concluded that while something about him had triggered some old memory, he had never before met the fellow. Nor did he think he had seen him around campus. He shrugged the incident off and put it out of his mind.

May and John waited, but while the place was crowded, they had arrived before the main rush, so they got a small table after only a few minutes.

"I'm really hungry," May said, "but first I need a drink."

May ordered whiskey on ice, and John ordered a beer. While they waited for their drinks they examined the menu, and John noticed the hostess seating that man and his companion at a table half way across the room. As the two sat down, the fellow glanced John's way and their eyes again met, and again the look on the man's face struck a chord of familiarity. It had been an unkind look that John thought he had seen somewhere before.

May ordered a full meal, but John wasn't terribly hungry so he just ordered a snack plate.

"Brighten up," May said. "Don't go all gloom and doom on me. You did fine, and you'll pass along with all the rest of us."

"I suppose so," John said. "The Kelk lessons got in the way of everything. And Professor Dirkson seemed to think that was the only thing I should study."

May shook her head. "I still don't understand why you're wasting your time with all that Kelk stuff."

John and May had had this conversation a number of times. "They were nice people," he said, "not at all like the stories, which makes me wonder how much of the stories are true. At this point I'm pretty sure almost everything we hear about them is wrong."

When the food arrived May dove into her meal with considerable gusto. John's small plate contained some cold cuts, cultured protein cheeses, bread, and a small knife he could use to cut off bite-sized bits.

Between bites of food, May said, "When Karya gets here, we're going to go bar hopping. You sure you don't want to join us?"

"I'd love to," John said, "but I'm bushed, and I don't want to show up tomorrow dragging my tail. When we're done here I'm going to call it an early night. But I'll take a raincheck for tomorrow night."

May shook her head sadly. "We really need to get you a girlfriend."

She paused and her eyes brightened. "Say, what about Celea?"

John didn't know any Celea. "Celea?"

"Yah, my friend at the door."

John recalled the brunette with blue eyes. "But . . . does she like . . . guys?"

May rolled her eyes and sighed heavily. "Not all my friends prefer women, you idiot. And I'm pretty sure she's still in the bar. I could hook you up, though I'll have to lie, tell her you're a lot smarter than you look."

John was tempted, but he wanted to stay in Primatov's good graces. "Give me a raincheck on that too."

When they finished the food May said, "Karya should be here shortly. Let's have another drink to kill time."

"Sure," John said. "I'll have another beer. Maybe it'll help me sleep, because I've got to be up early tomorrow and fight rush hour into Trafalgar."

While May tapped their order into the terminal at the table, John glanced at the two men seated across the room, and was careful not to be obvious about it. This time the fellow didn't look his way and their eyes didn't meet, and John didn't get that sense of familiarity. Like John and May, the two had finished their food and sat talking quietly over drinks.

They wore civilian attire, as did almost everyone there. But if John had to guess he would say they were military, if for no other reason than that they had chosen to eat in that establishment. This close to the academy, everyone present had some connection to ComSecCorps. But even had he been in a different part of the city, something about them said military, and definitely not academy cadets.

John tried to recall the look the man had given him, at the door when he first encountered him, and then again when they sat down at their table. It wasn't the man's face that had triggered a memory, but the look in his eyes, and that memory made John think of Novalis III and his rebel captor Cranoch.

To survive he had learned to read the brutal and sadistic man's looks and moods. Cranoch had a special gleam in his eye when he was about to do something really sneaky and hurt someone. It was a *tell* John had come to recognize, though it had taken him almost a year to do so. The man across the room had given John that same look, the Cranoch look of anticipated pleasure at someone else's pain.

There wasn't much left of the finger food on John's plate, just a piece of bread. He thought about walking back to the dorm alone, and didn't really like that idea. He reached out, picked up the small knife and tested its edge. It had a razor sharp, plast blade about as long his finger, basically a vicious little spike with a short handle. He knew he was being paranoid when he pretended to cut the piece of bread, then palmed the knife as he ate the last few crumbs. Under the table he experimented and found he could conceal the knife by sliding the blade into the cuff of his shirt, and cupping the handle in the palm of his hand. It wouldn't be much of a weapon, but he was probably just paranoid and really wouldn't need it anyway.

When Karya arrived she repeated May's invitation. "Come on, John, join us. I'm definitely in the mood to cut loose." She looked at May and said, "Let's find a place with some loud music."

May smiled at her. "Works for me. And with a dance floor."

John recalled the night blond-guy had assaulted him. Before that nasty incident he had spotted May and Karya out on the dance floor, and he recalled the way their eyes had been lost in each other's gaze.

Karya's eyes widened. "Dancing sounds great." She looked at John, "I'll even dance with Mr. Stick-In-The-Mud here. You are coming, aren't you?"

John grimaced and shook his head. "I can't. Gotta be up early tomorrow."

Karya gave an exasperated sigh and said to May. "We really need to get this guy laid."

"I'm trying," May said. "I've even got a girl picked out for him."

"Who?" Karya asked.

"Name's Celea, another cadet, but I don't think you know her."

John stood and said, "All right, you've had your fun. Have a good time, and I'll join you some other time."

Karya gave him a little hug and he headed for the door. He noticed the two men standing up from their table and preparing to leave as well, probably just coincidence. Nevertheless, he gripped the small knife handle concealed in the palm of his hand, and took some reassurance from that.

He ran into Nash Wakeland at the door to the restaurant. "Johnny-boy," Nash said. "Headed back to the dorm?"

"Yah," John said.

"Great," Wakeland said. "I'm headed that way myself. I'll walk with you."

"Calling it an early night?" John asked. "That's not like you."

"Nah," Wakeland said. "Just forgot something back at the dorm." He swaggered to the door and held it open for John. "Then I've got a date with a really hot woman."

John stepped through the door and Nash joined him out on the sidewalk. With Nash accompanying him back to the dorm, his paranoia subsided considerably.

••••

Anders had worked the afternoon-evening shift, and he didn't get off until a few hours before midnight. In the locker room, as he stripped out of his transit uniform and pulled on street clothes, Thoran approached him, gave him a friendly slap on the back and said, "I need a drink. Join me."

They walked out of the building together and up the street. At the first intersection, Thoran approached a parked delivery van and rapped on a small cargo port in its side. The port retracted and he stepped into the van, waving for Anders to follow him. In the front seat Hauptseergent Erika Kristensen sat behind the controls. Thoran closed the cargo port, he and Anders sat down in the cargo area, and Kristensen pulled the van away from the curb.

As she drove down the street she extended one arm over her shoulder. Her hand held a small package, and she said, "He may need this."

Thoran took the package and handed it to Anders. It opened easily, and from it Anders retrieved a waist holster containing a small pistol.

"It's a good carry piece," Thoran said. "Shorter barrel so it's a little less accurate, and a smaller load magazine. But you can carry extra loads, and it still packs a wallop, and you can conceal it easily beneath that coat of yours."

Anders asked, "What's the job tonight?"

Thoran grimaced. "We have to go pick up Gaertkine. He's been a bad boy."

Anders recalled the way some on their team distrusted Gaertkine because he was in it purely for the money. And Thoran had hinted the man hadn't been discreet with his pay.

Light spilled into the van through the windshield, and during the next few minutes it brightened considerably. Anders glanced out a window and saw a street lined with bars and nightclubs. Brightly flashing signs offered drink, drugs, and scantily clad men and woman. Kristensen had driven them into a section of Hyerdride known for sleazy night clubs, drug running, and prostitutes. The Larscom had long ago outlawed female prostitution, but anything could be had for a price in that district.

Kristensen pulled up to the curb in front of a bar and let the van hover on its grav fields.

Thoran showed Anders a small powered injector. "If I think he's going to give us trouble, I'll give you the nod, you distract him, and I'll give him a dose of this. He'll get real cooperative a few seconds later."

Anders nodded.

Thoran retracted the cargo port and they stepped out onto the sidewalk. A mixture of music, shouts of both anger and joy, cheers, grav cars racing by, police sirens in the distance; all of it combined to produce the din of the street. The scents of beer, cheap perfume, urine, and vomit assaulted Anders's nose. He and Thoran wove their way through a parade of gaudily dressed pedestrians to get from the curb to the bar's entrance. When Thoran opened the door, the grind of harsh music added to the assault on Anders's ears. But once within, with the entrance closed, the street sounds diminished to a faint background, and he found the volume of the music tolerable, though not enjoyable.

A long bar bisected a good portion of the room, with tables scattered about on the floor around it. At strategic points on the bar, dancers of both sexes undulated in various stages of undress. A very young boy wearing a considerable amount of makeup approached Anders. He reached out, touched Anders's arm and asked, "What's your pleasure?"

"Not you," Anders said.

The boy shrugged and said, "We don't offer women, because that would be illegal." He leaned close to Anders's ear and whispered, "Unless you're willing to pay the price, and you know how to be discreet about it."

Anders said, "No thank you. I'm here with a friend."

He followed Thoran across the room where they met one of the other team members seated at the bar, a man named Danekassel. Thoran had to shout to be heard above the music. "Where is he?"

Danekassel pointed, and Anders looked in the direction indicated. Gaertkine sat in a booth, his left arm around the shoulders of a woman. With his right he tossed back a shot of something, probably kirva.

Danekassel stood, and he, Anders and Thoran wove their way through the crowd. When they reached Gaertkine's table, he looked up and bellowed, "Thoran, old friend. Come to join the fun, eh?"

"Yah," Thoran said. "Going to have some fun."

Gaertkine looked at Anders. "It's the new guy, what's-his-name. Working for Thoran's a lot better than prison, isn't it? And pays a lot better too."

Thoran cringed.

Gaertkine waved both arms over his head and shouted, "Waiter. Waiter. Drinks for my friends here."

Anders had thought the music overly loud, but Gaertkine bellowed with enough volume for his voice to carry over it easily. He tossed a wad of script on the table as Thoran sat down beside him. "Drinks on me."

Thoran gave Anders a knowing look and nodded. Anders decided to pretend he had had too much to drink himself. "I can use another drink," he said, slurring his words a little. He leaned forward and put his hands on the table. He pretended to stumble and knocked the woman's drink over.

The woman shrieked.

Gaertkine tried to stand. "You clumsy idiot."

Thoran pressed him back into his seat, and Anders saw the glint of the injector in his hand.

"Whadoya," Gaertkine said, then his eyes rolled back and his head dropped forward.

A waiter stopped at the table. "What's wrong here?"

Thoran smiled at him pleasantly. "Our friend here has had a little too much to drink. We'll get him home."

The woman reached for the wad of script on the table, but Anders reached out and beat her too it. She gave him a dirty look.

Anders cleared Gaertkine's tab with the waiter and gave the woman a few notes. "For your trouble," he said.

Thoran and Danekassel got Gaertkine to his feet. To Anders's relief the fellow could stand, but couldn't stay on his feet without the support of the two men. It proved to be something of an ordeal getting him across the room, but Anders ran interference for them and they made it to the exit without incident.

Out on the street, Thoran asked Danekassel, "Was he doing that all night: flashing money, buying rounds of drinks?"

The man rolled his eyes and shook his head. "Yah."

They tumbled Gaertkine into the van and he immediately passed out on the floor. They climbed in with him, sat down, and as Kristensen pulled the vehicle out into traffic, Thoran leaned close to Anders.

"By the way," he said. "That young woman who testified against you at the tribunal . . ."

"Mistress Vreekande?" Anders asked.

"Yah, her," Thoran said. "You'll be glad to hear that bitch is going to get her due."

A lump formed in Anders's throat. "How do you mean?"

Thoran grinned unpleasantly. "She's asked a lot of questions she shouldn't. After tonight, she won't be asking any more questions. Thought you'd want to know."

Anders's mind raced. He didn't dare try to contact Viktra through citynet, not in the presence of these people. They had demonstrated repeatedly they could monitor and control nearby communications. He could only play along, then break away as soon as possible and try to warn Kristdokar.

Kristensen drove them to the building where they had first interrogated Anders. They turned Gaertkine over to the command eagle and four other members of their team, then climbed back into the van and Kristensen drove away.

Thoran said. "I'm thirsty. Let's go have a drink for real."

"Can't," Anders said. "Viktra's expecting me."

Anders tried to think of anything but Mistress Vreekande, and forced himself not to fidget and appear nervous. He asked Thoran, "What'll happen to Gaertkine?"

"Probably an industrial accident," Thoran said. "The fatal kind."

21

Abduction

"MISTRESS VREEKANDE . . ."

"Mistress Vreekande . . ."

"Wake up, Mistress Vreekande . . ."

Nikaela opened her eyes and blinked rapidly. She had dreamed something, and she couldn't recall what, which added to her confusion. She lifted her head off her arms and looked up into Kristdokar's face. The older woman said, "You fell asleep at your desk."

The day had started with that morning-long Lingua session with Velkerhaut, then the extended lunch with Kristdokar, Thordahl and Brynjar in the secure conference room. Nikaela spent the last few hours of the afternoon trying to dig up anything more on Norddansk. She remembered being the last one still at her desk in the large bullpen, but nothing after that.

"Go home," Kristdokar said. "Get a good night's sleep. You have my permission to sleep in and come in a little late tomorrow."

Nikaela walked back to her apartment building thinking only of a cold drink and a hot bath. The sun was setting and the night had begun to darken as she stepped into the lobby of her apartment building. She called the lift, waited a few seconds for it to arrive, and while doing so she changed her mind. Instead of a cold drink and hot bath, she would do cold drink, short nap, then hot bath.

The lift doors opened, she stepped in, and a second later stepped out onto her floor.

She had a little trouble with the lock on the door to her apartment. It took a few seconds to respond to her implants, and she decided to have the building superintendent check it out. He was usually much better about those kinds of things and frequently identified such issues before they became a problem. She hoped she wouldn't have to have an unhappy conversation with him.

When she stepped into the entryway of her apartment the light there automatically turned on. She closed the door, and this time the lock responded without delay. Perhaps she didn't need to contact the superintendent after all.

Normally, when first entering her apartment she immediately threw off her coat, then unbuckled the shoulder holster and tossed it and the weapon on a chair. But as

Nikaela walked through the small gathering room in her apartment, the lamps there didn't respond automatically. She felt her way by touch into her small kitchenette and was forced to manually switch on the lights. Some common electrical glitch had probably caused the malfunction in both the lights and the lock. She would contact the superintendent in the morning, and they would definitely have words.

Trying to think of what she wanted for that cold drink, she paused and yawned. It had been an exhausting day. Maybe she would just skip the cold drink and go straight to the short nap.

That was when her implants crashed, an odd sensation like trying to listen to a conversation with a finger shoved in each ear. She heard a soft thump in the empty apartment behind her, and in that instant realized someone had jammed her access to citynet, and to Kristdokar's secure military network as well.

Through reflex more than anything else, she let her knees buckle. And as she went down she spun while reaching for the weapon in the shoulder holster. She heard a strange, soft puff, and something ruffled the hair on top of her head just as she spotted a shadowy figure crossing the dark gathering room toward her. She leveled the pistol at him and pulled the trigger. The grav gun kicked in her hand and roared with the characteristic sound of a giant spring uncoiling.

She triggered the secure number Kristdokar had given her, but whoever had jammed citynet had also jammed her access to the secure military network they had set up. No one should be able to do that.

A loud pop sounded somewhere in her apartment, and a bullet slammed into the cabinet just above her head. A flashbang went off in her bedroom as she scrambled on her hands and knees across the floor, remembering she only had five rounds left in her pistol. Another loud pop, and it felt as if someone had hit her in the shoulder with a sledgehammer. She cried out as the bullet knocked her to one side and onto her back. She lifted the pistol and fired two rounds blindly into the darkness, then scrambled out of the light into a dark shadow in the corner of the kitchenette, leaving a trail of smeared blood on the floor. Another flashbang went off somewhere, and she heard shattering glass.

She heard that strange, soft puff again, and something stung her thigh. In the dim light she saw no apparent wound there, and the material of her pants remained undamaged. They had shot her with something, probably some sort of intramuscular drug. She had only seconds before it knocked her out, or killed her, or whatever it was supposed to do.

She pressed the grav pistol at a shallow angle against the spot on her thigh where she had felt the sting, and pulled the trigger. She screamed at the pain as the bullet tore a fist-sized chunk of flesh out of her thigh, and hopefully took much of the drug with it before it spread into her system.

Another shadowy figure appeared in the darkened gathering room, standing over the crumpled heap of the first. Her head swam and the floor seemed to tilt dizzyingly, and whether it was due to some drug, loss of blood, or the intense pain, it really didn't matter. She raised the grav pistol and fired blindly into the darkness.

The shadowy figure approached her, or maybe it was another shadowy figure. She raised her weapon and pulled the trigger again, but she had used up all six rounds and the gun just emitted an empty click.

The shadowy figure stopped and loomed over her. He held a large pistol in one hand and she figured he would now finish her off. She had trouble holding onto consciousness, and didn't really want to be awake when he did so. But he leaned down and said, "Want to know all about Norddansk, do you? That's a very unhealthy curiosity you've developed."

He straightened, and slapped her in the side of the face with the heavy pistol.

••••

Full night had enveloped the city while John and May ate dinner. Bright lights lit the street outside the restaurant, and people crowded the sidewalk shoulder to shoulder, everyone intent on going somewhere. With the end of finals, the strip near the campus had filled with a certain desperate energy.

John glanced over his shoulder, but saw no sign of the two men. In any case, with Wakeland walking beside him he didn't have anything to worry about. He chided himself for being paranoid. He'd have to go back to that restaurant and return the knife, maybe order something to eat and leave it on the plate when finished.

The crowds thinned as he and Wakeland left the commercial district. The streets were still well lit, but without the added illumination of glaring signs and advertising, more shadows intruded on the night.

Access to the grounds of the academy was relatively unrestricted, and guards manned the station at its entrance only during special events. When they passed the unmanned guard station and walked onto campus John felt as if he'd stepped into another world. Wakeland kept up a constant chatter about the hot girl he was going to meet. At one point he claimed, "I'd even take her over your red-hot Blacksword redhead."

John asked, "You know about her?"

Wakeland shook his head sadly. "Everyone knows about her, Johnny-boy."

They walked along a broad avenue for quite a distance before encountering another person, and when they did it was a lone cadet headed the other way on the opposite side of the street, probably going out to meet some classmates and let off a little steam. The cadets were all out looking for a little relief from their rigid curriculum of studies. John looked over his shoulder occasionally, just to be certain his paranoia wasn't valid, and wished he could join them.

Tall, leafy trees lined the street in front of their dormitory, with branches that arced out over the sidewalk beneath the street lamps, casting it in a mottled patchwork of light and shadow. As they walked toward their building, even with a friend at his side, John still had trouble controlling the paranoia, and he tried to tell himself he was just being foolish.

Well short of their destination, a lone figure stepped out of a black splotch of shadow and stood on the sidewalk, blocking their path. In that same instant John's implants said, "Line access is down. Exterior contact restricted."

Shadows partially hid the man's face, but John easily recognized the fellow from the restaurant with the Cranoch look. John and Wakeland stopped about ten paces short of the man. John tensed, while Wakeland stepped back as if to put John between him and Cranoch-Look. Wakeland had never before struck John as a coward.

"Don't move," Cranoch-Look said, raising a pistol and aiming it at John.

John froze. He couldn't outrun a bullet, not at that range, and not when fired by someone who knew how to use a heavy grav pistol. And from the casual way the man held the gun, John had no doubt this fellow knew his weapons.

Cranoch-Look stepped forward and stopped two paces from John, and there was that look again, the *tell*. "We're not going to hurt you. Certain people just want to talk with you."

They probably did want to talk to him, and perhaps that part was true. But the look on the man's face told John that when they finished, he and Wakeland would most likely disappear, or the authorities would find them face down in an alley with bullets in the backs of their heads.

He heard footsteps behind him. As two sets of hands grabbed his elbows and pinned them to his sides, a woman's voice on his left said, "Don't try anything, kid. You're way outclassed."

John looked over his left shoulder and found the pretty young woman he'd seen on the street arguing with blond-guy. She stood clutching his elbow in one hand, her other hand bending his wrist into a very professional lock-hold, the kind the academy taught in martial arts class. She gave his wrist a little tweak, and he grunted with pain.

"You were following me," he said.

She shrugged. "More like keeping an eye on you."

John glanced over his right shoulder, now knowing what to expect. Wakeland stood there holding John's elbow in a vice-like grip. With his added strength, and with the woman on the other side, and with Cranoch-Look holding the grav pistol at near pointblank range, Wakeland didn't need to bend John's wrist into a painful lock.

John said, "You set me up."

Wakeland grinned. "They pay me real good money, Johnny-boy."

Many of their interactions through the last year flashed through John's thoughts, and he understood now how gullible he had been to ever think Wakeland might be a friend.

Cranoch-Look approached and held the pistol aimed at John's chest. Wakeland and the woman raised John's arms and held them out to the side. Cranoch-Look frisked him with one hand while holding the barrel of the pistol against his chest with the other, and did a fairly thorough job of it. He touched John in several intimate places, but he did so with a cold-blooded, proficient attitude that confirmed John's earlier assessment that they were professionals. As the fellow ran his hands all the way out to the end of John's arms, with the handle of the small knife gripped in his hand, John pressed the flat of the blade against his wrist just inside his cuff. He felt a sharp sting as the blade cut a little into his flesh.

He tried not to appear relieved as Cranoch-Look stepped back. "He's clean, like I expected."

Wakeland said, "I told you he was too stupid to pack anything."

They had assumed John would go unarmed, and Cranoch-Look had missed the small spike of a knife because he expected to find something larger.

Cranoch-Look put the pistol away inside his coat as Wakeland and the woman locked John's elbows behind his back. Two grav cars raced down the street and pulled up to the curb. Cranoch-Look opened the back door of the lead car and climbed in. Wakeland and the woman bent John forward, pushing his head down, clearly intending to shove him into the seat next to Cranoch-Look. But at that moment John realized that chance, and their awkward positions, had put his right hand with the little knife between Wakeland's legs. As they shoved him toward the open door, he cut the blade free of his sleeve, and stabbed it into Wakeland's groin with all the strength he could muster.

Wakeland shattered the still of the night with a scream and released him. With the blade still buried in Wakeland's groin, John ripped the knife forward, going for maximum damage and hopefully the femoral artery. Wakeland staggered away from him, clutching at his crotch and wailing like a wounded animal.

The woman holding John's left arm glanced desperately at the shadows around them, clearly discounting John and assuming they were under assault from an external unseen opponent. With his right arm free, John twisted about and buried the knife in the side of her neck, then tore it forward, ripping out her larynx. She staggered away from him, gurgling and choking on blood.

John grabbed her by the front of her tunic, hammer-fisted the blade into the side of her head, then yanked it out. As she started to collapse he shoved her head-first into the seat next to Cranoch-Look, who fumbled at his coat to get the grav pistol out.

The front door to the car behind them shot open, and John spotted striking, pale-blond wavy hair. John sprinted toward it and plowed into the door just as blond-guy got a leg, a hand holding a pistol, and his head clear of the car. John's momentum slammed the door against him, pinning the asshole half way out of the car, and the pistol clattered to the sidewalk. Blond-guy struggled, trying to get the door open, but John stabbed the knife into his right eye, then gave him a crude lobotomy by slashing it side-to-side.

The window of the car's rear door shattered outward in a spray of glass shards, and a bullet punched into John's side. He staggered back a step, pain so intense he fell to his knees, leaving the knife still buried in blond-guy's eye. John's throat seized up and he couldn't breathe, couldn't even gasp. He wrapped his arms across his stomach where the bullet had scrambled his guts.

The pistol blond-guy had dropped lay on the sidewalk in front of him, and as a wave of dizziness washed over him, he fell forward and collapsed on top of it. Lying on the weapon, he heard car doors open and close as he wrapped his fingers around the weapon's grip, made sure the safety was off, and put his finger on the trigger. He tried to roll over, to make one last try at resisting them, but any effort on his part only intensified the pain, so he lay still.

His cheek rested on the concrete of the sidewalk, and he noticed a spatter of blood only inches from his face. He wondered if it was his or theirs. He tasted blood and saw little motes of unconsciousness dancing before his eyes.

A woman's voice said, "Is he dead?"

A man's voice answered her, "Fucking little shit better be."

"He's not supposed to be dead," the woman said. "This is a major fuck-up. We're supposed to bring him in alive."

The man said, "Help me roll him over to make sure, then we're out of here."

Someone grabbed John's left arm and rolled him onto his side, reigniting the pain in his guts. He found himself looking up into Cranoch-Look's face at almost pointblank range, but with his right arm and the weapon pinned beneath him he couldn't do anything about it.

"He ain't dead yet," Cranoch-Look said, "but I'm going to fix that right now."

Cranoch-Look rolled him over a little further, freeing his right arm.

The man must have seen the pistol in John's hand, because for a brief instant, as John angled the barrel upward, the fellow's eyes widened. John pulled the trigger, and the bullet punched a tiny, little hole in Cranoch-Look's neck, just beneath his chin. The top of the man's head exploded and rivulets of blood coursed out of his ears, nose and mouth. Then he collapsed on top of John.

The woman stood over them holding a pistol, her eyes wide with surprise. John's gun hand was free, but with Cranoch-Look's weight on top of him, he couldn't raise the pistol high enough for a kill shot, so he shot her in the leg.

Her knee fragmented into a cloud of meat, bone and blood, much the way his father's knee had disintegrated when the rebel Mercier had shot him. She cried out, dropped her weapon and fell to the sidewalk next to John, clutching her knee with one hand.

"You fucking maniac," she screamed as she scrabbled for her pistol.

John had a better angle now, so he shot her in the nose. She straightened up and froze for a moment with a distant look in her eyes. Then she toppled forward, and her face made a satisfyingly loud smack when she planted it into the concrete of the sidewalk.

Someone fired a grav pistol and a bullet thumped into Cranoch-Look's body. With the man's weight pinning him down, John waved the gun about wildly and shot at anything that moved. A man a few paces away clutched at his side and staggered. He raised a pistol toward John, but sirens in the distance interrupted him.

"Shit!" he said, then turned and limped away in a rush.

A few seconds later the whine of the generators in one of the grav cars rose in pitch. John fired several rounds into it as it lifted off the pavement and drifted toward him.

The pitch of the sirens rose in the distance, and John heard groans and whimpers nearby. It took him a moment to realize the groans and whimpers were his.

Someone rolled Cranoch-Look's body off of him, but the pain in his gut was so intense he couldn't sit up. He heard more sirens closer now, and another groan, though this time he wasn't sure if that one had been his or not. They would kill him if they got the chance, so he struggled to hold onto consciousness to defend himself. But consciousness wasn't cooperating that night, and it retreated to a distant place.

••••

When Anders stepped out of the lift on the floor of Viktra's apartment, he immediately opened a secure link to her. "Warn Kristdokar. They're going to do something to Mistress Vreekande."

"I'm sorry, Anders. You're too late."

22

Survival

IT TOOK NIKAELA a moment to realize she wasn't dead, then another moment to realize she had awakened. She could move her eyes and blink her eyelids, but nothing else, couldn't feel anything, couldn't speak, could only lay there and breathe.

The ceiling above her had been painted off white, and what little she saw of the walls around her were covered in the same dull shades. A bank of instruments above the head of her bed emitted an occasional beep, and little lights blinked here and there. But to see more than that she would have to move her head, would have to look to one side or the other, and that wasn't going to happen.

A handsome young man leaned into her field of view wearing the uniform of a medical tech. The stencil that would normally display his name above his left breast pocket had been removed. His bright-red irises would have been quite attractive had he not looked upon her with hard, angry eyes and an unyielding gaze. He spoke in a flat, rigid tone. "Right on time. You're system is responding the way it should—a good sign."

She couldn't move her lips to ask a question, and right at that moment, several came to mind. And if he gave her a few minutes to think about it, she could probably come up with a couple hundred more.

As he adjusted something on the instruments above her, he made no attempt to hide his anger. "There are a lot of people who'd prefer to see you dead." He didn't need to tell her she could count him among them. "But the higher-ups want you alive . . . for the time being. Just be careful to do everything you're told, because accidents can happen . . ." He hesitated as if unsure of his words, then blurted out, ". . . Blacksword-fucking slut."

She couldn't speak to tell him she hadn't fucked any Blackswords, though if she could have corrected him, it probably wouldn't have made much difference. And doing so might just aggravate him. He had said accidents can happen, so perhaps her forced silence had its advantages.

He checked readings on the instruments, paused every now and then and adopted a distant, faraway look for a second or two, probably using his implants to enter data into a central database. Then without further comment, the room went silent.

She didn't at first understand that he had departed. Possibly he had chosen to stand or sit nearby in inhuman stillness. But after several minutes of absolute silence, broken only by an occasional beep or chime from the instruments, that didn't seem likely. No one could remain so completely still for that long unless they were truly paralyzed like Nikaela. She concluded he had walked out without a final word, which was probably for the best.

After some minutes she realized she wasn't actually paralyzed. She felt a pulse here and there in her body and in her extremities, could feel her heart beating in her chest, the weight of her body pressing on the skin of her back lying in the bed. She wasn't paralyzed. She just couldn't move any muscle that wasn't part of an involuntary response.

The med tech had worn a naval uniform, but the place didn't feel like a ship: no vibration of a ship's engines transmitted through its structure. The fact that she couldn't hear corpsmen or doctors or anyone moving about meant they had placed her in a separate room with a door. She couldn't raise her head to count the beds, but she would bet that if somehow she did, she would see only two or three, probably an ICU somewhere. She didn't think her injuries were serious enough to warrant such care, so they must have put her there to isolate her from the rest of the staff.

She knew she was alive, held captive by a full-body nerve block, and hidden away somewhere in a naval medical facility.

••••

"Mistake! This wasn't a mistake. This was a colossal cluster-fuck of unprecedented proportions."

A male voice, that was John's first thought. And those were the first words he heard, though with consciousness returning, the pain also came back. He tried to ignore the unyielding pounding in his gut, tried to listen carefully, but the pain demanded his attention and he found it difficult to focus on anything else.

A second male voice said, "The little shit shot me, god damn it. He shot me."

A third, and much calmer male voice said, "He better not die."

"But he shot me. What else was I supposed to do?"

"If he dies, you'd better hope you die as well. Because if you don't, after this fuck-up we'll make sure you do."

John decided it was good to know they didn't want him dead. But then why the fuck had they blown a hole in his gut?

He felt cuffs on his wrists behind his back. He didn't want them to know he had awakened, so he carefully moved one ankle just the tiniest bit. He didn't think he felt cuffs there, but he couldn't be sure.

They had cuffed him and dumped him in the back seat of a grav car, but the voices didn't seem to be coming from inside the car. Trying not to move and give himself away, he opened his eyes and glanced up. Broken shards of glass framed the shattered opening of the car's rear window. In the darkness of the night he saw shadowy figures moving about just outside the car.

The calm voice said, "We're going to take the kid with us. You stay here and clean this mess up."

"But I'm shot. I'm bleeding."

"Too fucking bad," the pissed-off guy said. "And you don't look like you're that bad off, so deal with it."

The rear door of the car opened, and two sets of hands gripped John by his elbows. They weren't gentle as they dragged him out of the back seat, and at one point the pain in his gut blossomed anew and he screamed.

Calm-voice said, "We need to move quickly."

"Yah," pissed-off guy agreed.

They got John to his feet, though he could barely stand even with their help. With calm-voice on his left and pissed-off guy on his right, they half dragged, half carried, half walked him to another car, every step another exercise in agony.

They dumped him in the back seat, tossed him there like a bag of rocks. The pain blossomed anew and he cried out. He heard them open the doors of the car and climb into the front seat. As the car sped away, John's last thought was that *half dragged, half carried, half walked* added up to three halves, which wasn't possible.

He giggled, which caused the pain in his gut to spike, so he passed out.

••••

Colonel Primatov, Katrine's implants said, waking her from a sound sleep. *High priority alert.*

Earlier in the evening she had curled up on the couch in her small apartment to skim a bunch of really boring reports. She must have dozed off.

Still groggy, she sat up straight and tried to clear her thoughts. "What is it?" she asked.

There's been a soft hit in the CIS database for the name John Mathius. *His DNA was identified among blood samples from an active crime scene involving multiple homicides.*

She shot to her feet, dumping the portable comp terminal out of her lap and onto the floor. She had set up flags to be notified if John's name ever appeared in anything official.

"Details," she demanded. "Give me some fucking details."

The incident involved gunfire, but other than that, the crime scene was secured only ten minutes ago, so details are extremely limited.

"What's Mr. Mathius's status?"

Unknown. He was no longer present at the scene.

"Then give me a damn address."

Her implants recited an address on the academy campus located on a street the cadets called *dormitory row.*

She looked down at her clothing. Before sitting down for her exciting evening of boring reports, she had slipped out of her uniform, then into a comfortable robe and soft slippers.

"Get me transport, immediately, preferably by air." She didn't want to buck traffic in the city. As she marched across her small apartment she said, "And contact Colonel Blacksword, stat, code Blacksword one. Brief her fully."

In her bedroom she threw off her robe, pulled on fresh underwear, then selected khakis, boots, and a cap.

"Katrine," her implants said as she struggled into her pants, "Fran here. Transport is on the way. I've authorized high-priority traffic clearance so it'll be on the street in front of your building in a few minutes. And I'm including a protective escort."

"I don't need bodyguards," Katrine said as she pulled on her shirt, her words tainted by the hard edge of anger.

"Maybe, maybe not," Thealone said, sounding like a parent whose patience had been stretched to the limit, "but you're getting them anyway. From what little information I can get, this sounds like a fucked-up hit job, so it's not your choice."

Katrine didn't have time to argue the point. She sat down, and as she snapped the buckles in place on her boots, she recalled her conversation with Tarsik Obradour in his penthouse, and how he had offered to help if she had a *serious enough situation*. She had briefed Thealone on that conversation.

"Fran," she said. "Would you contact Obradour? Maybe his network of informants can help."

"Right," Thealone said. "You see what you can learn on the scene, I'll get hold of Obradour."

Katrine finished with her boots then stood, pulled her hair back into a ponytail and held it down with the cap. She grabbed a coat and was about to put it on, but hesitated. Thealone was right.

She returned to her closet, keyed the lock on a small arms locker and opened it. She retrieved a heavy grav pistol and a shoulder holster, checked the charge and loads in the pistol, then strapped on the rig and holstered the pistol under her arm pit. She jammed her arms into the coat, and raced out the front door of her apartment.

Out on the street in front of her building she saw no sign of the promised transport. Grav cars floated up and down the street, and traffic lights in the distance changed colors, nothing to indicate that several people had died violently some time that evening.

She paced back and forth on the sidewalk, unable to contain her impatience. Then the traffic light at the end of her block switched to a flashing blue emergency beacon. She stopped and turned around to look the other way. All of the traffic lights within view had now done the same.

The grav cars on the street in front of her came to a stop as the emergency network took command of their control systems. In front of her several cars backed up, while several more moved forward, opening a wide space.

There came a moment of unusual silence when all movement came to a stop. Then she heard the grating whine of heavy-duty grav field generators. She looked up and saw the flashing lights of her transport descending toward the open space on the street. The craft descending toward her bristled with gun turrets. Fran Thealone hadn't simply sent her transport.

Katrine whispered, "A fucking assault boat."

••••

"We've got to get him out of this city," calm-voice said.

John couldn't move. They'd done something to block signals traveling from his brain to his muscles, but they hadn't done the same for signals going the other way. The pain in his gut hammered at him, and he couldn't even groan.

Pissed-off guy said, "I've already made the arrangements." He sounded a lot calmer, though still pissed-off. "We should be able to—"

"Hold on," a female voice said. "He's conscious. He can hear you."

John had nothing to lose, so he opened his eyes; at least he had control over that. He had trouble focusing. Everything appeared in a smeared-out blur, and he couldn't make any real sense of what he saw. They had placed him on his back in a bed; that much he figured out.

A defocused blob leaned into his field of view. He saw the outlines of shoulders dressed in white, and a head framed by a brown splash of long hair. The blob spoke in the woman's voice. "His vitals are better. At least we've got him stable."

She did something out of his field of view. A shock of pain shot through his gut and he gasped.

Pissed-off guy said, "I thought he couldn't move."

Clearly, the woman was a doctor, or some sort of medical tech. "Involuntary response. Can't suppress that without suppressing all his breathing. What you just saw was the extreme limit of what he can do."

Pissed-off guy said, "Do we really have to fix him up? He took out five of our people."

John got a little satisfaction in hearing that. He hoped Nash, Cranoch-Look, and Blond-Guy were among the casualties. Waves of pain clouded his memory of the fight in front of the dormitory, but he thought he might have made all three men pay dearly. He was fairly certain Nash Wakeland's party days were over.

Calm-voice said, "Only four. I'm not counting that fuck-up Willis."

"Okay, four. But why can't we just put a bullet in the back of his head? The asshole's a fucking Kelk lover."

"It's this breschkada thing. They want to talk to him before we do that. After that you can kill him."

"But why fix him up? Just keep him alive long enough for that, then pop him and be done with it."

The woman said, "It's going to be at least a couple of tendays before they can question him. We can't leave him as-is that long. Peritonitis will kill him long before that. We fix him up now, or he dies before then."

Calm-voice said, "Can't let that happen. We've got friends we need to keep happy. How long to fix him up?"

"I've already started the cultures to grow new intestinal track. That'll take a couple of days, then we surgically replace the damaged portions. He'll be in reasonably good shape a few days after that."

Another blurry blob leaned into John's field of view. He got the impression of close-cropped dark hair. Calm-voice said, "When you're better, you're going to tell us what this breschkada thing is. It's got our special friends all bent out of shape."

23

More Surprises

AS THE ASSAULT boat descended toward the ground, Katrine keyed her implants and tapped into a vid pickup mounted in the nose of the craft. Trafalgar City's lights lit up the night for a hundred kilometers in every direction, but the commercial district near the academy drew her attention. Brighter than the rest of the city, she recalled her own nights out on the town when she had attended O-School. She tried not to think of how many years had passed since then.

The academy's campus showed up as a darker island of peace and tranquility within easy walking distance of the commercial district. The flash of lights from the emergency vehicles there drew her attention, and testified to the violence that had disrupted the serenity of an institution for which she had only fond memories.

"Dammit!" she said, her voice barely above a whisper.

One of her bodyguards looked her way. "Pardon, ma'am. What was that?"

"Nothing," she said. "Nothing. Just pissed off. Really pissed off"

At that, he raised an eyebrow.

She added, "At myself, mostly."

He nodded once and looked away.

When young Mr. Mathius left the safety of the training depot on Miriteen and made his way to Trafalgar, they had considered assigning a small protection detail to keep an eye on him. But security on campus remained unquestionably good, and the most secure city in the Commonwealth surrounded it, and they had kept his name out of just about everything. So they decided that bodyguards, no matter how discreet, might bring the unwanted attention to him that they so desperately wanted to avoid. She blamed herself, should have been smarter. But what had she and John done to help their opponents connect the dots that led to him?

With midnight still several hours off, the assault boat settled down on the lawn in an open area about a hundred paces from the flashing lights. As more information had come in, and it looked like they were dealing with an assassination attempt, Colonel Blacksword had ordered security details attached to all high ranking Blacksword officers on the planet.

Two of Katrine's bodyguards stood by the side hatch of the grav boat as it whooshed open. One stepped out, a few seconds passed, then he said, "Looks clear, but there could be shooters anywhere."

Whatever had happened, the incident was over, so Katrine didn't think she had anything to fear. And she thought it likely the anonymous *they* would not want to turn a muddled operation into something even messier. She stood, and the Blacksword trooper still waiting just inside the open hatch didn't offer her any assistance as she stepped out onto the soft grass—she would have docked him a stripe if he had dropped his diligence in that way.

Surrounded by four heavily armed actives, she walked toward the flashing lights. Four bodyguards seemed extreme, but from what she had heard so far, the assault on Mathius had also been extreme, so the extra caution might be warranted.

CIS had erected a secure crime scene barrier around a good portion of the street in front of several buildings. Its dome shape shimmered in the flashing lights of the emergency vehicles. It scrambled and blurred any images passing through it, preventing the news hypes from acquiring unauthorized vid clips, and it would admit only approved personnel. Katrine and her security detail stepped through it easily. She paused just within and surveyed the scene.

Crime scene techs crawled over a grav car parked at the curb, its doors open, several bullet holes in its side. Preservation blankets covered what appeared to be five corpses sprawled on the sidewalk nearby. She spotted a ComSec major from CIS kneeling over one of them, a man named Timmerson who had a reputation for having a level head, and a tenacious personality. Her implants identified a young woman standing next to him as Lieutenant Preekat, a civilian police liaison; ex ComSecCorps with a Type One clearance. O-School's campus was officially part of a military base, so the local authorities would be involved only peripherally. But no one could hush up an out-and-out firefight on the grounds of the military equivalent of a college campus.

As she approached the two, Timmerson looked up, saw her coming, and stood.

"Colonel," he said, extending his hand. "I'm Major Timmerson, CIS."

She shook his hand. "I know. I've been briefed."

She and Preekat introduced themselves and shook hands.

Timmerson said, "My orders state that you'll be taking over the investigation."

"Not, really," she said. "I'm not an investigator, not in the sense you mean. But the intended target is a Blacksword, and you may find yourself delving into some highly classified issues. I'll need to have access to everything you learn, and at some point I may instruct you to cease any further investigative work. I'll also be reviewing, and quite probably redacting, any information released to the public."

To Preekat she said, "I'm invoking a Class-One Blacksword security alert. Any reports you file will have to go through my office for redaction. And if your colleagues ask, you are to make it clear to them you are not allowed to discuss anything regarding this incident. Even the color of the leaves on the trees here is classified."

Preekat had dark brown eyes and an olive complexion. She nodded with a slight grin on her face. "I know the drill, Colonel."

Timmerson looked from right to left, noting the bodies draped in preservation blankets. "Can't hush this one up too much." He glanced over his shoulder at one of the nearby buildings. "Nothing but dormitories on this end of campus, and lots of witnesses." He nodded toward a small group of cadets standing inside the crime scene barrier talking with another CIS officer. "When the shooting started, they're the ones who called it in."

Katrine said, "I'll need to see your officers' notes on their interviews, and I'll personally want to interview them all again myself. And find Cadet Mathius's roommate. She's also a cadet, so you should be able to locate her no matter where she is."

She looked down at the body he'd been examining. The preservation blanket had been pulled aside to reveal the face of a dead man whose open eyes stared at nothing. "Have you figured out what happened?"

Timmerson glanced down at the corpse. "We have IDs on three of them. Two are ex Special Forces, and one is an active Zeta Company Blacksword."

"Active?" she asked, making no attempt to hide the surprise in her voice. She recalled her earlier fears that people in her own organization might be working for the other side.

"Yes," he said, nodding his head. "And I'll bet when we ID the other two, they'll be Special Forces as well."

She asked, "Do you know enough to walk me through it?"

In response, he lowered himself to one knee beside the corpse at their feet. The preservation blanket covered everything but the man's face. Timmerson reached toward the man's feet and peeled the blanket back. The dead man's crotch and pants were covered in blood, and a large pool of it had puddled between his legs.

"This was the first one," Timmerson said. "Your man completely severed his femoral artery. No doubt his implants tried to control the bleeding, but he probably bled out before the shooting stopped."

He looked up at her. "And we got a double hit on his DNA."

She squinted at him and said, "What do you mean by that?"

He looked again at the corpse. "Exactly what I said. He's a cadet named Nash Wakeland registered here at the academy; is a bit of a lady's man and has a reputation for partying and drinking."

Katrine recognized the name, knew he lived in the same dorm as Mathius and had befriended him.

Timmerson continued. "He's also an ex ComSecCorps Special Forces non-com named Nash Willis. Five years ago he got caught running guns to the insurgency in that uprising in the Heraclean Hegemony. For his efforts he received a court-martial, dishonorable discharge, and two years behind bars."

He stood and faced her squarely. "Between his release from prison and tonight he's operated below our radar."

He didn't say what he obviously thought. And from the look on Preekat's face the same thoughts had crossed her mind. He had just confirmed what Katrine had feared for some time now. Someone had enough pull to falsify highly secured information in ComSecCorps databases.

Without saying anything more, Timmerson turned, walked over to a blanket-draped corpse near the curb, and exposed a woman's face and neck. Her larynx appeared to have been shredded. "Ripped out her larynx and some of her trachea, then stabbed her in the side of the head. Hit her with considerable force and punched through her temple. We've already got a few video hits on her off citynet, and it looks like she's tracked your boy for some time now."

He walked a few paces down the sidewalk to another corpse lying beside the grav car, with Katrine and Preekat following. He exposed a man's face. The fellow had pale, wavy blond hair, and she recognized him immediately from the incident report about the bar fight he had tried to start with Mathius. His right eye had been destroyed and all that remained was a bloody socket. "This one was third, found him jammed up in the door of the car."

Timmerson sent her an image, and her implants showed her the crime scene as it had appeared when they first came upon it. The blond asshole had hung partially upright in the half-opened door of the car, the handle of some sort of weapon protruding from his eye.

"Stabbed him in the eye," Timmerson said, "then scrambled the hell out of his brains."

He pointed to blood stains on the sidewalk. "This is where your man took a gut wound. His shit and DNA is all over the sidewalk."

He leaned over another body. A good portion of the top of the corpse's head had been blown away. "Number four. Your guy took one of their weapons away from them and shot him just under the chin, though it looks like the guy took a little postmortem, friendly fire as well."

Next to that corpse he pulled the preservation blanket off a woman. She had a small, round hole just beside her nose, though Katrine saw a lot of blood clotting the hair at the back of her head. "Shot her in the knee first," Timmerson said. "That was clearly pre-mortem. Then finished her off with a face shot."

Timmerson stood and faced Katrine squarely. "One or more of them escaped in a car. We found it a few kilometers from here, blood all over the seats. But they wiped it with a DNA scrambler, so we won't be able to trace them. We found traces of gastric fluids on the back seat as well. It was consistent with a bad gut wound, and the contents match the shit we found on the sidewalk here, so we think they used it to carry your man away. But because of the scrambler we couldn't confirm that with absolute certainty."

He paused, looked her pointedly in the eyes and said, "Five Special Forces dead."
He handed Katrine an evidence block, a transparent case that preserved the present

state of an item. It contained a small knife. "We took that out of the blond guy's eye. Your boy took out the first three with that."

The knife was quite small, with a blade no longer than one of her fingers. She said, "A paring knife?"

Preekat asked, "What kind of a cadet is this cadet of yours, Colonel? Zeta Company, right? Maybe even Assault Team Null?"

The woman assumed Cadet Mathius was Blacksword Special Forces.

Katrine sighed, looked again at the small knife, then said, "He comes across as a little timid. Combine that with his apparent youth, and it's easy to take him for granted. But that young man has seen more death and destruction than most combat soldiers twice his age."

She glanced around to take in the entire scene one last time. "These people probably assumed he'd be an easy take-down and didn't take him seriously. And they triggered his survival response."

She paused and scanned the scene one last time. "That young man is even more resourceful than I thought."

"Full of surprises, huh?" Timmerson asked.

Katrine nodded. "The thing that surprises me most about our young man is the way he continually surprises me."

••••

Anders wanted to throttle Thoran, tie the man in a chair and beat on him until he revealed what they had done with Nikaela Vreekande.

"We have to do something," he demanded. It was one of the rare times he met with Kristdokar face to face. Also present were Thordahl and Brynjar, whom he had just met.

Kristdokar shook her head. "Thoran might not know anything of value. Or he might know what they've done to her, but not where they've taken her. That's the piece of information we need the most, and taking Thoran into custody might accomplish nothing more than exposing you and tipping our own hand."

Thordahl said, "We and our new friends have got people watching those addresses you gave us on Sarkovie. All four are warehouses, and the level of activity there leads us to believe they're using those as a base of operations for their interests in all the nearby star systems." He turned to Kristdokar. "It might not be a bad idea to put some firepower in the vicinity of Sarkovie."

Kristdokar nodded. "I can arrange for a ship, *Drakan Helgis*, a relatively fast destroyer. I've spent the last year carefully vetting its crew and reassigning a few here and there when it wasn't obvious. At this point we can be relatively confident none of her crewmembers harbors extremist thoughts regarding our Commonwealth associates."

Brynjar said. "I think we need a combat team on hand as well, one capable of boarding a hostile vessel, or assaulting one of those warehouses. I'd be happy to lead such a team."

"Excellent idea," Kristdokar said. "Select the people you want, and I'll make sure you get them."

The next morning Anders went to work at the transit depot with a feigned smile on his face as if nothing had happened. He thought he could get away with showing a small amount of interest in Nikaela Vreekande. After all, Thoran had volunteered the information that they were going after her.

At the end of their shift, Anders said to Thoran, "Let's go get a drink." Since he hadn't said it with exactly the words, "I need a drink. Join me," that meant he really wanted to get a drink.

"You're buying the first round," Thoran said.

The two of them discussed the paltry wages they received as transit engineers. Anders waited until they had downed a couple of drinks before he lowered his voice and said, "How'd it go with the Vreekande woman?"

Thoran shook his head, frowned, and like Anders, lowered his voice. "They got her, friend, but I'm sorry to have to tell you they didn't finish her."

Anders feigned a touch of anger. "Why not? I spent time in SecureMax because of that bitch."

Thoran said, "Keep your voice down," and looked over his shoulder. They were alone in a corner of the bar with no one nearby. "I know how much you hate her. But it turns out she's breschkada with a Blacksword."

At the mention of a hated Blacksword, Anders didn't have to contrive his distaste. "She's a Blacksword-fucking slut now? You must be joking."

"No, friend," Thoran said. "So they don't want her dead yet, not until they can interrogate both of them."

"How are they going to do that?"

Thoran grinned and again looked over his shoulder. "From what I hear, her breschkada will soon be on his way."

"Here?" Anders asked.

Thoran lowered his voice to a faint whisper. "Not here, but elsewhere, where they can question them without interference."

24

Useless Inquiries

KRISTDOKAR'S IMPLANTS CHIMED with an incoming call with so much priority, she had rarely seen it's like in all her years of service to the Supremacy. An officious looking young man appeared in her virtual vision. He sat at a desk, his hair tied back in a simple, unflattering ponytail. He had much more pepper than salt in his hair, and his cheekbones prominently emphasized the sharp features of his face. Her implants identified him as the chief administrative assistant to the Larscom Executive Council. It was rumored that one of the councilwomen had taken him as a lover, but the fellow wasn't that handsome, so Kristdokar wondered at the veracity of that information.

He looked her way with lifeless and unkind eyes. "Brigadier Skalde Kristdokar, by order of the Executive Council you are to report without delay to the council chambers."

Coming just one day after Mistress Vreekande's abduction, she had no doubt what had triggered such an order. She nodded once to acknowledge the directive. "How long should I plan to be away?"

His lips curled upward slightly, adding a lifeless smile to the lifeless eyes. "The Council did not specify an expected duration for your stay."

"It will take me at least three hours by air to reach Emkeldstadt."

He shook his head. "I've personally made the arrangements for your travel. The gate guards at Hyerdride Base will direct you."

"I will leave immediately."

When they ended the call, Kristdokar called a hired car. Then she retrieved a uniform from the closet in her office, and quickly changed into it. In the back of the closet she kept a small duffel stocked with items she might need on a sudden, unplanned trip. She carefully folded a second uniform, stuffed that and a few additional items into the duffel, then carried it with her as she left her office. When she stepped out of the offices of Friedrikdahl Import-Export, the hired car had just arrived.

The short drive to Hyerdride Base lasted only a few minutes. When Kristdokar identified herself, the gate guard pointed the driver to an aircraft on the tarmac, and he steered the vehicle in that direction. As they approached the plane, the pilot fired up its engines, and when the car came to a stop nearby Kristdokar didn't wait for the driver to open the door for her. She immediately climbed out of the sedan, then up a ramp and into the aircraft. A few minutes later it raced down the base's main runway and lifted off.

Kristdokar had expected a summons from Nygaard, her primary contact on the Executive Council, not a directive from the Council itself. When possible the vice skalde forewarned her of any prickly issues she might face. So why the change?

In the city of Emkeldstadt, Kristdokar's transport landed at Capital Airport, which was reserved for visiting dignitaries, prominent officials within the Larscom, and high ranking military officers, usually a lot higher ranking than Kristdokar. The aircraft taxied down an access strip, into a large hanger, and stopped beside a grav boat with the emblem of the Capital Guard on its side.

When Kristdokar stepped into the grav boat she found Nikaela's grandmother waiting for her. Slight of stature, Major Skalde Adeska Vreekande was not an imposing figure unless one did something to draw her ire. Already seated, she smiled at Kristdokar and patted the seat next to her. "Sit down. We only have a few minutes to talk."

The older woman had sponsored Kristdokar at the beginning of her career, and the two were still close. Kristdokar returned the woman's smile and sat down. "It's good to see you, Adeska, though I assume this is not a friendly visit."

They quickly established an encrypted link between their implants. "Watch out for Haugrund," Vreekande said. "She wants to shut down your operation."

"But why?"

"She's having trouble getting past the Blacksword thing, though at this point not even she doubts that the two young people are breschkada."

Vreekande gently placed a hand on Kristdokar's knee. "Now tell me exactly what happened to Nikaela."

Kristdokar described the bullet ridden apartment. "We found Nikaela's blood with traces of a drug that would paralyze her, and we think it quite clear they carried her away alive. Though if she still lives, we have no way of knowing that."

The older woman's brows narrowed in thought. "They clearly wanted her alive, and if they kill a breschkada it would look very bad for them, so they'll probably do what they can to keep her healthy, at least for the time being."

Vreekande leaned back in her seat. "Dornmier and Tiegnordan are neutral on the Blacksword issue, but they support your operation because they do want to know if there are rogue elements operating without official sanction, especially when they do something like kill twenty million people in such a way it appears the Supremacy was responsible. Nygaard and Veskarson support you fully, but don't make them look bad."

Kristdokar decided to tell her former sponsor what they had learned in their investigations. She spoke of Tiegnordan's possible involvement through Norddansk, and of the four shipping destinations on Sarkovie, though she kept Eindride's name out of it and simply referred to him as *a source.*

The older woman shook her head vehemently. "I don't believe for a moment Tiegnordan is involved. You're going to have to give the Council something to keep their support enthusiastic. I'd say give them Norddansk and Transmarin, but not those addresses on Sarkovie, or that you have an asset in the rogue operation. Don't mention Tiegnordan. Let them draw that conclusion themselves."

At that moment the grav boat settled onto the lawn in front of the old Hyvaldsborg palace. As a member of the Capital Guard opened the boat's hatch, Kristdokar stood while Vreekande remained seated.

Nikaela's grandmother gave her a conspiratorial smile. "I shouldn't be seen with you, so I'll have them drop me off elsewhere."

••••

"We went out dancing and he left the restaurant with Nash Wakeland," May said.

With her and Karya seated at a table in an interrogation room, Katrine paced back and forth in front of them. Both young women appeared quite frightened, or perhaps concerned, or maybe both.

The two really didn't have much to tell. Katrine had briefly entertained the idea that May or Karya, or both, were plants like Wakeland. But Timmerson had separated them and interrogated them individually at length. And in the hours since the shootout on campus, he and his people had scrubbed their records quite thoroughly. Something would have surfaced if they weren't really who they said they were.

Katrine stopped pacing, leaned forward, and placed her hands flat on the table. "Tell me about Wakeland."

Karya shrugged. "I met him briefly once or twice, but that's all. Don't really know him at all well."

May's eyes hardened with obvious anger. "And I know him well enough to know I don't like him. Did he have something to do with this?"

Katrine ignored the question. They had yet to release any details of the incident on campus, so neither May or Karya knew that Nash Wakeland—Willis—now lay on a slab in the morgue. She thought it best to keep it that way for a while.

Katrine said, "Why don't you like him?"

"He's a bad influence," May said. "It's like he wants to get John in trouble, always pushing him to drink more, once even tried to get him to fight an asshole in a bar. Pushed him pretty hard trying to do so."

"How so?"

May described the incident in the bar. Katrine had known the grosser details, because she received an immediate report on anything involving John Mathius. But she hadn't known Wakeland had pushed John to fight the blond fellow.

Karya said, "After that jerk sucker punched John, he was really pissed and I think he was ready to take the guy on, but May stopped him."

"I thank you for that," Katrine said. She didn't want to intimidate them too much, so she took her hands off the table, straightened, and stopped looming over them.

She quizzed them at length to fill in the blanks in her knowledge of the incident, but anything they might contribute ended when John and Wakeland walked out the door of the restaurant. And none of it would help her find John. If John hadn't killed the blond fellow, they would have hauled him in on general principle—if they could find him. In the hope of identifying the man's accomplice, Timmerson's people were reviewing the bar's records and any vid footage from that night, but Katrine suspected that would just be another dead end.

"You're both free to go," she said.

May asked, "Is John okay?"

Katrine shook her head. "No."

"How bad is he hurt?"

"We don't know."

Katrine looked pointedly at Karya, and there must have been something in her face because the young woman's eyes widened. "You're a journalist," Katrine said. "I've invoked a Class-One Blacksword security alert on this, so make sure you forget everything you've seen or heard tonight. When I'm ready to release information, I'll give you a one hour scoop. But before that, if I see anything that leads me to believe it came from you . . ."

Katrine hesitated; it wouldn't be wise to make threats.

Karya nodded, her eyes still wide with fear. "You don't need to say anything more, Colonel. Message received loud and clear."

May said, "You're really scary when you're pissed-off."

••••

"She is breschkada," Tiegnordan said, "a rare thing indeed. What did you do to protect her?"

Again, Kristdokar stood before the Executive Council with an empty gallery behind her. "When not in a secure facility, she went armed at all times. We found her grav pistol in her apartment; all its rounds had been expended. And we found evidence she had wounded one or more of her assailants, though they wiped the evidence with a DNA scrambler so we have no hope of definitively identifying them."

Tiegnordan drummed her fingers on the table in front of her for a second. "I assume you took more precautions than that."

Kristdokar wanted to say something like, *Of course we did*, but sarcasm would not serve her well. "We run a secure military network overlaid on citynet, with an emergency response number that triggers a rapid response team ready to deploy at all times. Mistress Vreekande's assailants jammed our network, which produced an alert when her implants went offline, but that did not immediately deploy the team the way the emergency response number would have."

At her words, all five members of the Council showed reactions varying from anger to consternation. Veskarson spoke carefully, "Did I hear you say someone jammed a secure military network?"

Kristdokar simply said, "Yes." She didn't need to spell it out for them. It was not the first time her opponents had demonstrated capabilities far beyond some petty criminal enterprise.

Nygaard said, "Shortly after her abduction, you diverted a destroyer to Sarkovie. Explain yourself."

Kristdokar had anticipated that question, and heeding Adeska Vreekande's advice, she had come up with a plausible explanation to keep Eindride's name out of the conversation. "We found evidence that a powerful Kelk company and a large Commonwealth conglomerate may be cooperating in a fairly sophisticated joint operation out of that star system."

Kristdokar had not had time to brief Nygaard beforehand. The councilwoman demanded, "What evidence?"

Kristdokar knew she could end her own career at a moment like that. "Mistress Vreekande uncovered an invoice trail that connected the two companies. We also obtained forensic evidence that both were involved in Novalis III and Reisenar, if not directly, then at least peripherally."

Haugrund slapped the palm of her hand down on the table in front of her. "Name these two companies."

Kristdokar couldn't help but grimace a little as she said, "Transmarin Industries in the Commonwealth, and Norddansk Weapons Systems here."

At the mention of Norddansk, Tiegnordan started. "Are you certain of this?"

Kristdokar needed to soften the blow a little. "I'm certain of the evidence, and it does point to culpability on the part of both companies, though that is a conclusion. We do not yet have a smoking gun."

Tiegnordan's eyes hardened with anger. "This should have been brought to my attention as soon as you learned of it. Why was I not informed of this earlier?"

Dornmier displayed a faint smile as she leaned forward and looked down the length of the table at Tiegnordan. "My dear Amita, I would guess you were not informed because she could not be certain you are not a traitor."

Tiegnordan looked ready to chew nails.

Dornmier continued. "And don't blame the brigadier. She had no choice but to move cautiously. But,"—Dornmier turned her attention to Kristdokar—"there is no doubt in my mind that if Norddansk is culpable, Vice Skalde Tiegnordan was not party to any of their rogue activities."

It was time to back down, so Kristdokar acknowledged that statement by closing her eyes and nodding her head once.

Tiegnordan appeared to regain her calm. "Sarkovie? Are you certain of that?"

Kristdokar shrugged. "We know only that Norddansk and Transmarin had something to do with Novalis III and Reisenar, and that they appear to be operating jointly out of Sarkovie, which is in the near vicinity of both systems. Beyond that, I can be certain of nothing. They clearly intended to abduct Mistress Vreekande, not kill her, and I would guess that by now they have spirited her off planet."

Veskarson looked right and left, carefully making eye contact with each of his four colleagues on the Council. "Does anyone have any further questions for the brigadier?"

They all voiced general agreement that they were finished with Kristdokar, though Haugrund and Tiegnordan got into an argument.

"Enough," Veskarson said, cutting them off. He focused on Kristdokar. "Brigadier Skalde Kristdokar, we thank you for your time and candor. We're going to discuss this matter in closed session, but we may have further need of your insight, so please wait outside in the hallway. We shouldn't be terribly long."

Kristdokar bowed, turned, and walked out of the room. An aide closed the doors to the chamber, and two Capital guardswomen took up positions on either side of the entrance. Kristdokar couldn't sit still so she paced up and down the hallway.

After about ten minutes, the doors to the chamber opened and the five councilmembers filed out of the room. Nygaard took Kristdokar by the elbow and pulled her to one side, establishing a secure, encrypted link between their implants. "Haugrund is rather hot-headed, and I often get the impression she would like war with the Commonwealth, but even her feathers have been ruffled by the machinations of these schemers and their accomplices. Interestingly enough, we seem to be more upset that someone is trying to manipulate us, than that they murdered twenty million people. Tiegnordan is going to cautiously look into what she can learn through her connections at Norddansk. And you and I are going to Sarkovie on a heavy cruiser with lots of teeth."

25

Advancement

WHEN ANDERS FINISHED his shift he desperately wanted to talk to Thoran and try to learn anything he could. But if he appeared too eager about information regarding Nikaela Vreekande, that could get him killed. As luck would have it, Thoran approached him in the locker room and said, "I need a drink. Join me."

Anders nodded, stripped out of his transit uniform and pulled on street clothes. He followed Thoran out of the building, and they walked to the bar where they usually met. Thoran selected a corner of the bar where none of the nearby tables were occupied. A waiter took their order for kirva, water, and shot glasses. They talked about the poor wages they made as transit engineers, and other work-related issues of no consequence. They continued the meaningless chat until the waiter delivered their drinks, then walked across the room to wait on another table.

Thoran filled two shot glasses with kirva, and raised his as if toasting Anders. "I've got good news for you, friend." He tossed the fiery liquid down his throat in a single gulp.

Anders needed to keep a clear head, so he merely sipped at his drink. "What news is that, my friend?"

Thoran grinned. "You have a chance to move up in the world."

"Really? How so?"

Thoran glanced over his shoulder, leaned close to Anders, and spoke softly. "A certain command eagle is impressed with your discretion. She would like to offer you a higher position in her organization. It will mean more money."

Recalling that Thoran and his covert friends had distrusted Gaertkine because of his singular interest in the money, Anders spoke in the same soft tones. "The money I'm getting now is more than sufficient."

Thoran grinned as if he approved of that answer. "It will mean more responsibility."

Anders lifted an eyebrow. "That might interest me."

Thoran's grin broadened and he lowered his voice to a whisper. "And maybe a chance to get even with that bitch that put you in SecureMax."

Anders leaned forward, nodding his head. "That would definitely interest me. But why me, why now?"

"We need to replace a certain off-planet asset. She was playing both sides, so she's been removed. You were an officer, and she's management, so you fit the job description."

"Off planet?"

Thoran nodded. "Yes. If you accept, we'll move you off Viktorkinde, and that'll happen very quickly."

"Where?"

Thoran shook his head. "You'll know that only when you get there, and you won't be able to take Viktra with you."

Anders shrugged. "Our relationship is one of . . . mutual convenience. We satisfy each other's physical needs. If we must end it, there'll be no tears."

"Then you accept?"

Thoran's words about it happening quickly made Anders cautious. He needed to make sure he would have a chance to communicate this information to Kristdokar. "Let me think about it."

"We have a ship leaving shortly. It's on a tight schedule, and if it leaves without you, the offer's off the table, so don't take too long to decide."

Anders raised his glass and tossed the rest of his drink down in a gulp. "I won't."

He took great care not to rush back to Viktra's apartment. When he got her alone and could set up a secure link between their implants, he told her what he had learned from Thoran.

When he finished she nodded carefully, then said aloud, "We're a little short on some groceries. I'll be back in a couple of hours."

She left him alone in the apartment, returned two hours later, and gave him the contact information for friendly assets on both Norandyne and Sarkovie. "Kristdokar says if you end up on either of those two planets, you can communicate with her through them. But if you end up elsewhere, you're probably on your own."

Anders and Viktra spent the night together enjoying each other's company, probably for the last time. The next morning he returned to his apartment and placed a call to Thoran. "That new career path we discussed yesterday evening. If the offer's still open, I accept."

"Good man," Thoran said. "We'll handle your resignation with the transit authority, and close down your apartment. Pack light and be out on the street in front of your apartment in two hours."

Two hours later, standing on the sidewalk, a sedan pulled up to the curb in front of Anders. He saw the dark shadows of the driver in the front seat and a passenger in the back. The rear door opened, and a female voice said, "Anders Eindride?"

"That's me."

"Please join me."

Anders climbed into the back seat of the car and sat next to a woman in civilian clothing. As the sedan sped away she handed him a package. Anders opened it and found a new DNA-tagged identity card listing him as Anders Karsten. When he touched it a small emblem flashed green.

The woman said, "You're now an employee of Norddansk Mining and Exploration, and you'll shortly be boarding *Sycorax*, one of their survey ships. The card contains a special code-block you should upload into your implants to support that identity."

Anders raised a skeptical eyebrow. To supersede the identification protocols, he would have to allow dangerously deep access, and he wasn't about to upload anyone's unverified code into the heart of his implants. It might include subvert-ware to make him a virtual slave.

The woman shook her head. "Don't worry, you don't have to give it ring-zero access; just ring one. That'll be sufficient for anything but a secure government or military facility."

She uploaded a summary of his new identity, including a short background and history. Anders Karsten was ex-military and had worked for a few years as a transit engineer, but recently hired onto Norddansk to manage a new operation off-planet. The history gave no hint as to his final destination.

"We made your background as close to the truth as possible. Less likelihood of a slip-up, that way."

After that, they rode in silence for more than an hour. The car took them to a large Norddansk Mining and Exploration facility outside of Hyerdride. After passing through security at the front gate, the driver pulled the sedan onto a taxiway running parallel to a large airstrip. A few hundred meters in the distance Anders spotted the squat shape of a heavy assault boat, with gun turrets protruding from its nose, sides, and tail. The driver stopped the car next to the boat, and the woman seated beside Anders said, "They're waiting for you. Have a safe journey."

Anders stepped out of the sedan, tossed his duffel over his shoulder, and walked the short distance to the open hatch in the side of the boat. A crewman in civilian clothing waited inside the hatch. He waved to an empty bank of seats designed to accommodate anything from simple civilian clothing to powered combat armor. "Take any seat you want."

One other passenger had taken a seat toward the front of the craft. He appeared to be wearing the uniform of a med tech. Anders wasn't in the mood for conversation, so he chose one of the few seats with a window. As the boat lifted off the tarmac, he watched the sun set and considered what he had learned in that car. Like Norddansk Weapons Systems, Norddansk Interstellar owned Norddansk Mining and Exploration. Did that mean someone in the parent company pulled the strings for the rogue operation in both subsidiaries?

To his surprise the boat didn't stop at Viktorkinde Prime, but spent over twelve hours driving out-system before rendezvousing with a much larger vessel. He didn't have any instruments in front of him, so he relied on educated guesswork and some simple calculations, but that would indicate they had travelled more than a hundred million kilometers from Viktorkinde.

As the boat approached the open docking bay of the exploration ship *Sycorax*, Anders caught a brief glimpse of the larger craft. He wondered why a mining and exploration survey ship would need gun turrets and transition batteries.

The boat mated to a docking boom that extended out of the open hatch of a large hangar bay. The boom then retracted, pulling the boat into its berth next to another heavy assault boat.

Survey ship indeed!

Anders waited while they sealed and re-pressurized the hangar bay, then opened the large troop hatch in the side of the boat. The other passenger in the med tech uniform stood and preceded Ander out through the hatch. When Anders followed and stepped onto the deck of the ship, a young female officer wearing a merchant spacer uniform greeted him. "Anders Karsten?"

Anders nodded. "Yes."

She hooked a thumb over her shoulder. "I'll show you to your quarters."

As Anders followed her across the deck, a small crew of technicians opened the cargo hatch in the back of the boat. The med tech supervised them as they carefully eased a portable med unit out through the hatch. Floating on its grav fields, the unit was about the size of a large coffin. Flashing lights on the unit's instruments told Anders it was occupied.

Allship blared, "Stand by for maneuvering."

Until that moment the ship's hull had been silent, but now he felt the vibrations of its engines through the soles of his boots. He briefly wondered about the occupant of that med unit.

••••

Katrine went down to the large bullpen where John had been assigned a desk as her aide de camp. She sat down at his desk and searched it carefully. She had already searched his dorm room but found nothing there beyond the normal stuff a young cadet might keep on hand. She found even less in his Armed Services Office Building desk.

She used her implants to tap into his call log, and her clearances to override the privacy settings there. She went through his log and found he had made a call to a senatorial aide named Charlie Maskers. She called Maskers and he answered immediately.

"Maskers here, Colonel Primatov. What can I do for you?"

"My aide de camp, John Mathius, spoke with you about a month ago. What did you talk about?"

"I interned at Transmarin Industries about five years ago, and he wanted to know what it was like."

"What did you tell him?"

"Not much. I mean I was about as low as they come in that organization. The work was even more menial than what I do here."

"Did anyone from Transmarin ask you about John's inquiries?"

"No, how would they know?"

Maskers knew less than nothing, and hadn't spoken to anyone from Transmarin in several years.

John had also made a call to an investment advisor named Theresa Vasquez. John's pitiful stipend as a cadet didn't leave anything left for investments, so that immediately drew Katrine's interest. She called the number, asked for Miss Vasquez, and was put through with only a slight delay.

"What can I do for you, Colonel Primatov?" Vasquez asked.

"About a month ago you spoke with Cadet John Mathius. What did you two discuss?"

"I'm sorry, ma'am, but I'm not allowed to discuss Cadet Mathius's investment inquiries with you unless he personally authorizes me to do so."

Katrine closed her eyes and rubbed her temples. "This is a Class-One Black-sword security issue. I need to know what you discussed with Mr. Mathius." Katrine sent the young woman a confirming authorization.

The young woman's eyebrows furrowed in thought. "That doesn't change any-thing."

They went back and forth a couple of times, but Vasquez refused to give her any information. Katrine realized the young woman was simply being stubborn. Katrine ended the call, then used her implants to trigger a Class-One security warning to the legal department of Vasquez's investment firm. Twenty seconds later her implants chimed. Katrine answered, and found herself on a three-way with Miss Vasquez, and the firm's chief legal officer.

She quickly learned John had inquired about Transmarin Industries. "There wasn't much I could do for him," Vasquez said, "so as a courtesy I registered his contact profile with Transmarin for investment updates."

"Did anyone at Transmarin contact you about that?"

"No," she said. "They're a big outfit. They must get a couple hundred registrants like that every day."

"Thank you," Katrine said, and ended the call.

She leaned back in John's chair, and said to no one in particular, "John, you poor, dumb, overly-conscientious fool."

Vasquez had registered his name with Transmarin, and that had probably trig-gered a red flag someone had set within their system. It might not have been based specifically on his name, but could have been triggered by his Blacksword status. And then there'd be the connection to her, which was publicly available information. There would be people in an organization like Transmarin who had the clout to dig quite deeply into a person's past, if they really wanted to. They had probably come up with some references to Reisenar, and maybe even Novalis III, and then someone connected the dots.

If Transmarin had abducted John, they would most likely try to spirit him out of the system. But the only way she could stop them would be to seize all Transmarin assets in Trafalgar nearspace, and the evidence she had wouldn't come close to supporting that. Within hours of any legal action on her part, Transmarin's lawyers would have a court order negating it.

Her implants chimed with a call from Thealone. "Katrine, as you suggested I contacted Tarsik Obradour. I'm going to put you on a three-way with him now."

Katrine closed her eyes and saw images of Thealone and Obradour as if they sat together in the same room.

"Colonel Primatov," Obradour said. "It's always good to talk with you. How have you been since we last spoke?"

"I'm fine, Mr. Obradour, but I'm feeling a certain sense of urgency right now."

"Yes," he said. "I'm told young Mr. Mathius was attacked."

"He was abducted."

Obradour continued as if ignoring her words. "I thought you might be interested to learn that the research vessel *Caliban* has filed a transition plan to a remote star system where they'll be spending months out of touch with the rest of the Commonwealth. They'll be conducting research that will hopefully lead to methods of manufacturing heretofore unheard-of, and previously non-existent, rare earth elements. Scientifically it's quite exciting, don't you think?"

"Well," Katrine said. "Yes, I . . . I suppose so. But I . . ."

Obradour smiled and said, "Of course, that's all bollocks."

"It . . . It is?"

"Yes," he said. "They're not going anywhere near that star system. *Caliban* is funded by Transmarin Industries, auspiciously a purely altruistic venture. And it's crewed by Transmarin employees, all ex ComSecCorps, and all hardline anti-Kelk, not a real scientist among them. Doesn't sound like a research vessel, does it?"

He didn't wait for her to answer. "And it's parked about four astronomical units out. I think the greatest danger your young man faces is if his abductors can get him off-planet and out of the Trafalgar system. Colonel Blacksword and I have discussed this, and she can make sure that doesn't happen on a ComSecCorps warship. And I've got my people scouring the docks, double-checking any commercial vessels scheduled to depart shortly. But Mr. Mathius's abductors wouldn't be stupid enough to try to pass him through Trafalgar Prime, because between us we can lock that space station up tight."

He paused and Katrine finished the thought for him. "And a ship parked four AUs out could avoid all that."

"Exactly," Obradour said. "And certain sources of mine tell me *Caliban* is ready to go, but they're waiting for a consignment of high-priority cargo to be delivered before they depart. Unfortunately, I don't have any information on the specific nature of that cargo, but I suggest you do what you can to prevent *Caliban*'s departure."

"I . . ." she said. "Well . . . uhhh . . . thank you."

"Oh, one more thing," Obradour said. "Don't believe what you see in the nautical registry regarding *Caliban*'s capabilities and complete lack of armaments. That's all bollocks as well. Bring a fast ship with lots of sharp teeth."

He withdrew from the call, and Katrine thought Thealone's eyes reflected her own surprise. Thealone said, "Hold for a few seconds."

She went offline, and about twenty seconds later came back into the call. "*Lightspear* is a fast hunter-killer scheduled to depart from Trafalgar Prime in about eight hours, destination Miriteen, captained by Commander Martin Neilosse. Admiral Harcourt owes me a couple of big favors, and if anyone goes all bureaucratic on me, Obradour offered to drop a hint or two to the right people. Given the circumstances, I'm sure I can get Harcourt to put *Lightspear* at your disposal. Pack your bags, Katrine, and get up there ASAP."

A hunter-killer; would that be good enough? Katrine's mind raced as she tried to consider the possibilities. "Without a court order, we can't simply waylay *Caliban* and board her."

Thealone winced. "Good point." She hesitated for an instant, clearly lost in thought. "I'll pull Mani Gascoigne into this. That sneaky bastard can get really creative at moments like this. You just worry about getting up to *Lightspear*."

••••

Nikaela woke up still lying on her back in a bed and realized they were controlling her sleep. The ceiling above her was no longer the off-white she recalled from her last awakening, but a drab gray-green, telling her they had moved her.

This time she could move her head, hands, and arms. With a little experimentation she learned her captors had now allowed her to have full muscle control and function from the waist up. She glanced to left and right and counted one other empty bed beside hers, confirming that they had isolated her from other patients, if there were other patients.

The door opened and the surly med tech entered the room. The tone of his voice made it clear his opinion of her had not changed. "Good, you're awake."

He helped her sit up in bed, then left without another word. A few minutes later he returned pushing a grav cart containing a hot meal. He floated the tray of food on its grav fields just above her lap.

She asked him, "Why no feeling from the waist down?"

He looked at her carefully for a moment, probably getting instructions through his implants on what questions he could answer. "The tissue damage to your thigh was quite severe. They tell me you did it to yourself. Why?"

"They shot me with something," she said. "I had to get it out of me before it did what it would do."

His upper lip curled into a snarl. "Too bad you didn't let it do what it was going to do."

She recalled also being shot in the shoulder. She reached up and tested the wound site there, but felt no pain or sensitivity.

The tech said, "That wound was much cleaner. We've already got that healed. The thigh wound though, we're going to be regenerating tissue for another day. Try to keep your hands away from it."

"Why fix me up," Nikaela asked, "if you're just going to kill me anyway?"

He shook his head. "I wouldn't know. I'm pretty low on the roster here. They don't tell me anything. But if I had any say in the matter . . ."

He didn't finish the thought, but simply turned and left the room.

Nikaela felt a slight vibration running through the bed. She guessed it came through the floor and the walls of her room, or more appropriately, the deck and bulkheads. In her short life she had spent many months on interstellar warships, and knew deep in her bones the way the faint vibrations of a big ship's engines propagated through its hull. They had put her on board a naval ship of some sort, and she was probably now quite far from Viktorkinde.

••••

When John next awoke, he lay in some sort of coffin-like chamber lit by very faint illumination. They had completely blocked his nervous system and he couldn't move at all, and thankfully they had blocked the pain as well. The coffin seemed familiar, and then he recalled a training session he'd attended while part of the marine contingent on the ComSecCorps destroyer *Defiant*. His captors had stuffed him into a mobile, automated med unit.

Something shook him from side to side. The med units he had trained on floated on their own gravity fields, but didn't include internal compensation to null out the effects of motion. More movement, more jostling; they must be moving him to some other location.

Time blinked and John awoke again still in the med unit. He felt the faint vibration of a boat's engines. They had a decidedly different character when compared to the vibrations of a big transition ship's drive. Not only had they gotten him out of the city. They'd spirited him off Trafalgar as well. He fell asleep wondering where he would wake up next.

26

Ahead of the Prey

KATRINE THREW A couple sets of fatigues and a selection of uniforms into a travel duffel. Since she was fully qualified in Naval Ops she could switch to naval uniforms at her discretion, but didn't have any on hand so her Infantry Ops uniforms would have to do. She added a few personal items, but kept it to a bare minimum. Anything else she might need she could probably requisition from ship's stores, or, if not, then she'd just have to live without it.

The assault boat again picked her up in front of her apartment building. Air traffic in the area prevented the pilot from simply firewalling the boat's drive and streaking up through the atmosphere to Trafalgar Prime. Traffic Control limited them to a one-G lift instead of the boat's full capability of thirty, at least until they got out of atmosphere. Katrine tapped into an exterior vid feed and watched the city drop away beneath her.

Her implants chimed with a call from Thealone. "Katrine, *Lightspear* is all yours. They're recalling the last of her crew now and she'll be ready to depart as soon as you get there. I don't know her CO's attitude on the Kelk issue, so I spoke personally with him and told him the whole thing is need-to-know. You can decide how much to tell him once you're under way."

Katrine's frustration at the restrictions placed on her boat by traffic control boiled to the surface. "Can you get us some priority through this traffic?"

Thealone shook her head. "I thought of that myself, but *Caliban* isn't scheduled to depart for another twenty-eight hours. It occurred to me that if they're monitoring emergency traffic, and they see someone coming their way in a hurry, that might spook them."

"You're right," Katrine said. "Should have thought of that myself."

It might take an hour or two to get up to Prime, another hour to make the transfer, but once the hunter-killer cleared the immediate neighborhood of the big satellite, the ship could do close to ten thousand G's in sublight. They could cross the four AUs to *Caliban* in about an hour and a half.

"Any luck with Gascoigne?" Katrine asked.

Thealone gritted her teeth and grimaced. "Yes and no. I'm going to bring him online so he can tell you himself."

Senator Manifort Gascoigne appeared in Katrine's virtual vision as if sitting next to Thealone. "Colonel Primatov," he said, "Colonel Blacksword is cutting you orders to take command of *Lightspear*. And the Intelligence Committee has issued a mandate for you to look into the new evidence we've uncovered regarding Novalis III."

Katrine was not aware of anything new, not something hard enough to take official action against a ship like *Caliban*. "What new evidence?"

Gascoigne gave her a big cheesy grin. "We're leaving that really vague. You've got a senatorial Class-One clearance authorization on this, which gives you a lot of room to maneuver. But wait until you're out in the boondocks somewhere before you try anything with *Caliban*. At a minimum, make sure you're not within transition-com range of any Commonwealth facilities, then do what you have to do."

He leaned forward and gave her a hard, unyielding look. "Don't get me wrong, Colonel. I'm not doing this for your young man. You and your Kelk comrades appear to be zeroing in on a much bigger issue, and that is of overriding importance. Remember, that takes priority over his life . . . or yours . . . or mine, for that matter."

Katrine nodded. "I understand, sir."

Gascoigne smiled and his tone softened. "But he seemed like a good kid, so if you can save his life, that would be nice."

Katrine returned his smile. "I won't forget my priorities, sir."

They ended the call, and Katrine got a message from central billeting telling her that her personal combat armor had been transferred to *Lightspear*. The orders Thealone had cut assigning her to the hunter-killer's crew had triggered a predefined sequence of events.

When they cleared atmosphere, traffic control let the pilot push the boat up to five G's. Seven minutes later he began decelerating, and seven minutes after that, as they approached the station, he slowed the boat to a near crawl.

Katrine climbed out of her seat and waited at the drop hatch as the assault boat docked at Trafalgar Prime. When her implants got the all-clear, she activated the hatch and it dilated with a whoosh. With her duffel over one shoulder, she hit the docks at a run and caught the periphery tube. Five minutes later it dropped her off at a station only a few minutes' walk from *Lightspear*'s assigned dock.

She marched down the dock to the hunter-killer's personnel hatch, and there she ran into a team of six Blackswords also boarding the ship. On their shoulders they wore the patch of Zeta Company, Blacksword Special Forces. But the Z on their patches lay on its side so it appeared as a distorted N; they had all come from Assault Team Null. They were known as nullheads, even called themselves that. But with few exceptions, anyone outside of Zeta Company who used that term in their presence might learn a very unpleasant lesson.

Katrine knew their leader, Captain Edward Fleming, but had never worked with him before, so she didn't know him well. He stood a few centimeters shorter than her, had dark brown hair, blue eyes and a pleasant smile. When he saw her coming his way, he turned to greet her. They exchanged salutes, and she extended her hand.

"Colonel," he said, shaking her hand. "I'm looking forward to working with you."

Katrine didn't try to hide her surprise. "I didn't know you'd be joining me." She hoped none of them had a problem working with the Kelk, if it came to that, but didn't know how to broach that subject with him.

He nodded. "Colonel Blacksword thought we might be of assistance. She told me to bring a select group of my best."

He glanced over his shoulder at his team of two women and three men. Then he turned back to Katrine, leaned close to her, and lowered his voice. "She also told me to pick among those who would have no problem working with . . . unusual comrades."

At that, Katrine couldn't hide a smile. "Have you been briefed?"

He nodded again. "Colonel Blacksword asked me to give you this message."

Her implants got a request for an upload and informed her that it was fully encrypted, and authenticated as Blacksword Class-One. She granted the request, and a virtual image of Fran Thealone appeared in her sight. "Katrine, I've fully briefed Ed on all the salient details of both Novalis III and Reisenar, including the information not on record. Ed's good, you can trust him."

The image disappeared and Katrine focused again on Fleming. "Your people have been briefed as well?"

"Yes, but to a lesser extent."

"Glad to have you with me."

He smiled. "You have a reputation, ma'am, a good one. You can count on me and my people for anything, especially if anyone is reluctant to give you their full cooperation." His smile widened into a shit-eating grin. "We'll politely nudge them in the right direction."

Fleming introduced her to the members of his team, and they stepped aside while she boarded *Lightspear*. She stepped through the personnel hatch, her duffel over one shoulder, then turned to the Commonwealth ensign draped from a bulkhead and saluted it. She turned to the officer of the deck, a female lieutenant j. g. with a name tag that read MERTAUGH. She saluted, saying, "Lieutenant Colonel Katrine Primatov requesting permission to board."

The young woman's eyes widened as she looked past Katrine at the nullheads standing behind her. The simple presence of a Null Team carried its own message to the crew.

Mertaugh returned Katrine's salute. "Welcome aboard, ma'am. Commander Neilosse, our CO, sends his respects and would like you to join him in his office as soon as you've stowed your gear."

Katrine turned around and extended her small duffel to Fleming. "Please dump this wherever they've got me billeted."

She turned back to Mertaugh. "Tell your skipper I'm available now."

The young woman's eyes focused in the distance as she relayed the message through her implants. Then Katrine's implants chimed. "Colonel, this is Neilosse. I'll be in my office when you get there."

Her implants projected a virtual overlay on the deck in front of her, with guidelines showing her the way. The commanding officer of every ComSecCorps ship bunked in a cabin next to the bridge to get there in an instant if needed. Katrine knew her way around a hunter-killer and didn't need the virtual directions, but they were standard procedure for anyone who had just joined the crew of a ship.

She found Neilosse's stateroom door open, with him seated at a small fold-down table. Even seated, she could tell he was a tall, gangly man. He pointed to a fold-down seat opposite him. "Close the door and have a seat."

She closed and latched his stateroom door, and as she sat down a loud clang echoed through the hull of the ship.

Allship blared, "Cast-off sequence initiated."

Neilosse didn't waste any time. "I know we're operating under a senatorial Class-One clearance authorization, and Colonel Blacksword told me this is all need-to-know, but what can you tell me?"

How much could she tell him? She pondered that carefully. Under Class-One, and as a fully qualified naval CO with experience commanding a hunter-killer, she could take command of the ship. But she didn't know the ship or the crew, and that could be a fatal mistake if they faced an armed engagement with *Caliban*.

She decided to keep it simple. "If you're wondering if I intend to take command of your ship, no, I do not. Beyond that, we need to intercept the research vessel *Caliban*."

He made no effort to hide his disdain. "A research ship? Couldn't that have been done with a police boat?"

Tarsik Obradour had supplied details on *Caliban*'s true capabilities. She instructed her implants to upload them into Neilosse's confidential log, along with the transition plan the research ship's navigator had filed with Trafalgar traffic control. One of Neilosse's eyebrows lifted as his implants obviously informed him she was transmitting.

She nodded. "Those are the details on that research vessel's capabilities, along with the transition plan they filed. We have intelligence that indicates they don't intend to follow that plan, at least not completely."

His eyes glazed over, and he sat that way for a good minute while he reviewed the data on *Caliban*. Then his eyes focused on her. "That's no research vessel. That's a fucking light destroyer, and she's got us outgunned. Her transition batteries can easily take us apart anywhere inside three hundred million kilometers. Is she manned by nice, law-abiding citizens that'll obey us when we order them to heave-to?"

Katrine grimaced. "I seriously doubt it."

"I take it this information doesn't correlate with that filed in the nautical registry?"

"No," she said. "Not at all."

He leaned forward, his eyes focused intently on her. "How did they manage that?"

She didn't try to hide her own discomfort. "That ship is backed by a very powerful organization, and some very powerful people."

"Powerful enough to falsify the registry?"

"Yes, and they don't care about the legality of their actions."

He leaned back and took a deep breath.

She added, "You should keep that in mind."

Allship blared, "Cast-off sequence complete."

Neilosse put one hand flat on the small table between them. "Right now my XO has the conn. But very shortly I'm going to have to give my people orders on where we're going and what we're doing."

The falsified nautical registry records might be sufficient evidence to get a senatorial warrant to board the ship. But Obradour had cautioned them that doing so might expose some of his sources, and he had specifically prohibited that course of action. The moment Katrine had seen the specifications on *Caliban*'s armaments, she knew the rogue research ship had the hunter-killer outgunned. In any case, they needed to put considerable distance between them and Trafalgar before taking any action. They had a solid connection between Transmarin and *Caliban*, but only a soft connection between the research ship and those responsible for the incidents on Novalis III and Reisenar. And attempting to board or detain the ship wouldn't really advance their knowledge regarding that. *Priorities*, Katrine thought, recalling Gascoigne's words. *Priorities*.

Katrine looked carefully into Neilosse's eyes. "Can you follow them without them knowing we're on their tail?"

His brow wrinkled as he considered the question. "Are they going to follow the transition plan they filed?"

Katrine couldn't be sure of anything. "Probably—at least at first. They'll want it to look good when they up-transit out of the system, so I doubt they'll deviate from it until they're far enough out that TC can't detect their transition wake."

Neilosse nodded. "That's at least five light-years out, seven to eight if they want to be conservative."

He continued to nod and think in silence for several seconds, then he grinned. "Then the best way to follow them, is to lead them."

Priorities, Katrine thought. From everything they had found at the crime scene, it appeared John Mathius's captors hadn't killed him, at least not yet. And transporting him up to a ship would indicate they intended to take him somewhere. Hopefully, he wouldn't be in serious danger until they got there.

Priorities.

Neilosse stood. "You're welcome to join me on the bridge, Colonel."

His offer had been simple, polite courtesy. Given her orders and the authorization from the senate, she didn't really need his permission for that, but she knew full well she should defer to him on such matters. If she circumvented his authority over his crew, that would reduce their effectiveness, and she needed a fully functioning warship.

On the bridge, Neilosse introduced her to his XO, Lieutenant Commander Belta Sharma. She gave Katrine a wary look, but didn't say anything.

With a crew of sixty-four, hunter-killers were notoriously cramped when it came to free space. They didn't support backup positions at bridge duty stations, so she stood behind the scan tech and looked over his shoulders. She took care to move cautiously so she didn't bash her head on an instrument cluster hanging down from above, or one protruding from another console.

Once they cleared the immediate traffic in the neighborhood of Trafalgar Prime, Neilosse instructed the helm to drive at five thousand gravities. "We're capable of close to ten kiloGs," Neilosse said. "But under normal circumstances I wouldn't push her that hard, and we don't want to look like we're chasing anything. We're just another, ordinary ComSecCorps ship headed outbound for up-transition."

Driving straight toward their target would obviously spook them, so Neilosse angled *Lightspear* on a vector to one side of *Caliban*'s line. An hour and a half later they passed the research ship, though they didn't get any closer to it than about a hundred million kilometers. Their prey showed no sign that they had taken notice of the hunter-killer.

Three hours out from Prime at a distance of thirteen AU's, Neilosse ordered, "Drones out."

The ship's hull echoed repeatedly as they launched the hunter-killer's combat drones. Several seconds later the scan tech said, "Parasitic feed is smooth and clean, sir. All six drones are green and go."

Neilosse barked, "Hold them at fifty thousand klicks."

The drones took up a complex dance of interwoven orbits around *Lightspear*, and with an effective scan baseline of a hundred thousand kilometers, their resolution improved dramatically.

"Sir," the scan tech said. "I'm detecting a small craft approaching our target. It's about the size of a drop boat and looks to be decelerating for a rendezvous. Should reach them in about two hours."

Katrine turned about to look Neilosse in the eyes when she spoke to him. "That's what *Caliban*'s been waiting for. They've got one of my people captive, and as soon as he's on board they may choose to leave earlier than their scheduled transition plan."

Neilosse gave her a faint smile. "Don't worry, Colonel. We've got time to spare now. As long as they stick to that transition plan for at least a couple of light-years, we'll be waiting for them."

Fifty astronomical units out, *Lightspear* pulled in its combat drones and up-transited.

"Okay, people," Neilosse said. "Let's put the coals to this boat. Firewall her and give me four thousand lights. And then we've got some maneuvering to do if we want to be in position."

Thinking of John Mathius, Katrine softly uttered, "Priorities."

The scan tech looked over his shoulder. "Pardon, ma'am, I didn't catch that."

"Nothing," she said. "Just thinking out loud."

27

Lying in Wait

THE CREW OF *Sycorax* wore merchant spacer uniforms, while the scientific team wore standard civilian clothing, all very appropriate for a mining and exploration vessel. And yet the entire ship operated at a level of discipline much like that of a Kelk warship.

Anders was assigned to one of twelve bunks in a room he shared with members of the scientific team. As he unpacked his gear, one of the team's members, a middle aged woman, introduced herself. "Welcome aboard, Maestra Karsten. I'm Agneta Aanberg."

Anders smiled and nodded, thinking she bore herself more like a senior NCO than a scientist. "Nice to meet you, Mistress Aanberg."

"Please, call me Agne. I'm in charge of the scientific team. And you're ex-military, I'm told. What rank?"

The new history they had given him had not gone into such specifics, so he stayed with the truth. "Command Superior."

She smiled. "Many of us here are ex-military. Do you play cards?"

A card game would be a great way to learn more about his new crewmates. "Yah, as long as the stakes aren't too high. My bank account is a little thin."

She dismissed his concerns with a shake of her head. "Don't worry, we keep the bets small. We've got a game going now. When you finish stowing your gear, join us. I'll introduce you to the others."

A few hours later, seated at a table in the mess hall with Aanberg and three others, as Anders considered the cards in front of him, one of his new friends said, "Anyone know anything about that prisoner they brought on board?"

"Prisoner?" Anders asked. "We're transporting prisoners?"

The fellow shook his head and kept his eyes on his cards. "Just one. Someone pretty special, I hear."

Anders hoped he might learn something. "Special. How so?"

"Don't know," Aanberg said. "But I hear when we get where we're going, we're going to take on another."

Anders kept wondering who the occupant of that med unit had been, but forced himself not to speculate on wildly improbable answers to that question.

••••

More jostling and movement woke John. He still lay in the med unit, and again they were moving him to some other location. He heard what sounded like the blare of allship, though muted and muffled by the med unit's cover. They must be transferring him to a much larger vessel.

Sometime later he awoke again, still paralyzed, but no longer in the med unit. They had put him in a bed with a bank of instruments overhead that emitted the occasionally beep or ping. The faint vibration of the ship's hull confirmed his suspicion that they had moved him to a larger ship. He heard the muffled sounds of allship and an alert klaxon. They wouldn't pipe that stuff into sick bay, wouldn't want to disturb recuperating patients.

"I still say we should whack him." John recognized pissed-off guy's voice.

Calm-voice said, "That's why you don't give the orders."

"I've excised the damaged intestinal tract." That was the woman doctor or med tech. "The cultures are doing well and we should be able to replace the damaged gut sometime in the next few days."

"Good," calm-voice said, "then he's all mine."

••••

Immediately after up-transition Neilosse ordered the helmswoman to give the ship a slightly starboard drift. "I don't want to get too far off *Caliban*'s line."

With their original transition vector angled in a slightly different direction from that of *Caliban*'s scheduled transition plan, if they didn't compensate a little, they would be too far off course to make the adjustment when the time came.

Two hours and a little less than one light-year later, *Lightspear*'s vector had taken them about ten thousand AUs off *Caliban*'s planned transition vector. Neilosse ordered the helm to begin a long, slow turn to starboard. Katrine knew the technique well. The harder they maneuvered, the more transition noise they generated. That would produce a much stronger wake, and make it easier to detect them at interstellar distances with a transition scanner. If they had raised the suspicions of *Caliban*'s CO when they up-transited out of Trafalgar nearspace, and the research ship's scan tech was tracking *Lightspear* closely, they might realize what Neilosse intended. Katrine could only hope *Caliban*'s crew was much too busy with preparations for their own departure, and didn't have time to pay attention to a lowly hunter-killer outbound on some sort of mundane mission for the Commonwealth.

A half hour later they reversed the process and began a long slow turn to port. The bridge grew silent as tension weighed heavily on all of them.

"Anything from our target?" Neilosse asked.

The scan tech shook his head. "Negative, sir. Plenty of transition noise and several transition flares coming out of the Trafalgar system. But that's to be expected, and nothing even close to *Caliban*."

In transition they could only detect grosser transition phenomena, like stellar masses, or flares emitted by ships up-transiting or down-transiting, so for all intents and purposes they were blind. At that moment *Caliban* might be driving hard in sublight to up-transit out of the system, and they wouldn't know until she did so. But to accurately track the ship, they needed to down-transit before then.

"Helm," Neilosse said. "Steady as she goes, and let's start dumping lights, but do it slow and careful."

They had swung around in a long, slow S-curve, first turning to starboard, and then to port. By doing so they had closed the distance between their vector and *Caliban*'s transition plan. They were now pushing lights directly away from the research ship along its expected vector for up-transition.

"One hundred lights, sir," the helmswoman said. "I'm seeing the first signs of transition instability."

A low-level gravity wave fluttered through the bridge, so faint it was almost below Katrine's ability to sense it. She knew from experience that if Neilosse and his crew were good, it would soon get worse, much worse.

"Fifty lights, sir"

Neilosse leaned forward, staring intently at his screens. "Remember helm, we want to keep our flare to a minimum. Your record is fourteen lights. If you can beat that, I'm buying an extra whiskey ration for the entire crew."

"Aye, aye, sir."

To minimize their flare they needed to get their transition velocity as close to one light as possible before down-transition, and then hold onto as much sublight velocity as possible once they did.

"Forty lights."

Katrine's stomach turned a somersault as a heavy gravity wave rolled through the bridge. She swallowed hard, and wondered if she still had her *transition gut*, the term hunter-killer crews used to refer to a spacer's ability to keep her lunch down during an exercise like this. It had been years since she had needed to prove she could, and she dearly didn't want to suffer the embarrassment of blowing chow on the bridge.

"Thirty lights."

Another gravity wave, stronger than the last, pushed at her gut. Katrine noticed she wasn't the only one gulping hard.

"Twenty lights."

A cluster of three gravity waves hit them in rapid succession.

"Nineteen . . ."

Larger ships experienced transition instability at about fifty lights, but hunter-killers were specifically designed to go well below that.

"Eighteen . . . seventeen . . ."

". . . and . . ."

". . . down-transition. We're at point eight-four lights and coasting, sir. Time dilation factor just under two."

Like a seasoned CO, Neilosse's voice showed no strain whatsoever. "Drones out. Scan, as soon as they're in position, get me what you can on *Caliban*."

They all waited in silence for the scan tech to position the drones in their complex orbits around *Lightspear*. Katrine almost jumped when he broke the silence. "Nothing, sir. And I'm not picking up a transition wake anywhere near her last known position, so I don't think they've up-transited yet."

"Good," Neilosse said. "Good. Steady as she goes and rig for silent running."

At least Katrine still had her transition gut. Now the waiting began.

••••

The surly med tech entered the room, but this time he had an unpleasant smile on his face that Nikaela thought might bode ill for her. One crewman, a crewwomen and a senior, female NCO followed him in. All three gave Nikaela a look that told her they shared the unpleasant med tech's opinion of her, and the name stencils above their left breast pockets had been removed. The two crewmembers carried short batons about the length of a man's forearm. She would not have recognized the neural prods for what they were had she not seen their like carried by the guards at SecureMax. She had never seen such devices put to use, but didn't need a demonstration to know the experience at the receiving end would be quite unpleasant.

The two crewmembers positioned themselves on either side of her bed, the woman on her left, the man on her right, and pressed the business ends of their prods against the sides of her throat. She flinched, tensing and preparing for the worst, but nothing happened. The med tech grinned, clearly entertained by her fear and discomfort. "If you do anything . . . if you even look like you're going to twitch the wrong way, you'll be quite unhappy with the results."

The looks the two women and two men gave her made it clear they all hoped she would try something. They wanted her to give them an excuse to put the prods to use.

The med tech reached up to the instruments above her, but paused. "You're healed well enough, so I'm going to remove the nerve block on your lower extremities . . ."

When he hesitated with a questioning look, she finished the thought for him. ". . . and I shouldn't take that as an invitation to try something."

"On the contrary," he said, "feel free to try anything you want."

With two neural prods pressed against her neck, she'd be a fool to do anything but cooperate. "Perhaps another time."

He shook his head. "There won't be another time."

She gave him her version of the unpleasant grin he had turned on her earlier. "You never know."

He ignored her and made some adjustment to the instruments. She felt a slight tingle in her hips and legs, and a few seconds later could once again wiggle her toes. "We've been stimulating your muscles, so at worst you might feel a second or two of weakness when you first stand. But after that, you'll be expected to walk on your own."

The crewwoman said, "We're not carrying you, Blacksword lover."

Nikaela did not miss the implied threat in her words. She would pay a dear price if she couldn't walk.

The med tech removed the sheets from the lower half of her body; she was naked from the waist down. The crewwoman on her left grabbed a fist full of hair on the back of her head and pulled downward, forcing her to arch her back and point her chin toward the deck overhead. The woman pressed the prod even more forcefully against the side of Nikaela's neck while the fellow on her right walked around the foot of the bed to join her. With Nikaela sandwiched between them, they told her to swing her legs off the bed and stand. When she did so, as the med tech had warned her, she felt a few moments of weakness, but that quickly passed.

The tech handed her a one-piece coverall and said, "Strip completely, then put that on."

She removed the hospital gown, moving carefully as she did so, conscious of the two prods pressed to either side of her neck. She tossed the gown on the bed, slipped her legs and arms into the coveralls, then sealed it carefully. The guards cuffed her hands behind her back with plast manacles.

The woman on her left said, "Can you walk?"

The man on her right said, "You better walk."

"I can walk."

The NCO led the way, with Nikaela following, and the two crewmembers following behind her, the output ends of their neural prods jammed into her back. Just beyond the door to the ICU she counted six beds in the main part of the ship's sick bay, still not enough information to give her anything more than a vague inkling of the ship's size.

Walking down a short, narrow passageway they came upon a crewwoman wearing a merchant spacer's uniform and headed in the other direction. "Prisoner walking," the NCO said, and the crewwoman pressed her back against the passageway bulkhead. As Nikaela passed her, the woman gave her a curious look, but nothing more.

They stopped at a grav lift, which confirmed her suspicions. Hunter-killers and smaller ships didn't make use of lifts. The deck beneath her feet had to be part of a vessel at least the size of a medium destroyer, or perhaps even larger.

When they stepped into the lift its doors immediately closed. The NCO must have programmed the lift through her implants, so Nikaela got no indication of the number of decks on the ship. But when the doors whooshed open the level onto which they stepped had the unmistakable feel of a ship's lower decks.

They marched her down a narrow passageway, then up to an empty security station where the NCO leaned over a bank of monitors. "We've got an empty house right now," she said, "so we'll put her in cell number two."

Just past the security station, the wall of the left side of the passageway was a blank, featureless bulkhead, its smooth surface broken only by the protrusion of rivets and welding seams. On the right, two heavy plast doors were spaced a few meters apart, and beyond that the passageway ended in a dead end. Each door had an open square about face high that would have been large enough for a small child to crawl through, had the opening not been blocked by heavy plast bars.

As the NCO and the two crewmembers led her down the narrow passageway, the last door on the right clattered open, driven by some hidden mechanism. The NCO stopped just beyond the open door and nodded toward the interior of the cell. "Your new home, Mistress Vreekande."

The guard behind her nudged her sharply in the back with the end of his prod. She stepped forward, then through the door and into the cell. She paused just within and surveyed her *new home*. Two grav bunks each held blankets and a thin mattress pressed against the wall by their gravity fields. A pressure toilet, pressure sink, two extrudable chairs, and a fold-down table were the only other features.

Nikaela wasn't prepared for the lightning bolt that slammed into her back and the shock of pain it sent arcing through her nervous system. She cried out, stumbled forward and fell to her knees. Someone grabbed her hair, pulled her head back, and she found herself looking into the face of the NCO. The woman had leaned forward so that only a hand's breadth of space separated their noses. The older woman's jaw muscles clenched as she spoke through gritted teeth. "This is what we think of Blacksword lovers."

The NCO produced her own prod, jammed it into Nikaela's chest between her breasts; another lightning bolt slammed her to the floor and sent her to the edge of consciousness. While lying on her side on the floor of the cell, they gave her a moment to catch her breath and recover. Then one of them jammed a prod into her throat just beneath her chin, and she couldn't even scream as the prod's output forced her jaw and throat muscles to seize up.

They followed that formula for an unknown length of time. After they jolted her with one or two of the prods, they gave her a moment to catch her breath, then they jolted her again. It would have been kinder if they had simply jammed the prods against her flesh and given her a continuous shock. She probably would have found unconsciousness that way, blessed, peaceful nothingness. They kept her conscious and screaming for quite a while.

28

On the Move

"COLONEL."

Katrine opened her eyes to a moment of confusion. She was lying on a grav bunk still dressed in her fatigues in a tiny room clearly not part of her small apartment on Trafalgar. A shallow gravity field held her pressed into cushions against a bulkhead like a fly on the wall. To give her a place to bunk, Neilosse had bumped his lowest ranking officer, an ensign, out of a stateroom the fellow shared with three other officers; the privileges of rank.

She dialed the bunk's gravity field back, pushed herself forward, and stepped onto the deck of the small stateroom. Her implants informed her she had slept for a little over two hours. It hadn't been enough. "I'm awake."

A woman's voice spoke through her implants. "This is Lieutenant Commander Sharma. Skipper asked me to wake you, and sends his apologies for that. We've detected an up-transition from the near vicinity of our target. We're tracking a transition wake now, though we can't be sure it is *Caliban*. But they are pushing about three thousand lights, which is a little extreme for a civilian vessel."

"I'll be right up."

"Commander Neilosse says to take your time. Right now they're ranging at just under one light-year, so they won't be here for well over two hours."

Katrine thanked the woman, took a quick shipboard shower, put on her service khakis, and reported to the bridge. She returned to her place standing behind the scan tech. His screens showed several transition wakes, but he highlighted one. "This is the bird we're tracking, ma'am."

She asked, "What about its transition profile?"

He glanced over his shoulder at her. "At this distance the data is still too noisy to tell."

"Care to take an educated guess?"

He gritted his teeth, clearly reluctant to refuse a request from a high-ranking officer. She understood his reticence. He didn't know her well enough to know if she might be an asshole about his reluctance to speak, or if he guessed wrong, would she be a jerk about that?

"That's all right," she said. "Let's wait until you're more comfortable with the data."

The rest of the bridge crew had been silent through her exchange with the scan tech. Perhaps that had been a test.

Neilosse said, "We're still well within range of our transition com, so I considered contacting Trafalgar traffic control. But it occurs to me asking specifically about *Caliban* might alert someone to our interest in the ship."

She didn't miss the hint regarding their earlier conversation concerning very powerful people. "Can you put me into contact with Colonel Blacksword?"

Neilosse grinned and turned to his com tech. "Make it happen."

"May I take the call in your stateroom?"

"Certainly," he said.

She nodded and smiled. "And if you can, please join me."

He returned her smile. "Of course."

From the scan tech, Katrine retrieved the exact time their possible target had up-transited. Five minutes later she and Neilosse huddled in his stateroom, and the com tech put her in contact with Fran Thealone.

"Change of plans," Katrine said. "Even if *Caliban* didn't have us outgunned, the best course of action is to follow them and find out where they're going. We're in position to do so, and we've got a bogie on our transition scan that up-transited from their near vicinity. But it could be another vessel with military capabilities, so we can't be sure it's our target. Without mentioning *Caliban*, can you find out if any military ships up-transited out of the system on or about that time? And if so, I also need their heading."

She gave Thealone the coordinates and timing of their bogie's up-transition.

Thealone nodded. "I see where you're going. Sit tight for a few minutes."

Katrine and Neilosse sat in silence while they waited, neither of them inclined to idle chatter. When Thealone came back on line, she gave Katrine a list of three ships and their headings. Katrine scanned the information. "Not one of these is on a heading even close to that of our bogie. So when it gets closer, if it has a transition profile consistent with a light destroyer, that's our *Caliban*."

Neilosse nodded and grinned.

Katrine wanted to speak to Thealone in private, but couldn't think of a polite way to ask Neilosse to leave his own stateroom. Neilosse beat her to the point. He stood up in the tight confines. "I'll be on the bridge. Please feel free to use my stateroom as long as you need." He left, closing the door behind him.

Katrine switched her implants to a special encryption key only she and Thealone used, and subvocalized everything after that. "Have you found out anything more about Neilosse?"

Thealone shook her head. "A little, but not much. He's got a spotless record, and excellent performance ratings. Fleet Operations Command has him on a short list for promotion to captain sometime in the next two or three years. He hasn't openly expressed sympathies one way or another regarding the Kelk. I dug a little deeper and he's never reported to an immediate superior with a reputation as hardline, anti-Kelk, and he's never been involved in an incident with the Kelk. You're just going to have to use your own judgement."

They ended the call, and Katrine sat for a moment considering her options. She decided to keep Neilosse and Sharma in the dark for the time being, while she looked for opportunities to gauge their attitudes regarding the Kelk.

••••

The crew of *Sycorax* made no attempt to hide the military nature of the ship. Even had they wanted to, it would have been impossible since they conducted a combat drill the first day out from Viktorkinde. Aanberg explained that since the ship explored the far reaches of space, they must be prepared for the possibility they might encounter Com-SecCorps warships. And it would be a disaster if they were defenseless under such circumstances. Since Anders was riding deadhead and not part of the crew, his assigned battle station was his bunk, and his operating instructions were, *Stay out of the way.*

Anders learned they would be in transition for close to twenty days, so he settled into shipboard routine with his bunkmates. Since Anders didn't have any shipboard duties, he read, worked out in the gym, and gambled at cards.

On the second day out from Viktorkinde, Anders's implants informed him he was to report to the office of Command Hawk Eskildsen on deck five. The rank didn't surprise Anders, since merchant spacer rank mimicked that of the military. And the captain would want to take the measure of any stranger in their midst, so Anders had expected such a summons. But the ship's CO would ordinarily have an office closer to the bridge in officers' country, not down in the bowels of the ship. Anders assumed Eskildsen was not the captain.

Anders made his way down to deck five, and he immediately came upon two spacers wearing actual military uniforms, not the merchant spacer equivalent. As his implants guided him to Eskildsen's office, every spacer he passed on that deck wore military attire and rank, and not one of them had a name stencil above their left breast pocket.

The door to Eskildsen's office stood open. Inside a woman sat at a small desk against a bulkhead, her back to Anders and the door, her attention focused on something on the desk in front of her.

Anders cleared his throat. "Command Hawk Eskildsen?"

She looked up from her work and focused her eyes on Anders. "Yes."

She had pale red irises, with more pepper than salt in her hair, which she wore shoulder length. Anders resisted the urge to snap to attention and salute her. "I'm Anders Karsten. I was told you wished to see me."

She pivoted on her seat to face him. "Come in, Maestra Karsten, and close the door."

Anders stepped across the threshold and closed the door, which made the tight confines of her office feel even more restricting.

She pointed to a small, extrudable seat. "Please sit down."

Anders touched the seat's switch, and it extruded out of the wall. He sat down.

She smiled pleasantly. "I'm aware of your true history, Maestra Eindride, though I'm the only one on *Sycorax* who is. Tell me about yourself."

Anders tried not to sound confused. "I don't know where to begin, mistress."

She frowned and looked at him for a long moment, as if evaluating him in some way. "Are you aware Mistress Nikaela Vreekande, who reported to you on Novalis III, claims she is breschkada with a Commonwealth soldier?"

Anders didn't try to hide his distaste as he said. "I was told she is breschkada with a Blacksword. But you said she *claims* to be breschkada. Is she not?"

She smiled again, but this time there was nothing pleasant in the look on her face. "I intend to find out. And perhaps you can help me."

She questioned him further, focusing mainly on his knowledge of young Mistress Vreekande. After she dismissed him, he paused at a ladder leading up to the next level. Quite possibly she had just confirmed his suspicions as to the identity of the special prisoner on *Sycorax*. And he now began to wonder if Thoran's superiors were really offering him upward mobility, or did they just want him on this ship, at this time, to help the command hawk with a certain young woman.

••••

The scan tech's eyes darted from one screen to another, his brow furrowed with concern. "I don't understand this."

Their target had held steady to its course and was now within four thousand light-hours of *Lightspear*'s position. Katrine had instructed Neilosse to hold off on briefing his crew about the true nature of *Caliban*. She wanted to see how the young man at the scan console reacted to the incoming data without any preconceived notions. "What's not to understand?"

"If I didn't know better . . ." He hesitated. "Their transition profile is nothing like it should be."

Katrine glanced at Neilosse seated at the command console, and he raised an eyebrow. Lieutenant Commander Sharma looked suspiciously from Neilosse to Katrine.

"They're pushing three thousand lights," the scan tech said. "That's way too much drive for a civilian ship. And their emission signature is all over the map, more like an armed warship."

Katrine wanted Neilosse's crew to understand it was not he who had chosen to withhold information from them. "Commander Neilosse, you have my permission to brief your crew on *Caliban*'s capabilities."

He nodded, and a moment later allship filled the air with his voice. "This is your captain. The ship we're tracking is a rogue with capabilities not listed in the nautical registry." He didn't go into a lot of detail, but he gave his crew enough information to know they faced a formidable enemy. "She has us outgunned, so we're going to move cautiously when we follow her."

He looked Sharma's way. "Sorry I couldn't brief you earlier."

She nodded and cocked an eyebrow in Katrine's direction. "Shall I sound general quarters, sir?"

He nodded. "Please do."

A loud, irritatingly unpleasant horn burped once. It was followed immediately by the steady clang of the alert klaxon, with Sharma speaking precisely over allship. "Watch Condition Red. All hands, this is not a drill. Repeat: this is not a drill." She repeated the message one more time.

While the klaxon continued to blare, Katrine looked at the scan tech's screens. In a little over an hour *Caliban* would pass within a few hundred million kilometers of their present position, basically right on top of them when it came to interstellar distances. The research ship's captain held her tightly to the transition plan they had filed, and would probably do so until six or seven light-years out from Trafalgar. Perhaps then, they would get their first inkling of *Caliban*'s intended destination.

Once all stations had reported in, Sharma killed the alert klaxon, and the bridge went silent, as if everyone there held their collective breath. Neilosse gave Sharma instructions to get them closer to *Caliban*'s line while he addressed the crew on allship.

Sharma instructed the helm to use their maximum sublight drive of ten kiloGs, and they accelerated perpendicular to *Caliban*'s vector, then decelerated to kill their sideways drift. In sublight the maneuver took more than thirty minutes.

"Scan," Neilosse asked. "What's our position?"

"Sir, if *Caliban* holds its line, she should pass twenty million kilometers to port."

Neilosse and his crew had positioned them in front of *Caliban*, and only slightly to one side. *Lightspear* coasted along *Caliban*'s line in sublight at point eight-four lights. It wouldn't take much to kick them into up-transition.

"All right people," Neilosse said. "We've got less than an hour before they get here. Let's go to work. Helm, firewall sublight on a vector parallel to *Caliban*'s line."

Katrine felt the faint vibration of the hunter-killer's engines propagate through the ship's structure as the helmswoman applied power to the sublight grav drive.

"Scan," Neilosse said. "Give me the details."

"Ranging at just over two thousand light-hours, sir," the scan tech said. "Driving hard at three thousand lights. Intercept in forty minutes plus."

With more than half an hour to wait, the bridge settled into a routine as they watched *Caliban* slowly close the distance between them. Waiting was always the hard part, watching the minutes and seconds tick by with agonizing slowness.

The scan tech gave them regular updates, and half an hour later he said, "Ranging at five hundred light-hours, sir. Intercept in ten minutes."

"Helm," Neilosse said, "you know the drill."

"Yes, sir. I'll hold her right at the edge of transition and let their wake pull us up into it."

Neilosse grinned. A good hunter-killer captain needed a certain amount of predator in his genetic makeup, and Katrine saw the anticipation of a warrior in the smile on his face.

The leading edge of *Caliban*'s transition wake hit them and a gravity wave rolled through the ship. It took an extremely experienced helmsman to properly execute the maneuver they hoped to achieve. She couldn't let the leading edge of the wake push them into transition too early. She needed to hold *Lightspear* just the right amount below the required threshold and wait until the bogie passed over them.

"Ranging at fifty light-hours, sir. Intercept in one minute."

Katrine didn't know anything about *Lightspear*'s helmswoman, but the fact that Neilosse didn't stand behind her looking over her shoulder spoke volumes for her expertise.

Neilosse barked, "Drone's in."

Several seconds later the hull echoed as *Lightspear*'s combat drones settled into their docking bays.

"Ten light-hours, sir, twelve seconds."

Another gravity wave rolled through the bridge, and another, and another. Katrine's mouth filled with saliva and she swallowed hard. Knowing what to expect, she had stayed away from any food for the last few hours, and guessed *Lightspear*'s crew had done the same.

"Ten seconds . . . nine . . . eight . . ."

Katrine watched *Caliban*'s blip on the screen approach. It seemed to meld with their position as a cluster of gravity waves tested her transition gut.

". . . two . . . one . . . intercept."

Nothing happened as Katrine counted the seconds. They wanted a little distance between them, so the helmswoman held back and let the bogie pass them. The seconds ticked by, and then the helmswoman barked, "Up transition," the strain in her voice almost turning her words into a growl.

"We're at twenty lights," she said.

Several seconds ticked by, then she added, ". . . thirty lights . . ."

Katrine forced herself to breathe evenly.

". . . fifty lights . . . one hundred lights . . . one thousand lights . . . we've matched velocity, sir."

The bridge remained silent as they waited for the scan tech to give them the verdict. He took a deep breath and said, "We're twenty-eight light-hours behind them."

Still, no one spoke as they waited for the most important piece of information. "No reaction from the bogie, sir. Just driving straight and clean."

"Perfect," Neilosse said. "An extra whiskey ration for the entire crew tonight, on me. And let's back off to a distance of about two hundred light hours. Wouldn't want to push our nose up their ass."

Now they would follow, and wait, and hope they didn't lose their prey.

Neilosse turned to Sharma, his XO. "They're following their transition plan, at least so far. I think it's safe to assume they won't try anything until they're beyond the range of Trafalgar's transition scanners, which start to peter out at about five light-years. That gives us a little less than eleven hours. Let's go to watch condition yellow and stand down."

"Aye, aye, sir," she said.

He continued. "Tell everyone to grab something to eat and get a little shut-eye. Keep scan operations fully manned in case they try something earlier, but we'll reconvene here in eight hours regardless."

29

An Unappetizing Meal

NIKAELA WONDERED AT the eerie silence that filled the cell, broken only by a rasping wheeze. It took her a moment to realize she was listening to her own breathing.

Dried tears crusted her eyes when she opened them. They had left her lying on her side on the deck of her cell, her head in a puddle of fluid that smelled of vomit. As she raised her head, her hair stuck to the floor, glued there by the half-dried former contents of her stomach. With a little experimentation she learned that they had removed the manacles from her wrists. She rolled onto her back and sat up, only then realizing she had lost control of her bowels at some point, and her coveralls were full of shit. Every muscle in her body complained as she struggled to her hands and knees, then to her feet.

They must have watched her, because at that moment the door to her cell clattered open. She recognized the two crewmembers who stepped into her cell. The female guard carried a neural prod, while the male dragged a hose capped by a heavy fire nozzle. The woman said, "Go stand in the corner over the drain and strip completely."

Nikaela slowly scanned the room and spotted the grate to a small drain in one corner. She crossed the room and stood over it, and under the eyes of the two guards she removed the one-piece coverall.

They hosed her down with water, then disinfectant, then again with water, and she learned the pressure in the hose was high enough to sting her skin wherever the spray hit her. She tried to ignore the pain and turned about quickly, desperately hoping to remove all the shit, piss and vomit. She even held the soiled coveralls up and managed to send most of the solid matter that clung to the garment down the drain, but not all of it.

When they finished, the woman tossed a fresh set of coveralls onto one of the grav bunks, and its gravity field held it pinned to the wall on top of the sheets. "You only get the two coveralls," she said, pointing to the wet heap of cloth lying on the deck. "You can clean those in the sink."

They left her standing there dripping wet, didn't bother to give her anything she might use to dry off. She pulled the blankets off one of the two bunks. They didn't make for a very absorbent towel but they did the job. She put on the new coveralls, and set to work cleaning the other pair in the sink.

••••

The Executive Council's decision to provide a heavy cruiser had elated Kristdokar. But her excitement quickly waned as she suffered through one delay after another.

The day after the Council meeting in which they decided to send the cruiser, in the morning they changed their minds and decided a single ship might not be a sufficient show of force. A large strike force would be much more appropriate. But by late that afternoon they decided a large strike force might be viewed as provocative by the independent systems in the neighborhood of Sarkovie, and by the Commonwealth as well. They dialed the strike force back to a large cruiser, a large destroyer, and a fast hunter-killer.

Two days after the initial decision to send Nygaard and Kristdokar to Sarkovie, they up-transited out of the Viktorkinde system on board the heavy cruiser *Konigsborge*, accompanied by the destroyer *Alvilddan*. Since the hunter-killer *Eldekarl* could push in excess of four thousand lights, they sent it ahead at maximum speed with instructions to make a hunter-killer approach to Sarkovie, and in the process drop a relay buoy about five light-years out. The cruiser and destroyer would follow at their own maximum pace of just over three thousand lights.

••••

Katrine set her implants to wake her after eight hours, and she actually managed to sleep the full eight. She awoke feeling reasonably refreshed, lay in her grav bunk for a few minutes and counted backward in time. A little over two days had passed since she had been called to the campus crime scene, and she had survived since then on stimulants, caff, catnaps and adrenaline. Eight full hours of sleep had been a refreshing luxury. She wondered how poor John Mathius fared.

She reviewed the Ship's Plan of the Day posted by the XO. It had been set up in anticipation of an extended period of elevated watch condition. It boiled down to relaxed formalities, informal cafeteria-style meals in both the wardroom and main mess, and a caution to eat lite because there would likely be gravity waves rolling through the ship challenging everyone's transition gut. Since Katrine was not standing a watch, she had no specific assignment or duty post. She would have to move carefully to make sure she didn't step on Neilosse's or Sharma's toes.

Katrine stepped out of the grav bunk's field and onto the deck of the four-person stateroom. She noted that two of the other bunks were occupied with slumbering officers, so she grabbed her fatigues and boots and stepped out into the passageway still dressed in her skivvies.

She carried her clothing down to the showers, but merely splashed a little water on her face, dressed, stopped by the wardroom for a light snack, then reported to the bridge. Neilosse and Sharma were already on station; she had purposefully timed her arrival to be sure of that. She reported to the Commander, then took up her post behind the scan tech. The young man acknowledged her with a nod and said, "Not so much as a twitch out of our bogie, ma'am, still steady as she goes."

Katrine smiled. "What's our position?"

"We're a little over four light-years out from Trafalgar, ma'am, still driving at three kilolights."

Katrine asked, "Is there a betting pool?"

The young man looked over his shoulder at Katrine and spoke cautiously. "I don't understand what you mean, ma'am."

Katrine smiled and shook her head sadly.

The young man grimaced and shrugged. "Most of the money's on eight light-years out from Trafalgar. But that bogie's just driving hard without a care in the universe, so my guess is they'll pull something before then. My money's on seven light-years."

Katrine did a quick calculation in her head. Three more light-years at three kilolights would take more than eight hours. Her presence on the bridge was not needed, and as much as she hated to admit it, having a high-ranking stranger on hand would not be conducive to optimal performance. Resolving to return in five hours just before they hit the six light-year mark, she approached Neilosse and made up an excuse. "Commander, I need a little gym time, and I've got some reading to do. I intend to be back before they do anything, but if the situation does change, I'd like to be notified immediately."

"Certainly, Colonel," he said. "I've already made sure the scan team and all officers know you're on the hot list with me and Commander Sharma. If anything breaks, you'll hear about it along with us."

Katrine excused herself and left the bridge. She would return in five hours, but she knew from experience that with no duty assignment, each tick of the clock would come with agonizing slowness. She put in three hours in the gym and tried not to think about how they had dropped the ball with regard to protecting John Mathius, but her mind kept returning to that failure.

After the gym she showered, put on her service khakis, and sat down in the wardroom to review everything she knew about Transmarin Industries. But just as she sat down her implants came to life, "*Caliban* is on the move."

In the same instant the alert klaxon blared and allship filled the air with Sharma's voice, "General quarters, watch condition red, all hands, this is not a drill."

Katrine shot to her feet as she checked the time; *Caliban*'s captain had chosen to move much earlier than anticipated. She knew better than to run, which was a formula for bruising her shins on an open hatchway, so she walked with as brisk a pace as she could manage. When she stepped onto the bridge Neilosse was already barking orders at his crew. Katrine took her place behind the scan tech, but didn't make the mistake of rifling questions at the fellow. Neilosse would inform her of the situation when he could, but that didn't stop her from looking over the tech's shoulders at his screens.

Caliban maneuvered hard, executing a serious course correction. While in transition *Lightspear* could only detect grosser transition signals. Had *Caliban*'s captain suspected they were being followed, he could have lost them by executing the course correction in a long slow turn over a period of hours. The resulting transition noise would be minimal and undetectable.

"Cheeky bastard," Neilosse said.

"Yah," Sharma said. "He's a confident one."

Yes, *Caliban*'s captain was confident. But to stay on the research ship's tail, *Lightspear* needed to maneuver just as hard, and if *Caliban*'s scan tech happened to be paying attention, his suspicions might be aroused.

"Sir," the scan tech said, "they've leveled off and are now running straight and clean."

"What's our new heading?"

As the scan tech responded to the captain's question, Katrine read the data off his screens without listening to him. She knew that heading, had traveled it quite a number of times in the last couple of years.

"Navigation," Neilosse demanded, "what have we got out there."

The navigation officer said, "Nothing close, sir. But the independent star systems are a little over a hundred light-years in that direction. That would include Norandyne, the Tollman Protectorate, the Mikotian Republic, Sarkovie, and the Heraclean Hegemony. Most of them are within thirty or forty light-years of each other."

In recent years it had become customary to no longer include all six of the independent systems in that cluster. No one liked to recall painful memories.

"You forgot one," Katrine said.

She turned around and met Neilosse's eyes across the cramped confines of the bridge. "Novalis III is out there as well."

••••

Anders received another summons to report to Command Hawk Eskildsen on deck five. When he climbed down to that level his implants did not direct him to her office, but instead sent him in the opposite direction. Again, the only spacers he encountered on deck five wore military attire.

He spotted Eskildsen at the end of a long passageway. She stood over a crewwoman seated at a bank of monitors. In the passageway beyond, two doors with barred openings were clearly the entrances to cells. Eskildsen had called him to the ship's brig.

She looked his way. "Maestra Karsten. I want you to see something." She pointed ed to one of the screens in front of the crewwoman.

It displayed the interior of one of the cells from a point near the back of the cell, and from a height somewhere close to the ceiling. A young Kelk woman lay curled up in a fetal position on a grav bunk, dressed in a one-piece coverall, her back to the vid pickup. He knew she was female because of the curve of her hip, and he knew she was young because her hair contained almost no salt. But all he saw was the back of her coverall and the back of her head.

Anders asked, "Can you switch to a different vid pickup so I can see her face?"

The crewwoman shook her head. "Only one pickup per cell. This ain't Secure-Max. We usually just deal with drunks and screw-ups here."

Eskildsen told the crewwoman, "Go wake her up, make her turn toward the camera."

"No," Anders said. "With your permission, I'd like to wake her up myself. If it's who I think it is, I have a few things I want to say to her anyway."

Eskildsen closed her eyes as if weary, and nodded her head once.

The crewwoman said, "She's in cell two."

Anders walked down the passageway to the second door and looked through its small barred opening. From that angle he saw her face in profile, and any question of the young woman's identity vanished.

For the benefit of Eskildsen, he hardened his voice. "Mistress Vreekande. Wake up."

She blinked her eyes, once, twice.

He shouted, "I said wake up."

She blinked her eyes rapidly and turned her head to look his way. She seemed dazed and disoriented so he waited. She shook her head as if to clear it, then uncurled from the fetal position, and stepped out of the field of the grav bunk. She walked unsteadily across the cell and stopped short of the door, keeping an arm's length of distance between them.

Her eyes slowly widened. "Maestra . . . Eindride?"

He gripped the bars in the small opening, pulled his face close to it, and angled his head slightly to one side so Eskildsen and the crewwoman would not see his lips move. He had considered this move carefully, knew that any tiny bit of information he gave the girl might help her in some way. In a rush, he whispered, "Only one vid pickup, ceiling high, corner, your back left side." Then he screamed at the top of his lungs, "Bitch."

She started and backed away from him a step, her eyes wide and blinking with fear.

He thought of the guards in SecureMax and the pleasure they had taken at his pain, used that memory to help him call forth fury the young woman didn't deserve. "Your testimony put me through hell."

A hand on his shoulder startled him. He turned to find Eskildsen standing next to him. "That's enough," she said.

He forced his thoughts to an uneasy calm. "Sorry."

Eskildsen gave him a pained smile. "It's quite understandable. But I think you should return to your quarters."

As Anders made his way back to the bunk room, he recalled that Mistress Vreekande's coverall had been open at the neck, and high on her chest he had seen what looked like a burn mark. Round and precise, it had been just the kind of burn the SecureMax guards had put on his skin with their overcharged neural prods.

••••

Anders Eindride! Only moments earlier he had stood in the passageway just beyond the door, and Nikaela now remained frozen in the middle of her cell, trying to understand what had just happened.

Since the tribunal at Erikdeg, she had only seen him twice: in the interrogation room in SecureMax, and on the street a few paces from his apartment building in Hyerdride. In the interrogation room his appearance had stunned her, but when she had approached him in Hyerdride that second time, night had enveloped the city, and by the dim light of the street lamps he had been little more than a dark shadow speaking in the voice of Anders Eindride. She had been able to convince herself he was still the same man. But now, standing outside her cell, his face clearly visible in the light of the passageway, he had aged far more than could be accounted for by the few years that had passed since that tribunal.

His fury at her had startled her as well, but not as much as his appearance. She thought carefully to recall the rush of whispered words he had uttered: "Only one vid pickup, ceiling high, corner, your back left side."

A small piece of information, but one that in some unknown way might prove to be of value. His fury had frightened her, but now she understood it had been a ruse to cover his actions, and perhaps to reinforce his assumed identity.

Conscious now of the location of the vid pickup in her cell, she turned and walked to the sink. She had washed the soiled coveralls and draped them over the sink to dry, but water alone had not completely eliminated the smell from the fabric, though it had muted the scent enough that she could wear them.

The door to her cell clattered open and she turned to face it. The male guard stood in the open doorway carrying a tray of food. "Time to eat," he said, but he grinned unpleasantly, as if enjoying a joke at someone else's expense. He placed the food on the small fold-down table, then turned and left. The door clattered shut behind him.

She caught the scent of something unpleasant, and for a moment wondered if the residual stink of the washed coveralls was worse than she had thought. She lifted the coveralls and sniffed at the fabric. No, that wasn't it.

She walked over to the tray of food, and the smell grew stronger. Her jailers had contaminated it with something quite disgusting and it smelled like a dirty latrine. The tea they had provided with the meal smelled of urine.

She carefully tested the water in the sink and found it drinkable. But she went hungry that day, and for the first time began to understand the depth of hatred so many of her countrymen harbored for the Commonwealth, and for those who did not share their hatred.

She killed time that day by drinking water from the sink and exercising.

30

Interrogation

JOHN HAD A hazy memory of repeatedly returning to a semiconscious state, always in a bed with med techs and doctors moving about. Each time he awoke he struggled to wake further, but just couldn't get there. And then time blinked, and again he awoke, and again he struggled, but to no avail. He had been awake for some time before he realized this time was different. He lay there for quite a while waiting for time to blink again, but that didn't happen.

He recalled calm-voice saying they would make him tell them about *this breschka-da thing*. Calm-voice had finished by saying, "It's got our special friends all bent out of shape." John decided that if questioned on the matter, his best chance at staying alive would be to plead ignorance. Hopefully, they had overlooked his Kelk lessons with Professor Dirkson.

A middle-aged woman leaned into his field of view. She wore civilian clothing and had brown hair that ended at her shoulders. "How are you feeling, young man?"

John recognized the doctor's voice and thought about her question for a moment. He didn't feel any pain, and with a little experimentation wiggled his fingers and toes, which he hadn't been able to do for quite some time, though his hands were cuffed to the sides of the bed. "How long?" he asked.

She glanced carefully over her shoulder, then lowered her voice. "We left the Trafalgar system three days ago."

"Where are we going?"

She grimaced and shook her head. "I don't know. Now you answer my question. How are you feeling?"

He didn't feel bad, just scared. "I'm not in any pain, if that's what you mean."

"That's exactly what I mean."

She delicately probed at his abdomen. "Any pain there?"

"No."

"Let me know if you do feel any."

She continued to probe, and while she did so he asked, "You don't seem like one of them."

She paused and again glanced over her shoulder before speaking in a lowered voice. "I don't know who they are, and I don't know what you've done to piss them off so much, and I don't want to know."

"But you work for them."

"They didn't give me any choice. I work for a medical device manufacturer. They needed a specialist in your type of injuries. My boss told me to report to an address and the next thing I know I'm on a transition ship going I-don't-know-where. Just keep in mind these people are really upset with you."

"I know that. It's just that—"

She held up a hand to silence him. "And I don't want to know why."

"I understand," he said. "What's the name of the company you work for?"

"Charterman Medical Devices."

He shrugged. "Never heard of 'em."

"We're a subsidiary of Transmarin Industries."

He didn't comment on that.

She helped him sit up, then stepped back from his bed as if he might be contagious. "You're well enough to be released. Be careful of the calm guy with black hair."

He nodded. "I will."

She turned and left, closing the door behind her. John hoped the poor woman survived this. For that matter, John hoped he survived this.

He had yet to see anyone wearing a uniform so he assumed he was on a civilian ship, and guessed they could do at most two thousand lights. Three days; that would put them over fifteen light-years out. Where could they be taking him?

The door opened and two men walked in, one average height with close cropped black hair, the other short and overweight with thinning, bright red hair that hung down to his shoulders in lank curls. The fat, red-haired guy hurriedly crossed the room and grabbed the front of John's hospital gown. "Okay, shit head,"—John immediately recognized pissed-off guy's voice—"what's this breschkada thing mean?"

Play stupid, John reminded himself. "What . . . what are you talking about?"

"The breschkada thing," pissed-off guy shouted, flecks of spittle spattering John's face. "What does it mean?"

John shook his head. "I don't know what you're talking about."

Still gripping John's hospital gown with his left hand, pissed-off guy back-handed him with his right, snapping John's head to the side. John instinctively tried to lift his hands to protect his face from another blow, but the cuffs clamping them to the sides of his bed prevented that.

"Enough," calm-voice said. "Back off."

Pissed-off guy released John and turned to calm-voice. "But he's—"

Calm-voice said, "I said enough."

Pissed-off guy cringed, which made it quite clear which of them gave the orders.

"Now shut up and get out of my way."

Pissed-off guy stepped aside like a beaten puppy.

Calm-voice looked into John's face. "I'm sorry about that, young man, but we do need to know about this breschkada thing."

Colonel Primatov had explicitly prohibited him from ever telling anyone of his breschkada status. And now this fellow and his pissed-off friend wanted to know about it. John again shook his head. "I've never heard that word before. I don't know."

Calm-voice stared at John for a long moment, then said, "It's a Kelk word."

"I don't speak Kelk."

"None of us do," the man said, "but we hope you might enlighten us a bit."

They hadn't called him on his lie about speaking Kelk, which hopefully confirmed that they didn't know about the Kelk lessons.

Pissed-off guy snarled, "I'll make him tell everything he knows."

Calm-voice ignored him. "It had something to do with that incident on Reisenar. You were there on your year of active duty, weren't you?"

John nodded. "Yes."

"Tell me about it."

John considered further editing the already edited story Primatov had approved. But he didn't know how much of that was publicly available information, and Primatov's redacted version was at least true, so he wouldn't be caught out in a lie. He repeated his carefully edited story, which heavily downplayed his role in their interactions with the Kelk.

Calm-voice asked, "So other than that woman on the subway platform, you didn't interact with the Kelk."

"I was just a grunt," John said. "Once I got to the embassy, and they patched me up, Colonel Primatov questioned me at length, then I want back to being a grunt on the injured list."

Calm-voice nodded thoughtfully. "He's probably telling the truth." He turned around to face pissed-off guy. "But just to be sure, you can go ahead and use your methods on him for a while, and we'll see if he changes his story."

Pissed-off guy grinned.

For the next hour John managed to keep to his story only because his implants helped block some of the pain, and because he knew they needed to keep him alive. He also pretended pissed-off guy was Cranoch; they were alike in many ways, especially the way they enjoyed giving pain. He found within himself an abiding hate for Cranoch, and anyone like him, and he would always refuse to yield to such a person.

••••

Food now proved to be always at the forefront of Nikaela's thoughts. Her jailers refused to bring her anything but contaminated food, and she had survived for the first few days on water from the sink, and exercise. But by the fourth day she had lost weight and no longer had the energy to exercise. She would have lost track of the days had she not been able to consult her implants.

At the beginning of the fifth day the female guard brought her another contaminated meal, and like the others she placed the tray on the fold-down table. Nikaela remained in her bunk unable to fight the lethargy that tugged at her constantly now. The stink of the food permeated the entire cell. If they followed the same pattern as previously, they would leave the tray sitting there for a couple of hours, so that even though she refused to eat it, she still had to smell it. Then they would come fetch it when they felt like it.

Nikaela thought of John Mathius, and hoped he was doing well in whatever academy the Commonwealth used to train their officers. She thought fondly of him, and wondered if she would ever see him again.

The metallic clatter of her cell door sliding open drew her thoughts back to the moment. A female command hawk stood in the open doorway. More by reflex than anything else, Nikaela stepped out of the grav field of her bunk to stand on the floor of her cell.

The command hawk frowned and wrinkled her nose. "You stink."

She marched forward and stopped with her nose only a finger's breadth from Nikaela's. "Have you no pride, young woman? You can at least bathe properly."

Nikaela shook her head. "It's not me. It's the food."

The command hawk frowned, leaned to one side and sniffed at Nikaela's shoulder. She leaned the other way and sniffed again, then straightened. She turned her head very slowly and deliberately to look over her shoulder at the tray of food on the table. She stepped back just as slowly, and crossed the short distance to the table as if approaching a dangerous animal. She leaned down, and with her nose only inches above the food, she sniffed again.

She jerked upright, covering her mouth and nose with a hand, then looked at Nikaela and spoke softly. "How long has it been since you've eaten?"

"I think . . . five or six days." Nikaela felt herself swaying from side to side and tried to stop the motion. She wasn't sure if she succeeded.

The command hawk nodded, turned away from Nikaela and walked calmly to the open cell door. She stood in the doorway, and the roar that came from her mouth blasted so loudly in the confined space Nikaela started and took an involuntary step back. "Oberseergent. I want you here front and center—nowwwwww."

The female NCO appeared as if by magic standing in the passageway in front of her. Nikaela recalled the woman easily, and the way she had applied the prod with such fervor.

The command hawk then spent quite some time discussing the NCO's parentage. Nikaela lost track of the time, but apparently some animal of which Nikaela had never heard had shit on the ground, and by the strangest stroke of evolutionary development, the NCO's parents had been born of that. Nikaela learned that was a hereditary trait, and that when it was time for the NCO to be born, her parents had created her by simply shitting together on the same spot on the ground. And since they were all evolved from shit, that particular genetic trait meant they liked to eat shit.

The command hawk finished by making the NCO sit down at the small table, telling her to, "Eat everything. If you don't finish every last bite, then I'll see to it you're fed nothing but your own shit for the rest of this journey."

Somehow the woman managed to down all of it, though her pale blue complexion turned quite green before she got to the last bite. When she finished, the command hawk ordered her to take the tray with her when she left. The woman walked rather stiffly out of the cell, and once out of sight, Nikaela heard the retching and gagging sounds of someone vomiting in the passageway.

Some minutes later, by order of the command hawk, the male guard brought a new tray of food. When he placed it on the small table, the command hawk sniffed at it carefully, then tasted a few bits here and there. Apparently satisfied she wasn't eating shit, she nodded and extruded one of the chairs next to the table. "Come. Sit down and eat."

Nikaela did so, and the first bite was glorious. "It's good. Thank you."

The command hawk nodded. "It's not a full meal. After six days without food you'll find it quite uncomfortable if you eat your fill. They're going to bring you four small meals a day for a few days. Then you'll go back to a normal diet."

Standing over Nikaela, she took a breath and sighed wearily. "I hate you for what you've done, young woman, and we will probably kill you before this is finished. But there's no need to be barbaric about it, is there?"

Nikaela chose to assume the question was rhetorical and didn't offer an answer.

••••

When John tried to open his eyes, he couldn't. He attempted to reach up to his face but his hands were still cuffed to the sides of his bed. After repeated efforts he managed to get his left eye open, and only then realized the eye lids had been glued together by dried, crusted blood. Try as he might, he couldn't get the right eye open, probably due to swelling.

He closed his eyes—eye. Pissed-off guy had been quite methodical and everything hurt.

John heard the door open, but didn't waste his time opening his eye to see who had opened it.

"Shit!" He recognized the doctor's voice. "Shit! Shit! Shit!"

He opened his eye.

She stood next to his bed, her hands partially extended as if she had started to reach out to him, but didn't know where to begin. She had tears in her eyes. "Why did they do this to you?"

"I guess they have to make sure I'm telling the truth."

She probed gently at his face, shaking her head as if trying to deny the reality they shared. "They told me you needed my help, but they didn't say . . ."

She reached up to the instruments above his bed and retrieved some sort of medical probe. Holding it a few inches above his skin, she carefully ran it down the length of his body, talking as she did so. "A partial, non-displaced fracture of the orbit of your right eye. A couple of broken ribs, some bruising to your left kidney, but no cranial damage, and no serious damage to internal organs."

John shrugged, which proved to be a mistake because it hurt to do so. "Sounds like he's a pro. I guess they need to keep me alive for some reason."

Her breath came out in shallow gasps. "I'm so sorry."

She brought in a couple of med techs to assist her. With speed healing and rapid regrowth, by late the next day she had him completely back to full health. He found it disconcerting that in a little over a day he went from lying in his own blood to feeling quite normal. That was when calm-voice and pissed-off guy returned.

"How are you feeling?" calm-voice asked.

"How do you think I feel?" John said.

"Hopefully, you feel like telling me the truth."

"I told you the truth." And that was true. He just hadn't told them all of the truth.

Calm-voice rocked his head side to side. "But I have to be certain of that. Let's go over it again."

Calm-voice repeated many of the same questions he had asked before, and John gave the same answers. At one point calm-voice said, "You're starting to sound like you've got this rehearsed."

"Of course it sounds rehearsed," John said, not feeling terribly brave at the moment and desperately wanting to avoid another beating. "I've had to tell the same fucking story so many times to so many people, I've completely lost count."

That appeared to satisfy calm-voice, at least as far as that issue was concerned. When he finished questioning John he turned to pissed-off guy and said, "Okay, he's all yours."

The second time around pissed-off guy did more than simply beat the crap out of John. He broke a few of his fingers, and it took the doctor two days to heal all of that.

She pleaded with the two men. "You don't understand. With repeated use of accelerated healing and rapid regrowth in a short period of time, his body will start rejecting those technologies."

They ushered her out of the room, calm-voice repeated the same questions and made John repeat the same answers, clearly looking for inconsistencies with his earlier answers. Then he turned John over to pissed-off guy with the same words, "Okay, he's all yours."

John stuck to his story by constantly recalling his abiding hatred of anyone like Cranoch. It helped to know that they needed to keep him alive, and he surmised that if he did start telling what he had held back, that would encourage them to think he had held back even more, and it would never end. John had told the redacted version of events on Reisenar so many times he had it down pat, and since he wasn't actually lying, there were no inconsistencies. He didn't think he could hate anyone more than Cranoch, but pissed-off guy certainly seemed to be vying for the honor.

After the third beating, the doctor fixed John up again. But that time it took her almost three days to get him back to normal, and her eyes frequently glistened with suppressed tears. He hoped she made it out of this mess alive.

The beatings ended and they put him in a private stateroom. But a prison cell was a prison cell. It might look like a small stateroom on a ship, but with the door locked from the outside, and an armed guard standing in the passageway on the other side of it, prison cell it was. They probably didn't have a brig on a civilian ship so they had to make do.

An odd thing happened the day after they locked him in the stateroom. A very military sounding alert klaxon blared and allship called all hands to battle stations. Battle stations! On a civilian ship!

Allship announced they had down-transited. Then a few minutes later he heard the unmistakable thrum of a big transition battery propagate through the ship's structure, followed by a little gravity wave that rolled through his cabin. In short succession he counted a total of twelve salvos and twelve gravity waves. It reminded him of training on the orbital weapons platform at Miriteen. Of course, the crewmembers manning the battery would have felt the gravity waves far more than he did in his prison cell of a stateroom.

An hour later allship announced up-transition, and again they were on their way.

No, nothing about this civilian ship added up to civilian.

31

Lost Prey

"*CALIBAN* IS BRAKING . . . braking hard."

Katrine slammed awake and stepped out of the field of her grav bunk. She had requisitioned a one-piece coverall from ship's stores and had taken to sleeping in that, which lessened the need to rush down passageways in her skivvies. It wouldn't do to give the spacers too much to look at.

When she stepped onto the bridge *Lightspear*'s crew was in the middle of trying to perform a crash stop. Going from pushing three thousand lights to down-transition as fast as possible was an exercise all ships practiced during shakedown, but one they rarely performed for real.

"Two thousand lights," the helmswoman said, speaking with the calm demeanor of an experienced professional.

Sharma said, "Maybe they're stopping for a navigation check."

Neilosse shook his head, his eyes riveted to his screens. "Not braking this hard. And they got a nav check two days ago. No need for another this soon."

Neilosse did not surprise Katrine with his next command. "Engineering, I want power priority to the helm. I want to beat them into sublight, but as soon as we down-transit, dump everything into the shields."

Hunter-killers could dump lights faster than larger ships, and Neilosse counted on that now. If *Caliban* beat them into sublight, then their enemy could get a precise targeting signature off *Lightspear*'s transition flare. *Lightspear* needed to down-transit while *Caliban* was still dumping lights, and half blind in transition.

"One thousand lights," the helmswoman said. "Five hundred . . . four hundred . . . three hundred."

Neilosse barked, "Helm, force down-transition if you can, and when we go sub-light all departments immediately rig for silent running."

"One hundred lights . . ."

A cluster of gravity waves rolled through the bridge.

"I'm pushing it as hard as I can, sir . . . and . . . we . . . are . . . down. Down-transition."

Knowing what to expect Katrine gripped the edge of a console. Utter silence descended on the ship as engineering cut power to everything but life support, with just a trickle fed to the sublight grav drive to keep it ready for maneuvering if needed. Katrine's spine, slightly compressed by the one G maintained on the bridge, decompressed when they went weightless. Holding tightly to the console kept her from floating away out of control.

"Drones out," Neilosse said.

The hull echoed with the launch of the combat drones.

"Transition flare," the scan tech said, "ranging at just over one light hour."

"Fire Control," Neilosse demanded. "Do you have a targeting signature?"

"I do, sir, and it's sweet."

"Colonel," Neilosse said to Katrine, "do we take the shot?"

She shook her head. "Negative."

Everyone there seemed disappointed.

The hull shrieked as a gravity spike punched through it.

"That was *Caliban*'s main battery, sir. They missed us by ten million klicks."

Neilosse nodded. "They didn't get a good targeting solution on us so they're trying long-shots."

Katrine focused on the scan tech's screens. *Caliban* fired eleven more salvos in rapid succession, but none of them came as close as the first.

Looking over the scan tech's shoulder, Katrine saw the blip of *Caliban* accelerate away from them at a sharp angle from its previous course.

"They're accelerating in sublight, sir, and taking a completely different vector."

"Yah," Neilosse said, sounding disappointed. "They know we're here, so they're not going to take a straight line to their destination."

"Do we follow, sir?"

Neilosse looked to Katrine for the answer to that. "Colonel?"

She shook her head. Now that *Caliban* knew they had an enemy on their tail, they would act more prudently than they had previously and lead them off in a false direction. After a day or two they would execute a long, slow turn that *Lightspear* couldn't detect while in transition. They'd end up following nothing.

On the other hand, *Caliban*'s original vector might have taken them to Sarkovie, Norandyne, or the Mikotian Republic. Novalis III was out there as well, but she didn't think anyone would choose that graveyard as a destination.

Katrine addressed her question to the navigator. "How far are we from Sarkovie?"

"Fifty-seven light-years, ma'am."

She looked pointedly at Neilosse. "We know they're not operating on Norandyne, and we have reason to believe they have allies on Sarkovie. And we have some assets there as well."

Neilosse grinned, reminding her of that bit of predator she suspected he had in his genetic makeup. "I have a feeling we're not done with *Caliban* yet. Sarkovie it is."

••••

Konigsborge and *Alvilddan* down-transited for a nav fix ten light-years out from Sarkovie, and to reestablish contact with the hunter-killer *Eldekarl*. Kristdokar suppressed her impatience as they pinged nearby space with their transition com, sending out a predefined encryption key to locate *Eldekarl*'s communications relay buoy, always a dangerous move, but one necessary under the circumstances. The buoy responded with a message from the hunter-killer's captain detailing her approach plan.

At that moment *Eldekarl* was in the latter stages of its hunter-killer approach, running silent and unable to transmit without potentially giving away its position. But in just under two days *Eldekarl* would down-transit two hundred light-hours off Sarkovie, hopefully undetected. They could receive while running silent, so through the buoy Nygaard transmitted their own approach plan to *Eldekarl*'s captain.

At Kristdokar's recommendation, Nygaard agreed to split up their small strike force. They sent the destroyer off in a different direction with orders to arc around and approach Sarkovie from a slightly different angle. *Konigsborge* would continue on in a direct approach with Kristdokar and Nygaard on board.

Both ships would attempt a hunter-killer approach. *Eldekarl* was much better equipped for such tactics, so *Konigsborge* and *Alvilddan* would only attempt to get to within eight hundred light-hours of the Sarkovie system before down-transiting. Once the hunter-killer did down-transit, the situation would be reversed. The cruiser and the destroyer would be running silent, but they could receive, though *Eldekarl* would have to be exceedingly careful about its transmitter splash. At that point the hunter-killer should be able to give them a good rundown on the situation in the Sarkovie system.

Wonderful plans, Kristdokar thought as the cruiser's captain and navigator set up their approach. She only hoped Sarkovie had been the right choice.

••••

Allship blared, "Down-transition in ten minutes and counting."

Anders looked carefully at his cards, then added a few pieces of script to the kitty at the center of the table.

Agneta Aanberg added a few more pieces while displaying an intentionally inscrutable look.

One of the men across from her looked carefully at his cards, then carefully at her. "You've got that look, but you're not going to beat my ass this time." He added more pieces to the kitty.

Anders tossed his cards face-down on the table and said, "That's it for me. I'm out."

Anders had cultivated a purely professional relationship with Agneta Aanberg. Senior NCOs knew everything that went on in their department, and because they were a tight-knit group, they often knew everything that happened in other departments as well. Anders hadn't tried to take their relationship any further, simply because she wasn't his type. When he learned she had a closer-than-professional relationship with another NCO, he knew he wasn't her type either, which was all well and good.

Anders downed the last of his kirva ration and stood. "I'm through for the night."

He left his new comrades in the main mess and made his way back to his bunk.

"Down-transition in five minutes and counting."

Sycorax's senior officers were exceedingly closed-mouth about their destination. But Anders had learned from Aanberg they were headed for Sarkovie. For some reason they intended to down-transit in the system, deliver someone or something to Sarkovie, then move to a position some distance off the planet.

In the bunk room, Anders stripped down, climbed into his bunk, and lay in the dark considering what he had learned. Because of the command hawk he knew their very important prisoner was Nikaela Vreekande, and rumor among the NCOs had it that when they got to their destination, they would take on another important prisoner. Senior NCOs were not prone to idle gossip, and he had learned long ago one did not take lightly any rumor among them. And two ship captains would much prefer to conduct a clandestine prisoner exchange well outside the bounds of any inhabited system. It all added up.

Anders resurrected his suspicion that they had put him on *Sycorax* for something more than merely transferring him to another location. That they weren't going to deliver him to Sarkovie when they had the opportunity was quite telling in that respect. What did Eskildsen want from him, and why couldn't she simply ask him for it outright? On the other hand, it was quite possible they didn't yet know what they wanted of him, had simply put him on board this ship to make him available for whatever the command hawk came up with.

••••

Katrine asked Neilosse to set up a hunter-killer approach to the Sarkovie system. Pushing four thousand lights, their transition wake could easily be detected at a distance of five light-years with a transition scanner. So at a distance of eight light-years they began to slow down, which reduced the strength of their wake, and the distance at which they could be detected. But they had to constantly reduce their drive as the distance narrowed, which meant that mathematically they would never get there. So at a certain point they were forced to take a chance and down-transit, trying to keep their transition flare to a minimum and hoping for the best. More often than not it was a trick used during war to sneak into the shipping lanes of an enemy and wreak havoc with their supply lines.

"Sir," the scan tech said, "we just hit one light year out from the Sarkovie system."

Katrine looked at the scan tech's screens. After thirty-six hours of decelerating on an exponentially decaying curve, they had cut their drive back to five hundred lights, a slow crawl for *Lightspear*.

"Okay," Neilosse said, "start dumping lights, but do it slow and easy."

In this case they didn't want to sneak into the system or a shipping lane, which would necessitate pushing much closer into the system on the declining deceleration curve and down-transiting several thousand AU's outside the system—much closer than they were at the moment—then coasting in sublight. Hunter-killer captains had been known to spend more than a month setting up such a shot. But all *Lightspear* needed to do was get close enough for them to put their transition scanner to use.

The helmswoman began carefully cutting their drive in a slow, steady, declining curve. Dumping lights too quickly generated a lot of transition noise, and would make them visible over a much greater distance

An hour later a gravity wave made Katrine's stomach turn a little somersault.

"One hundred lights," the helmswoman said.

"Keep that transition flare to a minimum," Neilosse cautioned.

With everyone's eyes locked to their own screens, the silence of the bridge was broken only by small beeps and pings from its instruments.

"Fifty lights."

The minutes ticked by as the helmswoman gingerly brought them closer and closer to the sublight threshold.

"Forty lights . . . thirty . . ."

Katrine gulped hard as a rapid cluster of gravity waves tested her transition gut.

". . . twenty . . . fifteen . . . and . . ."

"Down-transition at thirteen lights. Holding steady in sublight at point nine lights."

"Drones out and rig for silent running," Neilosse said. "And that's a new record. Extra whiskey ration on me tonight."

He looked Katrine's way and gave her that predatory grin. "If you're right, Colonel, and *Caliban* is coming here, we'll be waiting for them."

He turned to the navigation officer. "Nav, what do you think?"

The young officer at the navigation console had a predatory grin much like Neilosse's. "With our greater top speed, we should be two or more days ahead of them."

Again, the waiting.

Katrine spent some time in the gym, though on a cramped hunter-killer she had to limit her use of the facility. A day and a half after down-transiting one light-year off Sarkovie, Neilosse called her up to the bridge. She took her usual position behind the scan tech.

"Okay, scan," Neilosse said. "Tell Colonel Primatov what you've got."

The young rating said, "Bogie ranging at about four light-years, driving in at just under three thousand lights."

When they had first started tracking *Caliban* near Trafalgar, the young scan tech had been reluctant to hazard a guess at that range. Recalling that, Katrine said, "Still too far out for a good guess?"

"Not at all, ma'am. At this point we've acquired a complete transition spectrum on *Caliban*, and we've got a refined wake signature for comparison. We can't be absolutely certain until they get a little closer, but I'd bet good money that's our target."

Three hours later, the bogie had closed the distance to three light-years, and at that point all uncertainty had been laid to rest. Nine hours after that, *Caliban* passed *Lightspear* about a thousand light-hours off the hunter-killer's bow, driving hard toward Sarkovie.

Looking over the scan tech's shoulder at his screens, Katrine wondered if John Mathius had managed to stay alive. She wanted to believe they hadn't abducted him and put him on a transition ship simply to execute him in transit. But what did they have in mind, what did they hope to do with him?

"Sir," the com tech said, "I'm picking up a transition com signal about two hundred light-hours off Sarkovie, well outside heliopause. It's originating from a point not far off *Caliban*'s vector. That might be their destination."

Neilosse looked Katrine's way and their eyes met. "Can you decode it?"

"Negative, sir. It's heavily encrypted. But now I'm picking up a signal from *Caliban* with the same signature. It looks like a response."

A ship in transit operated in almost complete blindness, unless they had an ally coasting in sublight up-linking data to them.

"Steady as she goes, people," Neilosse said. "Let's just wait, and watch, and see what happens."

Katrine asked. "Any chance that unidentified ship spotted us? They were in sublight on our approach, might have tracked us."

Neilosse grimaced. "We used a very conservative deceleration curve, so they wouldn't have been able to detect our wake. It is possible they spotted our down-transition flare, but only if they were looking this way."

Three hours later, *Caliban* down-transited near the origin of the transition com signal. Almost immediately, the scan tech said, "Sir, I'm getting some transition noise from that ship near *Caliban*. Looks very much like the signature I'd get from a warship maneuvering hard with their sublight grav drive. And *Caliban* appears to be maneuvering likewise."

Neilosse nodded. "They're matching vectors for a rendezvous."

"Sir," the scan tech said. "I need to get a little more data to be sure, but that warship *Caliban* is approaching has an emissions profile much like that of a Kelk destroyer."

Neilosse's head turned slowly to look at Katrine and his eyes hardened with distrust. He didn't look away from her as he spoke to the scan tech. "Are you sure of that?"

"Not yet, sir. I need more data to confirm or deny."

"Take your time and make sure," Neilosse said, still looking at Katrine.

Katrine closed her eyes and gave a single nod of her head.

Several seconds passed, then the scan tech broke the silence. "Confirmed, sir. Definitely a Kelk warship."

Katrine opened her eyes. Neilosse had not moved, nor looked away from her. "Steady as she goes," he said. "Commander Sharma, take the conn."

"Aye, aye, sir."

Neilosse stood. "Colonel Primatov, in my office, if you please."

Katrine nodded. Everyone there wanted to ask the same question Katrine knew Neilosse was about to ask her, and their eyes tracked her as she followed him off the bridge. He led her to his office where he sat down at a small fold-down desk. He didn't invite her to join him and sit down as well. He also didn't need to tell her to close the door. She did so without prompting, then turned to face him.

"Colonel," he said, speaking slowly and precisely. "Tell me why a disguised Commonwealth warship is rendezvousing with a Kelk warship as if they're allies?"

"I don't exactly know," she said. "I will tell you they have taken one of my people as a prisoner, and I suspect they are delivering him to the Kelk."

The look on his face flashed from distrust to anger. "They're turning him over to the enemy? Are they betraying us?"

Katrine chose her words carefully. "If, by the use of the word *enemy*, you mean the Kelk Supremacy, I think the answer to that is no. That Kelk warship is probably as disguised as *Caliban*. I believe those two ships are both rogues, and together they are betraying the Commonwealth and the Supremacy."

He frowned and his eyes narrowed in thought. "I'm listening."

Katrine had no choice but to tell him about Reisenar, though she gave him a very concise and summarized version. She didn't go into the level of cooperation between her and Kristdokar.

When she finished he closed his eyes and remained silent for the longest time. After several seconds he opened his eyes and looked at her pointedly. "You're wondering where I stand on the Kelk issue. So I'll tell you . . . I don't know where I stand on the Kelk issue."

Katrine did trust him, but she needed to know more. "Can you stop viewing the entire Kelk race as the enemy?"

He pursed his lips and silently considered her question for a few seconds. "I don't know. Why don't you tell me who *is* the enemy. What are we dealing with in those two ships out there?"

She decided it was time to take a leap of faith. "We believe anti-Kelk hardliners on our side have found common cause with anti-Commonwealth hardliners on their side."

He shook his head as if she had just spoken in a foreign tongue. "Their racial hatred has overcome their mutual hatred?"

"It appears so," she said, "though they are supported by commercial interests on both sides, organizations that might benefit financially from a war."

His eyes widened. "Whoa! This is a fucking sticky mess."

"Yes, it is."

He abruptly stood. "As to the Kelk issue, I won't go out of my way to kill any I don't have to, or to start a war. You'll just have to trust I'll do my duty."

She shrugged. "I think that's the one thing I do know about you."

He grinned unhappily. "The open mandate from the Senate Intelligence Committee and the Class-One clearance authorization might have something to do with my duty."

32

An Echo of Pain

EIGHT MORE DAYS of pure boredom pacing the deck of his make-shift prison cell, and John was ready to climb the walls. Then allship announced down-transition, but this time no battle stations and no transition battery salvos. A couple hours later a faint clang echoed through the hull, followed by a sequence of similar sounds, as if they docked somewhere.

There followed an hour of silence, then the door to his stateroom opened and two armed guards walked in. They cuffed his hands behind his back and marched him out of his stateroom prison-cell. When they came to a ladder to a lower deck, with his hands cuffed behind his back, the two men carefully helped him navigate the steps downward. They marched him along a short passageway and through a bulkhead door, making sure he didn't bark his shins or bang his head. John had gotten the impression everyone on that ship would just as soon beat the shit out of him, so he found their concern for his well-being rather odd.

To John's surprise, calm-voice and pissed-off guy stood near an open personnel hatch talking with a female Kelk command hawk. Standing silently behind her, a female Kelk NCO and two Kelk crewmembers, one male and one female, watched the two converse with bored disinterest.

Calm-voice, pissed-off guy, and the command hawk went silent as John and his guards approached and stopped a few paces away. The Kelk officer had more pepper in her hair than salt, and John realized that in thinking of her apparent age that way, he had used a very Kelk way of thought. Professor Dirkson's lessons must have sunk in.

With a bland, bored expression on her face, the Kelk officer looked John over carefully.

Pissed-off guy approached John and stopped in front of him, standing quite close, a sneer on his face. "He's not much to look at, is he?"

Calm-voice said to the Kelk woman, "He's all yours."

Pissed-off guy gave John a nasty grin. "It's your dream come true, you fucking Kelk-loving piece of shit. See how you like the way they treat you, because you're all theirs now."

Pissed-off guy stood close enough that John felt puffs of breath as he spoke. John had nothing to lose, and he dearly wanted a little satisfaction. He head butted the asshole, slamming his forehead into the bridge of the bastard's nose, and feeling a satisfying crunch as it broke. Then he kneed the shit-head in the balls.

Pissed-off guy screamed, dropped to the deck and curled into a fetal position as the two guards behind John finally reacted and gripped his elbows.

Calm-voice held up a hand. "Don't hurt him. We have to deliver him unhurt."

John considered kicking pissed-off guy in the ribs, but they yanked him back a step before he could. Too bad!

Lying on the deck at their feet, pissed-off guy groaned piteously as blood poured out of his nose and formed a very satisfying pool on the deck. The Kelk officer had lost the bored expression. She looked John over again, but now he saw curiosity in her eyes.

John would gain nothing by revealing he spoke some Kelk, so he looked her in the eyes and spoke in Lingua. "I owed him that."

She lifted an eyebrow, nodded, and spoke in Kelk much too rapidly for John to follow her words. The two enlisted Kelk stepped forward and gripped John by the elbows. The command hawk turned and stepped through the personnel hatch. The NCO followed her.

It would be futile to resist, so with the female Kelk guard leading and the male following, John stepped through the hatch into a small airlock, then through another hatch into the body of a craft much like a Commonwealth assault boat, but this was all Kelk. He had entered just aft of the cockpit, and he caught a momentary glimpse forward into the control cabin. Looking past the pilot's head and shoulders, some of the gauges seemed familiar, though all the labels were written in that odd Kelk script. But the attitude yoke and thrust stick looked almost identical to that in the simulators and assault boats he had practiced in during advanced training. He couldn't see them, but he would bet good money there were yaw pedals on the floor in front of the pilot's seat. He had never considered it before, but he should have realized the main design elements of a boat's controls would be fairly common just about anywhere.

The glimpse into the cockpit only lasted for a second. They marched him toward the back of the boat between two rows of seats facing inward, the classic configuration for carrying armed troops. The NCO and command hawk had taken seats toward the rear of the craft. The female guard stopped about half-way there and pointed to a seat. John sat down, though he couldn't sit comfortably with his hands cuffed behind his back. They cuffed his left ankle to a cleat in the floor, and the two guards sat in the seats opposite him, facing him. The female casually slapped the barrel of some sort of baton against the palm of her left hand, repeating the gesture in a slow, steady cadence. The male guard carried a similar baton, but left it strapped to his side.

The Corps didn't use neural prods, but during basic John and his fellow recruits had been taught to recognize them because they might come up against one sometime. John decided he would take great care to ensure that his guards had no excuse to use the damn things.

The pilot sealed the airlock's personnel hatch, and a loud metallic clang rang through the boat's hull as it separated from the larger ship. For the first time in his life, he was the only person present not of Kelk lineage. He felt very alone.

They were only in transit for about ten minutes. Then he heard more clangs ring through the boat's hull. They sat still for a while, and he heard servo's whining and pumps chattering. The pilot opened the airlock hatches, John's guards uncuffed his left ankle and made him stand, and as they led him toward the exit he again caught a glimpse into the cockpit. Beyond its transparent plast windshield, he saw another assault boat resting on its docking boom in a large hangar bay. The doors of the bay were open to space, and several crewmembers in vac suits worked at securing the boat in which John had just arrived.

The female guard preceded him through the airlock, while the male followed, and John stepped onto the deck of a Kelk warship. The outer hatch opened into a passageway where two crewwomen paused when John and his captors appeared.

The command hawk stepped out of the hatch and barked something in Kelk that sounded like, "Prisoner walking."

The two crewwomen pressed their backs against a bulkhead as John's guards hustled him past them. Both watched him closely, one with a look of simple curiosity, and the other with open hostility.

The command hawk went her own way, leaving John with the NCO and two guards. They led John down the passageway to a grav lift. They called the lift, stepped into it, and a moment later stepped out onto another deck. They marched him down a narrow passageway, then up to an unmanned security station. The NCO leaned over a bank of monitors and touched a switch there, saying something in Kelk. John heard the words ". . . cell number one."

Just beyond the security station a short passageway ended in a dead end. The corridor would have been featureless without the two heavy plast doors in the right wall. Face high in each door, plast bars blocked a small open square that, even without the bars, would still have been too small to crawl through.

The first door clattered open as they led John down the passageway. They stopped at the open door, and one of the guards nudged him in the back with a neural prod. He stepped into the cell and paused. Two grav bunks each held blankets and a thin mattress pressed against the wall by their gravity fields. A pressure toilet, pressure sink, two extrudable chairs, and a fold-down table were the only other features in the cell.

John wasn't prepared for the lightning bolt that slammed into his back and the shock of pain that struck him. He cried out, stumbled forward and fell to his knees. Someone grabbed his hair, pulled his head back, and he found himself looking into the face of the NCO. The woman had leaned forward so that only a hand's breadth of space separated their noses. She spoke Lingua in a thick accent through gritted teeth. "This how like Blackswords we think."

The NCO jammed a prod between his legs and a shock of blinding pain shot through his groin. He screamed, and they kept him screaming like that for quite a while.

••••

Long journeys always tested one's ability to overcome boredom. Nikaela had learned that long ago, and like any experienced spacer had developed her own methods of keeping the monotony of shipboard life at bay. Study, training in a simulator, workouts in the gym, card games with friends and acquaintances, maintenance checks on her combat armor and equipment, almost anything helped alleviate the tedium. But she had never been forced to endure a long journey just sitting in a cell staring at four blank walls.

She asked for reading materials and they ignored her. She worked out quite a bit, improvising what she could with no exercise equipment at hand, but still found herself spending far too much time staring at the damn walls. She knew when they down-transited only because she heard it on allship.

Through experimentation she discovered that if she pressed her cheek tightly against the door of her cell, through the small barred opening she had a slanting view up the short passageway, and saw enough to know if anyone manned the guard station there. Her captors usually left it unoccupied. They brought her meals on a regular basis—thankfully no longer laced with shit. But other than that, the male or female guard might show up two or three times a day, walk down the passageway, glance briefly into Nikaela's cell, then leave her alone in the silence of the otherwise empty brig.

Two days after they down-transited, she was in the middle of a set of push-ups when she heard a commotion in the passageway outside her cell. She jumped to her feet, crossed the cell, and pressed her cheek against the door to see what she could. The male guard now sat at the security station.

Nikaela heard boot steps on the deck, but had no way of counting their number. The NCO said, "We'll put him in cell number one."

Nikaela strained to see what she could. She heard the door in the cell next to hers clatter open, and caught a glimpse of an NCO's shoulder, and that of one of the guards following her, probably the same NCO who had installed Nikaela in her cell. They entered the cell next to hers, there came a moment of silence, then a man screamed out a cry of pain that sent a shiver up her spine. She heard him gasping for breath, heard the guards struggling with him, then her heart went cold when she heard the NCO say in broken Lingua, "This how like Blackswords we think."

The man screamed again, and again, and again, and she heard something familiar in his voice. Time had allowed her to forget how she herself had screamed when the guards had tormented her with their prods. She had become desperate to see an end to the pain, and listening to him now she recalled that like him, she had abandoned all pride. She had begged and pleaded for mercy, and even now felt shame that she had not been stronger. She should have been stronger. And now the guards laughed at him the way they had laughed at her.

She tried to cover her ears. It had been a blessed relief to forget all that, to pretend she had been of stouter resolve, but now it came back to her. She sank down to the floor, sat with her back against a wall, tucked her knees up to her chest, and as he screamed and begged and pleaded, just the way she had screamed and begged and pleaded, she cried like a child.

She drifted off into a nightmarish haze of numbness, and the silence brought her back to her senses. The only sound she heard was the rasping wheeze of her own breathing. It took her a moment to realize she wasn't listening to her own labored breathing, but rather that of the poor fellow in the cell next to her.

She climbed to her feet and pressed her cheek against the door. The female guard sat at the security station. Nikaela listened carefully, desperately trying to pin down every sound that came from the poor fellow's cell. That bitch of an NCO had said to him, "This how like Blackswords we think."

Was he a Blacksword, perhaps even one of John Mathius's comrades? Standing so close to the small barred opening in the door to her cell, the smell from his cell hit her nose. The poor fellow hadn't fared any better than her.

She heard him groan, a gurgling, choking sound. He coughed, and then she heard him gagging and choking as he vomited.

The guard at the security station stood up. Nikaela didn't know how the woman might react to being watched by a prisoner, so she leaned a little away from the door, but could still see enough. The woman walked down the passageway, glanced into the fellow's cell, then returned to the bank of monitors.

A few minutes later the NCO showed up accompanied by the male guard. The NCO probably accompanied them this time only because she had some limited command of Lingua, a skill the two crewmembers were unlikely to possess.

The door in the cell next to Nikaela's clattered open. The NCO spoke in her broken Lingua. "Go stand flush grate. Become naked, no materials." She didn't have much command of Lingua, but it was probably enough, because several seconds later Nikaela heard the spray of the hose, and she heard the fellow gasp as it stung his skin.

When they finished hosing him down the NCO said, "You wear. Two materials only you get. You clean self, or be not clean."

The male guard spoke in Kelk. "I thought these Blackswords were supposed to be something to fear."

The female guard answered him. "Doesn't look like much, does he?"

With her cheek pressed to the door of her cell hoping to see something, anything, Nikaela saw the NCO and the male guard walk up the passageway away from the cells. The female guard had remained behind for some reason, and Nikaela heard her speak in Kelk. "Filthy, common-face breschkada."

Nikaela suppressed a gasp, couldn't breathe for a moment and staggered away from the door. Had she heard the woman correctly? Could it really be him?

••••

"Can you get us any closer?" Katrine asked Neilosse. She didn't need to also say, *without being spotted.*

In response to the questioning look he gave her, she said, "As I told you, we have assets on Sarkovie. I'd like to try to communicate with them. And with *Caliban* and a Kelk warship between here and there . . ."

He finished the thought for her. "The moment we fire up our transition com, they'll spot us, and think it very curious that a ship would sit in the middle of no-where one light-year out."

He turned to the officer at the nav console. "Anything incoming we might use for a tag-along?"

Katrine knew the maneuver well. With *Lightspear* coasting at point nine lights, they could use the wake of an incoming ship, with only a little help from the hunter-killer's transition drive, to pull them into up-transition with almost no detectable transition flare. Then they could *tag-along*, or hide, in the other ship's wake, and down-transit with it, using its down-transition flare to mask their own. Sarkovie wasn't the busiest of interstellar waypoints. But they had down-transited in the mid-dle of the shipping lane between Sarkovie and the Commonwealth.

The fellow at the nav console would be getting a direct feed from scan. When Katrine leaned slightly to one side, she saw the left half of his face through a gap in the instrument clusters. He grimaced. "Only one possibility, sir. We've got an in-bound ship ranging at two light-years and driving at a thousand lights. Very strong transition wake, so it's got to be pushing a lot of mass, probably a freighter. But it won't be here for over seventeen hours."

"Anything else?"

"One other ship, sir. It's a lot faster, but it's not on our line, probably inbound from Norandyne. We'd have to push the sublight drive hard to get lined up, and we still might not make it."

Neilosse looked at his screens for several seconds. "Colonel, if you please." He nodded to his screens.

Katrine edged her way around the scan console and stopped beside Neilosse. "That Kelk warship has me worried," he said. "They were here coasting in sublight before we got here. We made a good approach, so they wouldn't have been able to track our wake. But if they were looking our way they might have spotted our flare when we down-transited."

She shrugged. "There really isn't anything we can do about that but hope for the best, is there?"

"Exactly," he said.

"Then I guess it's the freighter."

"The freighter it is," he said.

33

The Whisper of a Friend

THE GOSSIP AROUND the card table proved to be invaluable, so Anders never turned down an opportunity to play. After more than twenty-three days in transit, and now parked off Sarkovie, Anders had become a familiar face and just another bored spacer. More often than not, he didn't have to ask or probe to learn something new, or important, or invaluable.

Anders looked at his cards, another losing hand. He tossed the cards face-down on the table. "I'm out." He leaned back, took a small sip of his kirva ration, and listened.

One fellow peered over the top of his cards at Agneta Aanberg, his eyes narrowing in concentration. "Heard we had some visitors from that common-face ship. How'd that go?"

She rolled her eyes. "Strange. And it doesn't get any less strange every time we meet."

Anders asked, "Come over a lot, do they?"

She nodded and tossed a few coins into the center of the table. "Yah, lot of back and forth between here and there. And one of those common-face guys is a real piece of work: fat, ugly, lanky red hair, always mad about something."

One of the other players glanced over his shoulder before speaking. "Management's real upset about something."

"Sure seems that way," Aanberg said. She glanced over her shoulder, then lowered her voice. "I heard the prisoner they brought over is a Blacksword."

••••

John awoke to a litany of sore muscles. He had heard of neural prods but had never before seen one, and had certainly never entertained the thought he might be on the receiving end of one—or had it been three? Under normal use they were supposed to provide just enough discomfort to discourage inappropriate conduct during an unstable situation like a riot. He had heard they were used only rarely in prisons, and almost never elsewhere.

His implants informed him he had slept for more than fourteen hours. He lay in the grav bunk and carefully tested his aches and pains. His captors had used the prods at such intensity his muscles had spasmed to the point of injury, and everything he tested proved to be sore, even the muscles in his jaw and chin. He carefully probed at a rather sensitive spot on the side of his neck, which turned out to be a mild burn from the discharge of one of the prods. He found similar burns on his torso, and on his arms and legs.

The door to his cell opened without warning, and out of pure caution John stepped forward out of the field of his grav bunk to stand on the floor of the cell. The male Kelk guard who had helped install John in the cell stepped into the small room carrying a tray of food. As the strange smells of Kelk food hit John's nose his stomach growled. The command hawk who had taken custody of John walked in behind the guard. As the guard placed the tray of food on the small fold-down table, the command hawk crossed the cell to stand in front of John.

He hadn't had a lot of experience at reading Kelk expressions, but when her brows furrowed he thought that indicated unhappiness just the way it would on the face of one of John's Commonwealth comrades. She reached out and touched the burn mark on the side of his neck and the frown deepened. She grabbed his wrist and he didn't resist as she lifted his arm to examine it. She slid the sleeve of the coverall they had given him back a few inches to expose another burn, and the look on her face seemed to morph from unhappiness to outright anger.

She released his arm, looked into his eyes for a long moment, then spoke in flawless Lingua. "They tortured you?"

He wasn't sure if it had been a question or a statement. He refused to be cowed, so he returned her stare with a hard, blank expression and said nothing.

She turned abruptly and walked to the tray of food on the little table. For some odd reason she lifted a tiny bite of food to her mouth, then repeated that several times as if sampling all the items present on the tray. She nodded once, then with the guard in tow, walked out of the cell. The door clattered shut.

John was famished, but still he waited for several seconds for something unexpected to happen. When nothing did, he crossed the cell to the small table, extruded one of the chairs, and sat down to eat.

The food looked quite strange. There appeared to be a main course of something with the texture and appearance of meat, except it was green. And to one side he poked at some sort of black tuber. The taste defied description as well, as if his strange Kelk captors flavored their food with a whole spectrum of spices completely foreign to him. It wasn't bad, just different, though one item emitted a pungent odor, and took a little effort to choke it down.

"John Mathius, is that you?"

He hesitated, a fork full of food half-way to his mouth. It had been a woman's voice speaking Lingua in a barely audible whisper, and he wasn't sure if he'd actually heard those words, or simply hallucinated them. The words had almost been below the threshold of hearing, and at that point he could no longer claim with any confidence he had a solid grip on reality. He waited for several seconds, but heard no more and decided he must be imagining things.

He put the fork full of food into his mouth and chewed the strange substance.

"John Mathius, is that you?"

He had heard it that time, or at least he was fairly certain he had. He didn't start or jump to his feet, but carefully and slowly put the utensils down and stood. He scanned the small cell and saw nothing obvious, though that didn't preclude hidden speakers. On the other hand the words might have come from outside his cell through the small, barred opening in the door.

Taking great care not to make any sound as he moved, he crossed to the door and looked through the opening at the passageway beyond. He saw no one there. He leaned to one side and looked up the passageway where he had a clear, slanting view of the security station. At the moment it remained unoccupied, so the words couldn't have come from a guard. He leaned the other way and looked down the passageway; again nothing.

"John Mathius, is that you?"

It had definitely come from the passageway, but only the faintest of whispers. He spoke in the same soft tone of voice. "Who's there?"

"Are you John Mathius?"

"Yes, who are you?"

"I am shit-of-bull Kelk woman, Mathius breschkada."

••••

A cluster of gravity waves hit them hard, and a young trainee at the nav console gagged, but kept the contents of his stomach where it belonged. He glanced sheepishly Katrine's way.

"Ranging at three light-hours, sir. Intercept in ten seconds."

Even though the lumbering freighter had a maximum velocity of a thousand lights, it pushed so much mass its transition wake had hit *Lightspear* like a raging storm.

Neilosse stared intently at his screens. "Don't let them push us into transition."

"Intercept in five seconds, sir . . . four . . . three . . ."

"Dammit," the helmswoman said. "They pulled us into up-transition, sir. Sorry, sir."

Katrine heard someone gagging into a vomit bag.

"One hundred lights," the helmswoman said. "Five hundred lights . . . and . . . we've . . . matched transition velocity, sir."

"Good job people," Neilosse said. "And helm, with that fucking monster of a wake, I'm amazed you managed to keep us sublight as long as you did. Good job. Now we've got a rough ride ahead of us."

They backed off to two hundred light-hours behind the freighter, but riding in its wake proved to be an ordeal. Neilosse's people were an experienced crew, so everyone had known what to expect, and had stayed away from any food for several hours before the intercept. Had they not, it would have been far worse. But still, for the next nine hours, two med techs constantly circulated among the crew, dosing them all with drugs to keep the nausea at bay.

One limitation to the tag-along strategy was that they couldn't just down-transit anywhere. Their transition flare would be visible and obvious to anyone within range. Neilosse's only option was to attempt to anticipate when the freighter would down-transit, close the distance between them shortly before that, then down-transit at the same moment as the freighter, masking their own flare in that of the larger ship. If the freighter captain followed standard procedure, he would down-transit near heliopause to get a nav fix before entering the Sarkovie system. That would be about twenty light-hours out.

"Sir, they're about three hundred light-hours out from Sarkovie."

"All right, people, let's close the gap. Helm, push it a bit."

"Aye, aye, sir."

From their position of two hundred light-hours behind the freighter, the helmswoman goosed their transition drive, and they started to close the gap.

"We're one-fifty light-hours behind them . . . one hundred . . . fifty."

"Steady as she goes," Neilosse said. "Hold us at fifty."

"Sir, they're about forty light-hours out, and that freighter's begun to decelerate."

Neilosse ordered, "Start dumping lights, and try to follow their deceleration curve. In this god-awful wake no one's going to see us."

"Sir, she's braking hard . . . nine hundred lights . . . eight hundred . . ."

"Helm," Neilosse said. "That freighter probably can't drop below two hundred lights without going unstable, and they're going to flare like a big warhead on a dark night. When they do down-transit, dump as much sublight velocity as you can."

"Three hundred lights . . . two hundred . . . one hundred . . . and . . . we're down. Sublight, coasting at point two lights."

"Engineering," Neilosse shouted, his usual calm demeanor broken by the dangerous situation they had just dropped into. "Power priority to the shields. We might be someone's target. Fire Control, watch your defensive stations."

With one Kelk warship rendezvousing with *Caliban*, Neilosse had to assume there might be others nearby. Katrine braced herself, ready to hear the shriek of *Lightspear*'s hull as enemy transition batteries ripped her apart. But several seconds passed in absolute silence and nothing happened.

"Sir," the scan tech said. "That freighter's transition drive is running dirty as hell. They probably masked us nicely."

They all knew they could end up an easy target. Hunter-killers depended upon speed and stealth for defense, and her defensive stations would be no match for the transition batteries of a Kelk warship.

As the minutes ticked by they all slowly began to breathe easier. They had down-transited seventy-two light-hours from Sarkovie's primary, and apparently had done so without being detected by their enemy.

"Stand down, people," Neilosse said. "Drones out, and rig for silent running. And let's get some food in our guts."

••••

Standing with his mouth pressed between two bars in the small opening in the door to his cell, John kept his voice to the faintest of whispers. "You are Mistress Vreekande?"

"I am. You must be careful. There is a single vid pickup in my cell near the ceiling in one of the back corners. Your cell is probably equipped the same way. Be careful, Mathius breschkada."

Only the real Mistress Vreekande had ever called him that, and only she had used the *shit-of-bull* expression to describe herself. But she didn't sound like the young woman he had met on Reisenar, the pretty girl with the pale blueish skin and bright red irises. He hadn't heard her speak for almost two years, so it wasn't the tone or character of her voice that bothered him, because he could barely recall such nuances. But whoever occupied the cell next to his had only the faintest of accents when speaking Lingua, whereas the young woman on Reisenar had mispronounced words, commanded a limited vocabulary, and frequently struggled with simple sentence structure.

Back then many of her comrades had heard the way she addressed John, and the way she had referred to herself. They might have coached someone else in those subtleties and planted a spy in the cell next to his. Were they hoping to learn something? They knew he had joined the Blacksword. Did they think he had some special knowledge? Did they even realize he was just a low-life cadet and not really an officer? He had trusted the real Mistress Vreekande, and would do so again, but not some phony impersonator.

"John Mathius, do you hear me?"

"I do."

"Why are you so silent?"

"Just thinking." John couldn't trust anyone or anything on this ship, so he decided he must err on the side of caution. "I need to finish eating."

"Are you shit-of-bull now, John Mathius?"

"No, just hungry."

He turned around and returned to the half-finished tray of food, sat down and continued the meal.

She raised her voice a little. "Are you ignoring me now?"

He ignored her.

"Do you distrust me?"

He ate another bite of food.

"You are my breschkada-sa."

He tried more of the black tuber.

"You taught me shit-of-bull on that subway platform, and you saved my life."

The tuber had an odd taste and a spicy burn to it. John finished the meal, and with a gut full of food, drowsiness set in. He had already slept more than fourteen hours in that cell, but his muscles still ached from his experience with the business ends of three neural prods, and he thought he could sleep fourteen more. He stood, crossed the short distance to his gravity bunk, stepped into its field, and fell asleep immediately.

When he next awoke he had slept for another eight hours. While he had been out someone had removed the empty tray of food. He lay in his bunk just staring at the cell door and listening to the silence of the cell block. He couldn't feel the vibrations of the ship's engines through its structure, so they must be coasting. And the imposter in the cell next to his had stopped trying to convince him she wasn't an imposter.

John stripped down and gave himself a sponge bath from the sink. While standing there naked and dripping wet, the door to his cell clattered open and the female guard entered carrying another tray of food. She paused just within the cell and he froze. She smiled, looked him over carefully, and made no attempt to hide the way her eyes stripped him of all dignity. She walked to the small table and put the tray of food there, then turned toward him and crossed the distance between them. She stopped one pace away and her smile turned into a grin.

She lifted the prod and used its business end to probe at one of his breasts. He flinched, waiting for her to activate the thing, but she didn't do so. She looked down at his genitals and her grin broadened into an unpleasant leer. He tried to act nonchalant about her scrutiny as she walked slowly around him, tracing a line with the end of the prod along his chest, then down his side and across his buttocks. She stopped behind him and ran the prod gently up and down the inside of his thigh. She continued around him and the end of the prod never left his skin as she finished the circuit.

He wondered if they had any taboos against interracial sex with a Commonwealth soldier. Would she use her neural prod to coerce him? Did their taboo against rape apply to a woman forcing a man to do something against his will? It was then that he realized he had unwittingly put her in the category of demonic Kelk monster. But still, he felt considerable relief when she finally turned away from him and walked to the cell door. She paused there, turned and looked at him one last time, then slowly lowered her eyes to look at his genitals again. She stood there staring at him for a long moment, then turned and left. The cell door clattered shut.

As he ate the meal he heard a whisper just below the threshold of his hearing, loud enough to know the woman in the cell next door had said something, but not loud enough to discern the words. She tried again a little louder, and he made out ". . . saved your life."

He hesitated, stood, slowly crossed the cell to the door, and pressed his face between two bars in the small opening. "What did you say?"

"I never told you how I saved your life."

His breathing quickened, because only she would know that. He had told Colonel Primatov he didn't know how, or if, the strange Kelk woman had saved his life, but the Blacksword officer had insisted she must have, or they wouldn't be breschkada. Other than Primatov, only Nikaela Vreekande would know she had never revealed that bit of information to him. She might have told some of her comrades, but he didn't think that likely. Or they might have extracted it from her through torture. But it wasn't the kind of thing anyone would think to ask, so that too seemed improbable.

"How did you save my life?"

"After you saved my life, when you left me on the subway platform, I saw you go right into the tunnels. When my squad caught up with me, they wanted to search both directions to hunt you down. You were badly wounded and could barely walk, and I knew they would find you and kill you. So I told them I saw you go left, and not to waste their time searching the tunnels to the right."

John had a vivid memory of staggering along the grav tracks in the tunnel, expecting that at any moment her comrades would catch up with him. He had thought the rest of his life might be measured in minutes, and couldn't understand why no shout echoed behind him when they caught sight of him, or why he continued to live and take the next step, or why he didn't hear the staccato burst of weapons fire that signaled the end of his life. Perhaps some of them might know how she had saved his life, but he thought it quite likely none of them knew she had never told him.

"You sound different, not like the woman I remember. Your accent is much better."

She raised her voice to an angry growl. "My superiors made me take lessons. They said my accent was horrible,"—she must have realized she had raised her voice, because she returned to the faint whisper—"and they didn't want me to represent the Supremacy sounding like an uneducated laborer."

Represent the Supremacy! "Are you going to be a diplomat, or something?"

"No. They assumed you and I would meet again. I don't think they anticipated we would be whispering messages between prison cells. They wanted—"

The sound of other voices somewhere up the passageway startled John. He heard boot steps on the deck, so he turned around and quickly crossed the cell. He sat down at the table, took up the fork, and began eating again.

Out in the passageway a woman said something in Kelk, though she spoke too rapidly for him to translate all of it. He caught the words *bring the girl*.

He looked up and saw the male Kelk guard looking at him through the barred opening in his cell door. The man disappeared from sight as John heard the clatter of a cell door opening. Then he heard Nikaela speak Kelk. She said something about *not resisting*, though he couldn't make out every word.

He saw a couple of heads walk past the barred opening headed out of the cell block. He jumped to his feet, crossed the cell and pressed his cheek against the door to get a slanting view up the passageway. He only caught a fleeting glimpse of her back, her salt and pepper gray hair tied back in a simple ponytail—mostly pepper. They marched her out of the corridor to some unknown destination.

John stood at the cell door looking out at the empty and silent corridor for a good five minutes. Then he heard voices and boots on the deck. He took one step back from the door.

The face of the male guard appeared in the small opening. He spoke in Kelk. "Step away from the door, Blacksword."

John remembered his earlier resolve to not let on that he spoke some Kelk. He looked at the guard with wide eyes and shook his head. The man stepped aside and the female NCO replaced him. She spoke in Lingua. "Walk from door back, Blacksword."

John backed all the way to the other side of the cell, and pressed his back to the bulkhead there. The door to his cell clattered open.

34

A Convenient Assassin

WITH *KONIGSBORGE'S* GREATER mass, it was difficult to make a hunter-killer approach in a cruiser and remain undetected. But by not trying to drive all the way into the system, and instead targeting a destination eight hundred light-hours off Sarkovie, *Konigsborge* stood a better chance of doing so. After down-transition, when the scan tech reported nothing nearby had shown any reaction to their presence, Kristdokar breathed a sigh of relief.

Nygaard asked *Konigsborge*'s captain, "Have you detected anything at all unusual in the vicinity?"

Command Eagle Holverzon was a man who displayed no outward emotion. "Nothing, Vice Skalde. Perhaps a little more shipping activity than usual for such a system, but nothing out of the ordinary."

"With your permission," Kristdokar said, "I'd like to contact my man Brynjar to see if he's learned anything."

Nygaard appeared to consider the request for a moment, then shook her head. "No, I think not. For the time being, it's all rather quiet out there. Let's maintain com silence and see if anything happens."

••••

With two guards gripping Nikaela's elbows tightly and her hands cuffed in front of her, which was a nice change, they and the NCO marched her to a small storage room. Racks of shelves lined the back of the room, but in an open space in front of them they had placed two simple chairs about two meters apart, both facing the single door. They sat her in a chair, then the male guard stepped behind her and pressed his neural prod against the back of her neck, saying, "Be a good girl."

She couldn't turn and look him in the eyes, but the NCO stood directly in front of her. Nikaela gave her a shit-eating grin. "I'm always a good girl."

The NCO and the female guard left, leaving Nikaela sitting in the chair with one guard behind her pressing his neural prod against her spine.

Several minutes passed, then the door opened. The NCO and the other guard escorted John Mathius into the room. Like her, they had cuffed his hands in front of him. They sat him in the other chair, then the female guard stepped back and pressed the business end of her prod against John's spine. The NCO spoke in Lingua. "Be good obeying, Blacksword."

She crossed the small room and put her back against a bulkhead near the door.

Allowing them to sit with their cuffed hands resting in their laps, and not restrained in any other way, was an overt demonstration of their contempt for Nikaela's and John's inability to do anything about the situation. Unfortunately, given the three-to-two odds, and the neural prods pressed against John's and Nikaela's spines, she had to admit they were right about that.

John looked her way and his eyes focused on her intently. While whispering back and forth between the two cells she had sensed his distrust of her, and while she understood it, it had still hurt a little. But when he questioned her about her accent, she had realized he couldn't be certain she was who she claimed to be, not when all he knew of her was the sound of a whispered voice that didn't have the accent he recalled. Now, he gave her a pleasant, boyish smile, and she watched the distrust melt off his features the way the residual air in a lock dissipates when opened to vacuum. She returned the smile.

The door opened, and in walked the command hawk and Anders Eindride. Nikaela managed to not flinch at his unexpected appearance. Eindride had taken an enormous chance telling her of the vid pickup in her cell. She hadn't told John he was an ally because she didn't dare utter those words on this ship, even in the faintest of whispers.

Eindride stepped to one side and joined the NCO with his back to a bulkhead. The command hawk stood squarely in front of Nikaela, ignoring John. "You and he are breschkada, they tell me. Is that true? Or is that just another lie?"

Nikaela nodded. "He is breschkada-sa. I am breschkada-se."

The command hawk's eyes narrowed angrily. "Tell me about it."

"What do you want to know?"

"Everything."

Nikaela considered her words carefully. "We were on a subway platform. A micro-nuke had damaged my reactor pack and scrambled its failsafes. I would have—"

"No," the command hawk barked, slashing her hand through the air. "Start from the beginning."

Nikaela wasn't sure what the woman meant by *beginning*. "From the beginning? How far back do you want me to go?"

The command hawk's face remained unreadable. "Start from the moment you first set foot on Reisenar."

Nikaela considered lying, but the command hawk had probably read the classified reports on the incident, and would catch her out on something. And if they uncovered one lie, they would then believe nothing she said.

She described how First Liaison Company had established their headquarters in a two-story building near Parliament House. She told them of the fake Kelk warships the hunter-killer *Reguskalde* had detected, the attack on the Commonwealth drop boats, and how she, Thordahl, and Brynjar had incorrectly concluded the whole mess was a diabolical Commonwealth setup. Because of that Thordahl had instructed Nikaela to attempt to capture a ComSecCorps soldier alive for questioning. And when John Mathius had fired on their rooftop positions, she and her squads had attempted to encircle and detain him.

The command hawk repeatedly interrupted Nikaela, asking her to clarify certain details or provide additional information. The woman interrogated her for more than an hour, much the way Kristdokar had questioned her regarding Novalis III. It seemed odd the woman would force Nikaela to repeat a story she must already know.

When Nikaela got to the point where her reactor pack was about to cook her alive in her armor, and John Mathius had staggered out onto the subway platform to help her, the command hawk cut her off and turned to the young man.

She spoke to him in Lingua. "Tell me of your experience on Reisenar. Start with your descent to the surface in the drop boat."

He hesitated as if he might refuse to talk. In that moment Nikaela thought she might have some idea what the command hawk wanted to learn. "Tell her the truth, John," she said, and realized that was the first time she had ever used his given name in that familiar way.

He nodded, and began talking.

Nikaela had never heard John's side of the story, at least not in any detail. She listened with rapt fascination as he carefully laid out the events that brought him to that subway platform. He described how, when Nikaela had told him the Kelk hadn't attacked the Commonwealth drop boats, and the two warships were fake Kelk, all the missing pieces made sense. But it was not until the command hawk focused on the details of his wounds that Nikaela fully understood the issue.

"Your first wound," the command hawk said, "armor splinters in your side from a torso breach caused by a Kelk assault rifle in that alley. Am I correct?"

John nodded, "Yes." He clearly didn't understand the line of questioning, but Nikaela now thought she might.

"And your second wound, flechettes from a Kelk rotary as you escaped the alley?"

Again, he nodded and said, "Yes."

"But the most serious wound,"—the command hawk sounded like an advocate at a tribunal who had just made a winning point—"the wound to your left hand, that was for all intents and purposes self-inflicted, was it not?"

"Yes," he said, and Nikaela's heart sank. He had just given the command hawk a tiny edge. But at that moment he closed his eyes and nodded. "Yes. I was weak from loss of blood, and the pain from the other wounds clouded my thinking. It was stupid, I know."

Nikaela's heart raced. John had just denied the command hawk the victory she had hoped to gain, and he clearly didn't realize what he had done.

The command hawk forced him to continue his story, but at a certain point she interrupted him, turned to Nikaela, and had her continue where he left off. Then she interrupted Nikaela, and transferred the telling of the story back to John. In that way, each of them told their own little bits of the conversation between them on that subway platform, until Nikaela finished by telling of the lie she had spoken to Oberseergent Geltkarl, the lie that John had gone left not right, the lie that had saved his life.

Throughout the entire exchange Anders Eindride had stood unmoving. His eyes never left John Mathius and stayed locked on him as if he might gain some deeper insight into the young man. On that subway platform, when Nikaela had asked John what he meant when he said he was *done with killing*, he had simply said, "Novalis III." During the telling of his story, and the command hawk's subsequent questioning, he had said nothing of his connection to that tragedy. Nikaela would honor his omission and keep that part to herself.

The command hawk stepped back and looked at both of them. She sounded tired as she said, "Do either of you have anything to add?"

John shook his head. Nikaela did likewise.

The command hawk turned to John and spoke in Lingua. "I have one last question for you, young man."

John didn't react, but simply sat staring at her, his face devoid of all expression.

The command hawk spoke without tone or emotion in her voice. "You were born and raised on Novalis III, am I right?"

••••

When the command hawk revealed that the young man was a survivor of Novalis III, Anders flinched. Even the NCO, who spoke such halting Lingua, seemed to understand the question, and her eyes widened fearfully. But Mistress Vreekande failed to react in the least, and Anders turned his attention away from the young Blacksword to look carefully at her. The young woman's eyes hardened, as if the command hawk's revelation angered her.

In SecureMax the prisoners weren't given regular updates on the latest news, so other than Thoran's information that Nikaela was breschkada to a Blacksword, Anders had previously heard nothing of the incident on Reisenar. Under Eskildsen's questioning, while Mistress Vreekande and the young Blacksword had told their stories, Anders had listened to every word with rapt attention. The command hawk had clearly hoped to discredit their account and prove they were not truly breschkada, and she had just as clearly failed to do so. And her revelation that the young man had survived Novalis III was an obvious effort to salvage something from the interrogation, but what?

The command hawk leaned toward young Mr. Mathius, as if inviting him to react in some way. "You were one of the few survivors. Did you lose anyone there?"

The young man didn't move in any way. He didn't flinch, didn't twitch, didn't breathe, but the look on his face morphed from uncaring emptiness to a cold, burning anger that frightened Anders, and clearly frightened even Mistress Vreekande. The fellow did not answer Eskildsen's question, but remained as still as a sculpture of stone and stared at the command hawk as if he could kill her with a thought.

The NCO sucked in a deep breath, and Anders realized he had not been the only one unable to breathe in that moment of silence. Mistress Vreekande's lack of reaction made it quite clear she already knew of the young man's history. And while the NCO and guards all reacted with obvious surprise, they weren't in play in this. That left only Anders. The command hawk had revealed that bit of information for his ears, but why?

At the young man's refusal to speak, Eskildsen turned to the NCO and spoke in Kelk. "Take them back to their cells and do not harm them."

Had she hoped to fuel Anders's hatred? Oddly enough, he had hated the Blacksword on principle, but he couldn't find any hate for the young man when he met him in the flesh. Obviously, Eskildsen needed an excuse to eliminate the poor fellow, and probably Mistress Vreekande as well. But why bring Anders into it? What did Eskildsen hope to accomplish using him?

As the NCO and guards led the two young people out of the room, Anders waited for Eskildsen to follow them, assuming he would follow her. But instead she turned to face him. "Maestra Eindride, a private word with you, if you please."

As the door to the room closed he nodded. "I'm at your service, mistress."

She gave him a pained smile. "This must be quite painful for you."

"How so, mistress?"

She pursed her lips as if undecided what to say next. "I know of your history. I know you hate the young woman because of her testimony at your tribunal. And no one would hold it against you if you hated the young man as well. He is, after all, Commonwealth, and Blacksword."

At that moment Anders played his part very carefully. It would not serve him to appear unhinged by anger or hatred, though he thought that might be what she wanted from him. "I certainly hold no love for the Commonwealth, and that applies especially to a Blacksword."

Her upper lip curled with distaste. "It angers me that they are breschkada, and even more that he is breschkada-sa. Doesn't it infuriate you? He makes us look weak at a time when we most need to appear strong."

At that moment Anders thought he might have some idea where the command hawk was going with this, and perhaps why they had put a cashiered ex-command-superior on this ship. Did they hope he would hate a survivor of Novalis III even more than he hated the young woman? "To become breschkada requires an act of great courage. It does anger me a Blacksword was the first to act."

"And now they stand in our way," she said. "If you can think of anything that might help, it would be most appreciated."

As Anders walked back to his bunk, he considered her words carefully. The two young people were too much of a symbol of cooperation between the Commonwealth and the Supremacy. Their existence might make any number of Kelk hardliners relent on their unwavering hatred of all things Commonwealth.

The command hawk and her comrades needed the young man out of the way, and probably Mistress Vreekande as well. But if they killed two breschkada without a compelling reason, it would be considered murder. On the other hand, if an unstable, ex-convict, ex-military-officer, took matters into his own hands, the command hawk and her superiors could walk away from the matter without suffering any ill effects. And they would wash their hands of one Anders Eindride. Would they send him back to SecureMax, or hold a nice, public trial and execute him, or maybe just quietly vent him to space?

No. Anders decided he would not help them murder the two young people, though it occurred to him they didn't really need him to do so. His superiors could simply kill them without his help, then blame it on him. Yes, he was too conveniently available for exactly that.

35

Join Forces

THE NCO AND two guards marched John and Nikaela back to the brig and deposited them in their cells. After the door to John's cell closed, he waited until their jailers had left the cell block. Then he pressed his cheek against the door and peered through the small opening at a slanting angle up the passageway; the security station remained unoccupied. He decided to wait at least an hour before attempting to communicate with Nikaela, so he stood there and kept an eye on the security station. Nikaela didn't break the silence of the cell block, so he concluded she had chosen to exercise the same caution.

About an hour later he heard a faint whisper barely above the threshold of hearing. "John Mathius."

He responded in the same quiet whisper. "Nikaela Vreekande."

"You didn't trust me before."

"I couldn't be sure it was you until I saw your face in that room."

"Don't we Kelk all look alike?"

Some of John's comrades shared that prejudice. But he would never mistake the pretty young Kelk woman he'd met on Reisenar for anyone else. When she had told him how she had saved his life, he had believed her on an intellectual level, but when he saw her seated in the chair in that room, even the faintest hint of doubt disappeared like a puff of smoke on a windy day.

He still didn't understand why the command hawk had questioned them. "Why interrogate us? I can't believe she learned anything new."

Nikaela didn't answer for several seconds, and when she did it was with some hesitation. "Breschkada is sacred to all Kelk, and there has not been breschkada for more than two centuries."

"Two centuries?" John asked. "That would be before the Kelk and Commonwealth first encountered each other."

"Yes. And there has never before been breschkada with another race, so that makes it even more sacred. They will lose face if they simply murder us. She hoped to find proof the bond between us was not strong."

"How?"

"One way would be to prove we weren't truly breschkada. Or if she proved you weren't breschkada-sa, they could get away with killing you because you aren't Kelk, and you are Blacksword. But she learned you are truly breschkada-sa, which is even more sacred than breschkada-se."

"Why was she so interested in my hand wound?"

"Because if your hand wound had been truly self-inflicted, we would still be breschkada, but the bond would not be as strong."

John recalled that Primatov had told him, ". . . the bond between battle-kin is considered especially tight if they came close to killing each other first."

"But it was self-inflicted."

"Not truly," she said. "When you said blood loss and pain from your other wounds had clouded your thinking—those other wounds were Kelk inflicted, so the hand wound was a direct result of those other wounds. We almost killed each other, Mathius breschkada."

"Sounds like she was clutching at straws."

"I don't know 'straw' word, John."

John tried to explain the phrase, and he must have succeeded because she said, "Ah, we say riding a reschcat to death. A stupid and desperate thing to do. Yes, she was riding a reschcat to death."

"What's a reschcat?"

"A nasty, dangerous, and very hard-to-kill animal. You will die before you ride it to death. Yes, she hoped to lessen the loss of face when they kill us. And she failed. But they will still kill us. They just have to think of how and when they can minimize the loss of face."

"Why did she bring up Novalis III?"

"That had something to do with Maestra Eindride, but I don't know what."

"Who is Maestra Eindride?"

He heard her breathe a long, slow sigh. "He was the civilian that came in with the command hawk. He was my command superior on Novalis III."

John's heart beat rapidly and climbed up into his throat. "You were on . . . Novalis III?"

For the longest moment she said nothing, and he said nothing to encourage her, or to make it easier for her to speak.

"It was my training mission between my third and fourth year at the academy."

She then told him a story of a naïve, young girl thrilled at the excitement of assignment to a covert team, and of her discovery of the unconventional weapons, and Anders Eindride's involvement in it all. "He did try to alert his superiors. He is a good man in all the ways that count. I—"

She hesitated. Then she spoke with the voice of a frightened little girl. "Do you hate me now?"

He paused to think for a moment about who he did hate. "No. I don't hate you. But someday I'll tell you about a man named Cranoch, and a man named Mercier. I truly hate them, still hate them, even though I killed them long ago."

At that point he had nothing more to say, and apparently neither did she. John leaned against the door of his cell and listened to the silence of the cell block, and in the stillness he thought he heard her intake and exhale of breath, soft, silent and restful. Then she raised her voice and shouted a single, angry Kelk word that resounded off the walls. It must have been some sort of curse, and he heard what sounded like the smack of her hand against the cell door.

"What's wrong?" he asked.

"I'm just frustrated. They have me locked out of shipnet."

Until that moment John hadn't thought the situation through. In his experience all crewmembers on a ship had certain low level access codes; in an emergency lives might depend on getting access to a restricted med locker, or a lifeboat. Nikaela was a Kelk military officer, and they were in the brig on a Kelk warship. John had never been an officer, just a grunt, then a junior NCO, then a cadet, but for emergency situations Commonwealth officers and senior NCOs had access to certain functions beyond that granted to the lower ranks. It must be the same with the Kelk.

His mind raced ahead of his words. "Do you have emergency access codes to this ship?"

"Yes, of course."

"What kind?"

She sounded uncaring and defeated when she spoke. "General low-level stuff common to all military ships: arms lockers, equipment lockers, assault boats, locks on some restricted hatches and doors."

The cuffs and manacles their jailers used to restrain them were locked and unlocked by an electromechanical key carried by one of the guards, so he didn't ask about those.

"Could you open the doors to our cells?"

"No. Those are controlled from the security station."

John tried to keep his voice calm. "But you could open other things?"

"No. Shipnet is blocking my implants from even simple functions."

John forced himself not to raise his voice. "What about vocal commands?"

"They've also nulled my vocal signature out of all ship's systems."

"But anyone can issue these commands if they know them, right?"

"Anyone but me."

John took a long slow breath to calm his excitement, and to make sure he kept his voice down to the faintest of whispers. "Do you think they nulled my vocal signature out of the ship's systems?"

"Maybe . . . probably not. Kelk systems won't respond to Lingua commands."

It couldn't possibly work, but he had to at least try. "But you can still tell them to me, and I'll say them."

"That won't work. You have to speak Kelk."

John switched to Kelk. "I do speak Kelk."

She answered him with silence. He waited, wasn't sure if she would speak at all, and then she said, "You have a shit-of-bull accent, Mathius breschkada."

••••

From seventy-two light-hours out, *Lightspear* aimed its transition com in the direction of Sarkovie with only a small chance they might be spotted by *Caliban* and its Kelk friends, who were farther out and therefore in the other direction. Even if one of the two rogues picked up a little transmitter splash, they couldn't decode it, and while running silent the hunter-killer wasn't emitting enough of a signature to be easily classified. They would be just another ship in the neighborhood of the Sarkovie system.

Katrine gave *Lightspear*'s com tech the transmit profile her contacts would be monitoring, then she and Neilosse adjourned to his office. She keyed her implants to the encryption key for the Blacksword station-head on Sarkovie, then established a direct connection to Neilosse's implants. In that way she didn't have to reveal the encryption key to him or his com tech, but he could receive an unencrypted translation and participate in the conversation through her.

When the com tech activated the connection, Neilosse's eyes widened as a voluptuous young lady appeared in the virtual image in their implants. She had glistening black hair and wore a dress that exposed a great deal of cleavage. The material of the dress was translucent enough to make the dark shadows of her areolas quite visible though the fabric. They nicely framed the points of her nipples which protruded noticeably. The dress ended just below her crotch. She was seated in a comfortable chair, and had her long legs not been crossed, Neilosse would have had an unobstructed view of the young woman's genitals. Prostitution was a highly regarded profession on Sarkovie, one to which many young men and women aspired. And quite a few of those who didn't ply the trade chose to dress like their more successful friends, a real style statement.

"Captain Miershall," Katrine said.

"Colonel," the young woman said. "I wasn't expecting you."

Katrine smiled. "Necessity forced me to put this mission together on rather short notice."

Miershall received an image of Katrine and Neilosse seated side-by-side, so Katrine introduced the two, telling Neilosse, "Captain Miershall is our head-of-station for covert operations on Sarkovie."

She gave Miershall an edited summary of John Mathius's abduction, but in the spirit of need-to-know, kept the details of Novalis III and Reisenar out of it. She said only, "The young man was involved in an incident of a highly classified nature."

Miershall nodded and smiled. "I understand, Colonel. But you say you're tracking a disguised renegade Kelk warship working with a disguised renegade Commonwealth warship?"

"Yes. What are you thinking?"

The young woman looked perplexed. "You have worked in the past with Command Superior Brynjar, have you not?"

Neilosse's eyes narrowed at the mention of the Kelk officer rank.

Katrine nodded. "Yes, I have. Why?"

Miershall appeared quite unsure of herself. "With your permission, I think it would be wise to bring him into this conversation."

"Brynjar is here?" Katrine demanded.

"Yes," Miershall said cautiously. "He is."

Katrine had trouble containing her excitement. "By all means, bring him on line." But then she saw the look on Neilosse's face and realized the two of them needed to have a little chat before the conversation included the Kelk officer. To buy them time, she added, "But first, fully brief Brynjar on what I've told you."

Miershall signed off with, "Yes, ma'am."

Neilosse demanded, "What the hell is going on here, Colonel?"

Katrine grimaced and spoke carefully. "Brynjar and his immediate superior were in command of the Kelk forces on Reisenar when our young man and their young woman prevented interstellar war. They've already demonstrated they can overcome any prior animosity toward the Commonwealth."

"And you trust him?"

"Yes, I do."

"And you want me to trust him?"

"Yes, I do."

He hesitated for a moment. "In the spirit of Reisenar, I guess . . . we can talk."

"He could be a valuable ally in this."

Neilosse waved a hand and shook his head. "We can talk. Let's just leave it at that."

She tried to keep the frustration out of her voice. "But if he can help, we—"

He interrupted her. "If he can help, we talk about—"

Miershall came back on line, which abruptly ended the argument—discussion. Brynjar appeared as if seated in a separate room, and he had made no attempt to disguise his appearance.

He smiled pleasantly, and Katrine dearly hoped Neilosse didn't see anything demonic in his face. "Colonel, it's always a pleasure to meet you."

She returned his smile and introduced him to Neilosse, who did a good job of not showing any signs of discomfort. "Captain Miershall briefed you?"

Brynjar maintained the pleasant smile. "Yes, she did. Exactly when did they abduct your young Mr. Mathius?"

Katrine gave him the date.

He closed his eyes, probably translating it to a Kelk calendar. "And at what hour did they abduct him?"

Katrine consulted her implants. "About three hours before midnight, Trafalgar City time."

"Very interesting," Brynjar said, nodding his head in a slow, thoughtful cadence. "They abducted our young Mistress Vreekande at almost the same hour. Three hundred light-years apart and they abducted the two young people within hours of one another."

Neilosse met Katrine's eyes with a look of fear and uncertainty. "What's happening here, Colonel?"

Brynjar continued. "Captain Miershall also tells me you have a rogue Kelk warship, and a rogue Commonwealth warship collaborating. And you can't act because they have you badly outgunned."

"Yes," Katrine said, keeping an eye on Neilosse for any sign of a bad reaction.

Brynjar grinned. "I may be able to help in that regard. I brought *Drakan Helgis* with me, a large destroyer, and I'll be happy to put her at your disposal."

Katrine had a sudden urge to jump out of her seat and shout, but again, the look on Neilosse's face dampened her enthusiasm. She looked into Brynjar's eyes and tried to be non-committal in front of Neilosse. "That's kind of you, Command Superior Brynjar. Commander Neilosse and I need to discuss logistics."

She felt quite confident Brynjar understood the issues she must deal with, and probably faced the same issues himself. He nodded. "I'll be waiting."

When they ended the call, Katrine opened her mouth to speak, but Neilosse held up a hand to silence her. "Just give me a moment. I understand. We're going to collaborate with—"

He went silent and his eyes widened even further. Then he closed his eyes and shook his head sadly, rubbing his temples as he did so. "I almost said, 'collaborating with the enemy.' But they're not the enemy, are they? Those two rogue ships are the enemy."

Katrine could almost see the wheels turning as he thought the matter through, and she decided the best thing to do at that moment was keep her mouth shut and let him find his own way there.

Neilosse stared at the floor as he spoke. "That Kelk officer said . . . Brynjar said . . . he's putting his ship at your disposal. Can you get him to agree you're in command of this . . . joint operation?"

Katrine knew where Neilosse was going with this: he'd have an easier time selling it to his people that way. "We've worked together before. Don't forget he's probably dealing with similar issues at his end, but I think I can get him to agree with that, even if it's only a pretense."

Neilosse nodded and held up both hands, palms out, as if trying to slow a juggernaut. "That'll do. Just make sure he knows not to contradict us in front of my people. Give me a day to spread this quietly through the crew. I don't want to make a big announcement. Let's you and I start with Sharma. I don't think she'll have a problem handling this. I want her signed up to this before we brief my officers and

NCOs, then I'll have the NCOs quietly spread the word that we're . . . that you're in command of a joint force, and that we're going to . . ."—he swallowed hard—". . . work with some Kelk allies."

36

Kelk Lessons

JOHN TRIED TO explain to Nikaela some of the more subtle nuances of the use of the word bullshit, and how words like *horrible* or *bad* or *terrible* would work better when describing his accent.

"But I like shit-of-bull," she said, sounding petulant. "It makes a good sound in Lingua, much better than Kelk profanity."

He tried again. "And it's not shit-of-bull. It's bullshit. One word."

"But I like shit-of-bull word better than bullshit word."

John wasn't getting anywhere with this conversation, so he decided to capitulate. "Then help me get rid of my shit-of-bull accent."

She laughed. He had heard her laugh on Reisenar, and it felt good to hear her do so again.

Luckily they didn't have to completely revamp John's abilities with the Kelk spoken word. He needed a few key phrases like "System command," and "System execute." Between those two phrases the access codes were simply strings of digits and letters, just like on Commonwealth ships, so he didn't need to clean up his accent for complete numbers.

Nikaela drilled him on pronunciation of numerical digits and the letters of their alphabet, repeating them over and over. Then he had to memorize the codes for basic locks on arms lockers, medical lockers, supply and equipment cabinets, lots of stuff like that. They had been at it for a couple of hours when they heard a guard coming to check on them. John dashed to the other side of the cell and stepped into the field of his grav bunk. He didn't try to pretend he was asleep. He put his hands behind his head and lay there like any prisoner killing time staring at four blank walls.

The face of the male Kelk guard appeared in the barred opening of his door and looked at him briefly. The fellow glanced right and left, scanning the cell as if somehow there might be someone else in the cell with John. Then he turned and walked toward Nikaela's cell. John waited, and several seconds later he saw the guard's head pass by the opening on his way out of the cell block.

John thought it best to adopt his earlier caution, and wait for at least an hour before trying to communicate with Nikaela again. And again, she exercised the same caution.

••••

When Katrine stepped into the gym, her spine compressed a little and her weight increased. Captain Edward Fleming and his nullheads had turned the local gravity up to something near two G's, and were drilling in hand-to-hand combat. Fleming stood to one side wiping sweat off his face while two of his people sparred in the increased gravity field. A quick head-count came up short by one, telling her one of his people had not accompanied them to the gym.

As she approached him, Fleming greeted her. "Colonel."

"Cap'm," she said. Since a ship had only one captain, when on board it was customary to corrupt Fleming's Infantry Ops rank. She nodded toward the gym's entrance. "A word with you, please."

"Certainly, Colonel."

He followed her as she turned and walked out of the gym into the passageway beyond. She stopped, turned to face him, and established an encrypted, secure link between their implants. At that he raised a questioning eyebrow.

She subvocalized her words. "I'd like you to take extra precautions to be sure no one separates you from your armor and weapons."

He raised the other eyebrow and she continued. "I don't anticipate any real difficulties, but I want to be prepared for the worst." She quickly briefed him on the presence of Brynjar and his destroyer, then detailed her conversation with Neilosse regarding the Kelk issue.

He frowned. "You think you might have trouble with Neilosse?"

"No, I've come to know him rather well and I don't think he'll be an issue, though I can't be absolutely certain of that. And when he and I briefed Sharma, she took it rather well, so I don't think she'll be a problem either. But I wouldn't be surprised if they have trouble with some of their crew."

Fleming rubbed his chin for a few seconds as he considered the matter. "We never leave our gear unguarded—Corporal Paltrow is with it now while the rest of us are here. But I'll elevate our preparedness. From now on, at all times at least one of us will be in full combat armor, and locked and loaded. And those of us not wearing our armor will gravity-lock it."

Katrine had heard of that trick, a special capability added to nullhead armor. Hanging static on a rack, it would not weigh anything more than usual, and the reactor pack would operate at idle so it didn't drain. But if anyone tried to move it without a special access code, its gravity fields would kick in, and it would feel like trying to move an object with the mass of a ten-ton grav lifter.

Katrine smiled and nodded. "Good. And please check in with me at least hourly. If you can't reach me, or if anyone tries to restrict your movements on this ship in an unusual way, or under extraordinary circumstances, you have my permission to use whatever force is necessary to reestablish contact with me. And then we'll decide where we go from there."

••••

Nikaela pressed her cheek against the cell door and whispered. "We're running out of time, you know?"

"I know." His voice sounded listless and uncaring.

She had drilled him on his accent throughout middle watch and into the wee hours of ship's morning. "I don't think they'll kill us here, not in these cells."

"Why not?"

She shrugged, and only after the fact realized it was a useless gesture since he couldn't see her. "Have you noticed that with few exceptions, we never see anyone beyond the command hawk, the NCO, the two guards, and Maestra Eindride."

"No," he said. "I hadn't. The fewer the better, eh?"

"Exactly. They're going to lose face, lose support, so they'll want to cover it up as much as possible, maybe take us off ship, vent us to space and say it was an accident."

"I've heard that's not a bad way to die." He sounded sad. "You lose consciousness after just ten or fifteen seconds."

"Yes, I've heard that too." She didn't tell him there was a good chance they would kill only him. Kill the breschkada-sa, the hated Commonwealth Blacksword. They just might get away with that, but Nikaela had promised herself she would not let them. She couldn't stop them from killing him, but she would fight them all the way, and leave them no choice but to kill her as well. She would die with her breschkada.

His next words told her he understood more than she thought. "I know that the next time they come for us, I have to try something, anything, even if there's just the tiniest chance."

Yes, he did understand. "Your accent is good enough now. Let's take a break before morning watch and get a couple hours of sleep."

"Yes, good idea."

She turned away from the door, crossed the small cell, and stepped into the field of her grav bunk. She set her implants to wake her in three hours, and lay there thinking it would be nice if she and her breschkada could spend their last few hours together. That train of thought didn't disturb her as much as she thought it would.

A mechanical clatter woke her, and she opened her eyes to see her cell door sliding into the bulkhead. The NCO and the two guards walked into her cell carrying their neural prods. They followed a procedure much like that when they marched her to the room where the command hawk had interrogated her and John. But this time they led her to a boarding passageway for an assault boat. They boarded the craft through a personnel airlock in the front section of the boat just aft of the cockpit. She caught a glimpse forward into the control cabin. The pilot sat flipping switches and doing other pilot things. Beyond the windshield she saw the doors of the hangar bay open to space, crewmembers in vac suits working at various tasks, another assault boat with a large number 2 painted on its side.

She spotted an arms locker in the boat at the front of the troop cabin. They marched her past it toward the back of the cabin, sat her in one of the last seats, and cuffed her ankle to a cleat in the floor. The male guard sat down opposite her, facing her, while the female guard and the NCO walked forward and out through the hatch, probably to retrieve John.

The time had come.

••••

John awoke to the sound of a cell door clattering open. It wasn't his, so it must be Nikaela's.

He heard a few words spoken in Kelk, and recognized the NCO's voice, though he didn't try to translate what she said. Several seconds later he counted four Kelk heads as they walked past the opening in his cell door headed out of the cell block. That would be the NCO, two guards, and Nikaela.

He stepped out of the field of his grav bunk, quickly washed his face and hands and cleaned up as well as he could. He had washed one of his two coveralls in the sink the day before, and during the night it had dried. He put it on and carefully sealed it just as he heard his jailers return.

The door to his cell clattered open, and in walked the female guard. She gave him the unpleasant grin she had displayed when she had scrutinized him while he stood dripping wet and naked. The NCO followed her in, and this time John watched closely as they cuffed his hands in front of him. The cuffs locked onto his wrists with a simple click, no use of a key to lock them. He had hoped to see one of them retrieve a key from a pocket, telling him where to look if somehow the chance arose, but no such luck. The guard pressed her neural prod against John's spine, the NCO led the way out of the cell, and John followed with the guard in lockstep behind him. They marched him out of the cell block and down a passageway.

He had only been outside the cell block twice; once when he first came to the ship, and again when they took him to the supply room where the command hawk interrogated Nikaela and him. Both times he hadn't known what to look for, or that he needed to keep his eyes open for arms lockers or something that might save their lives. And now he tried to fully scan his surroundings without being obvious about it. He spotted a maintenance closet, several first aid stations, and wondered if there might be something sharp in one of those he could use as a weapon. But with his hands cuffed, and the output end of the neural prod jammed against his spine, he'd be foolish to try anything.

They stopped at a grav lift, and when it arrived the female guard encouraged him to step into it by slapping him on the butt with her prod. He stepped in and turned about to face her, and again she gave him that unpleasant grin.

They took the lift to another level, then down a passageway and through a personnel airlock coupled to an assault boat with both hatches in the airlock open. As before, they entered just aft of the cockpit, and again John caught a glimpse into the control cabin. The pilot sat checking his gauges, while the copilot's seat remained empty. No need for a copilot for something as simple as a short trip out to vent two inconvenient breschkada to space. John felt a faint vibration in the hull of the boat. The pilot had its engines warming up and idling. He wished they weren't in such a hurry to eliminate him and Nikaela.

At the far back of the troop cabin John saw Nikaela and the male guard seated opposite one another, facing each other. John's guard pointed to a seat at the front of the cabin about as far from Nikaela as they could put him. He sat down and the guard cuffed his ankle to a cleat in the floor, with the NCO standing over them, her neural prod ready in case John tried anything. The female guard sat down opposite John, facing him and gripping the barrel of her neural prod as if she dearly hoped she'd have a chance to use it.

Above and to one side of the guard, a small red telltale on a locked panel drew John's attention. Just below the red telltale a stencil displayed a five-digit number in Kelk script. Nikaela had warned John that medical lockers, first aid kits, and anything that might be needed in an emergency were visibly labeled as such. But that was not the case with small arms lockers. They would simply have a five-digit locker number, and red and green telltales to indicate if they were locked.

The manacles they had used to cuff his ankle to the cleat in the floor had a plast tether about ten centimeters long. But they hadn't cuffed his right ankle, and he could easily bridge the distance to the locked panel with a single step. All John need-ed to do was say 'System command,' then read the lock number and recite the access code Nikaela had given him, then say 'System execute.' If they hadn't nulled his vocal signature out of the ship's systems, if Nikaela's access codes still worked, if John's accent wasn't too shit-of-bull, then the telltale would flash from red to green, and John could hit the latch on the panel and pop it open. At that moment he would learn if he would face the guard with a weapon, or a tape measure. It didn't really matter, because John knew that long before he finished that sequence, the woman seated across from him would give him a taste of that prod. And from the look on her face, she would take great pleasure in doing so.

Standing in the aisle nearby and speaking in Kelk, the NCO said something to the guard seated opposite John. It took him a moment to translate it into something like, "I'm going to check with Eskildsen."

The NCO touched two fingers to her ear, and for a few seconds she froze with her eyes focused in the distance. Then she focused on the guard and spoke in Kelk. John couldn't make out all her words, but he heard, "Eskildsen . . . late . . . something . . . twenty . . . minutes . . ."

The pilot looked over his shoulder and said, "Twenty minutes?"

The NCO and the pilot had a short conversation, speaking too rapidly for John make out more than a few disconnected words that made no sense to him. The pilot climbed out of his seat, saying, "Back in ten."

The NCO turned and walked toward the back of the cabin.

••••

Anders received orders to report to Eskildsen's office, and made his way down to deck five. As before, he found her seated at the small desk. She smiled and stood to greet him. "Maestra Karsten, thank you for indulging me."

He nodded. "Happy to oblige, mistress."

Again, she pointed to the small extrudable seat and invited him to sit down. He did so as she turned, closed the door to her office, then sat down herself and asked, "What did you think of Mistress Vreekande's story?"

He shrugged. "She is clearly breschkada-se, and he breschkada-sa."

She grimaced, as if he had revealed a painful truth. "Many believe a Kelk cannot be breschkada with a Blacksword."

Anders wondered if the word *many* truly applied, or if in fact there were only a small few who wanted to believe that. "I was not aware of such a limitation. But then, I'm no expert, so I wouldn't know. It's been what . . . more than two hundred years."

She clearly didn't like the answers he gave her and struggled for words. "At a minimum it is . . . unprecedented."

The correct word would be *inconvenient*, not *unprecedented*, but he didn't say that. "Does that present a problem for you?"

"Only a bit," she said, "though nothing insurmountable."

She held up a hand as if to stop their conversation. "One moment please."

Anders glanced around the small office while she took a call through her implants. It lasted for several seconds, then she finished by saying out loud, "I'll be there in twenty to thirty minutes."

She returned her attention to Anders. "Sorry about the interruption. As I said, while the young man and woman are a problem, it's not insurmountable. Do you think you might help in some way?"

She wanted to know if his bitterness extended to murdering the two breschkada, but she couldn't ask that outright. It would be dangerous for him to simply deny it. "I don't know. Do you have something in mind?"

She hesitated for a long moment and seemed to come to a decision. "We're transferring them down to Sarkovie, and we'll be transferring you there as well, for your new assignment."

She stood. "Please come with me."

37

The Spoken Word

NIKAELA WATCHED THEM bring John in and seat him at the front of the troop cabin about ten meters away. The seat they selected put him directly opposite the arms locker, though Nikaela had no idea if he had spotted it, or if he would make an attempt to unlock it. The NCO stood over the female guard and watched closely as she bent and cuffed John's ankle to a cleat in the floor. When the guard finished she straightened, then sat down opposite John, staring at him intently and gripping her neural prod.

A moment later the NCO reached up, touched her ear and froze for a few seconds. She and the pilot had a brief conversation, then the pilot climbed out of his seat, and walked out of the boat through the open airlock.

The NCO walked casually to the back of the cabin and addressed Nikaela's guard. "Short delay. Eskildsen wants to bring Eindride, said she'll be another twenty or thirty minutes." She turned and walked toward the front of the cabin.

If John had spotted the arms locker, and if he could open it, they might stand a chance. But Nikaela needed to do something to draw the attention of John's guard away from him, and keep the focus of both guards and the NCO off him while he made the attempt.

Nikaela's guard stood and arched his back, stretching his muscles. Then he leaned over Nikaela and said, "Why do you love a Blacksword so?"

Nikaela shook her head. "I don't love him. We're just breschkada." She didn't say that she had come to *like* John Mathius quite a bit.

The guard out-massed Nikaela by a good thirty kilos. He curled his upper lip into a sneer, and leaned down even closer. "What do you say to him when you're fucking him?"

It infuriated Nikaela that the man believed she thought only with her libido. She purposefully raised her voice. "I don't have to say anything, because when I'm with him I'm too busy enjoying myself. He's clearly got a bigger cock than you, you limp-dicked piece of shit."

Walking toward the front of the cabin, the NCO started and turned at the sound of Nikaela's angry words. Nikaela's guard raised his hand and shouted, "You fucking bitch," and slapped her hard enough to send her to the edge of consciousness.

The NCO rushed back toward them, shouting, "What's going on here?"

The guard's eyes flashed, he grabbed the front of Nikaela's coverall at the neck, and yanked her upward. As he lifted her out of her seat his strength gave her additional momentum and she kneed him in the balls. He grunted and screamed, and using the clump of material he'd gripped at the front of her coverall, he threw her to the deck. But on her way down she bounced off the row of seats, a shock of pain jolted through her ribs and she cried out. She landed on her side in the aisle, then rolled over onto her back, struggling to breathe as the pain thudded at her senses.

The NCO reached them at that moment and pushed the guard back. "What the hell do you think you're doing, you idiot?"

He shouted back at her. "But she said—"

The NCO faced the guard and stepped forward aggressively, backing him up a step and silencing him with a look. With her nose only a fraction of an inch from his, she bellowed, "I don't care what she said."

She turned her head to look down at Nikaela.

The guard had badly torn the front of Nikaela's coverall, partially exposing one breast, and she realized she could use that against him, make it look even worse than it had been. But with a lifelong prohibition against making false accusations, she said nothing. She simply took hold of the torn neckline of her coverall to draw the NCO's eyes toward the damaged material, and attempted to cover up the partially exposed breast.

The NCO's eyes widened and her face blossomed into an angry red. She turned on the guard and shouted in his face, "You moron."

The NCO looked over her shoulder and shouted, "Lindholm, get down here now."

The female guard in charge of John stood, shaking her head sadly. She turned and walked slowly toward the back of the craft.

The NCO said to the male guard, "I'm putting her in charge of the girl."

He shouted back, "But I didn't do anything."

Nikaela screamed and lunged for the NCO's ankles, wrapped her arms around them, twisted and rolled.

••••

When shouting erupted at the back of the troop cabin, both John and the woman guarding him looked that way. Halfway up the aisle, the NCO hesitated and looked back. Nikaela's guard cursed in Kelk and hit her with a slap that resounded throughout the troop cabin. The NCO spun on her heels and rushed back to the rear of the cabin as Nikaela's guard scuffled with her and threw her to the deck.

The NCO and Nikaela's guard shouted in Kelk at one another too rapidly for John to translate anything. Then the NCO turned and called back to the woman guarding John. John's guard shook her head sadly, rolled her eyes, stood and walked slowly toward the back of the craft. Then Nikaela screamed, grabbed the NCO's ankles, and pulled the woman down with her. The male guard tried to intervene, and he went down as well. The female guard turned her casual stroll into a rush toward the twisted mess of arms and legs, and joined the struggling, grunting and screaming.

John tried to ignore the free-for-all at the rear of the cabin, tried not to hurry his movements, tried to remain calm, knew if he let panic guide his actions he and Nikaela were dead. He stood and took one step with his right leg, leaving his left ankle tethered to the cleat in the floor. He didn't know where they had placed the voice pickup for the locked panel—if there even was a voice pickup—so he leaned toward the red telltale, and taking great care to enunciate his Kelk the way Nikaela had taught him, he spoke in a normal tone of voice. "System command, clear lock number . . ."

He hesitated and glanced toward the struggle at the rear of the cabin. The female guard had dropped to one knee with her back to John and was pounding on something with her fist, probably pounding on Nikaela.

John carefully read the five-digit lock number, then followed that with, "Access code," and recited the code Nikaela had given him. He finished with, "System execute." The telltale remained red.

He glanced again at the melee at the back of the boat. The female guard had gone down, but the male guard had stood and looked John's way. His eyes widened and he started forward, but he had to climb over the pile of struggling bodies to get to John, and he fought to do so, entangled in arms and legs.

A faint beep drew John's attention back to the locked panel, and he snapped his head around to look at the telltale. It flashed a bright green.

He hammered his fist into latch and the panel popped open. He glanced back; the male guard had just cleared the struggling women.

Inside the cabinet John saw two heavy grav pistols. He reached for one, struggled for a moment to pull it out of its clips, then got it free. He cleared the weapon's safety and spun toward the aft end of the boat. The male guard was only two paces from him and running at full speed up the aisle.

John raised the weapon and fired. The man's head jerked as he plowed into John and the pistol flew out of his hands. The fellow was larger than John and slammed him to the deck, landing on top of him with painful force. John struggled, but the man didn't resist him, didn't fight back.

The guard lay on top of him like a lover, and John looked into his face. The bullet had entered his skull through his left eye, turning the socket into a ruined mess. The other eye had already glazed over in death.

John pushed, but the man considerably outweighed him. He finally tumbled the body to one side, rolled over and spotted the grav pistol a few paces away. He scrambled on his hands and knees the short distance toward it, but came up short when the cuff tethering his left ankle to the cleat in the floor went taught. Behind him he heard the three women screaming and cursing.

He lunged, stretching out flat on the deck as far as he could, heard the NCO scream a curse in Kelk that he couldn't translate. He barely managed to squeeze the end of the pistol's barrel between the tips of his thumb and forefinger, and pulled it an inch closer. He got a better grip on the barrel, pulled it even closer, grabbed the handle, rolled over onto his back and sat up.

In the back of the boat, Nikaela lay on top of the female guard, struggling with her. The NCO had broken free of them and climbed to her knees. She held a neural prod in both hands, her teeth gritted, her face a mask of fury. She raised the prod high over her head to club Nikaela in the back of her skull.

John raised the pistol, aimed for a body shot, and in that moment the NCO glanced his way and their eyes met.

He pulled the trigger. The pistol kicked in his hand, and the NCO staggered as the bullet punched a hole in her chest. John aimed for her face and pulled the trigger again. Her head rocked back and she toppled backward.

Nikaela and the female guard continued to struggle, lying on the deck in the aisle between the two rows of seats. With Nikaela on top John saw her face, smears of blood darkening her cheeks and chin. All John saw of the guard beneath her was the top of her head. It was a risky shot, a dangerous shot, but he had already killed the NCO and the male guard, taking their implants off line. Someone would investigate, so he needed to take the chance.

••••

Lying on top of the female guard, Nikaela and the woman both had their hands wrapped around the neural prod. But the guard had control of the prod's trigger and kept trying to jam the output end beneath Nikaela's chin. That also meant it wouldn't do Nikaela any good to jam the damn thing up under the guard's chin.

Since she was on top, Nikaela had the advantage of gravity, so she took a chance, arched up, stopped pushing on the prod and pulled it upward. The change surprised the guard and it came up easily. Then Nikaela put her weight behind it, and slammed the barrel of the prod into the woman's nose. Blood splattered from the guard's nostrils and her grip on the prod slackened. Nikaela pulled the prod up with the guard's hands still attached to it, and hit her again and again and again.

"Nikaela!"

At John's shout she looked up the aisle to the front of the troop cabin. He sat on his butt on the deck of the boat, a pistol held in a two-handed grip and aimed her way, blood streaming from a cut on his forehead. The male guard lay in a sprawl in front of him.

The woman beneath Nikaela groaned and her eyes rolled dizzily. Nikaela pushed up off her just as she heard the report of John's grav pistol. The woman's body jerked as blood erupted from her eyes and ears, and then she went still.

Nikaela staggered to her feet, couldn't understand why John had stayed at the far end of the cabin and taken such a dangerous shot. But when she tried to walk his way, the cuff on her ankle went taught, bringing her to a stop, and back to her senses. They were cuffed at opposite ends of the cabin.

It took her a second to get her bearings. John had stood, then knelt down beside the male guard and was busy rifling through his pockets.

The key! Nikaela had to get the key.

She bent down over the NCO, wasted precious time searching her and didn't find anything. The female guard laid silent and still, a pool of blood forming around her head. Nikaela knelt on her chest, checked her shirt pockets and found nothing there. Testing the outside of the woman's pants pockets she felt something small and square in one of her thigh pouches. She dug into it and retrieved a small, metal device with an electromechanical interface at one end. Looking at the key slot in the cuff on her left wrist, it appeared it would fit, so she carefully inserted it into the opening. The cuff snicked audibly and popped open. It didn't take long to remove the cuff on her other wrist, then that on her ankle.

She staggered to her feet, saw John limping down the aisle toward her. He had a cut over his right eye, and a bruise on his cheek looked like it might swell badly. A trickle of blood from his left nostril had drizzled down to his chin. He stopped a few paces from her and held up a key he must have taken off the male guard. "Looks like you don't need this."

At that moment he was the best-looking guy she had ever met.

••••

Nikaela's eyes blinked rapidly for a moment, and John thought she might pass out so he reached out and gripped her elbow to steady her. The left side of her upper lip had begun to swell, and he thought he saw cuts on its inside edges where it had been mashed against her teeth by some blow. Blood reddened her lips and teeth, and trickled down to her chin. Some of her hair still remained in the ponytail, but some of it had been pulled loose from whatever held it in place, and it stuck out in a frazzle of disarray. At that moment she was the prettiest girl he had ever met.

She straightened, took a deep breath, and shook her head as if to clear it. "We have to get out of here." She pulled her elbow out of his grip and pointed to the dead woman at their feet. "She and her friends are dead, so their implants are off line. Someone's going to investigate."

She spun on her heel to the back of the troop cabin, hit a latch on a locker and a panel slid open to reveal two, general-purpose vac suits. "They're not customized, but they've got straps and expansion joints to adjust the fit, so they'll do."

Her actions confused John. "What are you doing?"

She looked over her shoulder. "It's our only way out of here. We can't go back into the ship, so that leaves the hangar bay. And it's under vacuum."

"No," John said. "No, that's suicide."

She spun toward him and snapped. "What else can we do?"

John took a certain pleasure in his next words, like a boy boasting to a pretty girl. "Why don't I just fly this fucking boat out of here?"

Her eyes blinked rapidly for a moment, then widened. "You can fly this thing?"

"Yes."

"You're a pilot?"

"Yes, fully qualified."

"You can fly a Kelk boat?"

His confidence wavered. He dearly hoped they had as much automation built into their flight control systems as a ComSecCorps boat. Otherwise, he might not overcome his complete lack of cockpit time in a Kelk boat. "Let's go find out."

She smiled, though a bit crookedly because of the swollen lip. "Lead the way, Mathius breschkada."

When John had gone down under the weight of the heavier male guard, he had twisted his knee and the best he could do was a staggering limp up the aisle of the troop cabin. He stepped over the dead male guard, but stopped at the small arms locker, retrieved the remaining grav pistol and handed it to Nikaela. He passed the airlock with its hatches dilated and that bothered him, but behind him he heard Nikaela stop, do something, and the hatches cycled shut. John sat down in the pilot's seat, and was glad to see he had been right: the boat had yaw pedals on the deck in front of him. The simple coverall didn't have clips for the side arm so he set the safety on the pistol and jammed it between his hip and the seat.

Nikaela leaned into the cockpit. "What next?"

John pointed to the copilot's seat. "Sit down and buckle in. I'm going to need help deciphering these gauges."

As she strapped herself in he scanned the instruments in front of him. He hadn't studied Kelk technical terminology, so he had no hope of decoding them. "Is there one labeled *launch*, or something like that?"

He pointed to three switches with protective covers on them. "It's probably one of those."

She shook her head. "Launch? No, nothing with launch."

She frowned and looked more closely at one switch. "It's a loose translation, but one says, 'Detach.'"

"Could that mean leave?" he asked.

Her eyes widened, she looked at him and nodded.

He grinned. "Then hit the damn thing."

She popped the protective cover and hit the switch. Red telltales flashed on the screens in front of them. Behind them a sound echoed through the hull coming from the vicinity of the airlock. It sounded like the ship's systems sealing the inner hatch in preparation for detaching the boat from the ship's passageway. Then the boat lurched sideways, and its docking boom moved it slowly across the hanger bay toward the open doors and open space, orienting its nose outward.

John gave a whoop.

Nikaela looked at him fearfully and said, "We are fucking, right? We are really fucking."

John hesitated, not sure if that was an invitation combined with really bad timing, or something else, though at any other time he might have seriously considered such an invitation.

She added, "It doesn't really matter, does it. We are just fucking."

The look on her face certainly didn't have any invitation in it, and then he realized she meant something else. "No, we're not fucking. I think you mean we are really fucked. And yes we are."

"Fucked is bad?"

He nodded. "Fucking is good, fucked is bad, very bad."

She gritted her teeth, gave him a hard look, and grinned. "Then let's fucked them before they can fucked us."

"Okay," he said, thinking that if they lived through this, he'd have to explain the more subtle nuances of fuck, fucked, and fucking. "Let's go fucked them good."

"Fucked them good?" she asked, shaking her head uncertainly. "I thought you said fucked is bad, and fucking is good."

38

Escape Aborted

WHEN ANDERS AND Eskildsen left her office, an armed guard stood outside the door waiting for them. Anders followed the command hawk, knowing he was probably walking to his own death, but powerless to do anything about it. The guard followed behind Anders, and at least the fellow wasn't so obvious as to draw his weapon and aim it at Anders's back.

Eskildsen led them to the lift. Her strategy had become quite clear: she intended to put him on an assault boat with the two young people, all under guard. The boat's crew would be personally selected members of her team, those who shared Eskildsen's hatreds, and could be counted on to be discreet. They'd kill Mistress Vreekande and the young man, though he hoped they did find a merciful way to do that. Then they would blame it on him. They might even keep him alive to conduct a public trial, then a very public execution.

They took the lift up to *Sycorax*'s hanger deck, then walked down a passageway to a closed personnel hatch. The command hawk paused at the hatch and frowned. She hit the lock on the hatch, but a telltale above it flashed red and nothing happened. Anders heard servos whining and gears ratcheting on the other side of the hatch's bulkhead.

The command hawk turned to the guard. "They're leaving without us. What is that idiot pilot thinking?"

At that moment an unterseergent wearing pilot's wings strode down the passageway toward them. When he saw the command hawk he stopped short and his eyes widened. "Command Hawk Eskildsen, I . . . uh . . ."

Eskildsen demanded. "Are you the copilot?"

He shook his head. "No, mistress, the pilot."

Her eyes flashed a very angry red. "You left your post?"

He kept shaking his head. "It was just a—"

She took an angry step toward him and he backed up a step. "Why is the copilot leaving without us?"

His eyes blinked rapidly. "There is no copilot, mistress. Just me."

She stood there for a moment and her brow wrinkled as she tried to process what she had just heard. Then she jerked as if struck by a bullet, put a finger to her ear and shouted into her implants. While she did that the guard pounded on the personnel hatch, the pilot cringed, lowered his eyes to the deck, found the tips of his boots of abiding interest, and backed away from them.

Anders backed slowly up the passageway away from the three people at the hatch. If Mistress Vreekande and her young man had managed to make some sort of escape, perhaps he could help them from inside the ship.

••••

As the docking boom lined the nose of the boat up with the open doors of the hangar bay, Nikaela pulled on a headset. While her implants had been locked out of ship's systems, with the headset she could still manually monitor com chatter.

The docking boom pushed them gently out into open space. John gripped the controls and did pilot stuff she didn't understand, and they accelerated slowly away from the ship. Nikaela didn't know their position, and didn't see a nearby star bright enough to stand out. A quick look at their screens showed that they were about two hundred light hours off Sarkovie. At its maximum acceleration the boat could cross that in twenty or thirty days, but the ship wouldn't give them anything close to that much time.

"*Sycorax One*," a board male voice said, and Nikaela recalled seeing a large 2 stenciled on the side of the other assault boat in the hangar bay. "This is *Sycorax* com central. We have three personnel who have gone off line, last known position on board you. Please explain."

Nikaela waved at John and got his attention. She pointed to the headset earphones, then pressed her hand over her mouth. John's eyes widened and he nodded.

Nikaela manually keyed the mic hanging from the headset in front of her mouth. She tried to sound as bored as the com tech on the ship. "One here. We'll have to see if there's a malfunction in our local shipnet."

"Very good, One. Please do so and advise—"

The com abruptly went silent. A moment later a female voice addressed her over the come. "*Sycorax One*, this is Captain Bjorkstrum, commanding *Sycorax*. Cut your drive, decelerate and return immediately to *Sycorax*. That is an order."

Nikaela didn't key the mic as she said to John. "Now we're really fucked. They know, and they've ordered us to come back."

The look on John's face turned sad and he said, "We really have nothing to lose, do we?"

She smiled. "No, we don't."

John nodded, gripped the controls, did something, and the whine of the boat's engines rose an octave. He had firewalled the boat's drive, though it didn't really matter. Thirty G's was nothing compared to the five or ten kiloGs a transition ship could put out.

The voice in her headset responded immediately. "This is Bjorkstrum. I said cut your drive and return. Do so, immediately, or we'll fire upon you."

Nikaela didn't bother to relay the message to John, and a moment later a massive gravity spike punched through the boat. It stunned Nikaela badly enough to disorient her for several seconds. When her head stopped reeling, she realized *Sycorax* had fired a shot across their bow, the first time she had been at the receiving end of a transition battery. The whine of the boat's engines had dropped back to almost nothing. John had killed its drive.

John gripped her arms and shook her to get her attention. "Tell them we're complying. Tell them we've stopped driving outward, we'll decelerate, then return."

She couldn't believe her breschkada would be so weak. "We can't just give up."

He shook his head and grinned like a school boy. "We're not giving up. I've got an idea, but we'll need those vac suits. We're still going to fucked them."

••••

"General quarters, watch condition red, all hands, this is not a drill."

Katrine slammed awake, and even without conscious thought, stepped out of the grav field of her bunk. Her old warship reflexes had returned in full force.

Two of the three officers she shared the stateroom with had also just awakened, and the three of them scrambled out through the stateroom door. Katrine headed to the bridge, while the two officers went in another direction. She rushed up a ladder to the next deck with a spacer close on her heels.

With his stateroom next to the bridge, Neilosse had beaten everyone there. As Katrine took her customary position standing behind the scan tech, he announced, "One of those bogies fired a salvo from its transition batteries."

A virtual image of Brynjar aboard *Drakan Helgis* appeared in her implants, relayed to her by *Lightspear*'s com tech.

Katrine leaned to one side and glanced over the shoulder of the nav officer. Neilosse had already given orders for *Lightspear* to accelerate hard in sublight toward the two rogue ships. They could up-transit and cross the 150 light-hours to *Caliban* in just over two minutes, but doing so from inside the heliosphere of Sarkovie's primary could produce considerable error in their vector. *Drakan Helgis* had responded in a similar fashion, but they had been in orbit around Sarkovie so their error might be even greater.

"It's your call, Colonel," Neilosse said.

Katrine turned to the com tech. "Connect me with Cap'm Fleming."

The com tech nodded, and a moment later the Null team leader appeared next to Brynjar. "Cap'm, get your team armored up, and I want you locked and loaded."

Fleming nodded. "Yes, ma'am."

Katrine said to Neilosse, "With your permission, I'd like Commander Sharma to keep him fully updated on an ongoing basis."

Neilosse looked at his XO. "You heard the colonel."

Sharma grinned. "Aye, aye, sir."

The virtual image of Brynjar nodded. "May I make a recommendation, Colonel?"

"By all means, Command Superior."

He grinned, the only time she'd ever seen a Kelk look demonic, and she realized he had the predator in his genetic makeup as well. "If your *Lightspear* is equipped like our hunter-killers, the only serious weaponry you have is a lot of large warheads. And if they have our two young people captive, we don't want to use those. But at close range *Drakan Helgis* may be able to target accurately with her transition batteries, and merely disable those ships. You should remain in sublight and help us make a more accurate jump."

He was right. With an ally in sublight feeding the Kelk destroyer accurate navigational corrections, they could cross the distance to the two bogies in about four minutes and overcome much of the distortions caused by transiting within Sarkovie's heliosphere.

Katrine looked to *Lightspear*'s captain. Would his crew cooperate that closely with a Kelk warship? So far direct interaction with the Kelk had been through Katrine and Neilosse, but to carry out Brynjar's plan, some lower ranks would need to interact directly with their blue-skinned counterparts on *Drakan Helgis*.

Neilosse nodded and grinned much like Brynjar. "We can do that."

Katrine felt rather predatory herself. "Please set it up."

Brynjar asked, "And do we transit as soon as we are ready?"

Neilosse had said it earlier: the call was Katrine's to make. Do they up-transit now, or hold? "Set it up, then let's hold, but keep driving in sublight toward them and be ready to up-transit on a moment's notice. Once *Drakan Helgis* down-transits near them, we'll follow on your heels. And your people will have to feed us corrections to make our jump accurate."

••••

As Anders climbed a ladder to the deck above the hangar bay, he asked himself what he might do to help the two young people. If they had somehow managed to commandeer the assault boat, they really didn't stand a chance against *Sycorax*'s main battery. The ship would cut them to pieces in very short order. But Mistress Vreekande was smart enough to know that. So perhaps all they really intended to do was die fighting. And if Anders must die with them, then so be it.

The alert klaxon sounded, calling all hands to battle stations. Since Anders's battle station was his bunk, he ignored it and walked quickly as if rushing to some assigned duty. What could he do? How could he help them? His implants were locked out of shipnet for anything but the most rudimentary functions.

A flashing red telltale in the wall of the passageway drew his attention: an emergency intercom. Under normal circumstances, only the lowest grade of spacer would use such a device, one whose rank did not yet warrant military grade implants. But in a combat situation, if shipnet went down, a hard-wired connection like that might be the only way to communicate with the ship's systems. And under full alert status it provided enhanced emergency functions.

The hull echoed with the thrum of its main battery firing a salvo. He hoped the two young people were still alive as he slapped the switch on the intercom, leaned close to it and said, "Damage control. Hull breach. We're losing pressure—" He cut off in mid-sentence, as if the emergency had interrupted him.

Damage control would get an alert flagged with the intercom's location, and while local pressure sensors would not confirm the hull breach, they would still have to respond to it regardless. A hazard alarm sounded as he hurried up the passageway. He found a ladder, climbed up to the next deck, and didn't have to look far for another emergency intercom. As alarms blared around him he reported another hull breach, then headed aft.

••••

"We detected a transition battery salvo about two hundred light-hours off Sarkovie."

Kristdokar stood next to Nygaard on the bridge of *Konigsborge* as Command Eagle Holverzon briefed them. "*Eldekarl* is three light-hours off Sarkovie. They have identified a ship that left orbit around Sarkovie and is driving hard in sublight toward the coordinates of the detected transition salvo. They're close enough to it to get a good noise profile from its drive, and it matches that of *Drakan Helgis*. They've also detected some transition com splatter from her and another ship about seventy-two light hours off Sarkovie. They began communicating with one another immediately after the transition battery salvo. By tracking the second ship's com splatter, we've determined she's driving at about ten kiloGs toward those same coordinates, but she's too far out for *Eldekarl* to profile her based on sublight drive noise alone."

Kristdokar walked to the scan console and stopped there to look over the shoulders of one of the scan techs. She didn't look Holverzon's way when she asked, "Do we have another ship in the vicinity that *Drakan Helgis* might have allied with?"

"No, mistress."

Nygaard crossed to the scan console and stopped next to Kristdokar. "It appears your man Brynjar has found an ally not of Kelk origin. And driving at ten kiloGs, that ally can only be a warship."

Kristdokar nodded, her thoughts racing. "Yes, and there are very few people outside the Supremacy with whom he would collaborate that way. I recommend *Eldekarl* drive in sublight toward the coordinates of that salvo and be prepared to up-transit on a moment's notice."

"I agree," Nygaard said. "Should we have *Eldekarl* attempt to contact *Drakan Helgis?*"

If Brynjar had found an ally in a Commonwealth warship, their cooperation would be tenuous at best. And then to have three Kelk warships reveal themselves, giving Brynjar overwhelming firepower superiority; that could spook any potential ally. Kristdokar shook her head. "I think not. Let's not reveal ourselves, at least not yet."

••••

When the alert klaxon went silent, the alarms Anders had triggered still continued to blare. He climbed up to the next deck and stopped at a maintenance closet. It wasn't locked and he slipped into it without being seen. The closet's interior measured about one meter by two, with lockers against one bulkhead that gave no indication of their contents. A selection of small tools were racked on the opposite bulkhead and secured against weightless maneuvering.

He grabbed a wrench and stuffed it into a thigh pouch on his coveralls. It wouldn't be much of a weapon against a properly armed guard, but spacers were rarely issued real weaponry, so the wrench should give him an advantage if he faced anyone trying to stop him.

Racked high on the bulkhead he spotted a portable seam welder meant for small repairs. He retrieved it and checked to make sure it had been fully charged. He rifled through the lockers on the other bulkhead, looking for anything flammable, found a pair of dirty coveralls stained with spots of oil. One of the maintenance team probably kept it there to put on for messier jobs.

Anders retrieved the wrench from his thigh pouch, triggered the seam welder and smashed the wrench into its switch until it jammed on. He wrapped the dirty coveralls around it and tossed it into a corner. It wouldn't make much of a fire, probably just a lot of smoke, but that would trigger an alarm and provide one more distraction for the crew.

He opened the closet door a crack and checked the passageway to be sure it was empty. Then he returned the wrench to the thigh pouch and slipped out of the closet.

39

Party Time

WHILE NIKAELA RUSHED aft for the vac suits, John reversed the boat's heading and fired up the drive to decelerate. But he didn't firewall it. They needed time to get sealed into those damn vac suits. From his own experience he knew the slower return would not seem unusual to *Sycorax*'s crew. A pilot might race away from a ship, but never toward it; too much danger of a collision that could cost a lot of lives. He didn't know how to manually trigger the boat's autopilot, but when he released the controls it reacted just like a Commonwealth boat, and automatically maintained the course and acceleration he had set. He left the grav pistol in the pilot's seat and headed aft to join Nikaela.

When he got there she was speaking into her headset, keeping someone at the other end happy. She had already donned the lower half of her vac suit. She paused long enough to show him how to get into his, then returned to her own preparations, though every few seconds she froze and responded to something in the headset.

The vac suit wasn't much. Meant for simple maintenance work or emergency use, it didn't have any tools or a harness to carry added gear, just a tool belt with a few empty clips for tools, and a reel of thin, plast safety line. He didn't think he'd find much use for that. As he pulled on the lower half of the suit, she hissed, "What's this idea you have?"

He adjusted the expansion joints at his knees for a better fit. "Do you know how to operate the gun turrets on this boat?"

She tugged angrily on a strap in her suit. "Of course."

The leg length in his suit was wrong. "As soon as we mate with the docking boom, we each take a turret, and once inside that hangar bay, we shoot the shit out of everything we can, cause as much damage as possible."

Her eyes widened with delight. "Yes. I like that. We can do a lot of damage from the inside when we don't have to punch through the powered shields on the exterior hull."

He hooked a thumb toward the cockpit. "I've got to do turnover. Warn them I'm maneuvering."

John rushed forward to the cockpit, his vac suit still a poor fit. He retrieved his pistol from his seat. The suit didn't include dedicated clips or a holster for the grav gun, so he attached the weapon to a clip on its belt, then buckled into the pilot's seat. He hesitated and shouted, "Are we good?"

She shouted back. "They said okay. You can turn over."

He cut the drive, turned the boat over and fired up the drive again to decelerate. He set it up so they would come to a halt about a kilometer short of *Sycorax*, then hurried aft.

Nikaela made adjustments to the straps and expansion joints on her vac suit, then helped him make the same adjustments on his. They carried their helmets with them and made it back to the control cabin with only a little time to spare. John didn't want the boat to come to a complete stop, so he cut the auto pilot two kilometers out, turned the boat's nose toward *Sycorax*, and let it drift slowly toward the ship.

"Give me your helmet," Nikaela said.

John handed it to her. "What are you doing?"

"Checking the helmet coms."

John shook his head. "*Sycorax* can probably monitor that. We can't use the coms."

She grimaced. "We won't, not until the end, not until it doesn't matter, and then it may buy us a little time."

She showed him how to manually trigger his com with his chin.

He helped Nikaela get her helmet on, though she discarded the headset to do so, and she helped him with his. They dilated their helmets' visors and kept them open so they could communicate by shouting, at least for the time being.

Nikaela jammed an earbud from the headset into one of her ears and held the mic close to her lips through her open visor. She kept responding in Kelk to someone at the other end. They passed the one-kilometer mark, then the half-kilometer mark, then four hundred meters, three hundred, two hundred—

Nikaela abruptly grabbed John's arm. "They said to halt right here. Told me to come to a complete stop or they'll take us apart with their transition batteries."

Transition batteries could range on targets at a couple hundred million kilometers. A hundred meters was point blank range. John grabbed the thrust stick and brought them to a halt about fifty meters from *Sycorax*'s hull.

"Did they say why?"

Nikaela nodded and looked stricken. "They're going to come out and board us. They don't trust us."

John closed his eyes and lowered his head. "They probably won't even take us back to the ship. Just vent us here."

"Fucking reschcat offspring," Nikaela said. "We need to fucked them."

Point blank range, he thought. But it could also be impossible to target on a quickly moving enemy at extremely short range.

John opened his eyes, looked at Nikaela and said, "Back to plan A. Get in the nose turret, and once we're inside that hangar bay, shoot the hell out of its door seals so they can't close it."

Her eyes widened with excitement, not fear. "What are you going to do?"

At that moment he regretted that her earlier confusion on word tense had *not* been an invitation, though the timing was still atrocious. "I'm going to back-assward ram the mother fuckers. So get in that turret, be prepared to seal your vac suit when I shout, and hang on."

••••

John gave the boat a fraction of a G of acceleration for one heartbeat, nudging it forward so it drifted toward the open hangar bay at about a meter per second. Hopefully that velocity was slow enough that no one on *Sycorax* would realize what he had done, at least not for a while. Ten seconds later their distance from the hull of the ship had dropped to forty meters.

John did some quick calculations using his implants. If he firewalled the boat's drive, at thirty G's they'd cross the distance in a fraction of a second and be traveling several hundred kilometers an hour. From inside the hangar bay that would do a lot of damage to the ship, but the boat would disintegrate, taking him and Nikaela with it. He wasn't into suicide, not unless they didn't have any other choice, and if it came to that, he wanted to take a lot of the assholes with him.

As they drifted closer to *Sycorax*'s hull he continually updated his calculations. They were just under thirty meters away when Nikaela shouted, "They told us to stop drifting and retreat to a hundred meters."

John shouted back, "Seal up and hold tight." He triggered the visor on his helmet and it contracted, sealing his suit.

Assault boats were meant to take a lot of punishment and still function. With Nikaela in the nose turret, and him in the cockpit, he spun the assault boat on its axis and aimed its aft end at the open hangar bay. He set the boat's drive for a reverse thrust of ten G's, and yanked on the thrust stick just as a massive gravity spike sent John's senses reeling. *Sycorax* had fired its main battery at them again, and missed again.

The boat rocketed backwards toward the hanger bay, then shot through the open bay doors and its stern slammed into the bulkhead at the far end of the deck, assaulting his ears with the sound of tearing, twisting, snapping plast struts and plating. The boat's internal gravity compensation failed before it came to a stop, slamming John back into his seat during the last instant of the collision. A heavy chunk of torn plast whirled across the hangar bay. It cut one of *Sycorax*'s crewmen in two, his vac suit emitting a cloud of vapor as it depressurized. A piece of girder careened across the bay into the other assault boat, still resting on its docking boom, and tore off its starboard gun turret. Then the air around John turned into a thick, white mist as their boat depressurized. He prayed that Nikaela had gotten her suit sealed quickly enough.

John floated in his seat, held there by the pilot's acceleration harness, and from that he realized they'd cut gravity to the hangar bay, or maybe it had failed because of the damage. The white mist dissipated as he popped the clips on the acceleration harness. His only thought was he must get to Nikaela and make sure she had survived. But at that moment the nose turret detached from the boat and went autonomous. It rose up on independent gravity fields to the height of the cockpit windshield and turned to face him, its two large-caliber weapons aimed his way. Those guns could rip through heavy combat armor with ease, though they would eat up the turret's limited, onboard power reserves quickly.

John could see nothing of Nikaela inside the turret. She must have had the same concern about him, and decided to check on him. He waved at her and gave her a thumbs-up.

She spun away from him toward the hangar bay doors, then unloaded several bursts of fire into their seals. It struck John how eerily silent the heavy weapons were in the vacuum of the hangar bay.

John floated upward and turned toward the back of the boat. The craft's troop cabin had been compressed from a length of ten meters to less than half that, and it was canted heavily to one side. The body of the male guard floated in the middle of the cabin, while pieces of the NCO and female guard were visible in the mangled chaos of twisted metal and plast at the rear of the boat.

He had to get out of the crippled boat so he gripped a handhold and tried the personnel airlock. But when he hit the switch, the hatch retracted a few centimeters into the boat's hull, then it came to a stop and something in its mechanism snapped hard enough that he felt the vibration through the handhold. He shoved his fingers into the narrow opening and groaned with effort as he tried to open it further, but it refused to budge.

The gun turrets! Maybe if he climbed into one and went autonomous like Nikaela.

The collision had badly damaged the starboard gun turret and partially separated it from the boat. The port turret appeared to be intact, but a broken metal strut with a viciously sharp spike blocked his way completely. Next to that a tear in a plate of twisted and bent plast exposed a sharp edge with a jagged spear point. He'd have to navigate that while floating in zero G and not tear his suit. He took one last look around the troop cabin for any alternative. Nothing! He turned back to the port turret.

With both hands he gripped the strut blocking his path, then used that leverage to swing his feet down to the deck. He pulled and the strut gave a little. He pulled harder, put his back muscles into it, and it broke free, sending him careening across the cabin. He slammed into the twisted mess at the rear of the boat and something sharp stabbed him in the arm, producing a fiery lance of pain.

As he broke free of the mess of twisted metal and plast, his suit computer spoke to him in Kelk. He didn't need to waste time translating. A jet of air produced a small cloud of condensing moisture from the hole he had punched through the left forearm of his suit. The suit was telling him he had a forearm breach, and probably giving him a countdown of his oxygen reserves. He watched the self-healing fabric attempt to close the breach by oozing a sticky substance that hardened instantly, but the tear in the material was too big and that didn't work.

He pushed off and floated across the cabin to the port turret, listening to the Kelk words his suit's computer spat at him, and trying to filter numbers out of it. He thought he heard eighty-something percent. He didn't know if that was eighty percent remaining, or eighty percent used up.

Removing the broken strut had given him reasonably clear access to the turret's hatch, though he still needed to be careful of the spear point of torn plast. He edged around it carefully and got the turret's hatch open. He climbed into it, sealed the turret, and its systems automatically began pumping air into the confined space. Like its power reserves, it would have a limited supply, only enough for a brief period of autonomous operation.

He strapped into the control couch, and wished he was encased in full combat armor, instead of a simple vac suit. He dilated his helmet visor, hoping the suit would react like its Commonwealth counterpart. Sensing the helmet visor open, and an exterior supply of breathable air, the suit stopped trying to supply him with something to breathe, allowing him to use up the turret's air supply first. The tear in his forearm had stopped emitting the cloud of condensed moisture, though when he moved his arm, drops of blood floated up away from it. It hurt like hell, but he could live with that.

The turret's attitude yoke and thrust stick were familiar enough he thought he could operate it, but the labels on all the instruments had been stenciled in Kelk script. One switch with a protective cover bore the same word Nikaela had pointed out earlier as meaning something like *Detach*.

"Fuck it all," he said, and hit the switch.

••••

When *Konigsborge*'s scan tech detected the second transition battery salvo, Kristdokar turned to Nygaard. "I think it's time we act quickly and decisively."

The vice skalde nodded. "I agree."

Nygaard looked Holverzon's way. "Captain, tell *Eldekarl*'s captain to proceed with all due haste and use all means possible to protect the breschkada. Instruct *Alvilddan* to drive in-system at maximum transition velocity, and let's do the same."

To Kristdokar she said. "Did I miss anything?"

Kristdokar nodded. "We should make Brynjar aware of our presence."

Nygaard smiled. "Good idea."

••••

Lightspear's scan tech started and spoke, her voice rising with excitement, "I just picked up another transition battery salvo from that bogie."

Katrine looked at Neilosse, then at the virtual image of Brynjar. "Go, Brynjar. Go, go, go!"

There had been a lot of sideways looks and surreptitious glances from *Lightspear*'s crew when they had learned they would be cooperating with the blue-skinned Kelk demons. But once the action had started, the reflexes of a well-trained combat crew had kicked in. It certainly helped that Brynjar had tapped Kelk officers who spoke excellent Lingua to man stations that interacted directly with *Lightspear*'s crew. And they were only transmitting data and verbal communications, no visual links, so *Lightspear*'s people didn't have to look at red-eyed monsters. She'd have to thank him for that, something she might not have thought of had she been in his shoes.

The scan tech said, "*Drakan Helgis* is in transition. Four minutes to target."

No one had said it, but they all knew the Kelk warship was extremely vulnerable. *Drakan Helgis* couldn't target accurately while in transition, but for the next four minutes their transition wake made them a very visible bull's eye. One big warhead could take out the Kelk destroyer with her entire crew.

"Captain," the scan tech said, the tension in her voice rising considerably. "I just detected three up-transition flares, one of them three light-hours off Sarkovie, and two approximately eight hundred light-hours out."

Neilosse demanded, "Can you identify them?"

The scan tech worked frantically at her instruments for several seconds. "The profile on the one close to Sarkovie looks like a Kelk hunter-killer. Farther out we've got . . . a Kelk destroyer . . . and a Kelk cruiser, driving hard in-system, but they won't be here for about fifteen minutes."

Neilosse's eyes flashed angrily at Katrine and he opened a secure link between their implants. "Is your man Brynjar playing us for fools?"

••••

From the nose turret Nikaela had an unobstructed view of the ship and its open hangar bay about thirty meters in front of her. Just as John shouted, "Seal up and hold tight," a boarding party consisting of three Kelk soldiers in full combat armor pushed off from its deck, and drifted slowly toward the boat. She could take them out with her turret's weapons, but John had some sort of plan, so she decided to let him play it out.

She triggered the visor on her helmet and it contracted. He had said something about *assingward backing*. At least that's what she thought he said. She knew the *backing* word, but the *assingward* word confused her so she braced herself, not knowing what to expect. Her ears popped as her suit ran a pressure check. It occurred to her if it failed the check, it was a bit late to do anything about it.

Assingward backing?

The hangar bay, the boarding party, *Sycorax*, everything in front of her spun crazily and snapped out of her field of view, replaced by a dark landscape of distant stars. She hadn't felt a thing because the boat's internal gravity fields had compensated. The boat shot backwards, and as it did so another massive gravity spike shot through the boat from *Sycorax*'s main battery; they had missed again.

The boat's aft end crashed into something to the sound of twisting, tearing plast. Its internal gravity field failed during its last instant of deceleration, and her momentum slammed her into her acceleration couch.

The air around her turret blossomed into a white mist. When it cleared, her turret's forward vid pickups showed the interior of the hangar bay, with the bisected lower half of a vac-suited crewmember tumbling out through the open bay doors. She saw nothing of the three armored soldiers.

Assingward backing; now she understood what John had done, though she'd still have to ask him about the assingward word.

John! Was he even alive?

She hit the *Detach* switch for her turret, explosive bolts fired, and she went autonomous. She drove the turret forward and up, spinning it about in the same motion and bringing it to a stop facing the windshield of the boat.

Nikaela hadn't really understood John's plan, which seemed to be nothing more than: *crash the boat into the ship and get them both killed.* She hadn't argued because she didn't have anything better to offer. At least they could do some hurt to the assholes on *Sycorax* before they died. But looking now at the wrecked assault boat, she understood fully.

With the aft end of the boat buried in the ship's structure, John had smashed a massive hole in the bulkhead at the back of the hangar bay, and taken with it several structural supports. Jets of air leaked around its margins, condensing into a cloudy mist that dissipated quickly. The boat was buried so deeply in the one bulkhead it had probably damaged another beyond it. *Sycorax* might still be able to operate under drive, but her crew couldn't know that until Damage Control assessed the structural damage. Her captain had to assume the warship's structure might catastrophically collapse under the stresses of drive, so for all intents and purposes, John had badly disabled the warship.

Rapid movement drew Nikaela's attention to the assault boat's windshield. John waved at her, then held his thumbs up in some sort of Commonwealth gesture that probably meant he was okay.

Nikaela spun her turret around, brought her weapons to bear on the hangar bay doors, and fired five three-round bursts, ripping away a good portion of the door seals. The turret computer said, *Power reserves depleted to eighty percent.* Once disconnected from the boat, the turret had only a limited supply of stored power.

She turned her attention to the other assault boat, just in case someone decided to use its turrets against her. Its starboard gun turret, the one closest to her, had been torn away by the ejected debris from the other boat's crash. Its other turrets couldn't get a good line-of-fire at her, so she didn't have to worry about them. There were signs of other damage on its hull, but it appeared to be intact.

The port turret from their wrecked boat detached and floated free for a moment. Then it darted forward and bumped against the damaged boat. It pulled away from the boat, moving in sporadic starts and stops. Either John didn't know how to handle a turret very well, or he had trouble deciphering the Kelk labels on its gauges, or he was hurt. She dearly hoped he wasn't hurt.

Something pinged off the outer shell of Nikaela's turret. Her screen showed an object behind her flagged as a friendly and headed her way.

She spun her turret around. One of the boarding party rocketed her way using the gravity fields from his armor, his assault rifle spitting a stream of rounds at her.

40

Desperation Time

THE DECK OF the maintenance closet jolted to one side, and to keep from falling Anders pressed a hand against a bulkhead. *Sycorax*'s hull shrieked and thrummed like a massive drum, a sound unlike anything he had ever heard. It reminded him of a transition battery breaching the outer shields, but multiplied ten-fold. He paused in the process of starting another fire.

Alarms squawked throughout the ship. Something had caused a momentary disruption in *Sycorax*'s internal gravity fields, which meant the ship had suffered serious damage. It was time to retreat to his bunk and try to stay alive.

Anders abandoned his efforts at sabotage. He opened the closet door a crack and checked the passageway to be sure it was empty. While committing his little diversionary acts of sabotage, he had always moved closer to the bunk room, and only a short time had elapsed since they had sounded general quarters. Had he been confronted he would have claimed to be heading there, and probably gotten away with it.

He stepped out into the passageway, closed the maintenance closet, then climbed up one more deck and stopped at an emergency locker he had identified earlier. From it he retrieved an all-purpose, one-size-fits-all vac suit. The damn thing would be uncomfortable as hell, but it might keep him alive, though it wouldn't matter much if the ship's internal gravity completely failed and subjected him to a couple thousand Gs.

There were three other suits in the locker. He retrieved their reactor pack cells. He'd use them as spares, if the need arose. Carrying them and the suit, he continued aft.

As expected, his roommates were assigned to emergency stations and he found the bunk room empty. He quickly donned the vac suit, didn't expend much effort to adjust the fit because he could fine tune that later, then pulled on the helmet. He needed to conserve the suit's oxygen supply so he dilated his visor. He'd breathe shipboard air as long as possible. If his compartment depressurized or the partial oxygen pressure dropped too low, and he happened to be asleep or unconscious at the time, the suit would automatically contract the visor, and feed him air from its supply.

He had thought carefully about what he would do in a disaster situation like this. Since he wasn't crew he couldn't wander about the ship during an alert. They wouldn't let him near the assault boats or life boats, and there was no other way off the ship. His best chance to maximize his chances of staying alive would be to sit out whatever happened and hope for the best.

He climbed carefully into his bunk, buckled its restraints about him so he wouldn't float away if the gravity failed, and closed his eyes to wait.

••••

John had some trouble controlling the turret's motion. It was both like and not like the turrets he'd trained in. Basic control seemed to be the same, but he didn't have the time to carefully translate the gauges—if he even could—so anything beyond the simple stuff was probably not going to happen. And setting up advanced functions—like pupil monitoring so the computer controlled aiming of the turret's weapons by tracking his eyes—was out of the question. He'd have to aim the weapons by aiming the turret. It didn't help that he needed both hands to control it properly, and that everything he did with his left hand produced a shot of pain in his forearm. Blood oozed from the tear in his vac suit's fabric.

His first effort at piloting the turret shot it forward to bump against the damaged boat. He didn't see any red telltales flagging damage to the turret, but maybe the Kelk didn't use red as a damage indicator. He recalled that the telltale on the small arms locker had flashed red for locked and green for open, so maybe they were the same, but he couldn't be sure. He backed up, moving in sporadic starts and stops.

One screen appeared to be a scan readout. If so, it showed two green objects moving nearby. He turned the turret that way in time to see one of the boarding party rocketing toward Nikaela's turret, firing a continuous burst from a heavy assault rifle, bullets ricocheting off the skin of her turret. She darted to one side as the fellow raced past her. He tucked his knees in and somersaulted to get his heels aimed in the opposite direction and decelerate. He clearly intended to come back for another run.

No time to figure out how to fire the damn weapons. John drove his turret forward, and just as the fellow came to a stop, plowed into him, then kept going and sandwiched the asshole between the turret and a bulkhead near an airlock. He backed the turret up and the fellow floated free but didn't move. John drove the turret forward and slammed it into him again.

He backed away slowly, lining up the turret to aim its weapons at the armored figure. But the man didn't move, and jets of vapor from one of his shoulder seals made it clear he'd suffered a torso breach, and probably other serious injuries.

John slid the turret to one side, and now saw that he had rammed the fellow with so much force he'd warped the bulkhead and put a hairline crack in it. At several points along the crack small jets of condensing moisture pinpointed locations where air leaked from the compartment on the other side of the bulkhead.

John's ears popped. The screens in the turret were a kaleidoscope of flashing red signals demanding his attention, and the computer shouted all sorts of Kelk words at him. Unfortunately, just like Commonwealth equipment, that was probably an indication he'd done bad things to his turret. He caught twenty-something percent and thirty-something percent, didn't know which was power reserves and which was air, or maybe they were something else.

John needed to make sure of the boarding party asshole, so he backed the turret across the hangar bay. A joystick with thumb triggers on it looked like a fire control stick. He grabbed it and swung it side to side. His weapons barrels moved with it and a targeting cursor on his main screen tracked with them.

He aimed at the armored figure floating in front of the weakened bulkhead with the airlock, and thumbed one of the triggers. Instead of firing the large caliber weapons, a defensive missile launched.

He managed to say, "Oh shit," just as it hit the far bulkhead, then a blast of debris and ejecta slammed into his turret, sending it bouncing around the interior of the hangar bay like a rubber ball in a small box. When it came to a stop his ears popped again, the turret depressurized and filled with a white mist, and his helmet visor contracted. The suit had detected the drop in air pressure around it and automatically sealed itself.

The mist cleared in a few seconds. His screens were blank and lifeless. The small tear in his suit again emitted a jet of white mist.

Combat armor would seal off a breach by pressure clamping the limb just above the rupture. Better to sacrifice the limb below the clamp than allow the body to die. John's simple vac suit wasn't that sophisticated, so he'd have to improvise.

He reached for the reel of wire-thin plast safety line on his suit's tool belt, and pulled out a couple of meters. He would have to wrap it extremely tight for it to do any good, so he locked the reel to provide tension at one end, then strung it around his forearm just above the tear. One loop and he pulled it painfully tight, another, and again he pulled it tight. By the third loop the jet of air had diminished, but not until the fifth had it dropped back to a trickle, though his left hand had begun to throb and ache. He locked the end of the line to his belt to keep pressure on it.

John hit the turret's hatch lock and it popped open. His turret had come to rest jammed beneath the nose of the boat he'd rammed into *Sycorax*. He climbed out, gripping the edge of the hatch so he didn't float away. He looked around and saw no sign of Nikaela's turret, hoped she was still alive.

There must be an airlock somewhere to allow the hangar crew to pass in and out of the bay while it was under vacuum. He recalled seeing one at some point, had to think for a moment to remember he had slammed the boarding party guy into a bulkhead right next to it, then blown away the bulkhead and the airlock with a missile. As his suit computer gave him a lot of bad news in Kelk he couldn't understand, he realized he was truly fucked.

Maybe the remaining assault boat. Maybe it would still hold pressure, or maybe he could climb into one of its turrets and stay alive a little longer.

He hooked the toe of his boot under the edge of the open turret hatch. During training they had practiced weightless maneuvering extensively, but it was all very different with the pain in his wounded arm hammering at him. He pushed off from the turret hatch and floated across the hangar bay toward the other assault boat, purposefully aiming low so that if he missed the boat he could still snag the docking boom on which it rested. As the distance to the boat narrowed, he felt weak and lightheaded, wasn't sure if that was due to the pain, or the initial stages of oxygen hypoxia.

He had aimed a little too low, and ricocheted off the hangar deck about five meters short of the boat. That sent him into a spin, but with his left arm he managed to snag one of the boat's landing struts and came to a stop.

The small personnel airlock on the other side of the boat was mated to the ship. His only chance was the troop hatch, much larger and no airlock, though he had no idea if he could open it.

His ears popped again and he had trouble thinking. With the boat resting on its docking boom, the bottom of the hatch was about waist high. He hooked the toe of his boot under the strut and straightened up, and miraculously, the hatch dilated without any effort on his part.

Standing on the deck of the boat in its gravity field, two Kelk crewmen in vac suits loomed over him. One shook his head sadly from side to side, and spoke over the helmet com. John only recognized the words, ". . . bad boy."

Then the fellow raised a grav pistol and aimed it at John's face.

••••

When John crashed his turret into the fellow from the boarding party, Nikaela had a momentary epiphany. Both that asshole and John's turret had shown on her screens as friendlies. That meant her turret would show on the ship's screens as a friendly, or at least she hoped it would. And then John fired that missile, blasting another void in the ship's structure, and blowing her turret out through the open hangar bay door.

Her reflexes kicked in and she brought her turret to a stop just beyond *Sycorax*'s outer hull. She tapped into the ship's command grid, something she should have done earlier. Most of the compartments adjacent to the hanger bay were now under vacuum, but Damage Control had also flagged several unconfirmed hull breaches and fires elsewhere in the ship. More importantly, extensive structural damage on the hangar deck and the decks nearby had everyone's attention. She had no idea how the captain had prioritized power for Engineering, but quite probably they focused on maintaining the structural integrity of the ship. She might have a small chance to do some damage against the outer hull.

She moved slowly, holding the turret about a meter off *Sycorax*'s hull. As long as she showed up on screens as a friendly, they might assume the green blip was nothing more than a repair skiff. She edged the turret around a defensive pod, and just to be sure stayed as close to the ship as possible, making it difficult to target on her.

Power reserve at twenty-five percent, the turret's computer said.

She eased her turret up the side of the ship, and paused just before clearing it. She moved about a meter higher and had an unobstructed view of the bridge, and *Sycorax*'s main battery.

Power reserve at twenty percent.

The high-caliber grav rifles on her turret ate copious amounts of power, but she didn't need power for this. The turret had a magazine of six defensive missiles that carried their own punch. She armed them, sighted at the base of the main battery, lifted her turret up to get a good angle of fire, launched them all, then drove her turret down along the side of the ship. The distance was so short she caught a momentary flash of explosion just before the bridge and main battery slid out of her field of view.

Assuming she had now been flagged as a non-friendly, she moved quickly, but kept the turret close to the hull to minimize any ability to target on her. Two defensive pods tried and came close, sending gravity spikes through her gut, but she made it back to the open hangar bay door, pulled the turret just inside the bay, and brought it to a stop.

She scanned the hangar bay looking for John. The place was a wrecked mess, their original assault boat a twisted jumble of torn plast and steel, and canted to one side with its nose protruding from a bulkhead. John's missile had also cratered another bulkhead on the far side of the hangar bay. Everywhere jets of air leaked into the vacuum of the bay.

She spotted John's turret jammed beneath the nose of the crippled assault boat, its hatch lying open. Movement drew her attention to the other side of the hangar bay. John clung to the landing strut of the other assault boat, a small plume of atmosphere jetting from his left forearm. Two Kelk crewmen stood in the open troop hatch above him. One of them raised a grav pistol toward John's face.

Power reserve at fifteen percent.

Nikaela drove her turret sideways into the hangar bay. With John effectively standing on the landing strut, his torso blocked the lower half of the open troop hatch and she didn't have a clean shot. She'd have to shoot over him and go for head shots, so she locked her eyes on the helmet of the crewman raising the weapon, her turret guns tracking with her pupils. Over her helmet com she heard the man say, "You've been a very bad boy."

At that moment she had no choice but to take the shot, so she fired a three round burst. The man's visor shattered and wisps of atmosphere erupted from his chest. He fell back and collapsed in the open hatch.

Nikaela locked her eyes on his companion's helmet, but just as she fired another three-round burst the fellow moved. She thought she hit him, but he disappeared into the boat's interior.

Power reserve at five percent.

Nikaela hit a switch to depressurize her turret as she drove it toward the open hatch. She brought it to a stop one meter short of John, then rotated the turret to aim its hatch at the open troop hatch on the boat. She popped the clips on her acceleration harness, unclipped the grav pistol from her tool belt, popped the hatch on the turret, and pushed out of it toward the open troop hatch.

Her aim was good. She floated through the hatch into the boat's internal gravity field and bounced painfully off the boat's deck. Toward the front of the boat the other crewman staggered drunkenly. He raised a grav pistol and fired. A bullet zinged off Nikaela's helmet and another punched into her side. It felt like she'd been stabbed with a hot metal spike.

Helmet and torso breaches, her suit said as she rolled to the side, raised her pistol and fired twice. A puff of air erupted from the crewman's chest and he went down. She heard the whistle of air escaping from her helmet, and saw a jet of it shooting from the side of her suit just above her tool belt.

Oxygen reserves at fifty percent and declining, terminal decompression in three minutes and counting.

She climbed to her feet and looked toward the aft end of the boat. It appeared she was now alone in the boat with two dead bodies. She rushed forward to the personnel airlock, made sure it was closed, then rushed back to the troop hatch.

She laid her pistol on the floor of the boat, then climbed out through the hatch into the zero-G of the bay, carefully keeping hold of the strut John clung to. He moved languidly, and said something that didn't make any sense.

Terminal decompression in two minutes and counting.

She would never have been able to lift him in full gravity. But in the weightlessness of the hangar bay, she untangled him from the landing strut, floated him up to the level of the troop hatch, then gave him a shove. When he passed into the boat's gravity field, he thudded onto the deck and lay still.

Terminal decompression in one minute and counting.

Nikaela climbed into the boat, closed the hatch, keyed her helmet's com, and shouted, "Computer, pressurize the cabin. Execute."

Pumps whined and the jets of air shooting out of her suit disappeared as pressure returned. Until that moment she hadn't known if they had nulled her vocal signature out of the system for even rudimentary emergency functions.

At a little over half an atmosphere she broke the seals on her damaged helmet and threw it aside. She popped the seals on John's helmet and removed it.

He opened his eyes, though he clearly had trouble focusing. "You're the best looking girl I've ever seen."

41

In Pieces

IF NEILOSSE HAD a temper, Katrine hadn't seen any signs of that earlier, but at that moment he looked like he was ready to blow his stack. She replied to him on the secure link he had punched through to her implants. "I trust Brynjar. I trust him with my life."

"And the life of my crew?"

"Yes. Please captain. Believe me, he is a straight shooter." Perhaps that wasn't the best figure of speech to use at the moment. She could take command of his ship, but that would be a damn foolish thing to do just then, so she didn't go there.

Perhaps that was why he calmed, and said, "It's your play, Colonel."

"Sir," the scan tech said, "*Caliban* is on the move."

Standing behind the young woman, Katrine turned her attention back to the screens. *Caliban* had up-transited on a vector out of the system, though its options had been limited and the two Kelk warships farther out might be able to intercept it, if they were inclined to do so.

"They're making a run for it," Neilosse said. "Too many Kelk warships on hand for them. A few too many on hand for me too."

On the screens *Caliban*'s Kelk accomplice hadn't moved, hadn't made a run for it as well. Why not?

At that moment the unknown Kelk hunter killer down-transited thirty light-hours off the bogie's position. They had missed badly, and it would take them time to set up and execute a correction. *Drakan Helgis* was only seconds from down-transiting, but would be right on top of the rogue Kelk ship because Brynjar had the advantage of navigational corrections fed to them by *Lightspear*.

On the tech's screens Katrine watched *Drakan Helgis* converge with the rogue ship then down-transit with a visible flare.

"*Drakan Helgis* is sublight, sir."

Now it was *Lightspear*'s turn.

"Okay, people," Neilosse said. "Navigation, have you got a good data feed from *Drakan Helgis*?"

"We do, sir."

"Stand by for up transition. Helm, execute at your earliest possible opportunity."

••••

Konigsborge's com tech said, "*Eldekarl* reports she missed the target by thirty light-hours due to in-system gravitational distortions."

"Damn!" Nygaard said, echoing Kristdokar's own thoughts. "Can they correct?"

"No, mistress, not before we can get there."

"Then tell them to remain in sublight and feed us correctional data."

"Yes, mistress."

Command Eagle Holverzon had been in direct contact with *Eldekarl*'s captain. "*Eldekarl* also reports *Drakan Helgis* has just down-transited in the immediate vicinity of the target. They've made contact with *Drakan Helgis*, and Command Superior Brynjar reports the target consists of two rogue warships: a Commonwealth destroyer disguised as a research vessel named *Caliban*, and an unknown Kelk destroyer, probably also disguised as a civilian vessel. The Kelk destroyer is not moving, and it's emission's profile shows some signs of damage. *Caliban* is making a run for it and driving out-system now. *Eldekarl*'s navigator believes we and *Alvilddan* may be in a position to intercept."

Standing behind the scan console next to Kristdokar, Nygaard stared at the tech's screens for a moment. While still in transition *Konigsborge*'s scan systems were all but useless, but with a data stream from *Eldekarl* coasting in sublight, they had all the information nicely visible on their screens.

"Brigadier," Nygaard said, turning to Kristdokar, "You know this Brynjar fellow and I do not—your recommendation?"

Kristdokar didn't take her eyes off the screens in front of the scan tech. "Send *Alvilddan* in to support Brynjar, and tell Brynjar to engage. The two destroyers working together will give them overwhelming firepower superiority, while we intercept this rogue Commonwealth ship coming our way. A heavy cruiser like *Konigsborge* should have no trouble engaging a destroyer."

Kristdokar turned to look pointedly at the com tech. "And ask Brynjar about that ship from the Commonwealth he appears to be allied with?"

The com tech worked frantically at her console, and Kristdokar forced herself to be patient. When the young woman finally spoke, her voice held a note of fear in it. "Mistress, Command Superior Brynjar reports he is allied with Blacksword Lieutenant Colonel Katrine Primatov, in command of the ComSecCorps hunter-killer *Lightspear*."

Nygaard looked at Kristdokar and raised an eyebrow. "Do you know this Commonwealth officer, this . . . Blacksword?"

Kristdokar wished Brynjar hadn't included the Blacksword part. She took a deep breath and met Nygaard's gaze. "I do. Not personally, but I have worked with her from afar for more than a year. And I trust her."

Nygaard stared at her without blinking. Then she nodded once and said, "Then I trust her as well . . . at least as much as I can trust a Blacksword. Though I'm not sure how much I would trust her if we didn't have overwhelming firepower superiority."

Nygaard grinned like a predator anticipating a meal.

••••

John's beautiful shit-of-bull Kelk woman leaned over him and helped him untangle the mess of plast safety line wrapped around his left forearm. Returning circulation proved to be even more painful than the throbbing numbness of a few seconds ago. He leaned back, closed his eyes and took deep breaths until the pain receded to the simple hurt of the stab wound in his forearm. He wiggled his fingers, was relieved to learn he could do so with only a bit of residual numbness.

When he sat up he saw the bloody smear on the side of Nikaela's suit just above her waist.

"You're hurt," he said. He staggered to his feet. His knees wobbled a little, but he managed to remain standing.

Nikaela popped one of the seals on the side of her suit and shoved a hand into it. Clearly in a great deal of pain, she spoke through gritted teeth. "I can't reach it."

John reached out and opened the seal on her suit a little wider. "Let me see."

Like John, she wore a simple coverall beneath the suit, and the side of it was soaked in blood. He stuck his finger in a hole in the material and tore it to get a better view of the wound site. The bullet had punched a hole in her side just above her waist, and exited after passing through a few inches of flesh. Blood oozed from both wounds, but neither pulsed.

"It passed straight through," he said. "The wounds aren't pulsing, and I don't think it's deep enough to have hit any vital organs."

"Good," she said. "We have to get out of here. Can you start this thing up?"

He shook his head. "What good will that do? The minute we try to leave, they'll just tear us apart with their transition battery."

"Maybe not," she said. "If we're lucky, I might have done some damage to it. But even if not, at least we should decouple from the ship so they can't board us easily. If nothing else, we'll park it in the middle of the hangar bay, lock ourselves into a couple of turrets, and keep fighting."

"Okay," he said. "Let's give it a shot."

They quickly checked the bodies of the two crewmen to make sure neither would wake up and make trouble. Both were dead.

John headed for the cockpit and Nikaela followed. Again he sat in the pilot's couch and she in the copilot's. She helped him identify a switch that might be interpreted as *Ignition*, or *Initiate*. When he hit it, nothing happened. He couldn't just sit there punching switches at random, so he tried the *Detach* switch. In a Commonwealth ship, launching the boat would initiate a sequence to automatically fire up its engines, but that didn't happen.

Servos whined, pumps clattered, red telltales flashed on the screens in front of them, and the boat's personnel airlock detached from the ship. Then the boat lurched sideways, and its docking boom moved it slowly across the hanger bay toward the open bay doors, carefully orienting its nose outward. The boom gave them a gentle shove and they drifted slowly out into open space.

Nikaela shook her head. "We are so fucking. We are so fucking."

It still wasn't an invitation, but if it had been, he wasn't sure how he would have handled it. The timing was a little better, but still rather dismal.

••••

"Down-transition," *Lightspear*'s helmswoman announced.

Neilosse looked Katrine's way. "Brynjar reports he is close enough to the rogue to target with high accuracy and is engaging. Do we engage, Colonel?"

Priorities, Katrine thought, recalling Mani Gascoigne's instructions. "Negative, Captain. We engage only if absolutely necessary."

••••

The assault boat drifted away from *Sycorax* at about three meters a second, and Nikaela noticed it had a slight tumble. Once a minute *Sycorax* rolled into view through the windshield, then rolled out again. Each time it was farther away.

Nikaela translated labels for John while he tried to get the boat's engines started. Every second they sat there she expected to feel a gravity spike from *Sycorax*'s main battery. It would tear through the hull, depressurize it, and they would die.

After a few frustrating and unsuccessful attempts at starting the boat's engines, John shook his head. "We're wasting our time here."

"You're right," Nikaela said. At that moment the pain in her side flared and her wound demanded all her attention. She grimaced and barely got the words out. "Let's try again later. If they hull this boat and we haven't replaced these damaged vac suits, we're dead."

As if to confirm that statement, a sharp gravity spike sent her senses into a spin. She clutched at the console in front of her and saw John doing the same.

"That was a transition battery," John said.

Nikaela's sense of equilibrium steadied. "But not as close as the last time."

John pointed through the windshield at something in front of them. "Look."

Sycorax had rolled into view again, and ejecta now formed a visible debris field on one side of the destroyer. Nikaela shook her head. "I don't think my turret missiles caused that much damage."

Without warning *Sycorax* accelerated away from them and disappeared from their view in the windshield. They had identified one screen as a scan readout. In it Nikaela watched the ship drive beyond the limited range of the boat's equipment. Something had caused *Sycorax*'s captain to make a desperate move.

"Vac suits," John said. "We need vac suits."

••••

A gravity spike punched through *Sycorax*, and the hull shrieked with a sound Anders recognized all too well. An enemy ship's transition battery had successfully penetrated *Sycorax*'s hull.

He felt a vibration in the ship and touched his hand to the bulkhead next to his bunk. Even through the vac suit's gauntlet he recognized the thrum of *Sycorax*'s sublight grav drive. Her captain had decided to make a run for it. As a precaution Anders contracted his visor and sealed his suit.

The hull groaned like an angry animal badly wounded, then gravity shifted, pushing him upward against his bunk restraints with crushing force. He couldn't breathe, and thought his ribs might splinter out of his chest. His eyeballs wanted to burst out of their sockets.

Sycorax shrieked as plast and metal tore and snapped, and with his last thoughts Anders recognized the death throes of a dying ship.

••••

"Sir," *Lightspear*'s scan tech said, his voice rising. "That Kelk warship is on the move. They're accelerating toward Sarkovie, probably going to try . . ."

The young man froze and stared at his screens, his mouth open with a frown on his face, a very unusual reaction for an experienced tech. Katrine turned away from Neilosse to look over the scan tech's shoulders. His screens showed several blips where there should only be one, all ranging at a quarter million kilometers. Katrine didn't understand what she saw there.

"Helm," Neilosse said. "Follow, dammit."

"Sir," the scan tech said. "I don't think we have to follow very far. That rogue Kelk warship just broke up."

••••

Anders regained consciousness slowly, floating in zero G and held in his bunk by his restraints. Everything hurt, his eyeballs, his muscles, his gut, his balls. He swallowed blood. He had bitten his tongue and almost taken off a good piece of it. He lay there for a while, taking slow, steady breaths and waiting for the pain to recede.

He had heard of other spacers who had experienced extremely high G forces. They survived only if the force didn't exceed a few hundred Gs, and only if it lasted for a mere fraction of a second, though they came away from it with some internal hemorrhaging. Some required surgery to stop the bleeding, some not, though they often recovered without any lasting effects.

He opened his eyes to complete darkness, not even a hint of light, and a silence so still he wondered if his eardrums had burst. But he heard little pops and ticks from his suit's systems, and that reassured him somewhat.

"Computer," he said. "Suit status-check, execute."

It took several seconds, and then his suit reported that it remained undamaged and operating at one hundred percent. It also reported breathable atmosphere in the bunk room, with no toxic contaminants, so his compartment remained intact.

He turned on a helmet lamp and dialed it down to minimum illumination to save power. He popped the latches on his bunk restraints and floated up off the thin mattress. He moved cautiously. He didn't know what debris might be floating in the bunk room, and it would be best to assume anything might puncture the material of his suit.

He eased his way out of his bunk, and holding onto its lip, he oriented himself to look around the compartment. He spotted the wrench he'd removed from his thigh pouch when putting on the suit, and a few personal items from his bunk mates, but nothing that might damage his suit. He carefully pushed off and floated across the compartment to the closed door in the far bulkhead. A telltale above it remained unlit—no power—so he didn't know if the compartment on the other side was under pressure or not. He tried the latch on the door but it wouldn't budge, so he gripped the wheel used to manually seal it when the power failed. He braced his feet in the base of the hatch, but couldn't turn it. Either it had jammed, or the compartment on the other side was under vacuum.

His suit would dissociate the carbon dioxide he exhaled and retrieve most of the oxygen for reuse. With three spare reactor pack cells, he wouldn't suffocate for quite a long time. But under the circumstances he should use every resource at his command, so he dilated his helmet visor to take advantage of the compartment's air and save his suit reserves. Only then did he hear a faint sound, a repetitive tap, almost below the threshold of hearing. He pressed the side of his helmet against the bulkhead, and it sounded louder, but not by much.

He scanned his surroundings, spotted the wrench floating in the middle of the compartment, pushed off and snagged it out of the air. When he reached the far side, he pushed off again and returned to the door.

Holding onto the latch in the door he slammed the wrench against the bulkhead five times. It clanged loudly, and he hoped it would transmit far enough through the hull to be heard, if there was actually anyone alive to hear it

Again, he pressed his helmet against the bulkhead. He heard nothing for several seconds, then the faint tap, tap, tap. He used the wrench again, then listened again, and did that twice more, but got no response from the tapping.

He sealed the wrench into a thigh pocket on his suit, pushed off and floated across the compartment to his bunk. He climbed into it and buckled the latches on his restraints. Someone had fired on *Sycorax*, so there were more ships out there than just *Caliban*. He dearly hoped they would attempt to rescue *Sycorax*'s crew. He turned off the helmet lamp and closed his eyes to wait in the dark.

42

Dead in the Water

KONIGSBORGE'S POSITION PLACED it sixty light-hours to one side of *Caliban*'s outbound transition line. If they hoped to intercept the smaller ship, they needed to kill their inbound velocity and make a hard turn, all in transition, the kind of maneuver that would light up the entire system with transition noise. It was a desperate move that would make them an easy target for anyone not in transition, but it was their only chance. And it would not have been possible without *Eldekarl* in sublight feeding them positional data.

Kristdokar wanted to shout commands and issue orders, but her interference would only hinder Captain Holverzon and his crew. She glanced at Nygaard; the councilwoman stood next to her with her teeth gritted and jaw muscles bunched, probably fighting to suppress the same reflexive impulse to take command. Both remained silent as the minutes ticked by and Holverzon orchestrated the maneuver.

He looked their way and addressed Nygaard, "At best we're going to have a long-shot, and then probably only one chance at it. Earlier you said we don't want to completely destroy them, so only transition batteries, no big warheads. Does that still stand?"

Nygaard looked at Kristdokar as she answered him. "Yes, only transition batteries. But do arm a large warhead and have it ready in case I decide you should use it."

Kristdokar raised a single eyebrow, and in response Nygaard lowered her voice. "If our breschkada-se is aboard that vessel, we don't want her to fall into Commonwealth hands."

Kristdokar didn't need the woman to tell her that the existence of the breschkada was an ongoing inconvenience for the Larscom. On Reisenar the two young people had averted interstellar war, and initiated valuable channels of communication between the Commonwealth and the Supremacy. But among Kelk, the distasteful interracial aspect of their relationship brought with it certain unavoidable liabilities. And while breschkada were in many ways sacrosanct, no one would fault them the use of a large warhead when in hot pursuit of an armed enemy. And that was doubly true for a Commonwealth rogue.

"Vice Skalde Nygaard," Holverzon said. "We'll get a better targeting solution if we down-transit, so I'm going to take us sublight."

He turned his attention to the helmsman. "Helm, crash stop. Start dumping lights. Fire Control, standby all main batteries."

Kristdokar looked at the scan tech's screens. The data stream *Eldekarl* fed them indicated they had completed the turn and now ran perpendicular to the rapidly approaching rogue warship's outbound vector.

"One thousand lights," the helmsman said.

Holverzon said, "Force her into down-transition as soon as you can."

"Yes, maestra. Five hundred lights . . . four hundred . . . three hundred . . . and . . . we're down."

Down-transiting at three hundred lights had lit up the system with a massive flare.

"Fire Control," Holverzon demanded. "Give me that targeting solution."

"Maestra, ranging at close to three hundred million kilometers . . . and . . . we have a solution, though it's a long-shot."

"Fire all main batteries."

Konigsborge's hull thrummed with the combined release of energy from her four main batteries. Kristdokar found herself holding her breath while looking over the scan tech's shoulders. A few seconds passed, then the blip on his screens disappeared. "Maestra," he said, "it looks like a hit."

Kristdokar thought the young man a little optimistic. A near miss could disrupt the rogue's transition wake and force them into down-transition with damage ranging from nothing, to complete destruction.

They waited for several seconds, then Holverzon said, "Helm, let's go in—"

"Maestra," the scan tech said, "they just up-transited again."

"Fire Control," Holverzon said, "stand by main batteries. Let's try another—"

"Belay that, Captain," Nygaard said. She gave Kristdokar an apologetic look. "Let's end this. Use that warhead."

Holverzon issued the orders, Fire Control computed a targeting solution, and they launched the missile. Kristdokar watched the blip of the missile converge with the rogue warship, then blossom into thermonuclear file.

If she herself were ever elevated to the Larscom, she hoped she would not become so pragmatic as to sacrifice a promising young life for political expediency. She also hoped Nikaela Vreekande had not been on board that vessel.

••••

Nikaela's side wound was clearly more painful than John's forearm wound. He helped her out of the copilot's seat, then followed her to the back of the troop cabin. She hit a latch on a locker like the one in the other assault boat. John expected to see two undamaged vac suits hanging there, but the locker was empty. They both had the same thought, and turned to look at the two dead crewmen lying on the deck of the boat. They checked carefully, and confirmed that the two men had retrieved their suits from the locker.

A massive gravity wave rolled through the boat and they both staggered. Nikaela clutched at John's arm. "That wasn't a transition battery."

"No," he said. "Big ship passing close by, really close—"

Another big wave rolled through the boat. John's stomach did a somersault, and Nikaela fell to one knee. "Another ship," she said. "Where did they come from?"

John helped her stand. "I have no idea. What do you think, good guys or bad guys?"

She gave him a look empty of hope. "I don't know. But it doesn't matter, does it?"

They considered using a patch kit for the suits, but all four were too badly damaged for that. John's suit was the only one without a torso breach, but the trick of wrapping safety line around his arm had been a short-term measure of limited success, and would only keep him alive a little longer than Nikaela.

Nikaela shrugged and sighed. "We might as well get comfortable."

They helped each other out of the unwieldy, one-size-fits-all vac suits, and it was a relief to remove the extra weight.

The boat had a small supply of water. They used it sparingly to clean their wounds and wipe the blood off their faces.

Nikaela raided an emergency medical kit. Bandages were bandages, but like the labels in the cockpit John needed help to decipher the use and application of many of the items in the kit. Nikaela showed him how to apply a wound sealant, and when he dabbed it on the cuts in her upper lip, the swelling immediately began to recede. When he sprayed it onto the two holes in her side, she let out a long sigh, and her face relaxed. "It contains a local anesthetic as well," she said. "It's quite effective for the first few hours after taking the wound. But the pain will come back."

John's forearm wound was a deep puncture with a jagged tear in the skin. When she applied the sealant to his arm the throbbing receded considerably, and only then did he realize how much effort he had expended to accommodate the constant demands of the pain. The sealant also helped considerably with the cut over his right eye.

As Nikaela applied a bandage to his arm she looked into his eyes and said, "You fought like a crazy Kelk man, John Mathius."

John wasn't sure what that meant. "Is that good?"

She nodded. "For Kelk it is."

"A compliment, huh?"

"Yes, a compliment."

"So crazy is good? I learn something new about you Kelk every day."

"How long did it take you to learn we don't eat your babies?"

He shook his head. "Don't patronize me. No baby eating. No scaled lizard tails either."

"Scaled lizard tails?" she asked. "They say that too?"

He nodded and grimaced. "Yah, some of them go pretty far."

"Well at least you know we don't have demon eyes, scaled lizard tails and forked tongues."

"Of course," he said. "Your eyes look rather nice."

She smiled in response to that.

He leaned to one side and looked at her butt. "And I think I'd spot the lizard tail, like it would stick out, don't you think?"

He straightened and looked again into her eyes. "And I'm absolutely certain no forked tongues."

She started and her eyes narrowed. "You're . . . absolutely . . . certain?"

"Yes, of course."

She squinted at him and her eyes hardened. "Absolutely certain . . . doesn't sound like you really *know* it . . . as fact."

"I am certain." He tried to explain it to her the way he'd explained it to May and Karya. "But I've never seen a Kelk tongue so I couldn't swear to it in a court of law."

"Court of law," she demanded, and he realized everything he said dug a deeper hole for him, because at that moment her eyes did look a tiny bit demonic, though kind of sexy at the same time.

She shouted, "Absolutely certain." She leaned forward and slammed the palms of her hands into his chest, pushing him back a step and knocking him against a bulkhead. She stepped forward aggressively and stood facing him almost chest to chest.

"Well then we should make sure you can testify in a court of law."

She reached up, and for an instant he thought she would either stick her tongue out at him, or hit him, or possibly both, but instead she wrapped her arms around his neck and kissed him.

From that moment forward, John would have no trouble testifying in a court of law her tongue was not forked. It was a very human tongue. He could now testify to that with absolute certainty, though, if pressed to explain exactly how he knew that, it could be embarrassing to tell the truth, so he might have to lie a bit.

The kiss lasted a lot longer than necessary, and he rather enjoyed repeatedly reconfirming his new knowledge of that subject. Nikaela melted against him and he wrapped his arms around her. He ran his hands down her back and along her very human waist and hips, taking care to avoid the wound in her side. And then his thoughts went places he had never thought his thoughts would go. He recalled the moment he had looked at her butt during the scaled-lizard-tail part of the conversation, and it occurred to him he had rather enjoyed—

Without warning she pulled her tongue out of his mouth, pushed against his chest and broke out of his arms. She grinned and said, "If we live through this, I'm going to find out if anything on you is forked."

She turned and walked away from him, a little extra sway in her hips, while he stood there wondering what the hell she had meant by that. And then it hit him.

She stopped, looked over her shoulder and said, "If I'm forced to testify in a court of law, I'll want to do so with absolute certainty."

Damn, he thought. *She is so fucking human.*

••••

Neilosse gave Katrine a very unhappy look. "I'm inclined to simply fire up our drive and run like hell."

With three Kelk warships amassed only a few hundred thousand kilometers away, Katrine was inclined to agree with him, though she was not going to admit it. And with the big cruiser returning from its pursuit of *Caliban*, the situation would get even more lopsided.

They had retired to Neilosse's office for a confidential discussion. At least that was the spin Neilosse had put on it for the crew, when in fact they were there for him to vent on Katrine.

She met his eyes and spoke very carefully. "So far, have they displayed any aggressive intent toward us?"

"No," he snapped. "They haven't. But they're Kelk. They're the enem—"

She raised a single eyebrow, a look she had perfected for upbraiding junior officers without shouting.

He pursed his lips and gritted his teeth. "Okay, they're not the enemy, but they're Kelk so I don't trust them."

She let the silence draw out for a long moment before speaking. "There are two people on those Kelk warships I do trust implicitly: Command Superior Brynjar, and Brigadier Skalde Kristdokar. They have been close allies for more than a year."

His eyes blinked rapidly, something she had observed before when he paused to think carefully. "A brigadier skalde, huh?"

"Yes."

"Is she in command of their operation?"

"I don't think so, but she certainly has a lot of influence over the woman who is."

She let him process that for a moment, then, thinking of Mani Gascoigne's admonishment to her, she continued. "This is more important than my life, your life, or the lives of your entire crew. So I must insist we join the recovery effort in the debris field of *Sycorax*."

She had used a secure implant link to warn Captain Fleming he and his nullheads might have to fight their way out of the lower decks. If need be, she would arrest Neilosse, confine him under guard, and take command herself. If they didn't have to kill anyone, then afterward they'd release him, and pretend it never happened. That way both she and he would still have careers.

He slowly rose to his feet and took a deep breath. "As you wish, ma'am. I'll not have it said I can't obey orders."

He was a good man, a good officer. She'd have to talk to Fran Thealone. Maybe they would offer him the Blacksword.

••••

When *Konigsborge* ended its pursuit of *Caliban* they were only about four hundred light-hours from the recovery operation. Kristdokar begrudged the hour it took to reverse their previous vector, but she could do nothing about that. Then they made a short transition hop, and ten minutes later down-transited in the vicinity of the other ships. But as they decelerated for a rendezvous, the scan tech blurted, "Maestra, I just picked up an up-transition flare at the last known position of *Caliban*."

"Damn," Holverzon said.

The scan tech continued. "They're only driving at about fifteen hundred lights, so I think we damaged them."

"Navigation," Holverzon demanded. "Can we intercept?"

Nygaard shook her head. "Belay that captain. By the time we reverse direction again, they'll have enough lead to easily lose us."

She leaned close to Kristdokar and lowered her voice. "I do hope they don't have Mistress Vreekande with them."

••••

Nikaela returned to the copilot's seat, and John to the pilot's. He pointed to one screen. "That scan readout doesn't show anything other than some minor debris nearby. *Caliban* was about a hundred thousand kilometers off, and they're gone too."

Nikaela nodded slowly, trying to think the situation through. "Those gravity waves, big ships passing way too close. Someone else is on the scene. But who?"

"Maybe some locals," John said.

She didn't believe that any more than he did. "Let's try to get these engines fired up."

Nikaela rapidly translated the labels in the cockpit one by one. John ignored many of them and shook his head, but on a few he questioned her further or tried something. At one point their efforts brought a blank screen to life. John ignored it and pointed to another label.

"Wait," Nikaela said. She looked carefully at the newly lit screen. "It's a damage assessment schematic."

She scrolled through pages of diagrams. Four items flagged yellow were punctures in the hull, probably caused by stray bullets from her gunfight with the two crewmen inside the troop cabin. The boat had automatically sealed up smaller holes like that. If anything larger had punched through the hull, the boat wouldn't have been able to re-pressurize, and she and John would have suffocated in the vacuum of the hangar bay.

There were far too many items flagged red, but thankfully the hull was intact and they had plenty of oxygen reserves. After a few minutes examining the damage assessment, that screen went blank as well, and no matter how hard they tried they could not resurrect it.

It only took them about a half hour to review every dial, label, gauge, and switch in the cockpit, since many of them were quite mundane, and clearly of no use for what they needed.

John leaned back in his seat and stared for a long moment at the console. "It's got to be that one labeled *Ignition*, or *Initiate*, or whatever it means."

Nikaela had come to the same conclusion. "There were a lot of red flags in the damage assessment schematic. I wish I'd had more time to examine it, but we probably did a lot of damage to this boat as well."

John pointed to a blank screen. "That screen was lit earlier. It was the scan summary."

Nikaela glanced back over her shoulder. Earlier the troop cabin had been well lit, but now some of the lights had gone dark. She recalled all those red flags in the damage assessment. "John, I think the boat's systems are failing one by one."

John looked at her and frowned, then followed the direction of her gaze and looked over his shoulder. "Fuck."

"We are really fucking, aren't we?"

He looked into her face. "Yah, but we've got new players on the scene. Maybe we should try a distress signal."

She shrugged. "We've got nothing to lose."

"The way I figure it," he said, "we've got a fifty-fifty chance they won't execute us out of hand."

Nikaela tried not to feel fatalistic. "If they do, that'll at least be faster than dying slowly out here."

That was when they learned the boat's com had already failed. They tried the turrets, thinking they might launch a couple missiles at some debris. Hopefully, someone would notice the explosions and investigate. But the turrets' systems were as dead as the com.

Fourteen hours later the boat's gravity failed, and as the craft cooled and they found themselves shivering, they donned their damaged vac suits to keep warm. They didn't bother with the helmets. Thankfully the cabin hadn't lost pressure. If it did, the damaged suits wouldn't do them any good.

43

Recovery

KATRINE LOOKED AT Brynjar and the two Kelk women next to him, all standing before her in her virtual vision. Brynjar had arranged for her to meet Kristdokar and her *immediate superior*. He wouldn't say more about the immediate superior, probably because he had been ordered not to, and that intrigued Katrine.

With Neilosse's permission she borrowed his office, sat down, and with the help of *Lightspear*'s com tech, established the link through her implants. And while she wore her service khakis and was seated, the image she transmitted to them was of her standing respectfully in her service dress blues. It would be good to finally meet Kristdokar.

Of the two women standing next to Brynjar, the brigadier skalde would be Kristdokar, and the vice skalde her immediate superior. Kristdokar wore a uniform not unlike Katrine's blues, had more pepper in her hair than salt, with high cheek bones and sharp, aristocratic lines in her face. The vice skalde wore a long, floor-length robe, with billowing sleeves and rank insignia on her shoulders, possibly a ceremonial garment. Her hair had almost turned completely to salt, she had an oval face, and almond shaped eyes. When younger she could have been a fashion model in the Commonwealth, even with blood red irises, though the look she gave Katrine did come across as a bit demonic.

Brynjar made the introductions, and Katrine learned Vice Skalde Nygaard was the third most ranking member of the Larscom Executive Council. Katrine would have to move very carefully.

Katrine and the two Kelk women traded courtesies, then Nygaard surprised her by acknowledging an obvious fact. "I thank you for having the courage to be here, Colonel. If the situation was reversed, and there were four Commonwealth warships facing a single Kelk hunter-killer, I would have a difficult time dispelling my officers' fears."

Katrine smiled and nodded once. "It has not been easy, but perhaps not as difficult as you think. *Lightspear*'s captain, Commander Neilosse, has repeatedly demonstrated the ability to discount the distorted myths we've all heard. He's a good officer."

Nygaard crossed her arms, sliding each hand up the opposing sleeve. "I would imagine you, like us, could use more officers like him. But enough of the niceties; I would assume you are wondering about your young man."

"Yes," Katrine said. "Have you found him?"

Kristdokar shook her head. "Unfortunately, no. We've almost finished the recovery operation, and we've questioned all the survivors we've rescued so far, though there aren't many. Most of them had heard rumors of two prisoners, and rumors one was a Blacksword, but so far none of them actually met or interacted with them. A command hawk supervised the rogue operation on *Sycorax*, and would probably have known more than the rest. But when the ship broke up, a gravity shear killed her, so of course we were unable to question her. We fear our breschkada were taken away aboard *Caliban*."

Katrine thought it interesting the way she had phrased that: *our breschkada*, as if both young people belonged to the Kelk. "How much more remains of the rescue operation?"

"*Sycorax* broke up into three large pieces," Kristdokar said. "We're searching the last of them now."

••••

Something woke Anders and he froze in his bunk, listening carefully. He heard nothing more than the occasional muted tick or pop as the hull cooled. Had it been a dream? Surprised he had slept, he couldn't recall any dreams.

A sharp clang sounded through the hull and he started. He waited and listened, and in a few seconds another metallic sound echoed through the hull. He unbuckled his bunk restraints and floated out into the compartment, gripping the edge of the bunk to orient himself. If someone had initiated a rescue and recovery operation, he needed to make sure they knew he was there. He pushed off and floated across the compartment to the door in the bulkhead. Using the door's latch to steady himself, he retrieved the wrench from the thigh pocket, then rapped it sharply three times against the bulkhead.

Several seconds passed with no response. A chunk of debris might have collided with the derelict piece of *Sycorax* and made the sound he had heard. After all, it had only been a single loud noise.

Again, he rapped the wrench three times against the bulkhead and waited. A second later someone responded, like him hammering something against the structure three times. He waited a few seconds, then did four taps, and a few seconds later they responded with four in kind.

They would work their way from compartment to compartment, stopping in each to see if the one beyond was under pressure. But he could save them time because he was suited. He contracted his visor and sealed his suit, then used its safety line to tie himself to the door in the bulkhead.

For the next four hours the sounds echoing through the hull grew louder and louder. At half hour intervals, they paused and rapped three times on the hull. Each time he answered them with three raps, and they continued on. He frequently dozed off into a light sleep, but their three-rap signal always woke him. And then one time when they signaled, he realized the three raps had been hammered on the other side of the bulkhead in front of him.

He pressed his helmet to the bulkhead and heard a steady grinding sound. After several seconds a small drill bit punched through the plast. The drill bit withdrew and he did not hear the hiss of escaping air. A small antenna wire replaced the drill bit protruding from the bulkhead, and his helmet com came to life.

"Identify yourself."

It occurred to Anders that whatever he said might get him killed. He considered giving them a false name, but they wouldn't have much trouble recovering the manifest from the ship's systems. They would quickly discover the lie, and that would bring the wrong kind of attention his way. "Anders Karsten. Not crew, just deadhead passenger."

"Are you suited?"

"Yes, all-purpose vac suit."

"Back away to the opposite side of the compartment. Hang on and keep your hands visible at all times."

Anders complied, though to keep from floating around he gripped the edge of his bunk with one hand. A few minutes passed, then the wheel that manually sealed the bulkhead door spun. The door opened and two Kelk soldiers in full combat armor floated into the compartment, both carrying heavy assault rifles aimed at him.

He slowly and carefully released his grip on the edge of his bunk and held his hands out to the sides, which meant he floated out toward the center of the compartment.

They cuffed him in both hand and leg manacles, then like excess baggage, floated him out of the compartment.

He wondered if they would simply execute him, or send him back to SecureMax. He tried not to think about that female guard and her neural prod.

••••

As they recovered the bodies of those killed in the breakup of *Sycorax*, they stored them in preservation bags on *Alvilddan* and *Drakan Helgis*. Survivors were put under deep electro sedation as soon as they set foot on one of the assault boats, then sent to *Konigsborge*. The cruiser didn't have a brig large enough to confine them all, so sedating them and storing them on portable cots in the surgical unit allowed a few guards and medical techs to keep an eye on them without difficulty.

Kristdokar began her morning each day by reviewing the list of survivors rescued the previous day. Then she had them carried one by one on their cots to an interrogation room, and only then were they awakened. When she completed the interrogation, they were again sedated and carried back to the surgical unit. In that way she ensured they had no interaction with the other survivors, nor did they even know who else had survived, if anyone.

That morning, while reviewing the list of survivors, Anders Karsten's name aroused her suspicions, especially since he was listed as a deadhead passenger and not crew. She pulled up a picture of him that had been recorded by the rescue team just before sedating him, and confirmed her suspicions. With a quick call down to the surgical unit, she informed them she would interrogate him next.

••••

John hadn't noticed it before, but Nikaela's lips were a lot bluer than the faint bluish tint of her skin. Maybe that was the norm and he just hadn't been that observant, or possibly it was due to the cold.

Nikaela's breathing bothered John, though he didn't know why. He watched her chest rise and fall as she took short, rapid, shallow breaths. There had been something in his training about that, but as he struggled to recall it, his mind kept drifting and he had trouble maintaining his train of thought. Blue lips, rapid breathing, together they meant something.

Blue lips, rapid breathing.

Blue lips, rapid breathing, something about oxygen and carbon dioxide.

Blue lips, rapid breathing, fix it with oxygen, fix it with oxygen.

"Fix it with oxygen," he said.

He unbuckled his acceleration harness. "Fix it with oxygen." Who had said that?

He floated up out of the pilot's seat, then pulled himself toward the troop cabin. "Fix it with oxygen."

Floating in the troop cabin were the dead guards and the helmets to their damaged vac suits. "Fix it with oxygen."

Why had he come back there? It had something to do with the suits. "Fix it with oxygen."

He reached out and snagged one of the helmets. "Fix it with oxygen."

He managed to get the helmet in place but his hands and fingers didn't seem to work as well as they used to, so he had trouble securing its seals. He paused and wondered why he was even bothering with the helmet, but after some time considering the matter, he decided he should finish the task.

With the helmet sealed he contracted the visor. Someone said, "Left forearm breach and excessive carbon dioxide levels."

The rush of fresh air felt good, and he thought he just might float in the troop cabin and sleep for a while.

"Carbon dioxide levels," he said. "Carbon dioxide levels."

A rush of coherent thought hit him like a slap to the face. The boat's oxygen re-cycler had shut down. They had consumed the oxygen in the cabin and now breathed air with a high CO_2 concentration.

John pushed off a bulkhead, grabbed Nikaela's helmet and headed for the cock-pit.

••••

Anders woke lying on his back with Kristdokar standing over him. She had a stern look on her face as she said, "Maestra Eindride."

As he sat up and swung his legs off the cot, she handed him a glass of water, and only then did he see the other woman in the room, a vice skalde. She did not acknowledge him, nor did Kristdokar introduce her.

He took a healthy gulp of water, then stood and placed the glass on a table in the center of the room.

"Sit down," Kristdokar said.

He did. The vice skalde remained standing while Kristdokar sat across the table from him. "So they put you on *Sycorax* to carry you to your new assignment."

"Yes," he said, "but not to carry me to my new assignment. At least I don't think so."

"Explain."

"There was a command hawk name of Eskildsen. She kept hinting it would be perfectly understandable if I wanted to kill Mistress Vreekande and her breschkada. I think she hoped I would do so, or barring that, they could kill them and blame it on me, the bitter and hate-filled disgraced ex-officer."

Kristdokar nodded. "Yes, they didn't want to lose face. Did you see the bre-schkada?"

"Twice," Anders said. He described how Eskildsen had shown him Nikaela Vreekande in her cell, and how he'd faked anger in an attempt to tell her about the vid pickup. Then he told them about the interrogation of the two young people. "I didn't know he survived Novalis III."

"She revealed that, did she?"

"Yes, I think she hoped it would inflame my hatred even more and goad me into murder."

Anders had a question he wanted to ask. "Have you found the two young people yet?"

Kristdokar's hard demeanor broke the slightest bit, and he saw sadness in her eyes. "No. We think they were carried away by *Caliban*."

"No," he shouted and leaned forward. "No, they were on *Sycorax* right up to a few minutes before the end."

The vice skalde started. Kristdokar's eyes widened and she demanded angrily, "What do you mean?"

He told them how he had accompanied Eskildsen to the personnel airlock of the assault boat, ostensibly to transfer him and the two young people down to the surface of Sarkovie. "But the airlock was closed and locked. The pilot had left his post and arrived to join us outside the airlock. And then the boat launched without a pilot. And then everything went crazy."

The vice skalde spoke for the first time. "Was Mistress Vreekande a pilot?"

Kristdokar shook her head. "No. But maybe the young man—"

She closed her eyes and went silent, clearly consulting with someone through her implants. She remained that way for a couple of minutes, then opened her eyes and said, "Colonel Primatov says the young man was a fully qualified boat pilot. And the head of our rescue operation reports they found one of *Sycorax*'s assault boats rammed into a bulkhead in her hangar bay, causing considerable structural damage. The second assault boat is missing, no sign of it. We've searched the debris field where *Sycorax* broke up, but not the location where she rendezvoused with *Caliban*."

••••

The reactor packs on the all-purpose vac suits weren't meant to operate for more than about half a day. John and Nikaela needed oxygen more than they needed heat, so they overrode the warmers in the suits and shut them down. But with the integrity of the two suits compromised, the oxygen dissociation system worked far less efficiently, and Nikaela tried not to think about their chances for survival. They were shivering badly when the reactor pack cells went dead. They replaced them with cells from the suits of the two dead crewmen, though with their hands shaking badly, it took a while to get them seated properly.

They wrapped their arms around each other in a lovers' embrace to conserve heat, tied a loop of safety line around them to keep them from drifting apart, and floated in the middle of the troop cabin, teeth chattering. Under other circumstances Nikaela would have enjoyed holding John that way. She didn't pass out or fall asleep, but as the hours slipped by, time became a concept without meaning.

At some point Nikaela stopped shivering, and she noticed so too had John. Something in her training warned her she should be concerned about that, but she couldn't recall what.

A loud noise brought her back from a place where her thoughts had shut down. A beam of bright light lit up the cabin. She turned her head to follow it to its source, shining through the windshield of the boat. It flashed about briefly, then the dark returned.

More loud noises echoing through the boat's hull, gears grinding and pumps chattering. Nikaela's shoulder bumped against something, and as weight slowly returned, she and John settled to the boat's deck. She should do something, find one of the grav pistols, make a last stand or something like that, but she just didn't have the energy.

44

A Little Payback

JOHN NEVER LOST consciousness, but at some point his mental processes shut down. He recalled shivering a lot, then not shivering, then a bright light, loud noises, clattering gears and pumps. Then gravity returned.

Someone separated him and Nikaela, put him on a grav stretcher and carried him through a ship's passageways. Kelk demons undressed him, stripped him down to his birthday suit. He wondered if they had some strange custom about only executing people when they were really cold and naked.

Warmth. Not a lot at first, just a slow steady warming that felt so wonderful he fell asleep.

He awoke to a blue-skinned Kelk demon leaning over him. Her face had high cheek bones and sharp features, and she wore a single four-pointed star on each shoulder, a brigadier skalde.

She smiled, and didn't look at all demonic. "Maestra Mathius, I'm Brigadier Skalde Kristdokar."

He had heard that name before, from Nikaela. "You're Mistress Vreekande's superior."

"Yes, she told you about me, eh?"

He shrugged. "A little. Is Mistress Vreekande okay?"

She raised an eyebrow as she nodded. "Like you, she's just fine. And like you, your condition was the first thing she asked about. She awoke about an hour ago."

John sat up and took in his surroundings. They had placed him in a medical bed in a compartment that contained nothing more than the bed, a small table and four chairs. He was on a ship, but it was not the sick bay of a ship. They had clearly moved the bed into it to isolate him.

None of John's training had included anything about the protocols required when interacting with Kelk officers of flag rank. Kristdokar stood in the background while a Kelk medical officer gave John a fairly thorough examination. They had fixed John's arm, and it had almost healed. To his surprise he could walk without feeling weak or faint, just hungry. They had dressed him in a simple coverall.

When the medical officer finished, they brought in a tray of food and placed it on the table. John's stomach growled as he sat down in one of the chairs, and Kristdokar watched him silently as he ate. He even recognized some of the food from the meals he'd eaten on *Sycorax*.

About halfway through the meal, the door to the compartment opened, and Nikaela entered. She saw John and hesitated, her eyes widening. John too hesitated.

Nikaela spoke rather formally. "Maestra Mathius."

He replied just as formally. "Mistress Vreekande."

"Oh come now," Kristdokar said. "By now the two of you must be on a first name basis."

Neither of them said anything in response to that. Kristdokar shook her head sadly. "I'll leave you two to catch up."

She turned, walked out of the compartment and closed the door behind her, leaving John and Nikaela alone.

Nikaela walked carefully across the compartment, pulled out a chair and sat down opposite John. "Are you okay?"

"Yes, are you?"

She nodded. "Yes."

John lowered his voice to a whisper. "Are we prisoners?"

She grimaced. "I don't know."

••••

Like all hunter-killers, *Lightspear* didn't have the space for anything close to a heavy assault boat, though it did have a small skiff that could ferry four people, including the pilot, to the surface of a planet. When Katrine got the call from Kristdokar and learned they had rescued the two young people, she didn't bother to change out of her service khakis into something more formal. Neilosse provided her with a pilot and she rode the skiff to *Konigsborge*.

Kristdokar greeted her in the hangar bay of the larger ship, and like Katrine she wore the Kelk equivalent of service khakis, though Kelk uniforms tended more toward gray than khaki.

"Colonel," Kristdokar said. "I haven't yet learned from the two young people exactly what happened to them. Would you like to sit down with them now and find out?"

Katrine nodded. "Lead the way."

As Kristdokar led her through the passageways of *Konigsborge*, they encountered a Kelk crewwoman. She paused, pressed her back against a bulkhead, and while she didn't stare at Katrine, she surreptitiously tracked her with her eyes as she passed. The same thing happened with several crewmembers before they reached their destination, a door flanked by two armed guards.

As Kristdokar approached the guards, one of them opened the door and held it for Katrine and her. Katrine followed the skalde through it into a compartment where John and Nikaela sat at a table, John working on a tray of food in front of him. At the appearance of the brigadier and the Blacksword, both young people shot to their feet.

Kristdokar waved a hand impatiently. "Sit down and relax." She pointed at John. "And you, young man, finish that meal."

Both young people moved tentatively as they sat down. Kristdokar pulled out a chair and sat down at the table with them, so Katrine did likewise.

"Now," Kristdokar said. "Let's hear what happened to the two of you."

Nikaela described how she was attacked and abducted from her apartment. John told of his abduction, and Katrine learned how the fellow in the restaurant had tipped his hand with a Cranoch-look. Katrine questioned John to learn exactly what he meant by *Cranoch-look*. It took more than an hour for her and Kristdokar to walk the two young people through their individual and combined stories.

When they finished, Nikaela hesitantly asked, "Are we . . . under arrest?"

"No," Kristdokar said. "Why would you think that?"

Nikaela nodded toward the compartment door. "The armed guards outside the door."

"Ah, that," Kristdokar said. "They're not there to keep you in. We haven't screened *Konigsborge*'s crew for their . . . attitudes regarding Commonwealth soldiers." She made a point of looking at John. "Especially Blackswords. Those two guards were selected from a small detachment that has been so screened."

Nikaela asked, "They're there to protect John?"

Katrine said, "I would guess they're there to protect both of you."

Kristdokar smiled. "Very astute of you, Colonel."

••••

Katrine followed Kristdokar to a conference room in officer's country, where Nygaard waited for them. The vice skalde wore what Katrine had come to think of as Kelk service grays. She sat at a large conference table with a Kelk version of a tea service in front of her.

Kristdokar and Katrine sat down. Nygaard offered them tea, and Katrine accepted, not certain if turning down the offer might be taken as some sort of slight. Nygaard stood and carefully poured tea into cups for all three of them, saying, "In the Supremacy, under formal circumstances, it is customary for the more senior person to serve tea to the more junior."

Katrine said, "I didn't know that. Thank you for telling me."

Nygaard sat down. "There is much we don't know about each other's cultures. Perhaps we should start learning."

Nygaard took a sip of her tea. "We installed a vid pickup in that compartment so I could watch and listen while the two of you learned the young people's stories.

Your young man is rather inventive. He destroyed a Kelk warship with nothing more than an assault boat."

"Yes," Katrine said. "One thing I've learned about him is that if someone pushes the wrong buttons, he can turn into a wrecking machine."

"Wrecking machine," Nygaard said, closing her eyes as if to consult her implants for a translation. "Demolition engine."

Katrine corrected her. "Very destructive demolition engine."

Kristdokar nodded. "Yes, and it appears the two of them together are a wrecking machine squared."

"Colonel," Nygaard said. "The Larscom wishes to invite you and Maestra Mathius to be our guests and accompany us back to Viktorkinde. You will be granted all the protections of the Larscom, and full diplomatic immunity."

To stall for time and a few seconds to think of how to say no, Katrine sipped at her tea, then carefully put the cup on the table in front of her. "Vice Skalde Nygaard, at this time Ensign Mathius should return to the Commonwealth. But I assure you such an invitation will be taken quite seriously, and we can then make the appropriate arrangements through proper channels."

Nygaard pursed her lips. "Colonel, rejecting the invitation is not an option, at least not for Ensign Mathius."

Katrine hadn't expected that. They had John, and they had overwhelming firepower superiority, so she had no choice. But would they really go that far?

Her hands were tied by the limits of her authority, and she thought it quite likely Nygaard really didn't want to actually use that overwhelming firepower superiority. "That does put me in a very difficult situation. I do not have the authority to establish diplomatic relations with the Supremacy. If Ensign Mathius and I accompany you without prior authorization from my superiors, it could be construed as an act of treason and will create a myriad of problems detrimental to any future relationship between the Commonwealth and the Supremacy. The same could happen if Ensign Mathius is forced to accompany you without my consent."

From the sly look on Nygaard's face, the woman knew exactly what Katrine was doing. "Then what do you suggest, Colonel?"

Katrine chose her words carefully to ensure that they sounded nothing like an invitation to establish formal diplomatic relations. "If you were to extend an invitation to the Commonwealth to send a diplomatic mission to Viktorkinde to initiate preliminary discussions on matters of mutual benefit, John and I could accompany you to establish the operating parameters for such discussions, and there would be no ramifications."

There damn well would be ramifications, but Katrine had to play the hand she was dealt.

Nygaard gave her a sardonic grin. "Like you, I cannot single-handedly establish diplomatic relations between our two governments. That would require a majority vote of the Executive Council. But I can invite you and your superiors to, as you say, 'initiate preliminary discussions on matters of mutual benefit,' if for no other reason than to reduce the number of encounters between our armed forces that result in loss of life. But see to it no warships are included in this diplomatic mission."

Katrine felt like a woman dancing barefoot on a floor littered with shards of broken glass. "Such a mission will be led by personages of considerable authority and influence, so a standard military escort would be appropriate. Let us say a private vessel to carry the dignitaries, plus two naval cruisers as escort, something I'm sure your forces near Viktorkinde could easily evict from Supremacy space, should the situation deteriorate for any reason. And the invitation would have to come through official channels, for example from the Executive Council to the Right Honorable Senator Manifort Gascoigne, Chairman of the Senate Intelligence Committee."

Nygaard leaned back in her chair and steepled her fingers in front of her. She considered Katrine for what felt like an eternity, then said, "I think the phrase you use in Lingua is, 'We have a deal.'"

Until that moment, Katrine hadn't realized she had been holding her breath. And the fact that Nygaard had agreed to that on her own authority, made it clear that the skalde and her colleagues on the Executive Council had already discussed something of that nature as a possibility. "Then I accept your gracious invitation for both myself and Ensign Mathius. However, am I correct in assuming there are factions within the Supremacy who don't care about diplomatic immunity, and are unlikely to honor it?"

Nygaard smiled. "I must agree with Brigadier Skalde Kristdokar, Colonel. You are quite astute."

Katrine returned the smile. "We have similar factions in the Commonwealth."

••••

After his interrogation by Kristdokar and the vice skalde, they didn't again sedate Anders and return him to a cot in the surgical unit. They did give him some new clothing. The tunic contained a visual distortion field generator woven into the fibers of its collar to disguise his appearance. Then they transferred him to *Drakan Helgis* and isolated him in a cell in the brig. He did learn from Brynjar that they had rescued the two young people, and the day after that, Kristdokar and Brynjar joined him in his cell.

Kristdokar didn't waste any time with small talk. "We want you to remain in the field."

Anders didn't really have a choice, but he still didn't want to end up with a bullet in the back of his head. "How can we make that work?"

Kristdokar nodded. "The derelict piece of *Sycorax* in which you were trapped also contained a few lifeboats. Your story is that when *Sycorax* broke up, you made your way to the lifeboats and took one. Each is equipped to keep ten spacers alive for a month. With the lifeboat's limited drive, the journey from where *Sycorax* broke up to Sarkovie will take about ten days."

Brynjar took up the narration. "We've retrieved one of the lifeboats, and we're checking it out to ensure that it's functional and fully equipped. Right now there's still a lot of confusion on all four of our ships as to who and how many we rescued from *Sycorax*. We need to get you off this ship now, before someone recognizes you, so we're going to stuff you in that lifeboat in fairly short order. We considered leaving *Eldekarl* behind as a backup for you, but we'd have to disclose your existence to more people, and that would put you in too much danger, so you're on your own. We are going to leave *Alvilddan* behind to finish mopping up here, but they won't know of you or your mission.

"The lifeboat is capable of one reentry on a planet like Sarkovie. Make your way to one of the four addresses they're operating from, and try to establish contact. If none of the four works out, you'll also have the name of friendly assets on Sarkovie. We will inform them we have someone working on Sarkovie, but to protect you, only our head of station there will know your identity. You can make contact with her through one of them, and they'll bring you in."

Anders had one question. "Is Vice Skalde Nygaard in on this?"

Kristdokar nodded, and her eyes narrowed with wariness. "She is, and has been from the beginning. We couldn't have gotten you out of SecureMax without her help."

That raised another question. "Who else knows about me?"

Kristdokar glanced momentarily at Brynjar. "Just we two, Nygaard, Command Superior Thordahl, and Mistress Vreekande. And we want to keep it that way, so that's why the sense of urgency."

And that raised the final question. "When does this end? When do I get to stop looking over my shoulder to see if I'm about to get a bullet in the back of my head? When am I a free man again? Will I ever be a free man again?"

Kristdokar seemed resigned and a little sad. "I don't know. Nygaard won't make any promises. She did say you've been an invaluable asset, and she told me I could quote her on that."

Anders sighed and shook his head sadly. "The gratitude of those old women is probably going to get me killed."

Kristdokar shrugged. "I don't think you want me to quote you on that, do you?"

••••

Nygaard understood Katrine's need to at least prepare a report for her superiors before leaving for Viktorkinde. And Katrine needed her kit and uniforms, so *Konigsborge* would not depart until after she retrieved her gear from *Lightspear* and returned to the Kelk cruiser. But she had an ulterior motive as well.

As soon as she stepped foot on the hunter-killer, she cornered Neilosse in his office. She briefed him on the situation and finished with, "I need uniforms for Ensign

Mathius. He's going to represent the Commonwealth to the Kelk Supremacy, and I will not have him doing so in a pair of sloppy coveralls. I need a couple pairs of fatigues, two service khakis, and at least one service dress blues."

Neilosse ran his fingers through his hair. "That's a tall order. We probably have some of that stuff in ship's stores, but not that much."

Katrine had taken some measurements off John before leaving *Konigsborge*. "Steal whatever you have to from your officers. Keep track of who and what, and I'll ask Colonel Blacksword to make sure they get reimbursed. If we can't find an exact fit go with something a little oversized. I can probably find someone to downsize them."

He shook his head. "I don't think we'll have any Blacksword patches."

Katrine threw her hands up. "I'd raid my own uniforms, but I'm going to need them. So I'll ask Cap'm Fleming and his nullheads to lend me some."

Neilosse nodded as if trying to convince himself. "You do your report and I'll worry about the uniforms."

"Thank you," she said, and turned to leave.

"Colonel, wait."

She turned back to face him.

He grinned. "It's been . . . a pleasure working with you, and . . . the most unusual assignment I've ever had. I do hope you come back alive."

••••

When Kristdokar informed John that he and Primatov would accompany them back to Viktorkinde, he looked at Nikaela for her reaction. She appeared to be as surprised as he felt.

He thought of the armed guards standing outside the door, there to protect him and Nikaela, and he wondered about visiting an entire planet full of people hell-bent on killing them.

There must have been something on his face because Kristdokar grinned and said, "Don't worry, young man. We'll take care of our breschkada."

"I sure hope you can."

She added, "Your Colonel Primatov returned to *Lightspear* to prepare a report for her superiors, but she'll be back in a few hours and we'll depart."

She turned and walked out through the door, but paused just beyond the threshold, looked back at Nikaela and said, "Please come with me, young lady."

Nikaela said, "Yes, Brigadier."

She started to follow, but John reached out, caught her elbow, and she turned back to face him. She had taken him completely by surprise when she had kissed him on that assault boat. Now it was time for a little payback. He lowered his voice. "You said if we survived, you'd have to find out if anything on me is forked."

Her eyes widened. He leaned close and stopped with his lips almost brushing hers. "Just let me know when you're ready to start the discovery process."

Her eyes widened even further and she turned a little bit purple. It took him a moment to figure that out. Start with skin tone that's a little bit blue, add a little bit red, and that would produce a little bit purple. "You're blushing."

Her eyes flashed angrily. "No I'm not." She stuck her tongue out at him, then said, "I almost wish it was forked."

She turned, stepped through the door, and closed it.

Acknowledgements

I'D LIKE TO thank Clyde, Tory and Dave for fixing all my dotted t's and crossed i's, and for their invaluable insight, criticism and advice, Karen for both supporting my dream and being my most valuable critic, and Steve Himes, and the whole team at Telemachus, for getting a quality product out the door.

Books by J. L. Doty

Series: The Treasons Cycle
Of Treasons Born
A Choice of Treasons

Stand Alone Novel
The Thirteenth Man

Series: The Gods Within
Child of the Sword
The SteelMaster of Indwallin
The Heart of the Sands
The Name of the Sword

Series: The Dead Among Us
When Dead Ain't Dead Enough
Still Not Dead Enough
Never Dead Enough

Series: The Blacksword Regiment
A Hymn for the Dying
A Dirge for the Damned
A Prayer for the Fallen
A Requiem for the Forsaken

Series: Commonwealth Re-contact Novellas
Tranquility Lost

About the Author

JIM IS A full-time SF&F writer, scientist and laser geek (Ph.D. Electrical Engineering, specialty laser physics), and former running-dog-lackey for the bourgeois capitalist establishment. He's been writing for over 30 years, with 15 published books. His first success came through self-publishing when his books went word-of-mouth viral, and sold enough that he was able to quit his day-job, start working for himself and write full time—his new boss is a real jerk. That led to contracts with traditional publishers like Open Road Media and Harper Collins Voyager, and his books are now a mix of traditional and self-published.

The four novels in his new hard science fiction series, *The Blacksword Regiment*, were released in July 2020. Right now he's fleshing out ideas for the next book in *The Dead Among Us*, he's writing another episode in *The Treasons Cycle*, and he's working on a new fantasy series *The Deck of Chaos*.

Jim was born in Seattle, but he's lived most of his life in California, though he did live on the east coast and in Europe for a while. He now resides in Arizona with his wife Karen and three little beings who claim to be cats: Tilda, Julia and Natasha. But Jim is certain they're really extra-terrestrial aliens in disguise.

Visit the author's website at http://www.jldoty.com
Contact the author at jld@jldoty.com

9 781951 744144